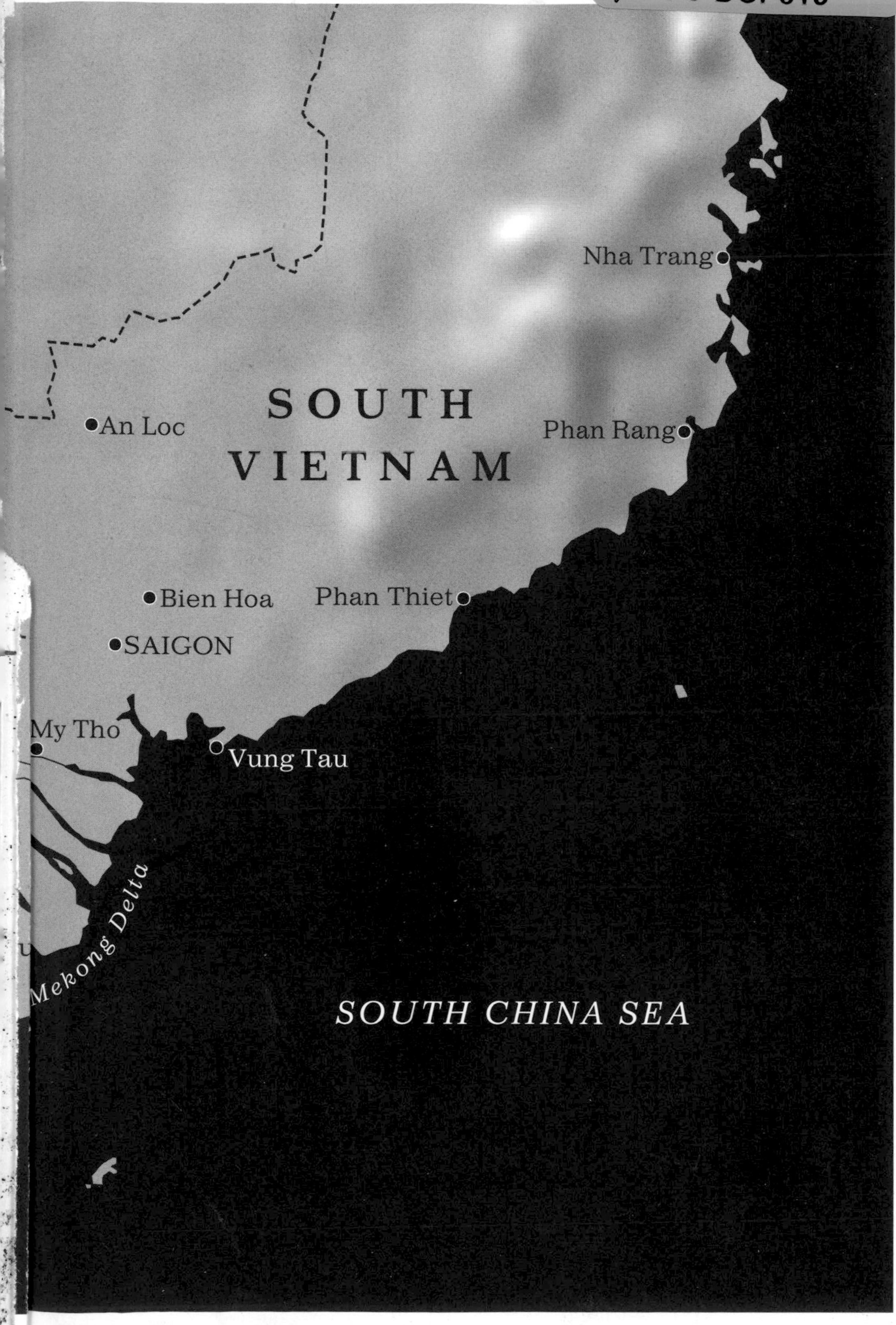

Nha Trang

SOUTH VIETNAM

An Loc

Phan Rang

Bien Hoa

Phan Thiet

SAIGON

My Tho

Vung Tau

Mekong Delta

SOUTH CHINA SEA

FINDING MOON

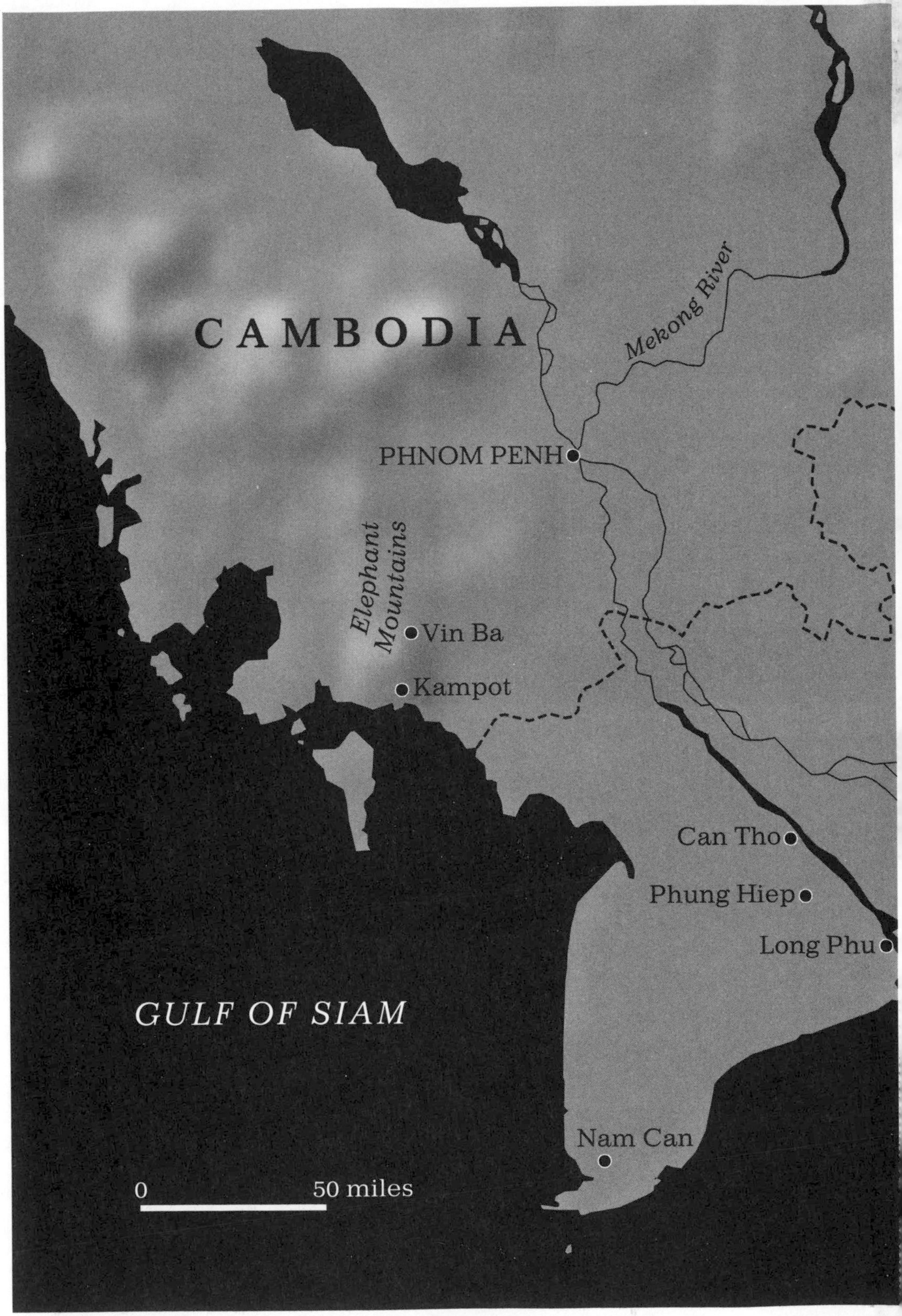

CAMBODIA
Mekong River
PHNOM PENH
Elephant Mountains
Vin Ba
Kampot
Can Tho
Phung Hiep
Long Phu
GULF OF SIAM
Nam Can
0
50 miles

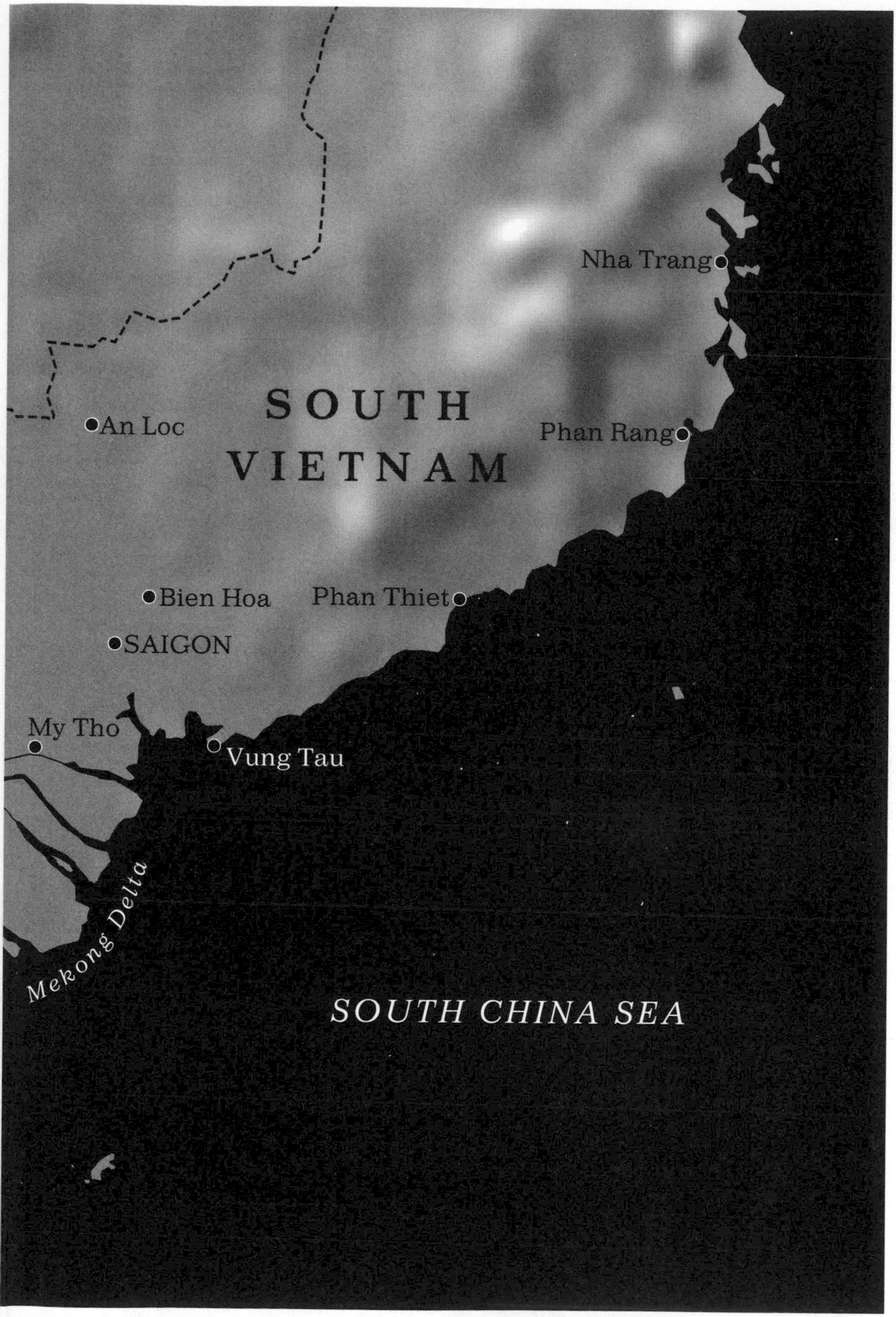

SOUTH VIETNAM

Nha Trang
An Loc
Phan Rang
Bien Hoa
Phan Thiet
SAIGON
My Tho
Vung Tau
Mekong Delta

SOUTH CHINA SEA

Also by TONY HILLERMAN

◈ ◈ ◈ *FICTION* ◈ ◈ ◈

Sacred Clowns
Coyote Waits
Talking God
A Thief of Time
Skinwalkers
The Dark Wind
People of Darkness
Listening Woman
Dance Hall of the Dead
The Fly on the Wall
The Blessing Way
The Boy Who Made Dragonfly *(for children)*

◈ ◈ ◈ *NONFICTION* ◈ ◈ ◈

Hillerman Country
The Great Taos Bank Robbery
Rio Grande
New Mexico
The Spell of New Mexico
Indian Country

TONY HILLERMAN

FINDING MOON

HarperCollins*Publishers*

 For information address HarperCollins Publishers, Inc., 10 East 53rd Street, New York, NY 10022.

HarperCollins books may be purchased for educational, business, or sales promotional use. For information please write: Special Markets Department, HarperCollins Publishers, Inc., 10 East 53rd Street, New York, NY 10022.

FIRST EDITION

Designed by Alma Hochhauser Orenstein

Library of Congress Cataloging-in-Publication Data

Hillerman, Tony.
Finding moon / Tony Hillerman. — 1st ed.
p. cm.
ISBN 0-06-017772-1
I. Title.
PS3558.I45F47 1995
813'.54—dc20 95-31309

---

95 96 97 98 99 ❖/RRD 10 9 8 7 6 5 4 3 2 1

AN APOLOGY, ACKNOWLEDGMENTS, DENIAL, AND DEDICATION

TO MY FELLOW DESERT RATS, my apologies for wandering away from our beloved Navajo canyon country. The next book will bring Jim Chee and Joe Leaphorn of the Tribal Police back into action.

I acknowledge the help of Professor Jack M. Potter, University of California anthropologist and author of *Wind, Water, Bones and Souls: The Religious World of the Cantonese Peasant*, and of Bernard St. Germain and Rick Ambrose, who patrolled the Mekong in the Brown Water Navy. Thanks, too, to Sgt. Chris Hidalgo of the New Mexico National Guard for familiarizing me with a vintage armored personnel carrier. Finally, thanks to my friend and cardiologist, Neal Shadoff, for helping my fictional physicians sound genuine.

The denial: While former members of C Company, 410 Infantry, will recognize some of the names herein as those of our fellow grunts, I have borrowed only the names of these old friends and not their personalities. All characters herein are fictional.

This work is dedicated to the men of C Company and to all those who earned the right to wear the Combat Infantry Badge.

FINDING MOON

PHNOM PENH, Cambodia, April 12 (Agence France-Presse)—The United States abandoned its embassy here this morning, with six helicopters sweeping into the embassy grounds to evacuate the ambassador and his remaining staff.

The action came as the last resistance of the Cambodian Army collapsed and Khmer Rouge troops poured into the capital, many of them riding on captured tanks and trucks.

The First Day

April 12, 1975

SHIRLEY WAS GIVING MOON the caller-on-hold signal when he came through the newsroom door. He acknowledged Shirley with the I'll-call-'em-back signal, threw his hat on the copy desk, sat down, and looked at D. W. Hubble.

"Nothing much," Hubble said. "AP has an early tornado in Arkansas. Pretty mediocre, but it could get better. Things are still going to hell in Nam, and Ford has a press conference scheduled for eleven Washington time, and Kissinger issued a statement, and General Motors—"

"What did Henry say?"

Hubble did not bother to look up from his duties,

which at the moment involved chopping copy from the teletype machine into individual stories and sorting them into trays. The trays were variously labeled PAGE ONE, SPORTS, FEATURES, FUNNY, SOB STUFF, and PIG IRON—the pig iron being what Hubble considered "seriously dull stuff that the League of Women Voters reads."

Hubble said, "What did Henry say? Let's see." He glanced at the top item in the PIG IRON file. "Henry said that Dick Nixon was correct in declaring we had won the war in Southeast Asia. He said the North Viets were just too stubborn to understand that, and the press was playing up the current setbacks to make it look like a disaster, and it was going to be the fault of the Congress for not sending more money, and anyway don't blame Kissinger. Words to that effect."

"What looks good for the play story?" Moon asked, and sorted quickly through the FRONT PAGE tray. The United States seemed to be evacuating the embassy at Phnom Penh. Moon saved that one. The new president of South Vietnam, something-or-other Thieu, was picking a fight-to-the-death bunch for his cabinet. Moon discarded it. A bill to put a price ceiling on domestic oil production was up for a vote in a Senate committee. That was weak but a possibility. The South Viets were claiming a resounding victory at Xuan Loc, wherever that was. He tossed that one too. Senator Humphrey declared that we should establish a separate U.S. Department of Education. There'd be some interest in that. The Durance County Commissioners had moved the road to the ski basin up a notch on the priority list. Most of the 28,000 subscribers the paper claimed would be interested in that one. And then there was a colorful, gruesome feature on the plight of refugees pouring into Saigon from points north.

It was good human interest stuff, but even as he read it

Moon was conscious of how quickly these accounts of tragedy from Vietnam had become merely filler—like the comics and Ann Landers and the crossword puzzle. A few years ago they had been personal. Then he'd searched through the news for references to Ricky's Air Mobile brigade, for actions using helicopters, for anything involving the Da Nang sector where Ricky's maintenance company was stationed. But since Ricky resigned his commission in 1968, Ricky had been out of it. And since 1973 the United States of America was also out of it. What was left of the war was a distant abstraction. As Hubble had described it once, "Just another case of our gooks killing their gooks." In the press across America, and in the *Morning Press-Register* of Durance, Colorado, the war was no longer page one.

But it was still page one sometimes at the *Press-Register*—until last month. Ricky was still in Nam, a player on the sidelines. That made Moon interested and made him think the *Press-Register*'s readers would also be. Now Ricky was dead, no longer running R. M. Air and fixing helicopters for the Army of the Republic of Vietnam just as he had fixed them for the U.S. Army. Probably the same copters, in fact. But as Ricky had said in one of his rare letters, he was "getting a hell of a lot more money and a hell of a lot less aggravation from division headquarters." There was a kickback to ARVN brass, but Ricky considered that "the equivalent of an income tax."

Ricky had said more. He had said, Come and join me, big brother. Come and join the team. Join the fun. It would be like old times. He'd said, South Nam is going under, and fast. Soon there'll be no more fat contracts from ARVN, but there will still be plenty of need for what R. M. Air can offer. Help me get this outfit ready for the change. And he'd said (Moon remembered the exact words), "R. M. Air is no good for slogans. We'll rename it M. R. Air, for Moon and Rick, and call it Mister Air. I'll do the business, you keep the engines running. Come on. With all that money she's married to now, Mom doesn't need you anymore. But I do."

Which was just Ricky buttering him up. Their mother had never needed him. Victoria Mathias wasn't a woman who needed people. And neither did Ricky. But bullshit or not, Moon had enjoyed thinking about making the move, even while he was wondering why Ricky had invited him. But he had never answered the letter. There hadn't been time.

"That Arkansas twister is looking better," Hubble said, inspecting the copy now emerging from the teletype. "The new lead says they got thirteen dead now." He waved the paper at Moon, looking mildly pleased with himself.

"It's still a long ways to Arkansas," Moon said. "Doesn't the city desk have anything better than the ski basin road yarn?"

Hubble described the local news menu without enthusiasm. A one-fatality car-truck collision, vandalism at an elemetary school, a roundup on candidates in an upcoming city council election. Hubble yawned and waved away the rest of it.

Moon picked up his stack of Please Call slips. The top one was from Debbie: *Call me right away. It's an emergency.* Debbie's emergencies tended to such matters as being out of fingernail polish. This one probably had something to do with reminding him of her birthday, which was tomorrow. But he dialed her office number. Her answering machine kicked in, her sweet voice inviting him to leave a message.

"Debbie, how about—" he began. But Shirley was bearing down on him, and Shirley did not approve of Debbie. "I'm at the paper," he said. "I'll call later."

Shirley handed him another Please Call note.

"I think it's your mother,"

"I'll bet it isn't," Moon said. Victoria Mathias did not make telephone calls. She communicated by letter, written in a neat, precise hand on socially correct stationery. Shirley's expression said she felt the kindness she'd shown by walking over with this message had been poorly received. "I mean it's *about* your mother," she said.

Shirley oversaw the telephone system and, unofficially, the office. She was old and tired and would have retired years ago if she didn't need the money. He felt a faint twinge of guilt at his mild rudeness. "Sorry," he said. "I'll call right away."

But the call-back number on the slip was not the number for Victoria Mathias. The area code was not Miami Beach. And the note read, *Pls. call Robt. Toland immediately in regards to your mother.*

Moon frowned. What the hell was this? He punched the button for an outside line and dialed.

"Thank you for calling Philippine Airlines. How may I direct your call?" It was the voice of a young woman pronouncing each word precisely.

"Philippine Airlines?" Moon asked.

"Yes, sir. This is Philippine Airlines." The tone had changed slightly to the one used for drunks, weirdos, and those who dial wrong numbers.

Moon swallowed his surprise. "Do you have a Mr. Robert Toland? My name is Malcolm Mathias. He left a call for me."

"Just a moment."

Moon listened to a telephone ringing.

"Security office," a man's voice said.

"Robert Toland, please," Moon said. Why would the security office—

"Just a minute."

Moon waited. No use thinking about this. No use speculating.

"Toland. What can I do for you?"

"I'm Malcolm Mathias," Moon said. "I had a note to call you."

There was the sound of paper shuffling.

"Mr. Mathias, your mother became ill this morning in the waiting room here. An ambulance was called, and she was taken to West Memorial Hospital." Mr. Toland, having exhausted what was written on his paper, stopped talking.

"Ill?" Moon said. "How ill?"

"I don't have that information," Toland said.

"What was she doing in your waiting room?" Mathias asked. "Do you know who she was meeting?"

"She was preparing to board the flight. At least she had luggage checked onto the aircraft. Would you like to have the hospital number?"

Moon considered what he had been hearing. Victoria Mathias would not become ill in an airport waiting room. Nor would she be boarding an airplane. He laughed. "There's been some sort of screwup," he said. "I think you have the wrong person."

"We take the next of kin from the passport," Toland said. "Am I speaking to"—a pause—"are you Malcolm Thomas Mathias, *Morning Press-Register,* Durance, Colorado?"

"Yes," Moon said. "I am."

And he was, of course, Malcolm Thomas Mathias, managing editor for the past two years of the *Press-Register*. And that meant his mother had gotten her passport out of wherever she kept it, and found somebody to look after Morick in their Miami Beach apartment, and had gone out to the Miami International Airport and bought a ticket to fly somewhere on Philippines Airlines. Another thought occurred to Moon.

"Where are you?" he asked. "Where is this?"

"What do you mean?" Toland said. "It's the airline security office."

"At Miami International? I didn't know Philippine Airlines . . ."

"LAX," Toland said, sounding irritated. "Los Angeles International Airport."

For some reason that made it all suddenly real to Moon. "She's alive? Was it something serious?"

"All I know is what I already told you," Toland said.

"What flight was it?" Moon said. "Where the hell was she going?"

"The flight goes to Honolulu, Manila, and Hong Kong," Toland said. "I could go get her ticket and take a look."

"Never mind," Moon said. He knew where his mother would be going. Somewhere toward Southeast Asia. Somewhere toward where her bright and shining younger son had been burned to ashes in a broken helicopter.

SAIGON, South Vietnam, April 13 (UPI)—President Nguyen Van Thieu announced today that government control of the provisional capital of Xuan Loc had been reestablished in what he called a "resounding defeat of Communist forces."

Yesterday Radio Hanoi had announced that Vietcong troops had captured the city, just 35 miles north of Saigon. Refugees pouring into the capital brought stories of bitter fighting between Communist tanks and ARVN paratroopers.

The Second Day

April 13, 1975

HIS MOTHER was asleep. No, she was unconscious. Comatose. Or perhaps sedated. She lay in a position which no sleeping person would naturally choose: flat on her back, legs extended straight and parallel under the sheet, arms extended tight to the torso.

A transparent tube emerged from plugs in her nostrils. Feeding her oxygen, Moon assumed. Four insulated wires from monitoring machines disappeared under Victoria Mathias's white hospital gown. One terminated under a patch of tape high on his mother's rib cage. Another tube linked her left arm to a bottle hung above the bed. She looked smaller than Moon Mathias remembered her. Surprisingly small. She had always seemed to him the largest person in whatever space she had occupied. Now she seemed to have shrunken, as if all those tubes had drained away her substance.

Someone was standing behind him. It was a woman about Moon's age, black, with a kind round face and a maze of wrinkles around her eyes. A nurse. What does one say under these circumstances? Moon could think of nothing that wouldn't sound inane. He attempted a smile.

"You're her next of kin?" the nurse asked. "Family?"

"I'm her son."

"They think she's going to be all right," the nurse said. "It seems to be a problem with her heart. Dr. Jerrigan's around here someplace. He can tell you about it."

"A heart attack," Moon said.

The nurse looked down at Victoria Mathias, up at the monitor, then at the bottle, and then at the chart. "Looks like they're still waiting for test results," she said. "Things are always slower on weekends. But when they brought her in here we were treating her for severe chest pains. It happened out at the airport, so the paramedics got there in a hurry. That helps."

"I guess so," Moon said. "Has she talked to you? Told you anything about what happened?"

"Not to me, she hasn't," the nurse said. "Maybe to the doctor. But it doesn't look like she's felt much like talking."

"I don't have any idea what she's doing here," Moon said. "Not the slightest idea. She lives in Miami Beach, three thousand miles away. Her husband's an invalid. Lou Gehrig's disease. Paralyzed. Stuck in a machine to help him breathe. She never leaves him alone. And she doesn't even know anyone in Los Angeles."

It occurred to Moon as he said it that he didn't really know if that was true. He had no idea who his mother's friends were these days. Or where they were. Or if she actually had any. Once she had had friends, of course, when they lived in Oklahoma. He remembered them from when he and Ricky were teenagers. Mostly they were neighbors, the parents of his own friends, people his mother did business with, people in St. Stephen's parish at Lawton. But they were older people, of no interest to teenage boys.

Long, long ago. Before the army. Before Victoria Mathias had given up her business, and Oklahoma, and her independence, to give him, her disappointing elder son, a second chance to do something with his life.

"All I know is I heard the ambulance brought her in from the airport," the nurse said. "Have you looked in her purse? Maybe that would tell you. A letter or something."

Victoria Mathias's purse was being held for her at the hospital business office. Moon showed his driver's license, signed for it, and carried it into the lobby. He stopped there and sat for a moment, holding it in his lap. Some childhood inhibition kept him from breaking the tape that the airline's security people had used to seal it. One doesn't pry into one's mother's purse.

"It's not something our family does," his mother would have said, not criticizing those nosy people who invade privacy but putting her two sons on a level at which better performance is expected.

He turned the purse in his hands. It was made of polished pearl-gray leather. Big and expensive-looking. His mother would have been wearing a tailored suit exactly compatible with this color when her heart failed her. Her shoes would have been tasteful and perfectly buffed. He turned the purse in his hands again. A corner was worn.

The leather almost imperceptibly frayed. Frayed? Could this be tbe purse of Victoria Mathias?

Moon fished his glasses from his shirt pocket and inspected the spot. It had been covered with some sort of transparent varnish. Fingernail polish, perhaps. Neatly and precisely applied, as his mother would have done it. He looked at the purse with new interest. Had it gained some sentimental value in the mind of Victoria Mathias? Was his mother less meticulous than his image of her? Was his mother short of money? He thought of the condo where she had moved with Tom Morick after their marriage. Lavish, with its tenth-floor roof garden and the long balcony looking down on the Atlantic surf. When he'd asked her about the rent she had looked embarrassed and said that Tom owned the building.

The scuff mark made opening the purse easier for him—as if it belonged to some stranger into whose affairs he had been somehow injected.

A faint smell came from the purse. Lavender? Lilac? Some flower that had grown in his childhood. They had taken her flowers, he and Ricky. Ricky had found them blooming in a field behind a neighbor's hay shed and picked them. Just weeds, Moon had thought. But they had found a bottle for the stems, and when Victoria Mathias came home from work she had transferred them to a vase and kept them on the mantel until the petals fell off.

Moon sorted through the purse. Something in it surely would tell him what had brought his mother across the continent. He extracted a thick plastic folder bearing the name of a Florida bank. He tapped it against the back of his hand, opened it. Hundred-dollar bills. He glanced around the lobby. No one seemed to be watching him. He counted. Eighty of them, mostly new. Eight thousand dollars. Another mystery. He replaced the folder in the purse and removed two envelopes. One had a Manila return address: Castenada, Blake and Associates, Attorneys-at-Law. It would be something to do with Ricky, Moon knew. Perhaps the law firm Ricky's company used. The other envelope was hand-addressed with no return. The stamp was a white heron in flight against a gaudy sky, canceled in Thailand. Then he noticed it was not addressed to his mother but to Ricky Mathias at Ricky's business address in Vietnam.

The letter inside was also handwritten, and as he unfolded it a photograph fell out. It was a black-and-white print of a woman in a white smocklike affair holding a baby dressed in what looked to Moon like pajamas. The woman was Asian—or perhaps Eurasian. Her face was turned slightly away from the camera. She was looking down, expression pensive. A pretty woman. The baby stared directly into the lens, eyes huge in a heart-shaped face. He felt a faint twitch of foreboding. There was something about the kid—

Moon turned the photograph. The back was blank.

The letter was dated March 12, 1975.

Dear Ricky:

I am writing this in Nong Khai and sending it out with George Rice, so do not attempt to reach me here because I'll be long gone by the time you get it. Our business here is done, and none too soon either, because the Khmer Rouge have been raising hell up in the hills. I go by bus down to Bangkok and fly over to Saigon if the situation makes that possible.

If things are wrong at Saigon, as I expect them to be from what we are hearing about morale in the ARVN, then I will continue to try to deal with things from Thailand and can be reached, as always, at the Hotel Bonaparte de l'Ouest.

> By the way, Eleth Vinh sends her love and says the baby is in fine shape and sent along a photo to prove it. As you guessed, she's uneasy about the gains Pol Pot's army (if you want to call it that) has been making and the dangers to her family. Considering what we're hearing about the conduct of Pol Pot's bandidos, that attitude is sensible. Frankly, I think you ought to get her out of there. Out of Nam, too, for that matter. I recommend that you pay close attention to this and forget the optimistic talk your high brass friends give you and what the U.S. ambassador has been saying on the radio. I'm hearing that certain people are already boarding flights from Saigon and taking with them very heavy luggage. Including, for example, valuable stuff out of the museums. I think time in Saigon is very short.

Moon skipped rapidly through the rest of it, which concerned details of shipping dates, billings, and other concerns of Ricky's business, all of which were incomprehensible to him. So was the signature: a scrawl that might have been B. Yager, or G. Yeyeb, or almost anything with the proper number of letters. He refolded the letter and slipped it back into the envelope.

His mind focused on a single phrase. "Eleth Vinh sends her love and says the baby is in fine shape." Who were they? The obvious guess was that Ricky had been attending to more than business. Had he fathered a child? If he had, that would explain what Victoria Mathias was doing. She was going to see the baby. Was this Vinh woman the mother or a nanny or what? And if Ricky had indeed become a parent, why hadn't he proclaimed the news to Victoria? She'd be the kid's grandmother, after all. Or perhaps Ricky *had* told Victoria. Why, then, had nobody told him? He would be the uncle. Uncle Moon. Why hadn't *he* been told? But he didn't want to think about that. Not now. He remembered that Victoria Mathias had always wanted grandchildren. She'd let Ricky and him, her two bachelor sons, know that without exactly saying it.

He inspected the photograph again. The baby still stared out, heart-faced and somber, directly into the lens. Probably a girl. His niece? Her hair seemed to be black, as was Ricky's. Maybe a trace of some of the facial structure Ricky had inherited from their mother. Nothing else, though. But then he rarely saw parental resemblances in any child. If she was Ricky's daughter, the mother was definitely Asian. Thai or Cambodian or Vietnamese, or Chinese, or Malay, or—

He slipped the print back in with the letter and opened the other envelope. This one was typed, neatly but on a machine with an imperfect *e* and a badly worn ribbon.

Dear Mrs. Mathias:

I am pleased to learn that the papers and other personal effects of your deceased son, my good friend and client Richard Mathias, have reached your hands safely and in good form. I agree with your analysis that these documents indicate that Mr. Mathias had been blessed with the birth of a daughter. I was not aware of this circumstance until I examined the papers which I sent along to you.

Pursuant to your instructions I have contacted your son's employees in Vietnam and am assured that arrangements are being made for the child to be brought to Manila. She will be received by the Sisters of Loretto Convent School here and cared for by the nuns until the proper papers can be obtained and her transportation to the United States arranged.

I regret to inform you that the deteriorating situation in the Republic of Vietnam has made travel difficult and expensive, with extraordinary means required, since many scheduled inbound flights are being canceled and outbound flights are fully booked many days in advance. Therefore I have taken the liberty of withdrawing from Richard Mathias's account at the Bank of Luzon the amount of $2,500 American to cover what I will call "extraordinary expenses," which I anticipate officials in Saigon may impose.

I am informed that arrangements to get a visa for the child and to place her on a flight from Saigon to Manila are being made by Ricky's associates at R. M. Air in Vietnam. I do not yet know details of those arrangements and will advise you by telephone as soon as I learn when the child will arrive in Manila.

Most sincerely, your servant,
Roberto Castenada Bolivar

Moon was feeling better. Ricky seemed to have kept his paternity a secret from just about everyone. He resumed his exploration of the purse and found a folded note.

Mrs. Mathias:

Three phone calls for you. That man called from Manila and said he was returning your call and would try again and then there were two calls from a man who said his name was Charley Ming, but he was calling for somebody named Lum Lee. He called again about an hour later, and this time the other man talked and he said it was terribly important to get in touch with you and would you please call him at the Beverly Wilshire, room 612. I will come in to help next week unless you contact me.

Ella

Two airline tickets were folded into an inside pocket. One was in the name of Mrs. Victoria Mathias Morick, a first-class round-trip to Manila via Honolulu. That was no surprise now. Nor was the second ticket, one-way from Manila to Miami International. The name on it was Baby Girl Lila Vinh Mathias. Victoria Mathias had been en route to rescue her granddaughter when her heart failed her.

WASHINGTON, April 13 (UPI)—As much as $700 million in military supplies has been abandoned by the South Vietnamese army in its disastrous retreat from the Central Highlands, a well-placed Pentagon source estimated today.

The officer, who declined to be identified, said, "It's all in the hands of the North Vietnamese now. We might as well have shipped it directly to Hanoi and avoided the wear and tear."

Still the Second Day

April 13, 1975

THE FIRST WORDS Victoria Mathias said were, "We have a granddaughter."

"Yes," Moon said. "I saw the letters in your purse. How are you feeling?"

"What day is it? How long have I been here?"

"Just one day," Moon said. "It's April thirteenth."

"I've got to go get her," Moon's mother said. She was in a different room now, moved to a different floor, in a different bed. But the wires were still there, and the tubes. Her skin had the pale, waxy look of death and her eyes the glaze of those who can barely discern reality. Moon took her hand. A cold and fragile hand.

"Ricky's dead, you know," she said. "Dead. But he had this daughter."

"I know," Moon said. "I know about Ricky and the baby." *My brother. My niece.* "Don't talk if it tires you. You take it easy now."

Victoria Mathias turned her head slightly and looked at him. She had said, *We have a granddaughter.*

We. There was that.

"I called Ricky's lawyer," she said. Her eyes closed. A long pause. Moon looked nervously up at the monitor screen. The lines on it still moved in a regular pattern, telling him only that his mother was still alive. She's just asleep, he thought. Good. But then she was speaking again, her voice so weak he could hardly understand the words. ". . . that man in the Philippines with the Spanish name. I don't think she ever got there."

"I saw the letter," Moon said. "She will get there, okay? It takes time. You take care of getting well. The nuns in Manila will take care of the baby."

"He didn't seem to know anything," his mother said.

"How about the mother?" Moon asked. "Why can't she bring the child?" He had other questions. Why isn't the mother keeping the baby? was one of them. But Victoria Mathias seemed no longer aware that he was there. Her body, already shrunken under the sheet, seemed to shrink even more.

She frowned vaguely, and her lips moved. "Very unsatisfactory," she seemed to say. But the voice was too weak to be understood and Moon thought he might have only guessed at that phrase. Victoria Mathias communicated by letter. To his mother, all telephone conversations were very unsatisfactory.

The person in charge of saving his mother's life was a doctor named Jerrigan. Dr. Jerrigan made his rounds from ten to eleven and should have been in this ward at about ten-thirty. Now it was fifteen minutes after eleven and Dr. Jerrigan had not arrived.

Moon had sat on the slick plastic chair in the waiting room for more than an hour. During the first thirty minutes of waiting he'd exhausted every possible speculation about his mother's condition and what he should do about it. He had devoted only a few minutes to considering what needed to be done about Ricky's daughter. Obviously, he would first call the lawyer in Manila for today's reading on that problem. The second step would depend on the first. With that decided, he let his mind drift back to the problems he'd left behind him in his rush to the airport.

First, as always, there was Debbie. He could take care of the birthday by finding her something special in Los Angeles—if he could ever get away from this hospital. And then there was the spaniel left in his custody by Shirley until Shirley was safely moved into her new apartment, where spaniels were tolerated. The spaniel had an appointment with a veterinarian and he was supposed to have dropped the damned dog off on his way to work. He'd forgotten about that until he got to the airport at Denver and had had to call the paper. It was Shirley's day off, so the burden fell upon Hubble. Hubble hadn't sounded happy about it, but he said he'd try to find somebody to take care of it. And he would. Hubble was grouchy but reliable. A little like himself, he thought.

So don't worry about the dog. Worry about the other responsibilities he'd left behind. Like J.D.'s truck. Moon inspected his knuckle, which seemed to be scabbing over nicely, and his hands, which despite heavy soaping in the shower still showed evidence of grease in deep cracks and under his fingernails. The grease and the scab were both evidence of J.D.'s failure to maintain his vehicle properly. The baby blue paint always glittered, but J.D's interest stopped with appearances. He never kept the engine properly tuned. Or cleaned it, which explained Moon's greasy hands, slippery wrench handles, and a bloody knuckle. In Moon's opinion, carelessness was only one of of J.D.'s several shortcomings. But he was a good-looking kid, good-natured, and great on the tennis court. And, according to Debbie, even better on the ski slopes. And now J.D's cute little GMC Jimmy sat in Moon's garage, its cute little diesel engine not quite reassembled. J.D. would be without wheels, which didn't bother Moon much. But Debbie was counting on J.D. to drive her up to Aspen this weekend.

The plastic of the waiting room chair crackled as Moon shifted his weight. His back ached. And suddenly the tension that had kept sleep at bay began draining away. He yawned. And when that was accomplished, he felt utterly exhausted. He looked at his watch, eyes barely in focus. Where the hell was Dr. what's-his-name?

Dr. Jerrigan was walking into the waiting room. He was about Moon's age, but a third smaller and a lot trimmer, with a California surfer's tan and the hard, wiry physique of the handball courts. He glanced at Moon, saw nothing to inspire interest, and looked down at his clipboard.

"Morick," he said. "Morick. It looks from this like he's suffering a coronary occlusion of some sort. The situation will probably require a coronary bypass. But we won't know until—"

"Wrong gender," Moon said. "It's Mrs. Victoria Mathias Morick. I am her son."

Dr. Jerrigan frowned at Moon.

"Whatever," he said, and checked his clipboard again. "Oh, yes. She's that woman they brought in from the airport yesterday. Emergency Room checked her in." He flipped through the pages on his clipboard. "We don't have the data we need back from the lab yet but—let's see—" Dr. Jerrigan studied his clipboard, frowned at it. "The EKG shows equivocal coronary abnormalities."

"So what's the prognosis?" Moon said, hoping that *prognosis* was the correct word. "How bad is it?"

Something on Dr. Jerrigan's belt went *beep-beep-beep.* Dr. Jerrigan glanced at his watch, walked about ten steps to a paging phone, picked it up, and talked awhile. When he returned, he looked again at the clipboard. "It doesn't look too good," he said. "But until we get the results of the tests they did last night, I can't really tell."

"Well, then," Moon said, "let's go get those test results. Right now. Let's go find somebody who *can* really tell."

Like many big men, Moon rarely had any need to show his anger and rarely did. But when he did, most people were properly impressed. Dr. Jerrigan was not one of them. He met Moon's stare with no sign of a flinch.

"Mr. Morick," he said, "your mother is not the only sick person in this hospital. She's not my patient. Dr. Rodenski checked her in at ER. This is Sunday. He's off today. I'm looking after her along with my own patients. There's not a damn thing we can do until we know more about her condition except keep her comfortable and stabilized. We can't get those lab reports until they're ready. And I've got a gunshot victim who seems to be trying to die right now."

"Well, goddammit, what's her condition?" Moon asked. "It sounds to me like she had a heart attack. Give me a rundown on her condition. Her chances for survival."

"You want a guess?" Dr. Jerrigan asked, his face slightly flushed. "How can I guess, not knowing any more than we do? But here is your guess. This was probably brought on by some sort of coronary blockage to the heart. A heart attack. Most people survive them."

"In other words, some don't?"

"Of course," Dr. Jerrigan said. "Some don't." Then his gadget was beeping again, and Jerrigan was hurrying away.

At the Pentagon, some senior officers compared the South Vietnamese rout with other military disasters: Napoleon's debacle in Moscow, the fall of France in 1940, the Chinese Nationalist collapse in 1949.

TIME MAGAZINE, APRIL 14, 1975

The Third Day

April 14, 1975

BY MOON'S UNCERTAIN CALCULATIONS of the difference between Pacific Standard Time and whatever time it was in Manila, it was probably the wrong hour to call Ricky's lawyer. But he placed the call anyway and heard an answering machine click on and a soft voice saying that Mr. Castenada would respond to a message when he became available. With Manila thus made to seem more real, Moon left a message asking Mr. Castenada to call him at the Airport Inn number where Shirley had made his reservation. Then he called a taxi and collected his mother's luggage from the Philippine Airlines security office.

The traffic noise here from jetliners overhead and the freeway below his window was thunderous. But he'd asked Shirley for convenience, not for comfort, and Shirley had delivered, as she always did.

He'd take a shower. Maybe that would revive him. He removed his shoes, his socks, and his trousers and then sprawled across the bed, dizzy with that odd sort of fatigue brought on by stress and sleeplessness. He pulled a pillow under his head, put the telephone on his chest, dialed the Colorado area code, then broke the connection and called West Memorial Hospital instead. The nurse who answered in the cardiac unit told him his Mrs. Morick was sleeping and doing as well as could be expected.

Then he called the paper. He asked Shirley for Hubble, but Shirley wanted to talk.

"How is she?"

Moon felt hazy, one step removed from reality. "As well as can be expected," he said. But that wasn't fair. Shirley was a friend. So he gave her the full report, accepted her sympathy, and asked for Hubble.

"He's not back from something or other down at city hall," Shirley said. "That's the meeting you were supposed to sit in on. And you've had five or six calls."

"Anything that looks important?" He asked it out of habit. What could be important today?

"Some long-distancers. One was from the AP bureau in Denver. Said they'd catch you when you got back to town. And then a couple from Los Angeles."

"Did they leave any messages?" Again, habit was speaking. Who cared about messages?

"One was from the airline. They want you to let them know about your mother's luggage. Do you want me to get that taken care of?"

"I picked it up," Moon said.

"And one from a man." There was a pause while Shirley shuffled papers. "A Lee Lum. No, I think it was Lum Lee. He had an accent. When I told him you were gone indefinitely, he said he was actually trying to reach your mother, and it was very important, so I told him he might reach you through the security people at Philippine Airlines."

"Okay," Moon said. The man must think his business was important to follow Victoria to Los Angeles. But what sort of business could it be? He was too tired to think. Add it to the list of puzzles.

"That it?"

"Except the usual stuff that somebody else can handle."

"Did Debbie call?"

A slight pause. "Let me see. Yes."

Moon allowed himself a tired grin. "And said what?" Moon asked.

"She said to tell you she hoped your mother was all right." Shirley's tone was precisely neutral. "And to remind you that Saturday was April twelfth. Was it her birthday?"

"If she calls back tell her I've been trying to call her." Which was a small lie but undetectable, because Debbie's office telephone was notorious for its busy signal, and so was the phone they shared at his house. Living with Debbie had taught Moon the value of small, undetectable lies told in the interest of keeping things peaceful.

"How old will she be?" Shirley inquired sweetly.

"I really don't know," Moon said, avoiding another small lie on technical semantic grounds. How old was Debbie? Twenty-two by her accounting, but since Debbie, too, sometimes told small lies, he really didn't know.

"Is Rooney in? Let me talk to him."

Rooney was working the slot, editing early and relatively unimportant copy to fill tomorrow's inside sections.

"I didn't hire on to do this kind of crap," Rooney said. "When are you coming back?" Rooney sounded sober, which was encouraging if not an absolute guarantee. "And how's your mother?"

"I guess she's going to have to have bypass surgery," Moon said. "But first I want to get a second opinion from a better doctor, and then if she needs an operation I need to find her a different surgeon. The one that has his hands on her now—I wouldn't even let him work on you."

"That bad, huh?" Rooney said. "The way you pick a surgeon is go out in the DOCTORS ONLY parking lot and find the custom-built Mercedes with the TV antenna and the chauffeur wiping the bird shit off it. There's the surgeon who keeps 'em alive long enough to get the bills paid." Rooney paused to consider this advice. "That's what my old granny told me."

Moon was not in the mood for Rooney at the moment. "What's on the menu?" he asked. "What story are you leading with?"

"I don't know yet," Rooney said. "We have a thing out of the State Police and the Game Department about dog packs worrying tourists up around the ski run. I told Hubble we ought to play that one. Give it eight columns, ninety-six points, all caps: TERRIERS TERRORIZE TOURISTS. Or maybe PET PACKS PROWL PARK. Or how about—"

"Get serious," Moon said. Rooney had been hired as a feature writer and did mostly special assignments for the city desk. But once, after too many whiskey sours at an office party, he had confessed to working in a former life as rim man on the *Kansas City Star*. That careless admission of editing experience had made him the paper's utility desk man, writing headlines and handling copy in emergency manpower shortages. It was a job he detested, and Moon had learned that his news selection tended to be eccentric if he was drinking. But now, as Rooney provided a rundown on what he'd been using on inside pages and what he was stacking up for potential front-page use, his judgments seemed reassuringly orthodox. There wasn't anything hot going on, either locally or statewide. Rooney had given big inside space to the Senate approval of price ceilings on domestic oil, which Moon would have used on page one, and the same sort of inside treatment to President Ford's request to Congress for more aid for Saigon. For the front, he was holding the daily Nam battle story, with a sidebar about refugees clogging the highways; a feature about a local kid building his own computer; a two-fatality collision on the Interstate; and a city council discussion of a proposed sewer bond issue. Not bad, considering that Rooney had written the computer yarn himself before Moon's departure had switched him from reporter to desk man.

"Then there's another sidebar on Cambodia that maybe ought to go on page one. Sounds like the Khmer Rouge is gobbling up Phnom Penh." Rooney's tone had lost its flipancy earlier in the recitation of the day's woes. Now it was grim. "Some of this stuff sounds like Attila the Hun is loose again. Everything but the giant pyramids of skulls."

"Yeah," Moon said. He felt a twinge of anxiety through the fatigue. "Well, tell Hubble I'm at the Airport Inn and that Shirley has my number. And switch me back to her."

"Debbie's been calling. Asking about you. I think she misses you." Unlike Shirley, Rooney liked Debbie. All males liked Debbie.

"What's she want?"

"To know when you'd be coming back."

"Tell her I've been trying to call her," Moon said. "And, look, did I ever tell you how nasty Shakeshaft gets about drinking? If I didn't, I'm doing it now. When he hired me I got the temperance sermon. My first job is to make sure nobody drinks in the newsroom. And my second job is to make sure nobody's been drinking before they come in. After that, I worry about getting the paper out."

"I'm not drinking," Rooney said. Coldly.

"Good," Moon said. "But did I tell you old Jerry has a habit of looking into desk drawers, poking around under piles of papers, and—"

"And smelling your breath," Rooney said. "I used to have a managing editor like that."

"You still do. I smelled it last Monday," Moon said, and dropped it there.

He called Colorado Mortgage and Title Insurance. The woman on the reception desk was somebody he didn't know. She said Debbie's line was busy. She took his hotel number and said, yes, she'd tell Debbie he'd called and to call him.

"You did say J.D., didn't you?" she asked.

"No," Moon said. "Tell her Moon Mathias called."

He looked at his watch. Probably too soon to try the Manila number again. Not the hour to sleep either. He was tired, almost dizzy with fatigue, but too tense to sleep. The shower would help. He rescued his shirt from the floor and inspected it. He'd packed without any real thought—shirts, socks, and underwear for a couple of days. The shirt he'd been wearing was knitted of something or other and could serve a second day. He carried it into the bathroom and carefully rinsed out a smudge below the pocket. He was hanging it up to dry when he heard a tapping at the door.

"Just a second," Moon said. He pulled on his trousers.

Two men were at the door, the one in front small, frail and old, the one behind big and young. Both Chinese, Moon thought and, as he thought it, amended the thought to Oriental, and amended that to Asian. It seemed clear that his dead brother was pulling him inevitably into a world where one would need to know the difference between Chinese and Vietnamese and Japanese, Cambodians, Indonesians, and all the rest.

The small man dipped his head slightly and looked up at Moon through thick round glasses. "Mr. Malcolm Mathias?" the man said. "I beg your pardon for this intrusion."

"Yes," Moon said, "I'm Malcolm Mathias. What can I do for you?" The man was wearing a brown suit made of some expensive-looking silky material which, so it appeared, had been slept in. Behind him, the big young man was smiling an apprehensive smile.

"My name is Mr. Lum Lee. I wish to express my concern about the health of your mother." He dipped his head again. "Also, I wish to express my condolences at the death of your esteemed brother, Mr. Richard Mathias." Mr. Lum Lee cleared his throat. "Your brother was a good friend to me. . . ." He paused, inspecting Moon, and added in a voice not much above a whisper, "And sometimes an associate in business." He cleared his throat again, looked at Moon, and added, "Sometimes. Yes. And I hope the health of your mother is improving."

"Yes," Moon said. "Thank you." He held out his hand. "Malcolm Mathias," he said. "How do you do. Come on in. Find a place to sit down."

Mr. Lee's hand was small and dry. Totally without strength. It made Moon think of bird bones.

"Excuse me," Mr. Lum Lee said. "I would present the son of my oldest daughter, Mr. Charley Ming. Mr. Ming has been good enough to be of assistance to me while I am in the United States."

Mr. Ming's hand, in contrast to his grandfather's, was a wrestler's: broad, hard, strong. But his smile was bashful. He held one of the room's two chairs for his grandfather, refused Moon's offer of the second one, and sat ramrod erect on the edge of the bed, holding his hat in his lap. Mr. Lee had placed his hat on the dresser beside his chair. His thick gray hair was cut short, into military bristles.

"I think your secretary will have told you I called," Mr. Lee said.

"Yes," Moon said. "But she didn't tell me anything about your business. She didn't say you would be coming to see me." How had this man located him? It must have been through either the airline security office or the hospital. And, if his courtesy went deeper than his words, why hadn't he called from the lobby to see if this visit was welcome? Was it because he didn't want to take a chance that Moon would want to avoid him? Moon found himself smiling at that. He'd seen too many movies about Oriental intrigue.

Mr. Lee looked abashed. "I am very sorry about this," he said. "I hope this visit is not inconvenient to you in any way. If it is—" Mr. Lee reached for his hat and started to rise.

"No, no. Not at all," Moon said. "I'm delighted to meet a friend of my brother."

"And a business associate as well," Mr. Lee added.

"We don't know much about his death," Moon said. "Just what his attorney told my mother, and what the American consulate told us. All about the same. But no details."

"It was a tragedy," Mr. Lee said. "A genuine loss. A fine young man. An honorable man." He shook his head solemnly. His eyes behind the thick lenses seemed even more watery and vague.

"Could you tell me anything more about it? All we were told is that he was in a helicopter in Cambodia, and it crashed in the mountains near the border with Vietnam, and Ricky was killed."

"I understand the wreckage was found by a unit of the Army of the Republic of Vietnam," Mr. Lee said. "The helicopter had burned when this unit arrived."

"Ricky was flying it?" Moon said.

"I think not. Another man was the pilot, I believe, excuse me," Mr. Lee said. "A Mr. Pol Thiu Eng, who works for R. M. Air. I believe it was him. I beg your pardon."

"They never told us anything," Moon said. "Just that it was an accident. Do you know how it happened? Or what Ricky was doing? They said he was flying out of Cambodia."

Mr. Lee looked thoughtful. "Business," he said. The sound of jet engines overhead engulfed the room. Mr. Lee sat patiently, studying his hands, waiting for silence. "I would think it would have been business."

"His business was helicopter repair and maintenance," Moon said. "Mostly avionics. Repairing the electronic gear on aircraft. He has a maintenance contract with the South Vietnamese Air Force. Or had one."

"With the Army of the Republic of Vietnam, I believe," Mr. Lee said. "With ARVN and with the RVN, the navy, too. Excuse me. With General Thang, I believe. Yes. But Mr. Mathias also had other business as well, and in Cambodia I believe it would be primarily the delivery business."

"Delivery?" Of course Ricky would have other businesses. Ricky wasn't the sort to be happy with just one iron in just one fire.

"A good business in recent times," Mr. Lee said. And added what sounded like "Unfortunately." But the word was drowned by another jet overhead. When it had passed, Mr. Lee allowed his small round mouth to shape itself into a smile. "Delivering things out of places where the Communists are coming in. Delivering property to Hong Kong and Singapore and Manila—places that are secure. People who own valuable things will pay well for such deliveries."

"Oh," Moon said.

Mr. Lee shrugged, his expression philosophical. "I myself have paid well," he said. "It is these terrible times we live in. Buddha taught us that one who runs against the wind carrying a torch will surely burn his hand. And yet we run against the wind."

"This is how you were associated with Ricky?"

Mr. Lee nodded.

"As a customer?"

"As a contractor," Mr. Lee agreed. "Mr. Mathias's company sometimes contracted to pick up an item somewhere for me and take it someplace else."

"In Cambodia?"

"In Cambodia. In Laos. In Vietnam. My home had been in Vietnam, in the highlands where it is cooler. But unfortunately, the war—" Mr. Lee shrugged again and lapsed into silence. Moon thought of the letter to Ricky. The details that had been incomprehensible when he'd read it must have referred to this delivery business.

"And now, where is home?"

Mr. Lee smiled. "Home?" He thought about it and smiled ruefully. "It is still in Vietnam," he said. "I moved out of the mountains to a place near Hue. It proved an unfortunate choice."

"I guess I meant the family home," Moon said, wondering why he'd bothered to ask that standard polite question.

"The family comes from South China," Mr. Lee said. "Canton. But the Nationalist Army defeated the warlord faction there, and my grandfather moved our family to the south. Then the Japanese defeated the Nationalists. My grandfather was killed, and my father moved the family down toward the border of Vietnam. Then the Japanese were defeated by the Americans and we moved again. And then the Communists defeated the Nationalist Army and my father was killed."

Mr. Lee sighed. "A long story," he said. "I moved the family into Indochina. But the French came back in when the Japanese were driven out, and the Viet Minh, who had been fighting the Japanese, began fighting the French. My two brothers and my son were killed then. After the French were driven out, the Americans came in, and my wife and one of my grandchildren were killed and we moved again—" Mr. Lee broke off the recitation with an apologetic look at Moon. "I beg your pardon," he said. "You were being polite. I was boring you with a family history."

"No, no," Moon said. "I am interested."

"But you are also a busy man. With many responsibilities. I must not waste your time. I must tell you that I am here because one of the very last transactions your brother and I engaged in was not concluded. Not totally completed. The tragedy interrupted it. The delivery was not consummated."

He peered at Moon through the thick lenses, his watery eyes seeking understanding.

"The goods were on the helicopter when it crashed?"

"I think not," Mr. Lee said, looking sad.

A jet came over, lower than usual. Mr. Lee waited.

So did Moon. It was the fatigue, he thought, that gave these two men, and the room, and everything else, a sense of unreality. He glanced at Mr. Charley Ming, who—caught staring—looked away. Mr. Lee was looking down at his small hands, folded in his lap.

"I want to learn where my merchandise has gone," he said. "I think Mr. Mathias put it somewhere for safekeeping. But the people at his company knew nothing about it. Your brother's papers had already been sent to his attorney in Manila. But when I got to Manila, again I was too late. He had sent everything to your mother in the United States." He shrugged, looking at Moon with the question in his face.

"You want to look at Ricky's papers to see if they'll help you find—whatever it was?"

"Exactly," Mr. Lee said. "For that I came to the United States. But when I reached Miami Beach, your mother had already left."

"She brought a few things with her," Moon said. "Mostly letters, I think. She wouldn't have brought business papers. In fact, I doubt if she would have received his business stuff. Whoever is running the business would need them. They would still be in his office, I'd think."

Mr. Lee looked at Moon, examining his face. He made a deprecatory gesture. "I think not necessarily so," he said. "Too bad, I think, but some business in some places must be kept very confidential."

Mr. Lee's expression said that he knew Moon, a sophisticated man, would have already known this, but he explained.

"It is not just in deference to the interests of his clients who don't want their privacy invaded, but in the interests of your brother. He wouldn't want too much unneeded information written down in files. Almost everybody can open files."

"Oh," Moon said, digesting this. "You're saying some of the things Ricky was doing were illegal?"

Mr. Lee looked startled. "Oh, no. No," he said. "Mr. Mathias was an honorable business person. But—" He paused, shrugged. "The helicopters, for example," he said, voice patient. "One of the assets of Mr. Mathias's company is control of helicopters of the Army of the Republic of Vietnam. And sometimes RVN helicopters. His people fix them and test-fly them, and then he notifies the army, and ARVN pilots come to fly them back to Saigon. Or sometimes pilots of R. M. Air return them to their bases."

"And who is to say where the copter was flown on the test flight?" Moon said. "Or how long it took to repair it?"

"Exactly," Mr. Lee said. "And who is to care? And, of course, a helicopter of the Army of the Republic of Vietnam can fly to places where flying other aircraft would be—" Mr. Lee searched for the right explanation.

"Not be allowed?" Moon suggested. "Or raise questions? Or provoke curiosity?"

"Exactly," Mr. Lee said again. "There would be much filling in of forms, and getting permits, and waiting, and—" Mr. Lee grimaced and rubbed thumb and fingers together, the universal symbol for bribery.

Moon nodded. Ricky was not the sort to overlook an opportunity.

"So one would not look for a file on the business he did with me in the business office of R. M. Air," Mr. Lee said. "One would expect more discretion."

"What was the merchandise?" Moon asked. It wouldn't be drugs. Ricky wouldn't deal with that. Not that Mr. Lee would tell him if it was. Some sort of contraband, though. Something that would require a bit of smuggling. But not something that would make you ashamed.

"An urn," Mr. Lum said. "Antique. Very old. Not very valuable to others, but priceless to our family."

For the first time the big man, whom Moon had come to think of as the bodyguard, spoke. "Yes," he said. "It holds our luck."

"Worth how much?" Moon asked, trying to understand all this.

"Beyond price," Mr. Lee said.

"And my brother seems to have lost it?"

"No, no," Mr. Lee said, agitated that Moon would read such an implication into this situation. "No. Mr. Mathias was a most efficient man. Most dependable. Worthy of complete trust. He would have placed it somewhere safe until he could complete the delivery. But then—" Mr. Lee shrugged, not wanting to mention Ricky's death. "Some things cannot be predicted."

"I'll go through all the papers my mother was sent," Moon said. "If I find anything, where can I reach you?"

Mr. Lee did not react to that. He reached into the inside pocket of his coat and extracted a flat case of well-worn silver. He opened it and held it out to Moon, displaying six thin black cigars.

"If you smoke tobacco you will find these excellent," he said.

"I've finally managed to quit," Moon said. "But thank you."

Mr. Lee reluctantly closed the case and returned it to its pocket. "You were wise," he said. "It is known to be bad for one's health."

"But look," Moon said, "it doesn't bother me. Go ahead and smoke."

Mr. Lee extracted the case, and from it a cigar, snipped off the end with a little silver tool designed for the purpose, gave Moon a grateful smile, and lit it with a tiny silver lighter that seemed to be built into the end of his fountain pen. He looked relieved. For the first time in months, Moon found himself yearning for a cigarette.

"Give me a telephone number where I can contact you," Moon said. "Or an address. I'll need that."

"That is most kind of you," Mr. Lee said, savoring the taste of the cigar smoke. "Unfortunately, I think it would not be practical." He turned his face away from Moon and exhaled a thin blue cloud. When he turned back he exposed an apologetic smile. "You see," he said, "I know something of your brother's business procedures. He was most careful. Not just in where he kept records but in what he wrote, when something had to be written."

Mr. Lee's smile apologized in advance again. "Not that this transaction was in any way illegal, you understand. But in Asia these days things are not normal. These days one does not encourage authorities to cause trouble."

"Because of the way he was using government copters?"

"Well, yes. There is that," Mr. Lee said.

"So why keep records at all?"

Through the blue haze which now shrouded him, Mr. Lee looked incredibly old. When he allowed the smile to fade away, his small round face sagged. "I do not know," he said, "but he did. I suppose it was necessary because other people worked for him. And with him. In various businesses. He would need to keep them informed. He wrote letters. He wrote in a way that would be really understood only by those who needed to understand. If I could see such letters, I would recognize any references to—"

The telephone by Moon's elbow rang.

Moon glanced at Mr. Lee, said, "Excuse me," and picked it up.

"Mathias," he said.

A moment of silence. Then a cough. Then, "Yes. Hello. Yes."

"This is Malcolm Mathias," Moon said. "Is this Mr. Castenada?"

"Yes," the voice said. "Roberto Castenada. How can I be of service?"

"I'm the brother of Richard Mathias," Moon said. "Your client." He hesitated, thinking he should correct that. Former client. Former brother. "I believe my mother made arrangements with you to bring Richard's daughter to the United States."

"Ah," Castenada said. "To Manila."

"Manila, then," Moon said. "Is she there?"

"Ah," Castenada said. "There are . . ." The telephone was silent except for the sound of breathing. Moon was tired. Here he was in a Los Angeles hotel room, hearing a man exhaling in Manila. "Complexities," Castenada said.

"Confusions. Many confusions. The child has not yet arrived in Manila. Or if she did arrive, I have not been informed and the child has not been delivered to the Sisters. I just called them and they said no. They have heard nothing."

"Then where is she?"

Mr. Lee had let his fatigue overcome him and sat with eyes closed, head tilted forward. The tone of Moon's question jerked him awake. He sat up, reached for his hat, and stood, signaling his intention to leave. Moon motioned him to sit.

"I do not know what happened," Castenada was saying. He spoke in precise English about the disorders in Laos, advances of the Khmer Rouge in Cambodia, a flood of refugees reaching Saigon, disruptions of communications, cancellations of airline schedules, unusual troubles with visas. "Perhaps they arrived in Manila but are staying with friends. Perhaps they are still in Saigon, having difficulties with exit papers and aircraft reservations. Perhaps. I have tried to make calls, to make inquiries, no one picked up the telephone, and since then I have not been able to get a call through."

"I see," Moon said.

"One cannot do anything," Castenada said, and, in his precise, prissy voice, explained why. Nothing was working in Saigon anymore without bribery. Planes that were scheduled to fly sat on the runways. Planes that were scheduled to arrive didn't arrive. Airports were closed. Borders were closed. Castenada droned on, describing chaos replacing civilization. Across the room Mr. Lee was slumping again, fighting off sleep, being overpowered by some terrible accumulation of fatigue. He sagged in the chair, face bloodless. Through the thick, distorting lenses his eyes seemed to waver out of focus. Moon glanced at Lee's grandson. The big man was watching his grandfather, looking concerned.

"What are you doing now?" Moon asked. "What steps are you taking to find that child?"

Silence while Castenada considered this. Lee sighed, removed his glasses, rubbed his eyes.

"Everything that can sensibly be done," Castenada said, finally. "We are waiting for information. When the child arrives at the school, the Sisters will—"

"Can't you do more than wait?"

"Mrs. Mathias arrives today. I will help her make contacts. There seems to be a need to trace this situation backward."

"My mother won't be there today," Moon said. "She's in the hospital. I think she had a heart attack."

Castenada expressed shock. He expressed sympathy and regrets. He would do what he could, but Moon must understand that might be very little. More was beyond his power. He could determine if the child had arrived in Manila. If she had, he would attempt to trace her. If she had been delayed en route, he would attempt to find where this had happened. But it was not likely that he, Castenada, would have the power to effect the outcome of this affair if the Asian mainland was involved. Perhaps someone would have to go. Sometimes the personal touch was needed. But he could not travel. He could serve only as adviser.

"Thank you," Moon said. "I will call you when I decide what to do."

"And I will keep you informed," Castenada said. "If I learn anything." His tone suggested he didn't expect that to happen. "Good-bye."

Mr. Lee's eyes were open again, his consciousness returned to this hotel room by some triumph of will.

"I beg your pardon," he said. "We have intruded on your privacy. A family matter."

Moon dismissed that with a gesture. "We were talking about records of your transaction."

"Yes," Mr. Lee said. "I was about to ask if you could allow me to look through your brother's letters. I hope that will help me determine the place where my family's little urn was left."

"That might be possible," Moon said. "I will get them from my mother and look through them and get in touch with you."

"You don't have them?" Lee no longer looked sleepy. His eyes shifted to the luggage beside Moon's dresser—a woman's matching blue suitcases, an expensive-looking leatherbound case, and Moon's grubby hanging bag.

Moon's distaste for deception warred with his fatigue and lost. He was tired. He yearned for solitude to consider what Castenada had told him. To decide what he must do about it. Besides, the sympathy he felt for Mr. Lee was overlaid with skepticism. None of this seemed real.

"I will have to get them," Moon said. "Where can I call you?"

Mr. Lee made a faint sound that probably would have become the first word in an argument. But he cut it off and rose shakily to his feet. He extracted a card from his wallet, a pen from his coat, and wrote.

"Here is where I am staying." He handed Moon the card and walked stiffly to the door, trailed by his grandson. There he turned back and looked at Moon. "This urn is very important to my family," he said. "I intend to offer a reward of ten thousand dollars for assistance that leads to its recovery."

"I'm not eligible for a reward," Moon said. "If my brother misplaced your urn, I feel responsible. I'll do all I can to help you recover it."

Mr. Lee made a movement that was something between a bow and a nod.

"Mr. Mathias," he said, "your brother talked of you often. From what he told me of you, I place a high value on that promise. And if I can help you locate your niece, I hope you will allow me to do so."

"Thank you," Moon said. "But first I have to decide what to do."

But he had a sick feeling. He knew what he'd have to do. He'd have to go find Ricky's kid.

BANGKOK, Thailand, April 15 (Agence France-Presse)—Two refugee South Vietnamese military officers said today that embittered ARVN troops used their tank gun to destroy the ancestral tombs of President Nguyen Van Thieu before they withdrew from Phan Rang, the home of the president's family.

The two, with seven other refugees, arrived at Bangkok airport yesterday in a military helicopter. They said their ranger battalion had been cut off and destroyed by Communist troops south of Phan Rang.

The Fourth Day

April 15, 1975

FROM THE LOS ANGELES International Airport to Honolulu, Moon Mathias alternated sleeping the sleep of the exhausted and reading through the papers he'd extracted from his mother's luggage. He'd been through them hurriedly in his hotel room, having called the number Lum Lee had given him and summoned Mr. Lee to join him.

The night before, when Lee and his grandson had finally left, Moon had decided to see no more of the two. The whole business seemed unreal, if not downright sinister. Lee, if that was his name, was probably involved in something illegal, and the so-called grandson was his bodyguard. But with the normal light of day, sanity had returned. Lee no longer seemed to be some renegade Chinese Nationalist general running opium out of the Burma poppy fields. He was just a tired old man on family business. Whatever he was, it was no skin off Moon's twice-broken nose. If he was engaged in something nefarious with Ricky, Moon wanted no part of it. He didn't even want to know about it.

And so he had called Mr. Lee. Mr. Lee had come, promptly and alone. He'd politely taken a chair across the corner of the bed and explained that his grandson was at work. Moon had hoisted his mother's heavy business case onto the bed, undone the straps, dumped out the bundles of papers, and sorted rapidly through the pile. Lee had leaned forward in his chair and watched, all senses alert, no sleepiness now. These papers are my brother's, Moon had thought, but they mean a lot to this old stranger and nothing at all to me. I am the outsider here, not Mr. Lee.

He worked grimly through the pile, looking for anything that might be painfully personal, or criminal, or which fell into some nameless, unthinkable category which would not be fit for the eyes of this crumpled little stranger. Looking for what? For something that would somehow relate to him, the brother, the other son of Victoria Mathias. And when he realized what he was doing, he had stopped looking and pushed the entire pile over to Mr. Lee.

To hell with it. His mother seemed to have been sent whatever had been found in Ricky's office by whoever had cleaned it out. "See if you can find anything useful," Moon said. "Help yourself. Take a look."

Mr. Lee had expressed gratitude and had taken a look, eagerly and efficiently. He made occasional notes, using a slim little pen that seemed to be genuine gold, and a slim little pad in a worn leather case. He seemed to be recording only names and addresses: a hotel in Bangkok; a shop in Pleiku; a village somewhere on the Thailand-Cambodia border; the name of someone who worked for Air America, which Moon recalled was supposed to be the ill-concealed cover airline of the CIA. Otherwise, names and places and numbers meaningless to Moon. And all the while Mr. Lee was jotting his notes he was explaining in his soft voice why the information might somehow lead him to the urn full of ancestral bones—his family's *kam taap*.

When Moon had called room service for coffee and sandwiches, Mr. Lee had added tea and fruit to the order and insisted on paying. He had done so with a hundred-dollar bill for which the bellman had insufficient change. Finally Mr. Lee had left, taking his notes.

"Did you find what you needed?" Moon asked. "Do you know where to find the urn?"

"Ah, no," Mr. Lee said. "But I have names now of people to call. Perhaps one of them can help. Perhaps not. Perhaps I will have to impose upon your time again." He removed his glasses and bowed to Moon.

"You have been kind to a stranger," he said. "The Lord Buddha taught that the deeds of a kind man follow him like his shadow all of his days."

Moon had gone for a walk then, out amid the roar of jets rising from the LAX runways and the whine of the freeway traffic. He walked twenty-seven blocks in what seemed to be the smog-diffused light of the dying day approximately north by northwest. Then he walked the twenty-seven blocks back again. He'd hoped the exercise would carry him back to some sense of reality—and it helped. He could think again of J.D's diesel engine waiting in his garage to be reassembled, of Debbie's disappointment at the missed birthday, and of how the paper—chronically shorthanded—would be handling his absence. He had even decided what to do about Victoria Mathias.

The next morning he handled most of it in an hour on the phone: having a dozen roses delivered for Debbie, leaving a message for J.D. that all he needed to do now was put in a new set of glow plugs and reassemble the engine, and trying to give Hubble some ideas for filling up the *Press-Register*'s annual nightmare—the vacation edition.

Rescuing Victoria Mathias from the jerk with the California suntan took two calls. The man he knew back home in the Durance General Hospital emergency room gave him the name and number of a heart specialist on staff named Blick.

"Good to talk to you," Blick said. "You'll be glad to hear that Sandra is doing just fine at Pepperdine. Nothing but A's."

Sandra? Sandra Blick? Oh, yes. They'd run a feature about her, with a picture. She'd won some sort of scholarship at the Colorado Science Fair. "I'm not surprised to hear that," Moon had said, and told him what had happened to Victoria.

"Where is she?" Blick had asked. "In West General in L.A.? I'll get you a good man on it. Somebody you can trust."

Within an hour, Blick had called him back.

"I reached the cardiologist you need," Blick said. "A woman named Serna. Great reputation. She wants to get your mother moved to Cedars-Sinai."

"I've heard of that one," Moon said.

"You should have," Dr. Blick said. "It's one of the four or five best hospitals in the country. Now, let me give you the telephone numbers you'll need. And I'll tell you how to make the transfer."

At West General, Moon found that Dr. Jerrigan was not at the hospital and the doctor who had checked Victoria in was otherwise occupied. His mother was barely awake. He signed the required forms certifying that he was checking her out "against medical advice." He scheduled the ambulance, collected her medical file, and signed financial forms. At Cedars-Sinai he checked her in and surrendered the file to a nurse at the desk in the cardiac ward. Then he waited thirty-seven minutes. Almost thirty-eight. A chubby woman with short gray hair and a round, serene face appeared, carrying the file he had delivered. She introduced herself as Emily Serna, sat down next to him on the waiting room sofa, and gave him the bad news.

All indications were that his mother had barely survived a severe heart attack. The circumstances suggested she might soon have another one. If she did, the odds were heavily against her living through it. A catheterization test was needed, an angiogram to determine the extent of arterial blockage and the damage already done to the heart muscle. "There's some risk with an angioplasty," Dr. Serna said. "Heavier because of your mother's condition."

"Angioplasty," Moon said. "That's running the fiber optic gadget up the artery to find the blockage?"

Dr. Serna nodded.

"How much risk?"

"Well, I'd say there's a ninety-five percent chance she'll have another heart attack—and soon—if we don't do anything. And I don't think she'd survive it. We need the angiogram to tell us what to do. Even in her condition the risk of the test being fatal is much, much smaller. If bypass surgery is indicated, then the risk might go as high as fifteen or twenty percent."

Moon considered. Dr. Serna waited, face sympathetic. She looked to him to be extremely competent.

"Okay," Moon said. "Is there a form I need to sign?"

"I have it," Dr. Serna said.

Moon signed it.

"Now I have a question for you," Dr. Serna said. "We had a call from Miami Beach transferred over from West General." She checked her notes. "It was from a Dr. Albert Levison. He said he was the physician attending Tom Morick. That's your stepfather? He asked to be provided a complete account of your mother's health. Does that sound reasonable?"

"It does. My mother is married to Tom Morick," Moon said, aware that his voice sounded stiff. "Morick has amyotrophic lateral sclerosis. He's pretty much paralyzed. In fact he's in an iron lung, dying fast. He'll want to know everything."

"We'll send Dr. Levison all the details, then. He can explain them to Mr. Morick. And your mother is more awake now, if you want to see her."

Victoria Mathias managed a smile, but just barely. Yes, she was feeling better. Less pain in her chest, but maybe that was the morphine. But what had he found out about the baby? Moon said nothing really definite, and that caused Victoria Mathias to give him a long, silent look.

"Malcolm," she said, "I'm a big girl. That means the baby hasn't arrived in Manila, doesn't it? Does it also mean that Mr. Castenada doesn't know where she is?"

"That's what it seems to mean."

"And that must mean she's still in Vietnam," she said.

"Or still en route," Moon said. "Castenada seemed to believe whoever was supposed to send her off in Saigon was having trouble getting her on a flight."

His mother studied him. "What did you think of Castenada?"

Moon shrugged. "Hard to tell over the telephone."

"He doesn't instill much confidence, I'm afraid."

"No. He doesn't."

She made a feeble effort to move her hand across the sheet toward him. Let it fall. Moon reached out and took it.

"Malcolm," she said, "I'm afraid you're going to have to go to Manila and take care of this."

"I will," Moon said. "But first we have to get you well."

"I don't think there's time for that. I was watching the television news out at the airport before this happened. Things seem to be going to hell in that part of the world."

"I can't just go off and leave you."

"Son," she said, "there's nothing you can do for me here. It's up to the doctor. You just have to go and get our granddaughter."

And so Moon went.

SAIGON, South Vietnam, April 16 (AP)—Communist rockets last night detonated an ammunition dump at Bien Hoa thirty miles north of here. The blast shook the capital and reinforced reports that the Bien Hoa air base, largest in Vietnam, had come under artillery fire.

The Fifth Day

April 17, 1975

THE JET DESCENDED THROUGH RAIN to the Manila airport. Out the water-streaked window beside his seat, Moon could see nothing but the bleak inside of solid cloud cover, then a lush green landscape blurred by the falling water, then puddled runways lined with weeds. His impression of the terminal was of roaring, clamorous confusion. A prematurely old building with flaking paint, cracks in too many floor tiles, and too much dirt. The air conditioner worked too well, making the humid air unpleasantly sticky.

Moon felt smothered, exhausted, uneasy. His mother's purse with eighty hundred-dollar bills in it was in his suitcase. What was the rule about bringing cash into the Philippines? Moon had a vague recollection of currency restrictions, but that probably concerned taking money out, not bringing it in.

The immigration agent was a skinny middle-aged man wearing what looked like a military uniform. He glanced at Moon's passport and at Moon and said, "How long in the Philippines?" in oddly accented English.

"Just a couple of days," Moon said, "maybe less." But the agent was already looking past him at the pretty girl next in line.

Customs was equally cursory. Moon handed over the declaration sheet he'd filled out on the plane and stood, shoulders slumping, while the agent read it.

"Nothing to declare?" the agent asked, without looking up.

"Just clothing," Moon said.

He opened Moon's dented old American Tourister, glanced in, closed it. Then he patted Victoria Mathias's briefcase.

"This?"

"Business papers," Moon said. "Letters, personal correspondence, things like that."

"Um," the clerk said. He motioned Moon to pick up his luggage and move along.

The door marked EXIT TO PUBLIC TRANSPORTATION was guarded by two teenagers in dark glasses, with the khaki uniforms and caps that Moon assumed were Philippine Army uniforms. Soldiers, surely, because they both held the same model M16 automatic rifles that Moon had trained with at Fort Benning. They lounged against the wall looking sinister in thelr glasses. He carried his bags past them, wondering if they were watching him. They didn't seem to be watching anyone.

Victoria Mathias's travel agent had made reservations for her at the Hotel Maynila, a shiny edifice of tropical-modern architecture. Moon explained to the desk clerk why Malcolm Mathias was claiming a room reserved for

Victoria Morick. The clerk looked bored, said, "Ah, yes," expressed sympathy, and handed Moon the key.

It hit Moon, finally, as he stood waiting for the elevator. Jet lag, he guessed. Too many hours without untroubled sleep. He leaned against the wall, eyes closed, surprised by the sound of the elevators doors sliding open. At the door of his eleventh floor room he had trouble making the key work. He slumped on the bed while trying to dial Castenada's office and screwed up the number twice before getting a busy signal. When he lay back on the pillow waiting to try again, sleep overwhelmed him.

He came awake slowly, conscious at first of the strangeness of the pillow against his face. Then he was jarringly aware of being on an alien bed. With his clothes on, even his shoes tied. Aware he was in a strange room, with no notion of where he was, or when it was, or why he was here. For Moon it was all too familiar, a skip back into the past of his last year in college and his time in the army. Drinking had become his hobby. Awakening in the wrong bed in a strange room with his head buzzing with hungover confusion had been a regular Sunday morning experience. But that had ended years ago. The last time he had suffered such an awakening had been the worst of all—a nightmare that had ended boozing for him forever.

He'd been aware at first of the bandages, of the pain in his head, of the tubes connecting his arm to something, that his left wrist and hand were encased in a cast. Hearing the breathing of the man asleep in an adjoining bed, the sound of a telephone ringing somewhere: hospital paraphernalia. And then a nurse was there. How did he feel? Was he well enough to talk to the policeman? The woman left while he searched for an answer. The Military Police captain replacing her beside his bed told him he had a right to call a lawyer if he wanted one.

Moon didn't want to be remembering that. He rolled off the bed. In the bathroom he washed his face and glanced at his wristwatch. But it told him only the Los Angeles time. Here it seemed to be morning. The digital clock beside his bed said nine twenty-two, but not whether it was A.M. or P.M. The sunlight filtering through high thin clouds over Manila Bay seemed to be morning light, and the traffic on the boulevard below—cars headed mostly toward downtown Manila—must be going-to-work traffic.

This morning the telephone in the office of Castenada, Blake and Associates rang only once. A woman's voice said, "Law offices"; the same words in the same tone one heard in Durance or Denver or—most likely—Karachi. But then Castenada's voice, with its exotic accent.

"Ah," Castenada said. "Mr. Mathias. Am I correct that you are in Manila?"

"Yes," Moon said. "As I told you. I came to pick up Ricky's child."

"Yes," Castenada said. Hesitation. "Can you come down to the office?"

"Of course," Moon said, puzzled by the tone of this. Of course he would have to come to the office. There would be papers to be signed, fees to be paid, expenses to be covered, arrangements to be explained. "The child," he said. "She has arrived safely?"

"Ah," Castenada said. "Not yet. You are at the Hotel Maynila, I think? Where your mother had made reservations. That is about fifteen minutes from here by taxi. Would it be convenient for you to come now?"

The cabbie looked surprised when Moon told him the address, and Moon was surprised at the direction it led them. They turned away from the bay and the towering buildings he'd seen from his hotel window and into narrow old streets where ramshackle apartment buildings were crowded between auto repair shops, mattress factories, even a chicken processing plant. People everywhere, children everywhere, a swarm of street vendors pushing their carts. Dirt, music from upstairs windows, a ragged man begging, color, vitality, the fetid smell of the drainage ditch running beside a broken sidewalk.

Something like a gloriously magnified version of the trumpet vine that had grown on the porch of his childhood grew here from the wall of a shuttered bar. Moon tried to compare it with Mexico, his only out-of-country experience. But Debbie had made their reservations at the Acapulco Pyramid. They'd seen nothing like this, not even on the drive through the barrio from the airport.

The cabbie was a short, skinny man with very black hair and a barber who had shaved the back of his neck unusually high.

"I wonder if I gave you the right address," Moon said, and repeated it. "Would there be law offices in this part of the city?"

"Oh, yes," the cabbie said. "One more block, I think. Then just around the corner. Then we will see." He laughed. "If not here, we try somewhere else. In Manila, lawyers you can find everywhere."

The cab stopped at a two-story structure of faded pink concrete block with the barred windows that seemed common to this part of Manila. A half-dozen signs lined the front door, a midnight blue that had weathered, but not enough to fit its pink surroundings. The first sign advertised an accountant, and the second read:

LAW OFFICES

CASTENADA, BLAKE AND ASSOCIATES

The cabbie turned enough to show Moon his profile. "Here it is," he said. He announced the fare in pisos. That reminded Moon he'd forgotten to change any money into Philippine currency. After laborious conversion mathematics, the cabbie took his pay in U.S. cash and Moon pushed through the blue door with the disgruntled feeling of the tourist who suspects he has been cheated.

The hallway was narrow and dark, floored with linoleum tiles. Moon walked down it, irritation replaced by uneasiness. The door at the end of the hall had a LAW OFFICES sign beside it. It stood partly open. *Alice down the rabbit hole,* Moon thought. At the hotel he had felt uneasy about going to this appointment wearing rumpled slacks and a shirt he'd rinsed in his Los Angeles hotel room. That worry had long since vanished.

The door opened into a small reception room. A chair, a padded bench, a secretarial desk with telephone and Rolodex but no secretary. Beyond the desk, another door with a little sign on it saying: MR. CASTENADA. No door for Blake. No doors for Associates.

Moon tapped on the only door.

A masculine voice said something in what Moon guessed was Tagalog and then "Come in" in English. Moon pushed the door open.

He had expected Roberto Bolivar Castenada to be as emphatically Old Spanish as the name. Although this man sat high behind a huge and heavy desk, he was small, frail, and very dark. Emphatically a Filipino. Black eyes prominent in a narrow face, black hair showing gray, a sharp prominent chin, a tentative smile showing large white teeth. About sixty, Moon thought. Maybe older. How could you tell with an unfamiliar race?

"Mr. Mathias," the man said. "Ricky's older brother. It

is good to meet you at last." The smile faded. "Even though the circumstances are bleak."

"You're Mr. Castenada?" Moon said.

The man nodded, made an embarrassed gesture. "You will please excuse me for not rising to greet you." He held out a slender hand, expression wry. Moon leaned forward to take it and saw why the man sat so high. He was propped on cushions in a battery-powered wheelchair.

"Malcolm Mathias," Moon said. "How do you do."

"Welcome to Manila," the man said. "Electra has gone out to get some coffee and sweets for our meeting. Otherwise you would have been greeted more properly."

"No problem," Moon said. "I have my passport and the papers our mother had with her if you need to look at those."

The man chuckled. "You are clearly the elder brother of Richard Mathias. You are exactly as he described you. And like this." The man slid open a desk drawer, extracted a photograph, and handed it to Moon.

The photograph had been enlarged to eight by ten inches, and from its glossy surface the face of Ricky beamed at him. And there he was, standing beside Ricky, wearing his standard stiff snapshot expression, clumsy in his dress uniform, looking slightly stupid, the bridge of his nose bent slightly to the left to remind him of a mistake he'd made trying to block a linebacker who was a half step faster than he'd expected. He hadn't seen this photo before. He stared at it now, remembering.

Ricky had handed his camera to Halsey, and Halsey had said, "Look brotherly," or something like that, and shot it.

Moon turned the photo over. Nothing there. It was the last time he'd seen his brother. They'd taken him back to Kansas City to catch his plane for Los Angeles and Tokyo and Saigon, and that was the end of Ricky. They'd driven back to the base and stopped at the General Patton Lounge for a few drinks—and that was the end of Halsey.

Moon cleared his throat. He handed the photo back to Castenada.

"Ricky gave you this?"

"Actually, he gave it to Electra. She asked him for a picture."

Moon didn't want to pursue that. He wanted to get his business done here and pick up Ricky's child, deliver the kid to his mother, and go home. But what was he going to do with Ricky's kid if Victoria Mathias was still in the hospital? As she would be, of course. And what if his mother didn't make it? What would he do with the kid then?

"You said the child hadn't arrived yet. When is she getting here? I was hoping I could pick her up today. Or at least get the paperwork done. Does she have a passport? Or does a child that young need one?"

Castenada's welcoming smile had disappeared while Moon was looking at the photo. Now his face was somber.

"The problem is we don't know where she is," he said. "She wasn't on the flight she was supposed to be on. So I have a man out at the airport checking all the flights coming in from Saigon. He is also checking everything that comes in from Bangkok or Kuala Lumpur or Singapore or anywhere else appropriate, in the event they could not get her onto a direct flight and took a roundabout way. All flights have been checked. And there are no flights any longer from Phnom Penh."

"You don't know where she is?" Somehow this didn't really surprise him. Somehow he'd half expected some awful screwup. It seemed fitting and logical. He just hadn't allowed himself to think of it.

Castenada was shaking his head. "Not in Cambodia, we think. And that is the very important thing. Because if she was still in Cambodia it would be very, very complicated. And maybe not in Saigon, which is where she was supposed to be placed on the flight. Thailand closed its border with Cambodia, and Ricky's people in Bangkok say they don't believe she came there."

"My God!" Moon said. "You're telling me you really don't have any idea where the baby is?" His voice was louder than he'd intended.

"Not yet," Castenada said.

"Not yet," Moon repeated. "When will you know?"

Castenada's expression suggested he'd not liked Moon's tone. He removed his hands from the desktop, leaned back in his chair, and examined Moon over his glasses. "Perhaps never," he said. "If you wish me to be realistic, perhaps never."

"I'm sorry," Moon said. "I just don't understand the situation. My mother was too ill to explain anything. I hoped I was just coming to Manila to pick up the girl and take her back to the States. All of this is—"

"Of course," Castenada said. "I should have taken time to explain on the telephone." He explained now, his expression cordial again but still leaning back from the desk. He said Castenada, Blake and Associates represented small international companies, mostly export-import, which operated across the various borders of Southeast Asia. Ricky had retained him first to incorporate R. M. Air in the Republic of the Philippines, then to handle the leasing of property where Ricky intended to establish a repair operation north of Caloocan City, to unravel a misunderstanding with a bonded warehouse in Singapore, and to recover an aircraft impounded by Laos authorities at Vientiane. Castenada delivered this recitation slowly, digressing to explain if it seemed necessary. He paused and threw his hands open in a gesture of finality.

"The point is that our relationship was primarily business. Which bureaucrat at Bangkok in which office did one need to approach? Which law in Malaysia was being enforced this year and which one winked at? So I know his business associates. But I do not know his friends."

He paused again, thinking, then added, "Only a few of them. And of course one's daughter would be entrusted to friends, not to business associates."

Moon could think of nothing to say to this.

Castenada waited, made a wry face. "I think to find the child you will need his friends. To help you."

"I don't know his friends either," Moon said. "Not his friends out here."

If Castenada heard this, he ignored it. "Because I think this person who was bringing out the child, I think he must have gone to earth somewhere. Somewhere safe until they could travel again." Castenada threw up his hands. "Everything is going to hell over there. Dangerous, dangerous, dangerous. Nothing can be counted on, nothing. Offices closed. Flights are canceled. Telephones go unanswered."

"So," Moon said, feeling totally out of his depth, "what do I do now?"

Castenada considered, looking first at the pyramid he'd made of his fingers and then at Moon. To Moon's amazement, Mr. Castenada was grinning.

"Oh, I know about you, Mr. Mathias," he said. "Ricky told me. I think you will find a way." The grin widened. "I think if Ricky's daughter can be brought to Manila, you will bring her."

"What the hell did Ricky—" Moon began, but the question was interrupted. A short plump woman slid into the room, bearing a black laquered tray. On it were two cups, a plate of rolls, and an oversized black Thermos.

"Ah, here is Electra," Castenada said. And with a

sweep of his arm: "Electra, we have with us Mr. Malcolm Mathias."

Moon stood. "How do you do," he said.

Electra's expression reminded Moon of a woman he'd seen on a television newscast being introduced to Queen Elizabeth.

"This is Moon Mathias," Castenada said. "This is the older brother Ricky has told us about."

Electra was blushing. She performed something like a curtsy. She said, "Oh, yes, I am so glad to meet you," and hurried out of the room.

Castenada poured, and served, and talked.

He assumed Moon knew Ricky had died intestate. That meant that in the absence of a will, and in the absence of any evidence that the child was actually Ricky's daughter, Ricky's heir would be his mother and—in most jurisdictions—his siblings. He said he understood Malcolm Mathias was the only surviving sibling. When Moon nodded, he said Ricky seemed to have been, as far as he could tell, a legal resident of Oklahoma, in the United States, even though his business address had been in the Republic of Vietnam. Therefore the estate would be adjudicated in an Oklahoma probate court and Moon would inherit—

Castenada paused, sipped coffee, eyed Moon over the cup, continued.

"—one half of the estate. Presuming, of course, that there is no litigation."

Castenada awaited a response from Moon, who had none to make. He hadn't thought about this. He didn't want to think about it now. How much could Ricky have accumulated—a retired army captain trying to get a business started?

"After legal fees, of course," Castenada said, grinning at Moon. "Lawyers are known to be avaricious. International lawyers notably so. Your mother has asked me to handle this. I've retained a Vietnamese lawyer who did some work for R. M. Air last year. Reasonably honest, I think. But"—Castenada threw up his hands—"where is he now? When I tried to call him about the child, telephone service was no longer offered to his office at Can Tho. I think perhaps the Vietcong are running the telephone exchange there now."

"Look," Moon said, "I don't want to talk about this. I want to talk about how to get the kid to Manila and from Manila back to the States."

"All right," Castenada said. "We talk about that. All I can do is give you the names of some of Ricky's friends. Maybe they can tell you where to go."

He flipped open a Rolodex file on his desk and began jotting notes on a pad. "Let us hope, let us pray, that they don't tell you to go find her in Vietnam." He glanced up at Moon, face somber. "Or, even worse, in Cambodia."

1740 hrs. 4/16/95
TO: Ofc Mgrs
FROM: McK. Embassy
STATUS: Eyes Only—Burn.
Rocket from H.K. this date orders top priority evacuation of nonessential personnel. Top limit essential U.S. citizens is 2000. Submit plan by 1400 hrs 4/17 listing essentials your mission and departure schedule for all others. Avoid any leak to non-U.S. personnel.

Still the Fifth Day

April 17, 1975

THE LIST OF FRIENDS MOON TOOK AWAY with him was short, and only three of those named on it might have been in Manila. First came George Rice, a name Moon remembered from the letter in his mother's purse. Rice, Castenada said, was in Manila "now and then, bringing things in and taking things out." He had called some time ago about difficulties he was having about an aircraft he had flown into Quezon City.

Castenada had been leaning forward, expression quizzical, remembering the details. "Yes," he'd said. "Mr. Rice said the customs people were talking of filing a charge and he wanted me to handle it. I told him this firm has no expertise in criminal matters and recommended another law firm to him."

"Criminal?"

Castenada raised a hand, rubbed thumb against fingers. "It seems to have been some problem with the papers. The manifest. The customs agents of President Marcos follow the example of their leader and handle such things informally." He smiled at Moon, making sure he understood. "And if the person involved is not willing to be sufficiently generous in rewarding this courtesy, there is sometimes the threat of arrest."

"Oh," Moon said. "So, what happened?"

Castenada shrugged. "The lawyer I recommended is experienced in such matters. I heard no more about it."

"So he may still be here?"

"Or he may be gone. He said he had flown in an old aircraft that needed some sort of equipment installed. How much time does that take?" Castenada's expression said he had no idea.

Next on the "possibly in Manila" list were Thomas Brock, who Castenada described as marketing manager for R. M. Air, and Robert Yager, at the Quezon Towers Hotel. Yager was the name Moon remembered seeing scrawled at the end of the letter to Ricky in his mother's purse. What did Yager do?

Castenada could only guess. "In Asia in these troubled times a business like Ricky's needs someone who knows everybody, has connections everywhere, can find out—" Castenada hesitated, looking at Moon quizzically again, seeming to ask himself how much this American would understand such things. "Someone would know if General A actually works for the CIA. If General B is about to be fired. If Imelda Marcos is fond enough of this third cousin to cut him in on a construction contract. That sort of thing. I think Mr. Yager is a person who—if he does not know everything—knows someone who does."

"I see," Moon said. If Mr. Castenada was giving him accurate information, Ricky's business seemed to be—well, less orthodox than he'd assumed.

"That is just an impression," Castenada said. "Just an impression." He made a deprecating gesture. "One hears things," he said. "Some true. Some not."

On the page he'd torn from his notebook to list the friends, Castenada now added the address of Ricky's Manila apartment. He creased the page into a precise rectangle and put it in a folder. Then he extracted a small envelope from his desk drawer, waved it at Moon, and said, "For you. It came this morning." He added the letter to the folder, then tore the top sheet from his memo pad and dropped it in.

"Someone named Lum Lee called for you," Castenada said. "Yesterday. It's all there on the memo sheet." He reached across the desk and handed Moon the folder and, with it, two keys on a ring.

"The keys to Ricky's apartment," he said. "You'll be more comfortable there than in the hotel, and it's cheaper." He glanced up at Moon. "Remember, I am at your service. And at your mother's. I think you will have to be here in Manila for a while." He considered that and nodded thoughtfully. "Yes, I think so."

And Moon had thought, Like hell I will! But now as he dumped the contents of the folder on his hotel room desk, he had a sick feeling that the frail little lawyer might be right. Maybe he'd be here forever. The alternative was going back and telling Victoria Mathias he'd failed her again. Not that she would be surprised. But this time he would have failed in what was likely to be the last opportunity she would ever give him to succeed.

He sat for a moment considering the wallpaper. It was brownish and gold in some sort of geometric design. Then he looked at the memo page. It was dated 10:20 A.M. yesterday.

> Please would Mr. Malcolm Mathias telephone to Mr. Lum Lee concerning a matter of mutual interest: room 919, Pasag Imperial Hotel.

Moon put the memo aside. Mr. Lee would still be hunting his ancestor's bones, or an urn full of cocaine, or whatever it was. A tired old man on an impossible quest. But no more impossible than his own. Moon smiled, remembering Lum Lee in Los Angeles, offering to help him find Ricky's child. Playing Sancho Panza to Moon's Don Quixote. The metaphor fit rather well. In this part of the world the old man would be the wise one, the one who knew the reality of Southeast Asia and the rules of the game. He'd call him. But first he picked up the letter.

The envelope was a standard business size, addressed to Mr. Moon Mathias in care of Castenada's office. No return address. The postmark was faint, but it seemed to read KUPANG, TIMOR. Timor? An island, Moon thought. Something like Ceylon. But where? And who there would know him as Moon? Know him at all? Have any business with him? He tore it open. The single sheet of paper was as plain as the envelope.

> Dear Mr. Mathias:
>
> I am a former client of Ricky's and I think of him as a friend as well. Only today did I hear the sad news of his death. First please accept my condolences. I am sure that the immense admiration Ricky felt for you was mutual and that the loss must be a terrible one. I, too,

have a brother with whom I am very close.

I am asking Mr. Castenada to forward this letter to you. By the time you receive it, or very soon thereafter, I will be in Manila at the Hotel Del Mar. Please call me there. I would not ask this of you if it was not a matter of extreme importance. In fact, it is a matter of life and death.

Sincerely,
Mrs. Osa van Winjgaarden

Moon found the Hotel Del Mar in the phone book, picked up the telephone, and then put it back. Life or death or not, it could wait until tomorrow. Mrs. what's-her-name probably wasn't even here yet. He did a bit of mental arithmetic and set the alarm beside his bed for two A.M. If he had the time zones right that would be ten A.M. in L.A. and eleven in Durance, a decent time to be ringing telephones there.

In fact, it was a little early for the person he most wanted to reach. Dr. Serna was in surgery and "not available." The nurse in his mother's ward reported her officially in serious condition but sleeping comfortably.

The receptionist answered Debbie's office number. Someone new. She reported Debbie was off today. She'd called in sick. Try her at home. Moon called his home number, let the phone ring twelve times, and hung up feeling uneasy. Sick? How sick? Debbie was never sick, not even during her period. But Debbie often didn't bother to answer the telephone. And sometimes Debbie wasn't home when people thought she was. And for Debbie, calling in sick would not necessarily have much to do with the state of her health.

Moon called the paper. Shirley sounded delighted to hear his voice. How was his mother? How was he? How was

Manila? When would he be home? Shirley was going by his house every day to feed her dog and wanted to know how soon—

"Why?" Moon asked. "Debbie can feed the dog until I get back." For Shirley, "going by" his house meant driving a dozen miles in the wrong direction. She was sticking herself with a long round trip just because she was too proud to accept a favor from Debbie. Downright silliness. Moon's mood had shown in his tone, and Shirley's tone showed she had noticed it.

"I think Debbie may have gone off on a little journey. Or something."

"Well," Moon said, wondering how he could make amends, trying to remember how he came to be tending Shirley's spaniel. Yes, it was because her apartment had changed ownership and the new landlord didn't allow pets. She needed a dog tender until she could work something out. "Maybe Hubble could feed the dog," Moon said. "What do you think? You know he rents a room from me."

Shirley laughed, placated. "I think he'd tell me to take care of my own damn dog," she said. "Or maybe something a little worse."

"You're right," Moon said. "But switch me over and I'll ask him."

Hubble said he'd be willing to haul Shirley's dog out into the San Juans and let the coyotes solve the problem. And how was Moon's mother? And were the Manila women as slick as they were when he did his navy time in the Islands, and when was Moon coming back, because it was time to get going on the damned vacation edition, and he was pretty sure Rooney was nipping at the bottle again.

"Bad?"

"You tell me," Hubble said. Papers rustled. Hubble read three of yesterday's headlines and started a fourth one.

"Lordy," Moon said. "Did they go to press like that?"

"Those were the ones I didn't catch."

"Let me talk to him."

"He just left," Hubble said.

"Tell the son of a bitch to stay sober until I get back or I won't just fire him, I'll whip his butt right there in the office."

"All right," Hubble said.

"What else? Any good news?"

"J.D.'s been asking about his truck," Hubble said. "Said he wanted to go to Denver."

"Tell J.D. it was the fuel injection pump. I fixed it, and all he needs to do is put in new glow plugs. He can put it back together himself. Or ask one of the guys down at the truck stop if he has troubles."

Hubble laughed. "Yeah," he said. "Can you imagine that happening? Getting his hands greasy?"

Moon couldn't, but he didn't want to talk about it. He told Hubble he'd be home as soon as he could. Then he just sat on the bed awhile staring at the telephone, mood somewhere between dismal, disgruntlement, and sleepy stupor. He fell back against the pillow, yawned hugely, and went to sleep.

The phone awoke him. Nine-ten. Who would be calling?

It rang again.

He picked it up and said, "Mathias."

"Hello. Is this Mr. Mathias?" The voice was hesitant, accented, and feminine.

"Yes. Yes," Moon said, "this is Mr. Mathias."

Brief silence. "This is then the room of Moon Mathias? Am I correct?" The voice was small, tone abashed. Moon had a vision of Shirley's spaniel when Debbie yelled at it.

"I'm sorry," he said. "I didn't mean to sound so grouchy. But, yes, this is Moon Mathias talking."

"I am Mrs. Osa van Winjgaarden. I had written you a letter. I hope I can talk to you."

"Of course," Moon said. What was the accent? Probably Dutch, from the sound of the name. "What can I do for you?"

Silence again. Moon waited. "It is too complicated for the telephone," she said. "I had hoped we could sit down and talk."

"Probably," Moon said. "Where are you calling from? And what will we be talking about?"

"I am at the airport. The Manila airport. I called Mr. Castenada, and he told me you were here. He told me he had given you my letter instead of mailing it on to America. And we would be talking about getting my brother out of Cambodia."

Good God, Moon thought. What next?

"Look," Moon said. "I don't know anything about Cambodia. Or getting people out. What makes you think—"

"I thought you would be taking charge of Ricky's company. And you are getting Ricky's daughter out," she said. "From what Mr. Castenada told me, I understand you are doing that."

Now the silence was on Moon's end. Was he doing that? He guessed he would if he could. He didn't have much choice. But, of course, he couldn't.

"I would if I could."

"It won't be much out of your way," she said. "And I could be of some help."

"How?" And what did she mean, *out of your way*? Did that mean she thought she knew where he was going? Did she know where the child might be?

"If you don't speak the Cambodian version of French, I could be useful there," she said. "And I speak one or two of the mountain dialects. A little, anyway."

"Hey," Moon said, "what did you mean, getting your brother wouldn't be much out of my way? Where is your brother? What's the—"

But now Moon was hearing Osa van Winjgaarden saying something to someone away from the telephone mouthpiece. She sounded angry and tired.

"I'm sorry," she said. "I didn't hear you."

"You're calling from the airport?" He was thinking, The woman has just got in from Timor, wherever the hell that is, and probably on some little prop-driven airline. She sounded exhausted.

"Yes. A coin telephone box here by the doorway. I am trying to hold a taxi. I'm—"

"Look," Moon said. "You go ahead. Check into your hotel. The Del Mar, isn't it? Take a shower. Get some rest. Then call me, and we'll get together tomorrow morning. Maybe you could come over here and have breakfast and we'll talk."

"Oh, yes!" she said. "Thank you!"

He paused. "But I think you are wasting your time. There's nothing I can do for anybody in Cambodia."

"Oh, no, Mr. Mathias," she said. "I don't think so. Ricky told me about you."

Special to the *New York Times*

WASHINGTON, April 16—Secretary of State Kissinger said today that the United States Embassy in Saigon had been ordered to reduce the number of Americans remaining in South Vietnam to "a minimum level needed for essential duties."

Evening, the Fifth Day

April 17, 1975

MOON WALKED DOWN THE DARK STREETS, emerged into the lights of Quezon Boulevard and the busy noise of traffic, and stopped to get his bearings. He loved to walk. It restored the spirit, cured him of whatever ailed him. But tonight it wasn't working.

This new task was one he could do absolutely nothing about until tomorrow. Only tomorrow would bring the information he had to have before he could decide what to do. Thus there should be no pressure until then. But the pressure was there. He'd watched the evening news on the TV in his room. Mostly Philippine stuff, but enough videotape of refugees flooding into Saigon to remind him that time was running out. So he went through it all again.

Tomorrow he would meet the woman from Timor. He'd

asked the hotel desk clerk the location of that island. The clerk had revealed ignorance even deeper than Moon's.

"It is somewhere way down on the south coast of Leyte," the man had said, after thinking about it a moment. "Dirty little port town, I think. Nothing much to see there." He had wrinkled his nose, made a motion of dismissal. "Smells bad. You don't want to go to Timor."

The woman with the Dutch name and the Dutch accent could clear up the geography question for him at breakfast. Beyond that, she'd either tell him something useful or she wouldn't. If she didn't, he would begin hunting Ricky's friends. Perhaps they would justify the optimism of Castenada. Until then there was nothing to do except walk. Carefree hours in a place new to him and exotic. He should be luxuriating in that. Why wasn't he?

He was nervous, that was why. He was nervous about Mr. Lum Lee for one thing. It was a rare feeling for Moon, and he tried to deduce the reason. Perhaps it was the Chinese-looking man in the lobby who seemed to be watching him. More likely the man had seemed to be watching him only because Moon was already nervous. He was an Oriental wearing a blue turtleneck shirt. Chinese, Moon guessed, but that was probably because Chinese had been his generic label for all Orientals who were not clearly Japanese. And why had Mr. Lum Lee followed him to Manila? He'd called the number Lum Lee had left for him. No one had answered.

"Who's the man sitting over there by the fountain?" he'd asked the clerk. "Wearing the blue shirt? Is he one of the guests?" And the clerk had looked, shook his head, and said, "Maybe. I think not so." And then when Moon had walked away from the hotel, past the line of waiting taxis, he'd seen Blue Turtleneck standing in the doorway looking after him. Or possibly just looking at the weather.

The weather was mild, dead calm, more humid than he'd ever experienced. Prestorm weather, he thought. Certainly far different from the high dryness of the Colorado Plateau. The surface of Manila Bay reflected city lights, the lights of traffic along Quezon Boulevard. Moon walked briskly, at the three-miles-in-fifty-minutes pace the U.S. Army had taught him, past dark warehouses and the twinkling mast lights of a thousand boats docked in the Manila yacht basin. He smelled fish, oil, flowers, salty ocean air, decayed fruit, a strange animal aroma. The perfume of the tropics, he guessed. Strange, exciting country. He should have been enjoying it.

The vehicles passing him were mostly World War II vintage jeeps, remodeled as taxis, garishly painted, honking for no reason he could understand. The sidewalk now was illuminated by the yellow glare of a streetlight. It showed him a shallow flood of dark water running down the concrete toward him.

Water?

Moon stopped, stared, sucked in his breath, and jumped to one side.

The stream was a multitude of insects: agile, light brown cockroaches. A migration of them flowing rapidly down the sidewalk. The crunching he'd felt under his shoe soles on the dark street behind him hadn't been dead leaves as he'd thought. Feeling slightly sickened, he hurried down the seawall away from this grotesque strangeness.

The rain caught Moon as he crossed the park in front of the Manila Cathedral. A drizzle at first, the tiny droplets oddly warm. But the drizzle quickly became a heavy shower. Moon ran across the grass and up the cathedral steps. In the shelter of the vestibule he stopped to catch his breath, looked back. A man was hurrying through the rain behind him, protecting his head with a newspaper. He wasn't wearing a blue turtleneck.

Moon sat at the end of the final pew. A dim red light at the main altar told him the Consecrated Host was there. An electric bulb cast a yellow glow on one of the side altars, silhouetting two kneeling men and a woman. But the body of the church was dark, lit only by a bank of offertory candles burning before an ornate crucifix in an alcove. The breeze brought in the smell of rain, of pollen, of mildew, seaweed, and decay. And then the breeze died. Moon found himself engulfed in the aroma of burning candle wax, furniture polish, old incense. Engulfed in memories.

Of sneaking with Eddie Tafoya and Ricky into St. Stephen's and salvaging guttered-out candles, melting them down, making their own candles which Eddie believed, erroneously, they could sell in competition with Father Kelly. Of swinging the censor in the sacristry, fanning the charcoal to red heat, producing a great blue cloud of aromatic smoke. Moon closed his eyes, trying to remember the sound of the Latin—*"Qui tollis peccata mundi, miserere nobis"*—and Ricky saying, "Who told us pick cotton Monday," and getting away with it because Father Kelly was too deaf to tell the difference.

"He who takes away the sins of the world," Moon said, "have mercy on us." He slid out of the pew, walked down the side aisle, looked out the doorway at the rain, examined the stained-glass window above him—the Holy Family in faded colors. He walked past the row of confessionals, the center door of each with its barred window curtained in black and the doors to the penitents' booths solid wood. Much like the ones in old St. Stephen's.

That was so Father Kelly could see who was coming, Eddie had always insisted, so he'd know which boy was admitting his awful crimes against God and society. Moon had asked his mother about that and she'd laughed. Actually, Victoria had said, it was because the priest had to sit in that hotbox for hours and needed the air to keep from smothering.

Moon opened the penitents' door. In addition to the standard kneeler, a little straight-backed chair had been crowded into the tiny space. Perhaps this booth was intended for the aged and infirm. At St. Stephen's one knelt, infirm or not. But times change. He sat on the chair, closed the door behind him, and let the memories come. The darkness was the same, and the silence, and the fear he could remember. And, most vividly, the shame. And finally, the despair.

Moon knelt and leaned his forehead against the wooden grating. The only difference between this and the confessionals of his boyhood was the sound. Closing the door had shut out the whispers and shuffling of the other students waiting for their turn. But through the closed privacy shutter behind the grate you could hear the indistinct, indecipherable mutter of offenses recited by the sinners on the other side, and of Father Kelly's instructions to the sinner. And then the shutter would slide open. The dreaded moment would arrive.

"Bless me, Father, for I have sinned," Moon whispered into the emptiness. "It has been—it has been a hundred thousand weeks since my last confession, and since then—"

A slight sound reached him through the grating, a polite, throat-clearing cough. The shutter was open. Moon felt his heart stop beating.

"How many weeks?" a soft accented voice said. "A long long time, I think you mean."

Moon sat back on the chair, drew in his breath. Of course. A priest had been sitting there thinking his thoughts, his night on duty in the confessional. "Sorry,"

Moon said. "I'm sorry. I was just . . . it was raining, and . . ." He stopped. Nothing to say.

"If I were a religious man," the voice said, and chuckled, "if I was that, I would say the rain drove you in. And since God makes the rain, perhaps God had a hand in this. In getting you here after one hundred thousand weeks."

The voice sounded neither young nor old and the accent had that odd cadence Moon had noticed in Filipinos speaking English. A little like reciting song lyrics. He'd heard it in Castenada's voice. The man behind the wooden grating is about my age, Moon thought. Maybe a little older. But he could think of nothing to say. He opened the door.

"Since we are here, and I have almost another hour, and since you don't want to get wet, why don't you just stay and talk? Or even make your confession?"

"Why not?" Moon said. "Because I'd be wasting my time. And your time."

"That bad, is it? You've done something even our God of Mercy could not forgive?"

"I don't think that's the trouble," Moon said. "Another priest told me you have to forgive yourself." It had been a chaplain at Fort Riley, a captain who had come to visit him in the stockade. He hadn't liked the captain, and the captain hadn't liked him.

The priest laughed. "In my long experience in here I've learned that's usually the easiest part. It is for me. I come to like my own sins. I find myself a reason for doing them. But is that why a hundred thousand weeks ago you stopped going to confession?"

"No," Moon said.

Silence.

The priest sighed. "I guess you're an American. A military man from the base, right?"

"American, but not military. Here on business. I was just out taking a walk."

"I peeked out a little while ago," the priest said. "The regulars have already been in to see me. I'm not going to have any more business. Not likely with the rain. I see three or four people out there. Praying for better lives and better luck at the side altar. And then there are a couple of poor souls who came in to stay dry."

Moon heard the sound of a sigh.

"I've said my evening prayers. I've meditated a little, and when you came in I was trying to remember what I was going to tell my students Monday about Thomas Merton. I have them reading *The Seven Story Mountain* and I've taught that book so often that thinking about it makes me sleepy. And my chair in here is just as hard as yours. So then you come in and sit awhile. But then there is nothing but silence. Ah, something different. I start waking up. And when you finally speak you tell me a hundred thousand weeks. That's a challenge. I think of how many commandments could be broken in such a long lifetime. I think, What could provoke repentance now for sins so fossilized? I was excited." He sighed again. "But now you are thinking of disappointing me. You didn't know a priest was lurking here. You were engulfed in nostalgia. I think you were remembering how it was that lifetime ago the last time you asked your God to help you." The mockery in the tone included them both and swept away Moon's embarrassment.

"You left out the important part," Moon said. "About telling God I was sorry. That I had repented. That I would go forth and sin no more." And as he said it, he realized that he was, in a strange way, confessing.

"And then next week, or next month, back again with the same litany of lust and avarice and anger and malicious gossip," the priest said. "Is that it? It is for me. It has always been my problem too. This business of feeling like a hypocrite."

"Sure," Moon said. "And do you also feel like you're wasting your time? The rule says you have to—what's the language—'make a firm resolve to sin no more'—and when you walk out of the confessional you know you're going to do it again."

"It's usually sex," the priest said. "With men, anyway. Adultery with the married men, or single men sleeping with their girlfriends, or trying to. With women, it's more often some sort of malice. Or it's laws of the church. Missing mass on Sunday without a good reason. It used to be eating meat on Friday, but since Pope John the Twenty-third that's off the list. God be praised for that. Anyway, women seem to have trouble forgiving somebody."

"Really?" Moon said. He was thinking of Victoria.

"Sometimes it's stealing, of course. Shoplifting. Taking a neighbor's chicken. But finally they get down to what's really bothering them. Her sister has insulted her and she has done so much for her sister. How can she be expected to forgive this? Surely the Lord would not expect it of her."

The priest sounded so troubled by this that Moon suspected he had just dealt with this question.

"How about men?" he asked.

"Little things. Things done in anger. God's name taken in vain. Illicit sex. Hardly ever does anybody confess cheating on the wages they pay, or taking bribes." He laughed. "In Manila if people confessed to taking bribes, I'd never get out of here." The tone of that canceled the chuckle.

"I guess you'll find avarice everywhere," Moon said. "We have some of it in Colorado."

"Nobody seems to think greed is against the rules. Or grinding down the poor." The priest sighed. "I wonder what President Marcos says to his confessor? 'I've been stealing a billion pisos a month from my people. I will give that back. I will stop torturing the political prisoners. I will—'" Brief silence. "Ah, well. I doubt if the president and Imelda go to confession much anymore."

"So women have trouble forgiving," Moon said. "How about mothers? Do they forgive their children?"

"How about you?" the priest asked. "Was treasuring a hatred that favorite sin of yours? The one that caused you to leave the church?"

"As you said," Moon said, "with men it's usually sex."

"Adultery?"

Moon laughed. "I was just a boy. Fifteen, maybe sixteen. With a heart full of lust."

"Impure thoughts? Or impure actions?"

"Fiercely impure intentions," Moon said. "Relentless. To make it worse, the target was usually the sister of a very good friend. Intention to betray as well as intention to fornicate. Thus a double load of guilt."

"So you stopped going to confession."

"I went," Moon said. "But I quit telling Father Kelly about the things I knew I wasn't going to stop. I'd just make up stuff. I'd tell him I'd stolen something. I'd lied to my mother. I'd been mean to my little brother. Cheated in class. So forth. Until finally I just quit going."

Moon heard the priest shifting on his chair. Then a long silence. Finally a sigh.

"And now, a hundred thousand weeks later, how do you feel about it?"

Moon thought about that. Remembering that facet of his childhood. His hopelessness. The certainty of damnation. The sense of loss. He grimaced. "Terrible at first. Now nothing much," he said. "I don't feel anything."

"But you did once, you say. I think that's usual. You've gotten used to it. People do."

A wise man, Moon thought. Or is it just experience—what you learn from sitting on the other side of the grill for a hundred thousand weeks, listening to someone else's sorrows? "Sure," Moon said. "I guess that's it."

"Now tell me about that big sin you mentioned. It has to be something besides sex. Jesus didn't say much against that. He was teaching us to love one another. How long since you've read the Gospels?"

How long? He didn't remember. "It's been a while," Moon said.

"Is anyone out there waiting now? Take a look for me."

Moon pushed his door open. Through the side doorway he could see the falling rain, a gush of water splashing off the entrance steps from a drain spout, traffic lights reflecting off wet pavement, time rushing past. Tomorrow he would have to deal with that. But not tonight. Not now. Inside the church, the three kneeling by the side altar had become a solitary man. Two women sat in the back row of pews, whispering. Across the church, a man leaned against the wall staring toward the main altar. If he wore a blue turtleneck, it was hidden under the yellow plastic of a raincoat.

"Nobody's waiting."

"Then why not help me pass the time? You can just satisfy my curiosity. A simple act of kindness." Moon heard the sound of the priest shifting in his chair. "Or why not make your confession?"

Why not? "I guess for the same reason I stopped in the first place."

"A sin you don't want to stop?"

"Yeah," Moon said. "Or can't."

Silence. Moon realized he was hungry. What time was it anyway? Would the hotel coffee shop be open? Why was he carrying on this dialogue with this odd man? He considered that. Because he was enjoying it, of course. And that surprised him. But then, it had been a long, long time since he'd had this sort of conversation with anyone.

"Why don't you marry her?" the priest asked. And chuckled. And said, "Allow me to quote Saint Paul: 'If they cannot exercise self-control, they should marry. It is better to marry than to be on fire.' You remember that one?"

"Sort of," Moon said. "But she won't do it. She says later, maybe, but not yet."

"But she will copulate with you?"

"Sometimes."

"For the pleasure of it," the priest said, thoughtfully.

It wasn't a question but Moon said, "Yes." And then he said, "No. Maybe not. I think she enjoys it but the way it is, she lives in my house. She is supposed to pay rent, but it usually doesn't get paid. I pay the bills, buy the food, take care of her car—"

"Yes," the priest said. "I see."

But Moon knew he didn't see. Not really. And suddenly Moon wanted this man to understand. Maybe to understand himself.

"She's a lot younger. Just turned twenty-two. And very, very pretty. High school cheerleader. Do you have those in Manila?"

"Not exactly, but I know what you mean."

"Not much education, and a sorry family situation. Her dad drank and beat her mother, and then he beat her. The family split up, and then her mother was—well, she got a reputation for being promiscuous. Anyway, Debbie moved out when she got out of high school."

Moon stopped there. How much of this was he going to talk about? And how could he describe it? Any way he told it, it would seem he was trying to justify using her. In a way he was. In a way they were using each other. How could he describe this relationship? Suddenly the oddity of all this struck him and he laughed.

"Yes?" the priest said.

"I am thinking," Moon said, "that you may need that hour to hear all this. It's about how a guy who has been a sort of total loser sees a woman who is just about as sexy-looking as women can get, and before he knows what's happening he's caught up in the kind of weirdness that would make a chapter in a psychiatry book. Is it love, is it pity, or is it a way to make amends for ruining another woman's life? Or is it just predatory testosterone at work?"

"Pity?" the priest said. "If it's based on pity, it's not going to be much of a sin."

"Why do we talk about stuff like this to a priest?" Moon asked. "If you're a good priest you haven't had much experience."

"Well, now. How about before the priest took his vows? Or how about slipping and repenting and being forgiven? All that's possible. Anyway, we hear a lot. You'd be surprised what we hear sitting here in the darkness. And we get to know the ending of these stories. Usually you only know the beginning. And we have enough testosterone to understand the urges."

So Moon talked about Debbie, how her beauty and her awareness of her beauty were part of the problem. It was all Debbie thought she had to offer, Moon said. Which was sad. He'd first seen her at Granddad's Tavern in Durance, dancing with a ski bum, wearing cutoff jeans and a T-shirt, object of desire of every male in the place. Including Moon Mathias. But she was too young for him; she attracted the predators and, clearly, was attracted by them. It hadn't occurred to him she'd give him a thought. He'd been wrong. He'd noticed her three times in the bar; then she appeared at the newspaper office. She'd asked for him by name. She handed him the sort of news release from the utility company where she worked that normally would have been mailed. She flirted. He'd asked her out to dinner and taken her home to bed, and within the month she had said she was looking for a room to rent. He'd rented her one.

"I can't see you in the dark," the priest said. "Are you a tall, handsome fellow?"

"Nobody has ever suggested that," Moon said. "I'm big, built like a barrel, broken nose, and I guess you'd say I look harmless."

"I don't think women are as interested in how men look as the other way around," the priest said. "What do you think attracted her?"

Moon had never answered that question before, not even to himself. He said, "I think she was afraid. I think sort of subconsciously she figured I wouldn't hurt her."

"Have you?"

"No," Moon said. "I haven't and I won't."

"But the predators would?"

"They will."

"You don't think of yourself as one of the predators?"

Moon felt his face flushing. Why the devil should he defend himself to this man? But he wanted to.

"I should explain the arrangement better," Moon said. "She has her bedroom, I have mine."

"You said that," the priest said, "but—"

"Let me finish," Moon said. "I stay out of her room. She doesn't always stay out of mine."

"The sleeping together then is when she wants to?"

"Or when she sees I want to."

Silence. The priest coughed. "Is anybody waiting?"

Moon checked. "Nobody."

"How about other men? The predators."

"She's free as a bird," Moon said. "She goes out with

other men. Probably she's out with one tonight." Even as he said it, Moon found it hard to think of J.D., the publisher's happy-go-lucky son, as a predator. Unless gerbils are predators.

"You said she wouldn't marry you yet. Does she say she'll marry you someday?"

"She doesn't say it, but I think so," Moon said. "Or one of them will take her away, and dump her, and she'll end up like her mother."

"Why do you think that?"

How could he explain it to this man whose only view of life was through a wooden grillwork into the darkness of other men's souls?

"Because she doesn't have any respect for herself. No confidence. A couple of these guys dump her and—" He let the sentence hang.

"Go on," the priest said.

"That's all," Moon said. "I'm finished."

"But you've left me with the question unanswered. What was the big sin you mentioned? And how did you ruin the woman's life?"

"I killed a man," Moon said.

Into the silence that this produced he added, "He was—" But he left the sentence unfinished. What more was there to say?

"The Fifth Commandment," the priest said. "The fifth. Thou Shalt Not Kill is not even number two. But serious, of course. How serious depends on the motivation. Was it ambition, lust, revenge, envy, a moment of fury, hatred?—"

"He was my best friend," Moon said. "I guess, outside my family, he was the only person I could ever say I loved. I could trust him. Absolutely trust him."

"So what was the motivation?"

"I was drunk," Moon said.

SAIGON, South Vietnam, April 17 (UPI)—A Saigon military spokesman announced today that "radio contact" with the fishing town of Phan Thiet has been lost following an assault by North Vietnamese infantrymen. "Loss of contact" is the term normally used by the South Vietnamese military when a position has been captured.

The Sixth Day

April 18, 1975

TO REACH THE DINING ROOM of the Hotel Maynila one took an escalator from the lobby, descended past a waterfall flowing over a granite pseudo-cliff, and surrendered oneself to an ornately uniformed fellow to be taken to a seat. Moon was assigned to a table adjoining the swinging doors from the kitchen. He explained he needed a quieter place for a business conversation. He suggested one of a row of empty tables by the glass wall with a view out into the garden. The uniformed fellow looked skeptical but bowed and made the new assignment.

Moon sat, elbows on the tablecloth, looking into a steady tropical rain and into a jungle of tropical flowers, none of which he could identify. The incident with the maître d' had confirmed a previous Moon conclusion. He must either get this jacket and these slacks to the cleaner and his socks, shirts, and underwear to a laundry, or say to hell with it, face reality, and fly home where it didn't matter how he looked. The opulence that surrounded him here reinforced another decision. He had to check out of this five-star hotel, whether or not he went home. He couldn't afford it. If he was going to play out this Don Quixote role to the end, he'd find Ricky's apartment and move into it until someone told him where to locate the baby. Or until he got sensible and gave up, a conclusion to this affair that had come to seem tremendously appealing.

Victoria Mathias had taught her sons that being late for an appointment was inexcusably rude, an arrogant declaration that you were more important than the one you were meeting. Moon, therefore, tended to be early and thus had become skilled at waiting. He studied the menu, but saw nothing to modify his decision to order bacon and scrambled eggs. Then he unfolded the *Philippine Daily Journal* he'd picked up in the lobby.

The banner story concerned construction of the Imelda Marcos Children's Hospital. A headline down the page declared that Pol Pot's new government in Phnom Penh was establishing a "national program of reeducation" to restore Khmer values to Cambodia. Moon read every word of that. It involved Khmer Rouge troops driving hordes of civilians out of cities and towns into work camps being set up in the countryside. It sounded like a hodgepodge of rumors, mostly incredible. He turned to a follow-up story on President Ford's request that Congress appropriate more money for weapons for South Vietnam. The writer saw no sign that Ford was twisting arms to get the funds, nor any indication that Congress would agree. From that Moon turned to REFUGEES FLEE HIGHLANDS. A photograph of ARVN troops crowding aboard a C-130, knocking down civilians, accompanied the story. Moon imagined himself caught in such chaos, baby under his arm. Here he was, wasting time. And if Ricky's child was still in Cambodia, how much time did he have? He put down the *Journal* and glanced at his watch. In fifty-eight seconds, Mrs. Osa van Winjgaarden would be late, as people usually were.

But when Moon looked up, a woman was walking toward his table.

She was tall, slim, dark, a narrow face, a straight, narrow nose, high cheekbones, and large black eyes, which, when he noticed her, were studying him anxiously. This was not the plump blue-eyed blond Dutch matron the name had led Moon to expect, but she was walking directly toward him. He pushed back his chair and rose.

"Mr. Mathias," she said. "I hope you haven't been waiting long?"

"Not at all," Moon said. "In fact, you're early. I've just been reading the paper and waiting for some coffee." He shook the hand she offered, pulled back her chair, and signaled the waiter.

"I hope you found some good news," she said. "We could use some good news." She smiled at him, a rueful smile. "Certainly *you* could."

Moon looked surprised.

"I mean your brother's death. And now your mother being so ill. Mr. Castenada told me of your troubles. I hope she is getting better."

"Oh," Moon said. "Thank you. It's her heart. They're doing some tests. Maybe they've already done them. To tell whether to do bypass surgery. Last time I called I couldn't reach anyone who seemed to know anything."

"The time difference," she said. "You can never reach anyone on the other side of the Pacific. But I want to express my sympathy. Ricky was a wonderful man. And his wife. Eleth was sweet."

Eleth? Eleth Vinh? Wife? "I really didn't know her," Moon said. "We hadn't met." He signaled for the waiter again, waited while the coffee was poured, offered this dark woman the cream and sugar, and, when she declined, applied it to his own cup.

"You saw the paper this morning," she said. "Pol Pot's mad children are in Phnom Penh. How does that affect your plans?"

Plans? Moon stirred, sipped. "Actually, it doesn't," he said. "I haven't any plans. Only to talk to you and find out what you would tell me. And then I will see if I can find some of Ricky's friends and see what they know. And if the child is somewhere here in Manila, I will get her and take her home to her grandmother."

Mrs. van Winjgaarden was looking surprised. "No plans," she said. Her lips parted slightly as if to speak again. Then closed.

"By the way," Moon said. "I don't know how to pronounce your name. Is it Dutch?"

"Dutch, yes," she said. "One would say 'wanwingarten.' But it is hard to say. I think it would be better if you call me Osa."

"Osa," Moon said.

She smiled. "Your name is Malcolm, I know. But Ricky always called you Moon. Would it be impertinent to ask? . . ."

"It's my nickname," Moon said. "When I was little they used to have these little things they sold in a cellophane sack. Moon Pies was the name. A round cookie on the bottom, then a layer of marshmallow covered with chocolate. Two of them for a nickel. I always spent all my money on 'em. So they started calling me Moon Pie Mathias. It got shortened to Moon."

Mrs. van Winjgaarden smiled politely, willing to change the subject. "Mr. Castenada told me that Ricky's daughter never reached here. You think not so?"

"That's what he said," Moon agreed. "But I hope he's badly informed. Maybe something went wrong with whoever was bringing her. Maybe somebody else completed the trip. Maybe they delivered her to one of Ricky's friends here. Mr. Castenada didn't have any recent news." Even as he was saying it the theory sounded inane. If the child had reached Manila, Castenada's man checking the flights would have known. If she had been brought in some other way, surely Castenada would know.

Mrs. van Winjgaarden's expression suggested she thought so too.

"Perhaps," she said. "But I think they would have got in touch with Mr. Castenada. You think not true?"

The waiter spared Moon the need to respond. Mrs. van Winjgaarden ordered toast and melon, Moon his bacon and eggs. He was trying to match this self-assured woman with the small shy voice he'd heard yesterday on the telephone. The difference of a night's sleep, he thought. Yesterday's trip must have been exhausting—getting to Manila from Timor.

"You're from Timor, I think," Moon said. "I'm not sure I know where—"

She was smiling at this. "No one ever does."

Moon realized the smile was wry; the amusement was at herself, at the obscurity of her homeland. Not at his ignorance. He found himself thinking he would like this woman.

"People know it's an island," she said. "It's the last large island in the Indonesian chain. Southeast of Borneo. North of Australia." She laughed, her expression apologizing to Moon for underestimating his education. "Of course, north of Australia. Everything is north of Australia. Say halfway between Australia and the Celebes."

"Oh," Moon said. "Sure." Pretending to remember, flattered that she'd presume he could place the Celebes.

"But I don't live on Timor. I was there arranging to buy things. To buy folk art for the export business. I live in Kuala Lumpur."

"Oh," Moon said. That's somewhere in Indonesia too, he thought. Or perhaps the Malay Peninsula.

"And you, of course, are from the United States. I think Ricky said from Colorado."

"From Colorado," Moon agreed.

"So," she said. "Today you intend to talk to Ricky's friends here. And you will learn if someone brought Lila to them but didn't tell Mr. Castenada?"

Moon nodded.

"And if Lila is not here, you will find out if they know where she would be?" she suggested. "Whether she was taken to Saigon. Or perhaps to Ricky's place at Can Tho?"

Moon nodded. Can Tho? Yes. He remembered the sound of that. Ricky had mentioned something about that place when he'd visited at Fort Riley. Halsey had turned the name around and made a joke out of it. And it was mentioned in Ricky's papers. "A town in the Mekong Delta?"

"Can Tho? Yes. Near the river's mouth. Where Ricky had his repair hangars. What are your plans if you find out Lila is there? How will you get there?"

He thought. "I guess the airports are closed." He tapped the newspaper.

"They were this morning, except for Saigon," she said. "I think getting into Saigon is still possible." She smiled wryly. "They say the planes are pretty empty going in. Getting out?" She shrugged. "And how do you get from Saigon down to the delta?"

"The rich folks leaving the sinking ship," Moon said.

Their breakfasts arrived. They buttered their respective slices of toast. Moon sampled his bacon. Excellent. The eggs tasted fresh. He savored them. Mrs. van Winjgaarden was looking down, toying with the melon. An interesting face, but her short hair looked as if she'd combed it with her fingers, and her jacket was rumpled. Like his own.

"Why did you want to see me?" Moon asked.

She looked up from the melon and down again. "I want to ask for your help. My brother is at a little place in the hills in Cambodia. With some of the Montagnard people. He has a medical station at Tonli Kong, a tribal village. I want you to take me there."

Moon's face showed his amazement. "Me? How?"

"I had called to talk to Ricky about doing it," she said. "That's when they told me he was dead. So I called Mr. Castenada. He told me you were coming to get Ricky's daughter. So I thought I would ask you to help me."

Help me. Always that. Why not the other way around? Why not, How can I help you, Mr. Mathias?

"I don't see how I can do that."

She looked up from the melon, surprised. "I thought you would be taking over Ricky's company. I thought you would fly us up to the hills and we would pick up Damon, and—"

"I'm not a pilot," Moon said. "I can't fly a helicopter. Or anything else."

Mrs. van Winjgaarden stared at him numbly, melon spoon frozen in midair.

"You can't? I assumed—"

"No," Moon said. "I'm no pilot. I took a few flying lessons once." He shrugged. It was one of the things he wasn't good at.

Mrs. van Winjgaarden put down the spoon, expression puzzled. "Then how did you hope to get out? How did you hope to get the baby out? Getting in would be, I think, fairly easy if we don't wait too long. But getting out . . ." She let the sentence trail off. Why say it?

Moon found himself taking a perverse pleasure in this; in defeating this overconfident woman's overconfident expectations.

"If you don't go in, there's no problem getting out," he said.

Mrs. van Winjgaarden picked up the spoon, put a bit of melon in her mouth, and chewed thoughtfully, looking at him. She reached a conclusion, swallowed.

"Oh," she said. "You'll go in. Alone." She nodded to herself. "You don't want me along. You'll have enough problems without excess baggage."

Moon's pleasure went away, replaced by irritation.

"Look," he said. "I will check with whichever of Ricky's friends I can find. If they know where the kid is in Manila, I collect her and take her home. If they know she's somewhere I can get to, I go get her. Otherwise, I go back to the States. Back to minding my own business."

Mrs. van Winjgaarden listened carefully to every word of this, smiling slightly. Moon's irritation edged toward anger.

"Believe what you like," he said. "What makes you think I'm so eager to risk my neck?"

The smile broadened. "I know about you," she said.

"That I'm crazy? Who told you?"

She shrugged. "Ricky. Ricky's friends. Mr. Castenada."

That stopped him. He sipped his coffee, remembering what the lawyer had said. Remembering Electra. Remembering old Mr. Lum Lee.

"What did Ricky tell you?"

"That you were marvelous."

Her face was dead serious as she said it, and Moon

realized that he was being teased. Victoria had teased him sometimes when he was a child, when he was angry or moody. And the woman who taught calculus when he was in high school did it. But no one since then.

"Ricky told us about your football playing. About knocking the other players down so he could run. About throwing the shotput when your back was hurt. About beating the big man who was drowning the dog. About the time—" She was ticking them off on her fingers when Moon stopped her.

"That was a little brother talking," he said. "In our family, in our town, Ricky was the star."

"And modest," she said. "Ricky told us about that too. He said when you played football, he just followed behind you. He told us, 'Moon knocked them over and I got the credit.' That's what he told us about you."

Moon felt his face flushing. He forced a grin. "More little brother talk. The scouts from the colleges recruited Ricky. They didn't offer any scholarships to me."

"Because of your knee," she said. "A knee was hurt. You had to have an operation to fix it. And you could always repair things. The car you boys bought. The machines at your mother's printing place. The—"

"Why can't your brother just come out by himself?" Moon asked. "Why do you need to go get him?"

Mrs. van Winjgaarden looked down at the melon. "Because he won't. He is a stubborn man. He wants to stay with those people in the mountains. With his tribe. He thinks of them as his responsibility."

"How about the Khmer Rouge? From what I read they're rough on Americans. On Europeans."

"Rough?" she said. "Yes. They kill them. And their own people too. We hear they usually tie them to a tree or something and beat them with sticks. Not using up their ammunition that way. They say Pol Pot's children kill everyone who is well dressed. Or well educated. Or wears glasses. Anyone who has soft hands."

"Surely your brother must know that."

"Yes." She looked directly into his eyes now, as if she thought he might have some explanation for what she was saying. "But you see, Damon wants to die."

Moon had nothing to say to that.

"He told me he wants to be a saint. Like the martyrs who died for their faith," she said. "I think that is true. Damon is a minister. A Lutheran missionary. He wants to give those people some proof that he believes the Gospels he has been teaching them. A demonstration of self-sacrifice." She said it all matter-of-factly, in a voice devoid of emotion. Then laughed. "Greater love hath no man," she said. "Do you play Monopoly? GO DIRECTLY TO HEAVEN. DO NOT PASS GO. DO NOT COLLECT TWO HUNDRED DOLLARS. Damon wants to go directly to heaven."

To his surprise, Moon found he was feeling disapproval. "You don't believe in that?"

"Oh," she said with a self-deprecating laugh, "I suppose I believe in the abstract idea. But I love him. Damon is my brother. When he was little I looked after him. I don't want Pol Pot's crazy children to beat him to death."

She attempted a smile but didn't quite make it. Her expression was folorn.

Moon thought, Here it is. Here is what always overwhelms me. Pity. Always pity. How do people sense that? How do they read me so easily? And Mrs. van Winjgaarden seemed to read even the thought.

"I wish I could help you," he said. It's just—"

"But first you must find Ricky's friends here. To learn about the child. Yes. I understand."

And so they went to find Ricky's friends.

BANGKOK, Thailand, April 17 (Agence France-Presse)—A blackout of customary news channels wrapped developments in Cambodia in uncertainty today amid rumors that the new government had ordered an evacuation of the capital and reports that some government army units were still resisting in the south.

Still the Sixth Day

April 18, 1975

FINDING THE ADDRESS Castenada had given him for George Rice proved relatively simple by Manila standards. The taxi driver repeated the street number doubtfully and asked, "In Pasay City?" Moon had simply shrugged. But Mrs. van Winjgaarden said, "Yes. Pasay City. It's off Taft Avenue. Close to the Manila Sanatorium."

Which proved to be correct and left Moon wondering how a woman who lived in Kuala Lumpur, wherever that was, was so familiar with this address. She took his surprise as a question and extracted a little book from her purse.

"I buy street guides," she said. "I keep them. I think I must have twenty by now."

The apartment with the Rice number on it was on the

second floor of a ramshackle cement-block building smothered with tropical vegetation. Its two windows facing the porch were open and so was the door. Moon's tap on the screen brought forth a small young woman clad in a loose pink housedress.

She stood behind the screen wordlessly inspecting them.

"My name is Mathias," Moon said, "and this is Mrs. van Winjgaarden. We are looking for George Rice."

Her neutral expression became a scowl. She shook her head.

"We were given this as his address," Moon said.

"Not now," she said. "No more."

"Do you know where we could find him?"

The expression changed. She knows, Moon thought, and she thinks it's funny.

"It is very important," Mrs. van Winjgaarden said. "It concerns the welfare of a child."

"I don't know," the woman said. She shut the door, and as they were walking away down the porch they heard her shutting the windows.

"Well," Moon said, "I guess we can check off Mr. Rice."

"The neighbors will know something," Mrs. van Winjgaarden said. "We will try some of the other apartments. I think someone will tell us something."

Someone did. But he wanted to start at the beginning. This man, he said, didn't actually live in the apartment. He came now and then, always driving a rental car, and then he would be gone for a long time, and then he would come again and stay a few days and then be gone again.

"This time, I think he will be gone a long, long, long time." He extended two skinny arms all the way, suggesting something like infinity. He waited for the question.

Moon asked it. "What happened?"

"It was about a month ago," the man said. "Maybe a little bit less. I work at night, at the sanatorium, and I was just going to bed when I saw him pull in over there and park. I was looking out and wondering where he had been, getting in just about dawn, you know. And they were waiting for him. Grabbed him just as he got out of his car."

The man telling them this was standing barefoot in the doorway of the apartment just below the one Rice had occupied. He was a very skinny fellow in walking shorts and short-sleeved shirt. It seemed to Moon that he was enjoying the telling of his story. He stopped now and looked from Moon to Mrs. van Winjgaarden, waiting for another question.

"Who grabbed him?" Moon asked.

"Police," the man said. "I counted five of them. Two in uniforms, and three of them looked like Marcos's men. Suits on. Neckties. They took him upstairs, and I could hear them thumping around up there. Moving furniture." The remembered excitement provoked a smile. "I thought it was political," he said, "but it was just dope."

"Just dope," Moon said.

"Well, maybe it was politics; the *Express* said it was heroin. But with the *Express,* it's whatever Imelda tells it to say. I think she owns it."

"Is he in Bilibad?" Mrs. van Winjgaarden asked.

"I guess so," the man said. "The paper said he got twenty-five years."

Back in the taxi, Moon gave the driver the address of Robert Yager, a hotel in Quezon City. "He probably won't be there," he told Mrs. van Winjgaarden. "Castenada said he lives in Phnom Penh mostly. But that's where he stays when he's here."

"Do you know how to go about talking to Rice in Bilibad?" she asked him.

"I'm not even sure I know what it is. A prison?"

"It's the hard-time prison here in Manila," she said. "I think they have another one way down south somewhere. They need a lot of prison space for all the political enemies Marcos is rounding up."

"I guess I can call the Associated Press and ask them to find out if he's in there," Moon said. "And they'd know what the rules are for talking to prisoners." And whether the charge was heroin smuggling. Heroin. How much heroin would fit in one of the Huey copters Ricky was repairing?

"I think you might try your embassy," Mrs. van Winjgaarden said. "The U.S. government and the Marcos people are very friendly. Very close. Unless they think this George Rice is a Communist, they could get you in." She laughed. "Heroin would not be as serious as politics. Unless maybe Mr. Rice forgot to pay whichever of Imelda's cousins has the cumshaw concession for heroin."

Heroin. It should be easy enough to tell heroin from ancestral bones if you looked into the urn Mr. Lum Lee was hunting.

Moon did not want to go to Bilibad and talk to George Rice. He wanted to go to Colorado. Tonight, if possible.

"Do you know this Rice? What did he do for Ricky?"

"I met him two or three times. He was a pilot for Ricky, and I think they were good friends too. I think he and Ricky were going to buy an airplane together. A little one. I think they both liked to fly around. Like a hobby."

"Not heroin?" Moon asked, and wished instantly he could swallow the question.

She looked at him. "You know your brother. What do you think?"

"I think not," Moon said.

She nodded. "Yes," she said. "Not heroin. Not Ricky.

Cambodia is full of it. And Laos too. And Nam. They bring it down out of Burma, the little Chinese armies that control the mountains. They say Ricky worked with your Central Intelligence Agency, and the CIA is tied up with the opium armies. But I think Ricky didn't like drugs. He saw too much in Nam. In the army. He talked about how it ruined his crews. And he said once he hated working with the CIA because they worked with the drug traffickers. I think he hated heroin."

"Yes," Moon said. "I think he would have." And when he spoke again it was to comment on the rain, which had started again. It pounded against the roof of the cab. They sat in silence, watching the windshield wipers work and the streetlights come on as darkness closed in on Manila.

The desk clerk at the Quezon Towers confirmed that Robert Yager kept an apartment on the twelfth floor. But Robert Yager was not now in residence there. Nor was he expected. He had sublet the suite through the end of April. But Yager might be reached, the clerk said, at the R. M. Air offices in Can Tho, Vietnam. That, the clerk said, was "Mr. Yager's usual place of occupancy." He had no other address.

That sent them back into the cab, down the glistening rain-wet streets to find the address of Thomas Brock on Cuenco Street in Makati. While they hunted that, they agreed that Yager could be checked off as impossible. Thomas Brock soon joined him.

Brock's block had been a mixture of middle-class apartments and small one-story business addresses. Now the street was limited by a LOCAL TRAFFIC ONLY sign printed in both English and Tagalog. The side of Cuenco Street that bore his even-numbered residence hotel was now piled with the rubble of buildings smashed to make way for larger buildings.

Moon gave the driver the address of Mrs. van Winjgaarden's hotel.

"Yes," she said. "You must be exhaused. We can do no more today. Tomorrow—" She paused, not sure how to continue.

"I don't know about tomorrow," Moon said. "I want to think about it."

"You said Castenada could give you nothing more? No better addresses? No more associates who might—"

"Three names. Yager, Rice, and Brock. Three addresses. He didn't seem to know much about them, just that they'd had some association with Ricky in the past. Worked for him or invested, or something."

"You would think a lawyer would know more than just names," she said.

"I could call Castenada in the morning," Moon said. "I could ask him." Could. But he didn't think he would. If Castenada had any more information he would have offered it. It would just mean more wasted time. Tomorrow he would try to wrap up this business. Then he'd call Philippine Airlines and see if he could get on the day-after-tomorrow flight. He could be home when? He'd gain the day he'd lost crossing the international dateline. Make it three days from today, then. He thought of Debbie. Would she be there? Maybe, maybe not.

"And ask about Mr. Rice. I think you should. Find out how to see him in Bilibad." Mrs. van Winjgaarden had been staring out the cab window at the rain, but now she turned to look at him. "I have been remembering," she said. "Rice. Like what they grow so much of in the Mekong Delta. I remember him better now I have been thinking. He was supposed to be their best pilot. Always making jokes. A short man with a short beard. White. It made him look old." She nodded. "Yes. Ricky said he could fly any of the helicopters."

The cab was stopping.

"Here's your hotel," Moon said. But the driver had made a mistake. This crummy little place, jammed in between a generator rewinding shop and a service station, wouldn't be where Mrs. van Winjgaarden would be staying.

She got out, shielding herself from the rain while she extracted cab fare from her purse.

Wrong again.

"I'll pay him when he gets me home. We can settle up later," Moon said, and watched her disappear into the crummy little place, leaving him with just the rain and the thought that his brother may have dealt with heroin.

SAIGON, South Vietnam, April 18 (UPI)—North Vietnamese troops began a furious tank, artillery and infantry attack today on Ham Tan, the capital of Binh Tuy Province and a 30-mile step closer to Saigon.

The Seventh Day

April 19, 1975

MOON HAD RISEN EARLY, had breakfast, called the Associated Press Bureau, got the day manager, identified himself, and explained that he needed to know how to go about learning if a U.S. citizen named George Rice was held in Bilibad Prison and, if so, how to go about arranging an interview. The day manager had once covered Denver city hall for the *Rocky Mountain News*. He'd see what he could find out, but it would involve dealing with both the U.S. Embassy and the Philippine penal bureaucracy, so delay was unavoidable. He took Moon's telephone number and said he'd try to get back to him by noon, but that might be optimistic.

With that step over, Moon took a taxi out to Caloocan City to check on the property Ricky had leased. Maybe someone would be there who knew something—such as where to find Brock. It was a long shot but better than waiting in his hotel room for the AP to call.

"Caloocan City?" the cabbie said. "That's a long ways outside. For that we don't use the meter. I just use this special rate card. So you get a bargain."

Moon had been warned about exactly this by the Maynila's concierge. "Make sure they turn on the meter. Those special rate cards are stuff they make up themselves to get more money out of tourists."

"I'll tell you what we'll do," Moon said. "Give me the rate card price now and turn on the meter. And when we get there, we'll compare them."

The cabbie gave Moon a huge gap-toothed grin. "My name is Tino," he said, "and I think you've been to Manila before."

They drove north through the teeming traffic on Roxas Boulevard, which for no reason apparent to Moon suddenly became Bonifacio Drive. They crossed the muddy Pasig River, left modern Manila and its middle-class housing district behind, and were surrounded by slums and the distinctive aroma of burning garbage.

"Smoky Mountain," Tino said. "Lots of poor people live here." He waved at the clusters of shacks they were passing and went on with the same tone of civic pride he'd been using to describe the glass and steel edifices along United National Avenue. "They build houses on the city dump. No rent to pay that way. And they collect stuff out of the trash and fix it up and sell it."

The city dump also provided the homes. They were patched together with sheet metal, odds and ends of wood, insulation board, bamboo. The architect of the hut they were passing now had used old carpeting to fill in a gap in the siding.

Caloocan City met expectations for a city no better than Smoky Mountain did for a mountain. They passed clusters of small fields being plowed this spring morning by men driving water buffaloes, followed by clusters of two-story business buildings, followed by great fields of sugarcane. The address they were seeking was surrounded by just such a field.

Castenada had written, *Caloocan City, Marmoi Road, Number 700; look for billboard Great Luck Development Corp. Look for warehouse of Seven Seas Worldwide Container, Inc.*

Great Luck had surrounded two or three acres of its property with a fence, to keep out the cane, and built two concrete-block structures. Judging from the signs, the smaller one housed the offices of both Great Luck and Seven Seas. The larger one looked new: an office wing attached to a triple-sized hangar. And above the high hangar doors was painted:

M. R. AIR, LTD.
HELICOPTER REPAIR, LEASING AND TRANSPORT

Moon stared at the sign. Not Ricky Mathias Air but Moon and Ricky Air. Ricky had meant it. That was hard to digest.

Tino looked around.

"This is it, no?"

"Yes," Moon said. "Wait for me."

The office door was locked, but through its window he could see that the room was furnished with two desks, a table, filing cabinets—the usual office furniture. The ashtray on the desk had two cigar butts in it. He pounded on the door. Waited. Pounded again. Then he walked across the gravel to the Great Luck Development Corp., encouraged by the whine of a band saw and hammering. The sign on the door said 700 MARMOI ROAD, and it opened just as he tapped on it.

A small, plump, and very pregnant woman looked up at him. "Good morning," she said. "You must be Mr. Bascom, and you are a little bit too early."

"My name is Malcolm Mathias," Moon said. "I'm looking for Mr. Brock. I think he works next door at the helicopter company."

"Mr. Brock?" she said, frowning. "Oh, yes. But I haven't seen him for days." She searched her memory. "Not for maybe two weeks."

"Do you know where I could find him?"

"Is nobody over there?" she asked, indicating M. R. Air with a glance. "I think Mr. Delos would know."

"No one was there."

"Oh, yes," she said, and laughed. "I forgot what day it is. Mr. Delos would be fighting his cock. He will be at the stadium."

The stadium was a mile or so beyond the cane fields, beside a creek that irrigated a narrow row of rice paddies. It was round, designed by someone with access to a large number of heavy timbers and a supply of corrugated sheet metal roofing. The timbers were erected exactly far enough apart to be spanned by the roofing material, which was nailed to it to form the walls. The roof was a steep thatched cone, and the single entrance was guarded by two small booths made of lumber. At one, admission tickets were on sale at ten pisos each. Over the other a sign declared POLLOS FRITOS, and from it rose a thin haze of smoke and the delicious smell of frying chicken.

"Tell you what we'll do," Moon said when the cabbie parked in a lot occupied by scores of bicycles and a couple of dozen cars and trucks. "I'll buy you a ticket and you help me find Mr. Delos in the crowd."

"Ten pisos," Tino said, voice scornful. "And you get a discount because a lot of the fights are already over."

"How do you know?" Moon said. "It's still early."

"Lots of losers," Tino said, pointing to the POLLOS FRITOS sign.

Moon paid full fare for both tickets—about ninety cents American—and they found a place on the top row, seven levels up, where the siding had been removed to let hot air and tobacco smoke escape. The stadium was about two-thirds full with a couple of hundred spectators: all males, all ages, almost all clad in the Filipino summer garb of short-sleeved shirts, cotton pants, and straw hats. The exceptions were those who held the seats around the ring. Most of them wore jackets, and most of them had custody of roosters.

The ring itself was a platform raised about three feet above the earthen floor and surrounded by sheets of transparent plastic. In it five men stood. In the center a skinny little man wearing a black suit, white shirt, and necktie was talking into a microphone. To his right and left stood two-man teams, which Moon identified as bird holder and assistant. The man with the mike spoke in what Moon guessed must be Tagalog and then repeated at least some of it in heavily accented English. The audience listened in rapt silence.

"He's telling about the cocks," Tino murmured. "The one with the red feathers around his neck—" Just then the master of ceremonies stopped talking.

He lowered the mike and the arena exploded into bedlam. All around them, all around the stadium, men were leaping to their feet, shouting, flashing hand signals, acknowledging hand signals. Tino was saying something in Moon's ear.

"What?" Moon shouted.

"I say if you wanna bet, bet on the one with the red feathers around his neck. Number nineteen. The maestro said he's won three fights."

"I'll just watch," Moon said. "Do any of those guys holding roosters look like Delos? She said he was short and fat and wore a long mustache."

"Two fat ones," Tino said, pointing.

Moon had noticed that. But both were sitting with their backs to him.

In the ring, the maestro raised the microphone. The clamor of betting stopped almost instantly. The rooster bearers advanced. The roosters pecked at each other while the maestro watched. Unsatisfied, he signaled the rooster bearers forward again. This time the cocks pecked with more satisfying ferocity. The maestro sent the rooster bearers back to their corners. They crouched, holding the roosters on the floor. One of the roosters waiting his turn outside the ring crowed lustily. The maestro's hand dropped and the combat began in a wild flurry of feathers of spurs. Red Feathers went for the head. His black opponent backed away, then counterattacked, encouraged by shouts and imprecations from the audience. There was another wild flurry, another, and another, and suddenly it seemed to be over. Red Feathers was down, wings extended, neck held out. Black Feathers took two wobbly steps and stopped.

"Looks like you picked the wrong rooster," Moon said.

"I think maybe a draw," Tino said.

The handlers picked up their roosters. The maestro called them together. They held out the birds, head to head. Red Feathers was obviously out of it. Another morsel for the pollos fritos stand. But the black bird had no fight left. Instead of pecking, he pulled his head back. Maestro ordered a retrial. Again, Black Feathers wanted no more combat. His backers in the audience groaned. Maestro made a washing gesture with his hands while the bird holders departed. He said something unintelligible into the mike and signaled the next fight.

Both fat men climbed into the ring, one with a handlebar mustache and holding a mostly white rooster. Mr. Delos, surely, since the other one was clean-shaven. The ritual was repeated, the birds pecked at each other, the uproar of betting resumed, and the fight began. This one lasted a little longer and ended with the white rooster prone and breathing its last.

Tino grinned at Moon. "Pretty good, huh?" he said. "I don't think you have anything in America like this."

"Just hockey," Moon said. "I guess that's as close as we get."

This time when the concluding test was applied, the winning bird had retained enough martial spirit to deliver a couple of farewell pecks. The maestro pointed to it and said the proper words into the mike, and bedlam again ensued. This time the yelling and pointing was accompanied by the passing of money up and down the rows and across the seats—the white cock's backers paying their gambling debts to the winners. The honor system in practice, Moon thought, which was something else now missing from American athletics. But he didn't have time to watch. Mr. Delos was carrying his deceased bird out of the stadium.

Moon caught Delos at the pollos fritos stand, in a glum conversation with the cook. But any grief Mr. Delos might have been feeling for his bird vanished when Moon introduced himself. The round brown face of Mr. Delos went aglow with delight as he pumped Moon's hand.

"At last. At last," he said. "Your brother told us he hoped you would be coming, and Mr. Brock said he expected you. I am so happy to meet you."

"Mr. Brock. Is he here?"

"He has gone back to Manila," Mr. Delos said. "There was a business arrangement to complete with Thousand Islands Airways. Ricky had made a proposal—" Mr. Delos remembered that delight was not appropriate. His expression changed. "We are so sorry about Ricky. What a terrible loss for you and for your mother. Please accept my condolences."

"Thank you," Moon said. "Where can I reach Mr. Brock in Manila?"

Finding that address required going back to the office. Delos checked in his Rolodex file. He extracted a card with the same address Castenada had provided. That and the telephone number with it had been scratched out and replaced only by a different telephone number. Mr. Delos was apologetic.

"His apartment, they tore it down so he moved, but it's just until he can find a new place so he didn't put down where he is now. Just the phone number."

Moon called it, and while he listened to it ring Mr. Delos talked about business. Ricky had persuaded Thousand Islands it should expand its copter fleet by tapping into the huge surplus that the end of the fighting in Vietnam, Laos, and Cambodia would make available. M. R. Air would do the brokering and the conversion from gunships to transports, would handle maintenance, and would even subcontract some island-hopping jobs.

"We have more than a thousand islands in the Philippines," Mr. Delos said. "Too rough for airstrips, just perfect for landing pads. And then we think maybe we can get maintenance work for the Manila police. The U.S. government gave them a dozen copters but I think only about two now are safe to fly. And then—"

The telephone was not going to be answered. Moon hung up and listened with pseudo-attention until Mr. Delos completed his account of business prospects. He asked Mr. Delos to have Mr. Brock call him at the Maynila if he checked in, shook hands, and left.

In the parking lot, Tino was squatting beside the left rear wheel of his little Toyota taxi, examining a very low tire.

Moon looked at his watch. It was already well past the noon hour when AP hoped to call him.

"A nail or something out at the stadium, I guess," Tino said, sounding disconsolate.

"I'll help you change it," Moon said.

"Okay," Tino said. "But the spare's flat too."

WASHINGTON, April 18, (AP)—The Senate Foreign Relations Committee today approved a $200 million appropriation for humanitarian aid for South Vietnam, but a $722 million request for military aid remained stalled in Congress.

Still the Seventh Day

April 19, 1975

IN THE GIFT SHOP OF THE HOTEL MAYNILA, Moon bought copies of the two English-language Manila evening papers with the least flamboyant typography. He sat in the lobby reading, watching the dinner-hour traffic pass in tuxes, cocktail gowns, and the formal wear of various desert sheikdoms. If getting Tino's multiple flats fixed hadn't made them so late he would have been tempted to ask Mrs. van Winjgaarden to join him for dinner. Not that he would have done it. Partly because he couldn't dress for anything more chic than a greasy spoon coffee shop but mostly because she would have pressed him to help her, probably in some fairly subtle way. Besides, she was several degrees out of his class and wouldn't be dining with him unless she wanted something. Even so, eating alone in a dining room surrounded by couples and foursomes had been a dreary affair. Equally dreary was the prospect that now confronted him: spending the evening watching the rain splash against the windows of his room.

The biological clock operating behind Moon's forehead had not yet compensated for Los Angeles–to–Manila jet lag. He'd been sleepy about noon. Not now. In fact, he doubted if he'd be sleepy until about Manila sunrise. He skipped through the papers again. Nothing he found in either made the prospects of flying off to the Republic of Vietnam or the former Kingdom of Cambodia seem promising. The South Viets' strategy, if they had one, seemed to be defending Saigon and the Mekong Delta, letting Uncle Ho have the rest of it, and hoping for the best. Floods of refugees were pouring out of the highlands. Floods of refugees were also pouring into Thailand from Cambodia, carrying terrible tales of Pol Pot's "Zero Year" campaign. The stories of slaughter and atrocities sounded to Moon exaggerated by a factor of about a hundred. But even when you discounted it, the news made any notion of joining Mrs. van Winjgaarden on her journey to extract her suicidal brother from the Cambodian hills seem stupid.

He refolded the papers and put them on the chair beside him. Not sleepy but tired. He'd tried Brock's Manila number as soon as he got back to the hotel, with no answer. He'd try it again tomorrow morning. The Associated Press day manager had left a message as promised. It was short and clear: "Bilibad says it has no George Rice. Media man at embassy (Del Fletcher) says he will check other possibilities tomorrow." Another thing to deal with in the morning.

Moon felt a stirring of hope. George Rice would have jumped bond and vanished from the planet. Brock would answer his telephone and report that he knew absolutely nothing about the whereabouts of Ricky's kid. Whereupon Moon would arrange his return flight to Los Angeles, express his regrets to the Dutch lady, and get the hell out of there. Or, better yet, Brock would say he had the child here in Manila and would Moon please drop by and pick her up? Then he'd go get the child and the two of them would fly home.

But what if Brock answered the phone and said the child was somewhere in Vietnam or Cambodia? What would he do then? He'd think about that only if he had to think about it. No need to think about it tonight. Instead he probed around for any other possibilities. Any loose ends he'd overlooked. Should he go back and cross-examine Castenada? Nothing to be gained from that. He imagined a recuperating Victoria Mathias sitting across a table from him, full of questions, looking for a reason to go over there and find the kid herself. Were there any loose ends he'd overlooked?

One. Ricky's Manila apartment. He'd have to find it and take a look. He dreaded doing that. Dreaded it. But something there might be useful. Probably would be. Old letters. Old notes with names of people, names of friends of a pretty young woman named Vinh who had borne Ricky's child, perhaps people who would take in this orphaned child.

From his pocket, Moon extracted the key Castenada had given him and checked the address on the tag attached to it. Then he walked out into the warm darkness and signaled a cab.

The address was Unit 27, 6062 San Cabo, Pasay City, less than three miles from his hotel. The building was a two-storied M-shaped structure surrounded by palm trees. Unit 27 was on the end of the upper floor. Moon climbed an external stairway and walked down the porch, checking numbers, hearing music through door panels, hearing laughter through opened windows, seeing the warmth of reading lamps through blowing curtains. Unit 23 was dark and silent. So were Unit 25 and Unit 27.

The key didn't seem to fit. Moon inspected it, listened to the rain pattering against the roof tiles overhead, turned the key over, and slid it in. The lock clicked. Moon turned the knob and stepped into the darkness. He inhaled, testing for the stale, musty air of a room closed too long, feeling on the wall for a light switch, finally finding it.

The air, which should have had the mustiness of a long-unused apartment, was not musty at all. He was inhaling the aroma of onions, of burnt toast, of coffee, of talcum powder, of human perspiration. He was hearing someone breathing.

Moon pushed the light switch. Across the tiny living room in the doorway to a bedroom a man was facing him. Naked. He was a thin man, with thinning red hair and drooping mustache. In his right hand he held a large black pistol pointed at Moon's chest.

"Hands on top of your head," the man said. "And turn around."

"Who the hell are you?" Moon asked. "What are you doing here?"

The pistol looked like one of those old army-issue .45-caliber semiautomatics, exactly like one Moon once carried in his own army-issue holster. The naked man clicked back the hammer. "Turn around, you son of a bitch. Kneel and get yourself facedown on the floor."

Moon turned around and knelt, hands atop his head. The carpet beneath him was grimy. Moon's anger offset his fear. To hell with this.

"If this is Unit Twenty-seven," he said, "then this is my brother's apartment, and what the hell are you doing in it? If it's not, I made a mistake. And I apologize."

From somewhere behind him Moon heard a woman's

voice. "Who is it, Tommy? Do I call the police?"

"Your brother?" the naked man said. Brief silence. Then: "What's your brother's name?"

"Ricky Mathias."

"Well, shit," the man said. "I'll be damned. Are you Moon Mathias? You look like you're big enough."

Moon stood up and turned around. "I'm Moon Mathias, and who the hell are you?"

"Tommy Brock." He shifted the pistol to his left hand and held out his right.

Moon shook it.

"Nina," Brock said. "If you're decent, get out here and meet the famous Moon Mathias, Ricky's brother. You've heard Ricky tell about him."

Nina emerged from the bedroom in a short white nightgown. She was small and dark with long tousled hair. She examined Moon with frightened eyes, nodded, said "Hello," and slipped back through the doorway into the darkness.

Moon found himself breathing normally again. Almost normally. Anger had replaced the fright.

"You're sort of trespassing, aren't you?" Moon said. "How the hell did you get in here? I want you to get your clothes on and get your asses out."

Tommy Brock was disappearing into the bedroom. From the waist upward he was brown, waist downward virginal white—the two-tone coloration of one who works shirtless in the sun.

"I mean right now," Moon said. "Out." But even as he said it, he realized he had questions to ask this man.

"Well, now," Brock said from somewhere out of sight in the bedroom, "what's the goddam rush? Get down to it, maybe *you're* the one trespassing. This place is on lease to R. M. Air. Or M. R. Air as we're calling it now. I've got the key. Everybody with the company picks up the key when they come to Manila."

With that Brock emerged, looking amused, khaki pants on now and buttoning a short-sleeved shirt. The pistol seemed to have been left behind. He padded barefoot past Moon into the kitchen. "Have a seat," he said. "I'll put on some coffee. Or do you want something stronger? Ricky said you swore off drinking, but maybe you'd make an exception after somebody points a forty-five pistol at you."

Embarrassment replaced Moon's anger. He cleared his throat, thought of nothing to say, seated himself on the edge of the sofa. The light had gone on in the kitchen. A clattering of utensils. "How about I heat up what we had left over? It's still sort of warm. Not really stale. We just got in from seeing a movie and were going to bed when you—when you got here."

"Warmed up's fine," Moon said.

Brock was leaning against the kitchen doorway, looking happy, good-natured, and amused. "You sure favor that picture Ricky had of you," he said. "You going to take over the outfit?" His expression turned wry. "Lordy, there'd be enough irony in that for anyone. Ricky always wanted to get you out here. Said we'd be the Air Express of this whole corner of the world. We wouldn't need the ARVN connection." He shook his head. "Now you get here and it's too damned late. Too late, anyway, for Ricky. Maybe not too late for the company, though. We're got several things working."

"How did it happen?" Moon asked. "With Ricky, I mean. We never knew much except it was a copter crash."

Brock frowned. "Nobody told you anything?"

"Just the official word from the embassy," Moon said. "No details."

"Well, then," Brock said, looking somber, "I think I'd

better start at the beginning. Skip back enough so you'll know why things weren't quite normal."

Brock said Ricky had concluded that they must move the R. M. Air repair base out of Can Tho. Can Tho was right beside the Hau Giang arm of the Mekong. The Vietnam navy had been slacking off its Mekong patrols and the Vietcong were raiding just upstream. That was in February. Ricky flew to Saigon and met with the ARVN general they'd been doing business with. The general and Ricky had agreed that R. M. Air would move its operations down to a building the general owned in Long Phu. An ARVN ranger battalion was based there, and it was practically on the coast of the South China Sea. A comparatively safe place and easy to evacuate when everything went to hell. So they started moving stuff. Their two regular pilots were flying Hueys loaded with spare parts and office equipment down to Long Phu when an old Chinese man came in and wanted a hurry-up flight into Cambodia to pick up a cargo.

Moon interrupted. "You know his name? The old man?"

"Lum Lee," Brock said. "We'd done some hauling for him before. Antiques, so he said." He smiled. "I think Mr. Lee is one of those fellows who catches big fish in troubled waters. You know, a temple gets looted, or a museum, or some maggot's house, and all of a sudden there's valuable stuff for sale at a bargain."

"Maggots?" Moon said.

"Rich moneylenders," Brock said. "Bankers. I think it's a Chinese word. Maybe Vietnamese. And I guess you're supposed to pronounce it *mah*-go. Anyway, Mr. Lee was in a hell of a hurry. He'd just heard that the Cambodian army was pulling out of a district up in the north, and he had some stuff he wanted to retrieve before Pol Pot's little savages got there." Brock grinned. "He said it was ancestral bones."

"Ancestral bones?"

Brock laughed. "Yeah. That's what he claimed." He studied Moon, nodded. "Your brother said you were good at figuring things out."

"Not really. Mr. Lee contacted me too. I thought it might really be ancestral bones he was after."

"Anything's possible out here. Maybe so," Brock said, grinning. "We were shorthanded, so Ricky flew a chopper up there himself. Then he radioed in and said to tell Mr. Lum Lee he had the cargo and he was going to stop at Vin Ba and then come on in."

"Vin Ba?"

"It's a little rice village up on the edge of the hill country. Next to the Nam border. It's where Eleth's family lives. They're in the charcoal-making business. She was visiting up there, and he was going to stop and pick her up."

Brock paused, thinking about it. No happiness in his face now.

"I guess he did," he said, and paused while the gusting wind blew rain against the windows. "Her body was in the wreckage with his. Eleth and Ricky."

For the very first time as Brock described this, it became real to Moon that his brother was dead. It was no longer an abstraction in which *Ricky dead* was merely a phrase that meant no more than *Ricky away*. For much of Moon's adult life Ricky had been away. Now Moon was conscious of a void that would never be filled. He closed his eyes.

But Brock was talking again, about the site of the crash, near the Vietnam-Cambodia border. About an ARVN patrol finding the wreckage after some farmer reported a fire. About flying over the place, looking down on the site, finding a place to put down, and walking up into the hills to see about the bodies.

"I called your mother about that. The soldiers had buried them right there by the wreckage. She said just leave them be. Let him rest in peace," Brock said. "That sounded like what he would have wanted anyway. You think?"

"Yes," Moon said. "Ricky wouldn't have wanted to be messed around with." He wiped the back of his hand across his eyes, opened them. "You talked to our mother about the little girl?"

"I didn't think about it," Brock said. "I guess she was in shock, hearing Ricky was dead. I guess she didn't think of it either."

His mother would have thought of it, no doubt about that. It meant she didn't know about the child. Ricky hadn't just kept the secret from him.

Brock had seated himself on the chair beside the kitchen door. "Coffee's steaming," he said. But he did nothing about it.

"It was an accident," Moon said. "That's what the embassy people told my mother."

"I guess so. Or maybe some of Pol Pot's Khmers were up that way and shot it just for fun. What's the difference?" Brock got up, disappeared into the kitchen. "Black or cream or what?"

"Everything," Moon said. "If it's handy."

"That Chinaman wanted to know about his cargo. I told him the copter was all burned up. Nothing in it. He wanted me to fly him up there to make sure. I said no way. If the Khmer Rouge had shot one copter they'd shoot another. But when I was away he talked Rice into flying him up. Rice'll do absolutely anything. Doesn't give a shit."

"I guess they didn't find it," Moon said. "Mr. Lee is still looking."

"Rice thinks he's immortal," Brock said. "Kismet. Fate

awaits. That's the George Rice slogan." He emerged from the kitchen with two cups, gave one to Moon, reseated himself. "But I was surprised Ricky flew up there. What for? What was he doing? Nothing up in those ridges but three or four little villages. Hill tribes. But the Vietcong hide out up there, and nowadays I guess the Khmer Rouge too."

"I heard Rice was in Bilibad Prison," Moon said. "I was going to see if I can get in there and talk to him tomorrow to find out if he knows what happened to Ricky's daughter. But they say he's not there. And I need to know what you know—"

Brock's expression went blank. He held up his hand. "What are you saying? You saying Lila's not here?"

Brock's wife was standing in the bedroom doorway, "Oh, God!" she said. "What happened to her?"

"What happened?" Brock repeated. "You telling me Castenada doesn't have her?"

"I don't know what the hell happened," Moon said. "Castenada said someone was making arrangements to bring her out, and Victoria—that's our mother—was flying out to Manila to pick her up. But she had a heart attack, and Castenada doesn't seem to have any idea what happened to the child."

"Son of a bitch," Brock said. "I guess Rice must have—"

"Screwed up? I guess he did," Moon said. "I heard he might have got distracted into another line of business. I heard he was arrested and stuck in Bilibad. But they say—"

"He's not in Bilibad," Brock said. "President Marcos and Imelda have Bilibad filled up with politicals. They sent Rice down to Palawan Island. To the prison down there."

"Oh," Moon said, not knowing how to react to this.

"You're looking for little Lila, then," Brock said. "They didn't get her on a flight to Manila? I thought that was all set up."

"By you?"

"By Rice," Brock said. "Well, sort of by me. After Ricky and his lady were killed, we were moving things down to Long Phu. We were sort of expecting you to show up and take over, but we figured you'd have made the move anyway. Too risky where we were and things beginning to go to hell at Saigon. And then one day the Vinh woman showed up. Eleth's mother. She said they were trying to get moved out to Thailand but they weren't having any luck because everything was blocked off, either by the army or the Khmer Rouge. She said Ricky and Eleth had planned to move to the States someday. They'd told her if anything should happen to them she should send Lila to her American grandmother. The old lady believed that with the Khmer Rouge coming they couldn't keep the baby anyway because Pol Pot's people were killing all the foreigners, and the baby looked American. So I called Castenada and talked to him about it and then I called this fella we work with in Saigon. I told him to get an airline ticket for the girl and fix up the documents she'd need and call me when everything was ready. Then the plan was for Rice to fly Lila up there and send her along to Castenada." Brock paused. "Now you're telling me Rice didn't get it done? Is that right?"

"Castenada says the child didn't arrive. So whatever you set up didn't work," Moon said. "Where's the girl now, do you think?"

Brock heard the anger as well as the questions. He sat staring at Moon.

"Well, it ain't as simple as I made it sound," he said, finally. "We couldn't get the goddam papers. We couldn't get an airplane seat. The wise guys in Saigon were hearing things that scared them, so the line in front of the U.S. Embassy was about a mile long and not moving. And the fat cats and generals' wives were filling up the outgoing traffic."

"And so you let it go," Moon said. "Just dropped it."

"I thought we'd get it fixed up. I had to come here to take care of problems. I told Rice to bypass the embassy and work on the CIA people. They owed Ricky a lot of favors. I said, Call in the IOUs, and I figured he would do it. I figured it was all taken care of."

"From what I hear, your Mr. Rice managed to get a load of heroin flown out to Manila," Moon said. "Why couldn't he leave a little of that behind and crowd the kid on?"

Brock took a sip of his coffee, eyeing Moon over the brim. From the bedroom came the sounds of the woman getting dressed. Brock put down the cup.

"You want to hear about this or you want to fight about it?"

"All right," Moon said. "Go ahead. Let's hear it."

"George must have thought he had it handled. I know for sure he took the girl up to Saigon with her grandma. Then he came back to Long Phu. There was a load of things there waiting that a customer wanted out. So George flew it down to Singapore. We had an old DC-Three we'd bought down there, getting it fixed. George picked it up and flew it over to Manila to pick up a spare engine and some spare parts we'd located there. And some Filipino customs people nailed him."

Brock sipped his coffee.

"And seized our DC-Three, of course. That's one of the reasons I'm still here in Manila: trying to get the damned thing released so I can fly it back. And working with this shyster lawyer trying to get George sprung out of prison. And trying to finalize a contract Ricky had started negotiating last winter."

"So the little girl, she's still there in Saigon, you think? With her other grandmother?"

"I don't know. Maybe so. Maybe not. The old lady's Cambodian. She doesn't have any connections in Saigon."

"Okay, then. Where the hell else would she be?"

"I guess you're going to have to talk to George," Brock said.

SAIGON, South Vietnam, April 19 (Agence France-Presse)—A spokesman for U.S. Ambassador William Martin told a Vietnamese television interviewer last night that the ambassador and his wife are still in Saigon "and have not packed any belongings."

The Eighth Day

April 20, 1975

GETTING INTO THE PRISON on Palawan Island and arranging a conversation with George Rice would be what the woman at the U.S. Consulate called "relatively simple."

"The Marcos government keeps the important criminals up here at Bilibad to keep an eye on them," she told Moon, looking up at him over her bifocals. "The Communists, the Huks, the wrong kind of politicians, old family types who have bad ideologies but good connections—they're kept up here in Manila. They use Palawan for the regular criminals: robbers, burglars, murderers, car thieves, smugglers, rapists, so forth. The ones the government doesn't have to worry about."

The consulate clerk paused with that, rubbed her plump and dimpled chin, and considered what she might add to make sure Moon had received her message. Thinking of nothing, she looked up at him again and nodded.

"I think we can get you in, under the circumstances," she said. "It seems to be a good cause. Finding a missing relative, I mean. And there doesn't seem to be anything political about this Rice fellow."

Then she suffered an awful second thought.

"There isn't, is there?"

Looking into her determined stare, it seemed to Moon that this was another of those rare times when fudging a little on truth was ethical.

"I think he's a Republican," Moon said, and restored the clerk's helpful attitude. She smiled at him.

"I don't think they'd keep anyone there they considered dangerous," she said. "I mean politically dangerous. I understand it doesn't have any walls. Just sort of a big rice plantation surrounded by the jungle."

"What keeps the prisoners from escaping?" asked Moon. The unexpected good news had stimulated his natural urge to be friendly.

The consulate clerk felt no such urge. "I have no idea," she said. "Leave me your number and you'll be informed when we get clearance." While she was saying it she closed the folder in which she'd placed the request Moon had typed out, a copy of the relevant page from his passport, and the rest of the paperwork, and opened another folder and pushed the button that would send the next problem into her office to be dealt with.

"How long do you think it will take to get clearance?" Moon asked. "Any idea?"

"Probably two days if you're lucky," she said. "But don't count on being lucky." And she dismissed him with her official consulate clerk's smile.

Moon had retreated to the Hotel Maynila to wait. He collected his laundry. He bought more socks and underwear. With the help of a vastly overweight cabdriver he solved the problem that large Americans have in Asian countries. The owner, either in ignorance or whimsy, called the shop L'Obèse Boutique, and in it Moon found two shirts, a water-repellent jacket, and jeans big enough to fit him. Then he got on the telephone to L.A. He talked to the nurse in the Intensive Care Unit and learned that Victoria Morick was still not ready for transfer to the Cardiac Care Unit but was "doing as well as can be expected."

He left word for her doctor to call him at the Maynila. He called his own number in Durance and reached Debbie. Debbie reported that J.D. hadn't been able to find anyone to put his engine back together, and what could he do about that? Shirley's dog was no longer on the premises, and no, she didn't know what had happened to it. She'd had his car washed. And don't forget he'd been gone for her birthday. Also, she missed him terribly.

"I miss you too," Moon said. "I dreamed about you last night." True. And, of course, it had been an erotic dream. After he hung up, he sat awhile on the edge of the bed, glumly thinking about that. Why did he kid himself about the Debbie relationship? Why? Because for some reason he had never been able to fathom, he always needed to think of himself as the guy in the white hat. Moon, the good guy hanging around to save the poor maiden when J.D. and the other predators dumped her. Never Moon the going-to-seed lecher kidding himself about his motives with this sexy youngster.

Enough of that. He called the newsroom and learned from Hubble that Rooney was threatening to quit, that their Sunday editorial about the ski basin had produced indignant telephone calls, that the Ford dealer on the school board was threatening to pull his advertising if the sports editor didn't lay off the football coach, that nothing much was happening on the vacation edition, and that they'd had an electrical fire in the darkroom and were farming out their photo printing until the rewiring was done. That was playing hell with the newsroom budget.

Those duties done, Moon considered what was left. He should call Mrs. van Winjgaarden and tell her about Rice. He should return the three calls he'd had from old Lum Lee. Instead, he walked to the window and looked out at the evening. Lights coming on along Roxas Boulevard and Manila Bay. Clouds blowing out to sea. Stars appearing.

He picked up the telephone. What would he say to Mrs. van W.? Now that it seemed likely he could find Rice and talk to him, he didn't want to do it. He didn't want to go to Palawan Island and visit this jerk in his jail cell, and she would certainly expect him to go. He didn't want to go to collapsing Vietnam. Or bloody Cambodia. He wanted to go home.

Failing that, he'd go for a walk.

He walked faster than his army regulation pace at first because he was tense and he needed to burn off nervous energy. But the mild air got to him quickly. April is April, even in a climate where winter hardly makes itself noticed, and yesterday's rain seemed to have provoked a sort of renewal. The perfume of flowers overpowered the aroma of decay. He could hear songs of frogs in the ditches, insect sounds, some sort of night bird he couldn't identify, other noises strange to him. And on a night like this, Manila slept with its windows open. Somewhere someone was playing a violin. He heard laughter. A radio far off to his right broadcast Bob Dylan exhorting Mr. Tambourine Man to play a song for him. He meet three boys on bicycles. He met a couple hand in hand, the man grinning, the woman giggling. He met an old man carrying a cat. He thought about the priest in the confessional.

The priest had said his name was Julian. If this stroll took him past the cathedral, he'd go in and see if Father Julian was waiting to absolve his evening quota of sinners from their guilt. If he was there, if no one was waiting to confess, he might go in and ask if Julian would like to continue their conversation. Moon guessed he would. After all, he'd left the confessional with the priest's curiosity unsatisfied. And he'd been rude. He'd like to apologize for that.

What was that big sin, Julian had asked, and he'd told him he'd killed a man. There had been silence then: Julian surprised, Julian shocked. The priest must have wondered if Moon was simply mocking him. His response, when it finally came, suggested that. The tone was light. As with the secular law, he'd said, the church has degrees for homicide too. Had he committed murder, premeditated and done with unrepented malice? Or had it been homicide committed in a sudden rage? Or perhaps Moon had left a fellow to starve stranded on some isolated cliff, simply out of forgetfulness. That would be another sort of sin altogether. Probably no sin at all. And the litany might have continued, had not Moon interrupted and cut it off.

It was murder by self-indulgence, he'd said. Far too many bourbons with water and then too much insistence on driving when Halsey wanted to drive and should have driven. Then driving too fast, losing control, flipping the jeep, killing Gene Halsey, killing the best friend he ever had.

And Julian had said, Ah, that is a terrible tragedy but not a terrible sin. To be a terrible sin it would need to be done with deliberation, an intentional, defiant violation of God's prohibition against killing one's fellow human being. And Moon had been able to bear no more of these sterile truisms. He had interrupted Julian again.

"I understand all that," he'd said. "I was an altar boy. I

memorized my catechism answers. That wasn't the terrible sin I meant. That only set the stage for it." And he'd stepped out of the booth and walked into the darkness and the rain. Tonight there was no sign it would ever rain again. The moon, about two days short of full, hung over the yacht basin and made a bright yellow streak across Manila Bay toward Moon. It cast his long shadow ahead as he walked down the broad path and sidestepped this evening's migration of roaches and turned onto the bricked corridor that led to the cathedral steps. But the moonlight didn't follow him inside. It seemed darker than he remembered.

And emptier. A fat bald man sat in the final pew at the back of the church. One woman knelt in the candlelight at the side altar. An old man in a white shirt leaned against the wall at the end of the confessional row, apparently waiting his turn.

Moon sat, stretched his legs before him, felt himself relax. The doors were closed at the confessional where Julian had been three nights before, and a little green light glowed above it. Julian was at work. The door to the cubicle where Moon had sat opened. A young woman emerged, made the sign of the cross, genuflected, and walked past Moon. She was smiling. The waiting man disappeared inside, taking her place. Moon considered how he would describe this incident to Halsey, how Halsey would react to it.

"Why did you go in there?" Halsey would ask. And then he would, Halsey fashion, answer his own question. "Because you wanted to recapture your misspent youth, I think. No, you wanted him to forgive you for not being nice to your mother. So then why did you cut out before you got to that part of your story?" And Moon would find himself pulled into a discussion about why he, and why Halsey, behaved in the way they did. And what it all meant. And why they couldn't seem to relate to the sort of women who appealed to them, and what life was all about in the first place.

The door of the other penitential cubicle opened and another woman emerged, this one elderly. She walked slowly toward the main altar and knelt. The door remained open, inviting another penitent. None appeared.

Moon's thoughts drifted back to Halsey. In retrospect their rapport seemed odd. Conventional wisdom says opposites attract. But, except physically, he and Halsey were very much alike. They would not try to defeat the world but they would survive. Their cuts would heal. Halsey was no more ambitious than he was. The three stripes on Halsey's sleeve were there by default. The same with Moon's rank as sergeant. The army was all right with Halsey. It was stupid, senseless, inefficient, full of the absurdities that Halsey collected and treasured. He'd found a home in the armored division. And so had Moon. And both for the same reason: the draft board lottery came up with their number. Halsey could have qualified for a deferment. Why hadn't he? A lot of trouble, he'd said. And he was curious. What else would he do? Fate had decreed it. The two of them had sat in the post exchange night after night drinking bad PX beer and discussing such questions. Going into town together in usually fruitless searches for women. Exchanging boyhood embarrassments, triumphs, and defeats, looking under it all for some hint of meaning.

The man in the white shirt emerged from the penitential doorway and departed, leaving it open. If the priest in the center cubicle was indeed Father Julian he would be idle now, looking out to see if another customer was waiting. Moon was aware that the priest was probably looking at him right now, wondering if he'd come in. Well, would he? Moon wasn't sure. It was a long, long time since he had

had a talk like the ones he and Halsey had shared. He hadn't realized how he hungered for them. He glanced back, saw that now the center door was open too, and a small priest, his cassock hanging loosely on his skinny frame, was limping down the aisle toward him.

"I decided that you might not be coming in," said Father Julian. "I decided I would bring you a personal invitation."

"You recognized me," Moon said, because he could think of nothing else.

Julian made a deprecatory gesture. "Biggest man in the cathedral," he said. "I wouldn't be surprised if you're the biggest man in Manila."

Moon laughed. "You exaggerate," he said.

"How big are you?" Julian said. "Six and a half feet, I'd say. Maybe two hundred sixty pounds."

"You're still exaggerating."

"But not by very much, I think. Anyway, I am happy to see you. I had hoped—" Julian paused, thinking.

"That I'd finish the story?"

"Oh, that. Yes. That would be interesting. But I had hoped, too, that you would tell me something that would jar my mind from its lethargy and I would somehow think of something wise to say to you. And you would say, 'Yes! Yes! Of course! This dinky little priest is absolutely correct. I should forgive myself for this awful sin of which I am so proud. And then I will allow God to forgive me."

Father Julian had seated himself in the pew beside Moon, and he looked at him sideways now, grinning.

"We priests sometimes entertain such grand delusions. It is something that happens to us when we receive the Holy Orders, when the bishop ordains us."

"It happens to all males, I guess," Moon said. "I used to enjoy some grand delusions." But when had that been? As a child, of course. But not much after that. He had time enough to think about it because Father Julian seemed to be thinking about it too. At least he wasn't talking. He sat, head slightly down, smiling slightly, a minuscule nod in agreement with whatever was passing though his mind. Relaxed. It skipped Moon back to post exchange evenings he and Halsey had spent.

"It's not a séance," Halsey had said after they'd finished a second beer without a word spoken, "because a séance requires some effort. And some outside interference from a spirit. I'd call it nonverbal communication—the ultimate in intellectual inertia." And Moon had said, But we don't communicate, and Halsey had said, "Sure we do. When the First Sarge came in a minute ago you raised an eyebrow. I looked. You smirked. I remembered how he tried to take the wrong gal home last time we were here. I nodded. We communicated." And Moon had said, Just call it comfortable silence.

And the silence now was comfortable. Father Julian, having heard his quota of sins for the day, seemed to feel no hunger to hear more. Moon was in no hurry to provide them. They talked about why Julian had gone into the seminary, and why he'd returned to it after dropping out. They talked about American journalism, and Manila journalism, and, eventually, about what Moon was doing so far from Durance and the cold, clean air of the Colorado high country.

"That's odd, don't you think?" Julian said. "That your brother didn't tell you he had a daughter? Didn't he tell your mother either?"

"Maybe he did," Moon said. The thought had hung at the edge of his consciousness for days, but it was the first time he'd allowed himself to really consider it. "If he did, she didn't tell me."

Julian seemed to notice how forlorn that sounded. He looked at Moon, expression sympathetic. "Maybe he thought you would disapprove. Big brother–little brother, you know. The infant born out of wedlock. Woman of a different race. All that. Maybe he told your mother to keep it a secret."

"Possibly," Moon said. "Who knows? Maybe she knew all the time. Maybe not telling me was her idea."

"And why would that be?" Julian said, but he was asking himself more than Moon, and Moon had no comment.

A woman came in through the side door, lit another candle before the alcove altar, and knelt. From somewhere far out in Manila Bay came the sound of a tugboat hooting; from Quezon Boulevard the sound of a siren; from somewhere behind them, someone coughing. Silence.

Julian sighed. Chuckled. "This is going to sound Freudian, I think. What I'm about to say. But is there something between you and your mother? Some rift? Some—some problem?"

"Well, yes," Moon said.

And as he said it he knew that this was what he had come for: to talk to another human being about how he had brought about the defeat of Victoria Mathias. To make this confession.

"Women have more trouble forgiving, you know. You told me that. Your experience from ten thousand weeks of hearing their confessions. I'll tell you what I did to my mother."

Julian held up his hand. "Wait. Think about it for a moment. I *am* curious. I would like to hear it. But do you really want to tell me?"

Moon thought about it. "Not exactly," Moon said. "I don't want to but I need to."

Julian nodded.

"I have to go back a ways," Moon said.

Julian nodded again. "Go back as far as you need," he said. "Nothing awaits me but an empty room."

But where to begin? "She was a small woman. Still is, for that matter. But I was thinking of when I was a boy. Little. Very neat. Very pretty. Our house was neat too. We lived in Oklahoma. In Lawton. We owned a little printing shop. My dad was a great big guy, like me. People called him Marty. For Martin. Looking back on it, knowing what I know now, I know he drank too much. Like me. When I was twelve he got sick. Very sick. They put him in the hospital and the doctors decided he had pneumonia. They treated him for that. Turned out they were wrong." Moon paused, tried to keep the bitterness out of his voice. "He got sicker and sicker, and finally they discovered he had tuberculosis and it had spread into his spinal column. They called it Pott's disease, and whatever it was it killed him, and it took a long time doing it."

Moon stopped. He could never talk about this without feeling a rage building up inside him.

Julian sighed. "Tuberculosis," he said. "An old-fashioned disease. They could probably have saved him now. Since about 1960 they have a drug that works."

"I guess he was a little too early or they were a little too stupid. The TB screwed up the vertebrae in the neck and upper back and caused abscesses and put pressure on the spinal column. We used to go visit him in the hospital, the three of us, and when Mother could finally bring him home he was paralyzed. Almost totally from the neck down. Just a little motion in one arm and hand."

Moon inhaled a great breath and let it out. Father Julian sat motionless just down the pew, head slightly bent. Moon inhaled the smells of spring in the tropics, and of an old, old church, and sorted through the memories.

"It gave me a chance to understand what love is all about," he said, and he described the way Victoria Mathias had cared for a husband who had become nothing more than a helpless talking head. How she kept the printing operation going to support them, working nights and Sundays on billing and the books, and, when she wasn't working, being always with Martin. Taking him out to the park in his wheelchair, reading to him, bathing him. Cleaning him up before the doctor came, shaving him.

"She had to do absolutely everything. As if he were an infant." Moon paused. He had come to the part he had never told to anyone except Halsey. Not even Ricky. Certainly not Ricky.

"You are describing perfect love," Julian said. "Unselfish. And perfect tragedy."

"And now the other half of the tragedy," Moon said. "My father's half."

"Yes," Julian said. "I was thinking about that."

"He wanted to die. He wanted to set her free."

"Yes. I would guess that. So would I."

"I didn't guess it. It didn't even occur to me," Moon said. "It got so I resented him. Ricky did too, probably. But we never talked about it. I'd think, *Why don't you just die?* I'd wish it all the time. I'd even pray for it. Pray that when I woke up in the morning he'd be dead."

"But you never said anything."

"Of course not," Moon said. "For God's sake. No. It didn't occur to me for a long time that my father was praying for it too."

"But you figured it out."

"I didn't. I wasn't that smart. Or that kind. I overheard them. Talking."

Moon paused again. But he knew immediately he was going to tell it all. And he did. He'd come back from the shop early because the printing order he was supposed to wrap and deliver had been canceled. It was Saturday afternoon. Early summer. Ricky had left his bike beside the house, and he decided he'd put it in the garage. That meant a detour that took him across the grass right under the window where Martin Mathias spent his days. He'd heard his parents talking, and the anger in his father's voice had stopped him. He'd never heard that tone before.

"I think she'd been cleaning him up. After a bowel movement, probably. Doing one of those humiliating personal things. And something must have gone wrong and he was yelling at her. Or actually, I guess he was yelling at himself. He was calling her names. I remember he kept repeating 'Stubborn as a damned mule.' And he said he knew Mother wouldn't put him out of his misery by killing him, easy as that would be. And he could understand that. He could understand the moral problem. But why wouldn't she give him a divorce? Would that hurt her pride? Make her feel she'd been a failure? Or put him in a nursing home. Would the neighbors think that was selfish of her? If she didn't want to have a life for herself, she should have one for Ricky and me. And then my mother said something too low for me to hear, and he said, 'That's not true. Dr. Morick is in love with you. He always has been. He could give you a decent life.' And she said something like, 'I'd be bored to death.' And I didn't hear any more of it."

"You went away?" Julian asked.

"I went back to the shop and got the pistol my father had kept in a cabinet there. A little twenty-two-caliber revolver. I loaded it and put it in my pocket and went home again."

"To kill your father?"

"When I had a chance. When my mother wasn't there."

Julian shifted in the pew, sighed. "The tragedy multiplies itself," he said. "Love and pity can make a terrible blend if faith is left out of it."

"Faith? Faith in what? Faith that God would mend a damaged spinal cord?"

"All right, then," Julian said. "I hope you can tell me that, without faith, this story of yours had a happy ending. You didn't kill him, did you?"

"Not me," Moon said, and laughed. "Not likely. Mother went back to the shop after dinner. It was my night to take care of Dad, so Ricky was off somewhere. I went in his room and he said something normal to me, like what was new down at the shop or something like that, and I told him I had overheard him yelling at Mother and I asked him if he really wanted to die, and he said—"

Moon stopped. He was having trouble with this. Julian sat motionless beside him, waiting. Moon cleared his throat.

"And he said he was terribly sorry I had heard that. That sometimes one just loses control and says things he regrets. And I said, But do you really want to die? Would you if you could, if no one would suffer for it, if you could just force yourself to stop breathing, for example? He didn't answer that for a while. Just studied me. And then he said, Yes, he would. It would be better for him and for Victoria and for all of us. Then I showed him the pistol. I told him I would do it for him."

Moon stopped again, remembering that moment as he had remembered it a thousand times, remembering fumbling the pistol out of his pocket, its oily smell, showing his father that it was loaded. And his father's expression. Every time he remembered it, it seemed that when the surprise had gone away it had been replaced by a kind of longing. And then by pride. That's what it looked like. But how could it have been?

"Tell me why you didn't," Julian said. "You were—what? Thirteen or fourteen? Not wise enough yet to see why you shouldn't."

"Thirteen by then," Moon said. "Well, we talked about it, the pros and cons. He said it would be better if he did it himself. Asked me to put the pistol in the hand he could move a little. He could hold it down in his lap, but he couldn't raise it up to his head. Then he said nobody would believe it anyway. How could I explain his getting the pistol? Too many people would know he couldn't have shot himself. He told me to take the pistol, and I did, and he asked if there was still that box of rat poison on the high shelf down at the plant. I told him that Mother had said it was too dangerous to have around and got rid of it.

"He said then he guessed we'd have to wait a little while, but not long. Dr. Morick had said his liver was failing fast and he wouldn't live long anyway. Victoria would not have to put up with him much longer. But if I killed him, I would be her burden for the rest of her life. Her heart would break for me."

"Indeed," Julian said, "it would have. Your father was a wise man. So you put away the pistol?"

"Mother came in while we were talking. I must have been terribly upset. I didn't hear the car."

"And she heard you?"

"I was still holding the pistol. Dad saw her standing there in the doorway. And he said, 'Victoria. Malcolm overheard me yelling at you this afternoon and has offered to solve our problem for us. I think I've persuaded him it would just make a bad situation worse.'"

Moon took a huge shuddering breath.

"And she came in and took the pistol out of my hand and hugged me and started crying. We were all crying, all three of us."

"Catharsis," Julian said. "So you did have a happy ending. Sometimes love can be as effective as faith."

Moon cleared his throat again. "Ah," he said. "But that's not the ending."

"It couldn't be," Julian said. "Your story hasn't come yet to the great sin you've teased me with. Did that involve your father?"

"He died the next year," Moon said. "When I was fourteen. And my mother mourned for him."

"And so did you," Julian said.

"So I had the example. A brave man and a brave woman and some notion of what you give up for love. So I didn't have any excuse."

"Excuse for what? Oh, for what you are about to tell me you did?"

"For what I did," Moon said. "I had killed a man. I was driving drunk and driving an army vehicle off the post without authorization. We did it a lot, but the crime is being caught at it. So I was awaiting trial. Clearly guilty. The charge was homicide committed during the conduct of a felony. Drunk driving being the felony. I was assigned a first lieutenant as defense attorney. He advised me to plead guilty, saving the court time, and plead for leniency. The most I'd get was twenty years. I was terrified."

"I can see why," Julian said. "How old were you then, early twenties?"

"I don't know why I was so frightened. Not for sure, anyway. I think maybe it was because I didn't know myself very well yet. It seemed that a military prison was not the place I should be spending so much of my life. I felt like I was going to be buried alive."

"Reasonable," Julian said.

"My mother was notified, of course, and she came to see me. I told her about the lawyer. What he had said. She said that was intolerable. I said it was also inevitable. And she said surely something could be done. I said no it couldn't be done, because we had no money for the big law firms and no political clout. I gave her the whole self-pity business. If I couldn't have freedom, have my life back, at least I could wring some sympathy from my mother. And I did."

Moon hesitated.

"I even cried," he added. "I'll never forget that. I actually cried."

"Twenty years in prison," Julian said. "I would have cried too. Who wouldn't?"

"So my mother went home, and almost right away I got a letter from her. She was marrying Dr. Morick."

"Ah," Julian said.

"I told you Morick was Dad's doctor. But he also had inherited real estate, and he was smart, and he'd made great investments in California land and in Florida beachfront. And was chairman of the county Democrats and a great friend of a congressman on the House Military Affairs Committee and had all sorts of connections. A lawyer showed up at the stockade, a white-haired man with an assistant carrying his briefcase. He took about fifteen pages of notes on what happened, and who questioned me, and what went on in the military hospital. And—guess what—a little later somebody at a higher level reexamines the charges, and they are reduced to conduct unbecoming a noncommissioned officer, unauthorized use of a military vehicle, and so forth. The penalty becomes loss of rank, loss of six months' pay, and a general discharge."

That finished the story for Moon. His confession had been made. He was tired.

Julian considered it. "Someone might say that was a happy ending," he said. "But it wasn't. Not for you."

"She never liked Morick. He was Dad's doctor and that

gave him an excuse to be there a lot, to keep lusting after her. And he was a stuffy, boring, self-important old bachelor more interested in his real estate projects than in practicing medicine. But she wasn't a very lucky woman, my mother. Her husband gives her a vegetable to care for, and then, when he dies, she has to marry another one to save a weakling son."

"You don't think she would have—"

Moon pounded his fist into his thigh. "Never. Never. Never!" Moon said. "She *never* would have married him. She did it to save her pitiful boy."

Special to the *New York Times*

WASHINGTON, April 21—Defense Department officials concluded today that the situation in South Vietnam was deteriorating so rapidly that the United States must plan an immediate evacuation of all Americans and their dependents.

The Tenth Day

April 22, 1975

FOR MOON MATHIAS, the flight from Manila to Puerto Princesa was in the aisle seat of one of those twin-engine prop-jet aircraft that short-hop commuter airlines favor. Moon had already learned to avoid such aircraft when possible. The planes were fitted out for small people and intended for short trips. So used, they were barely tolerable for someone of his dimensions. But the flight from Manila on Luzon Island down the Philippine archipelago and then across the Sulu Sea to Puerto Princesa was anything but short.

While waiting for the consulate to call and tell him he had clearance to visit George Rice, Moon had bought a map of the Philippines and a tourist guidebook. And then, on an uneasy hunch, he bought a large-scale map of Vietnam, Cambodia, and Laos. He put that map in his bag, hoping never to need it. On the Philippines map, he took a scale of distances he marked off on a sheet of hotel stationery and made some calculations. A direct flight from Manila to Puerto Princesa, the capital of Palawan Island and site of its only airport, was just about four hundred miles. But, of course, there was no direct flight. The only one scheduled from Manila took one first to Iloilo, three hundred miles southeast on Panay Island. From there one flew two hundred and fifty miles southwestward across the Sulu Sea to Puerto Princesa. That made five hundred and fifty miles, broken by an hour sitting in an airport in a tiny town, which, Moon's guidebook said, "had little to offer the tourist except an open-air market where exotic tropical products may be purchased."

The guidebook made Palawan itself sound equally unpromising, unless one loved to rough it in the tropics. It called the island "one of the world's few remaining unspoiled paradises." Its economy was based on fishing "with some subsistence agriculture." Its population was described as "light, scattered, and largely Malay in ethnic origin." Looking at it on the map made Moon wonder why the cartographers and politicians had included it as part of the Philippine cluster. It lay like a line drawn from Borneo to Luzon, almost three hundred miles long, from Bugsuc on the south to the tiny settlement of Taytay on the north and only about fifteen or twenty miles wide. It looked to Moon like Bugsuc was a hell of a lot closer to Borneo than Taytay was to any dry land in the Philippines. He measured it out, and it was. Not that it mattered. What mattered was four and a half hours' flying time in a small seat designed for someone half his size.

Moon Mathias had quit fitting small seats since he started growing seriously in about the fifth grade. But he had made himself proficient at enduring. He sat, legs cramping, neck hurting, expression bland, and listened to the small Filipino who occupied the window seat.

The small Filipino wore a thin mustache that had turned gray. He said his name was Mr. Adar Docoso. He had been a platoon sergeant in the Philippine Scouts. He had fought the Japanese "until General MacArthur sailed away and abandoned us." Now he was in the scrap metal business. He was flying out to Puerto Princesa to see about buying a Panama-licensed freighter that had been more or less abandoned there because it wasn't worth fixing its worn-out diesels. He had four sons, all unusually intelligent, and one remarkably beautiful daughter. This out of the way, he wanted Moon to explain to him why the United States of America had chosen to make Hawaii the fiftieth state instead of the Philippines.

"Hawaii is just three or four little insignificant islands, and not many people, and most of them are Japanese." In describing his adventures as a Philippine Scout, Mr. Docoso had already made it clear that he considered the Japanese savages. "We cannot understand why you made those people a state and not us. You tell me so I can know that."

"I don't have the slightest idea," Moon said.

"I know lots and lots of Americans," Mr. Docoso said. "Nice people. Like you. I deal with them in my business. They bring their old worn-out ships in here, and run them ashore or set them on fire, so the insurance companies will pay them something, and then I buy the scrap metal. Good for everybody. Good people. But why did they do that to us? Why did you turn us away like dogs, and give us gangsters for our government, and then have the CIA teach the government how to torture people so we can't get rid of them? I wish somebody could tell me why that is."

"What would you think if I told you I was an agent of the CIA?" Moon asked.

That seemed to work. Mr. Docoso lapsed into silence. Moon edged a cramped foot from under the seat ahead of him and flexed it. He thought about how to deal with Mrs. van Winjgaarden, who, unfortunately, was occupying a seat three rows ahead of him.

"But I know Mr. Rice," she'd said. "Of course I should go along. I know that part of Cambodia, that part along the border just above the Mekong Delta. I've been there visiting my brother. I will know what to ask Mr. Rice."

And he had said no deal. He'd handle this alone. She couldn't go. She couldn't get into the prison even if she did go. And she had said they would probably let her in if she was with him. They would think she was his secretary, or something like that, and he had said, Maybe, if I would be stupid enough to lie to authorities of a foreign prison.

But anyway, there she was three rows up the aisle, head bent slightly forward. Asleep, apparently.

Mr. Docoso poked him with an elbow, grinning up at him. "You are joking me," he said. "You are never with the CIA."

"No?" Moon said. "Why not?"

Mr. Docoso clutched his throat. "No necktie," he said. "CIA they wear nice clothes. Clean. Pressed. Expensive suits, vests, shined shoes." He pointed to a man who Moon had thought to be a Japanese businessman in the aisle seat two rows up. "Like that one. Or the other kind of CIA, they wear sports shirts and leather jackets. Two kinds of CIA but neither kind is like you." Mr. Docoso was grinning broadly at this, shaking his head in affirmation of his wisdom.

And so Moon flew across the Sulu Sea listening to Mr. Docoso's vision of the state of the Filipino nation circa April

1975. He learned that Fernando Marcos's father hadn't been a poor Filipino as his press releases and biographers insisted but the son of a wealthy Chinese loan shark, and how Imelda had the airport at Puerto Princesa enlarged because one of her cousins was building a tourist resort on the beach up at Babuyan, and a great many other things about the presidential couple's kith and kin and their nefarious dealings.

Finally, the blue water below them converted itself into the deep green of tropic jungle.

"Puerto Princesa," said Mr. Docoso, pointing downward. And below there appeared a cluster of wharves, barnlike warehouses roofed with red tin, a docked ship that looked to Moon like some sort of navy auxiliary vessel, a very small and very dirty freighter, and a hodgepodge of anchored small craft, among them a pencil-slim two-masted sailing ship, which seemed from high above so white, so clean, so tidy that Moon thought of a swan in a yardful of dirty ducks.

The town itself reinforced that impression. One- and two-story buildings, some thatch-roofed, some bamboo, some of more or less standard concrete-block construction, clustered along narrow dirt streets. It was a very small town with trees everywhere, a small open square where a public market seemed to operate, a dilapidated church with a cross atop each of its double spires. Moon could see no sign of anything that looked formidable enough to be a government building.

"That's Puerto Princesa?" Moon asked. "It's the capital for the island?"

"It's a very long island," Docoso explained, "but it is also very thin." He demonstrated thinness with his hands. "And nobody lives here but mostly Malays."

The airport was also thin, a single runway closely bordered by palms, bamboo thickets, and assorted tropical vegetation strange to Moon. He wondered how it must have looked before Imelda ordered it enlarged.

"The hotel here at the airport is the best," Mr. Docoso said as they crowded down the exit stairway. "Very modern. Toilets and bathtubs in the rooms and every room is equiped with refrigerated air-conditioning." Docoso seemed to feel that this recitation of assets might seem incredible. He shrugged. "Imelda owns it," he explained.

SAIGON, South Vietnam, April 21 (Agence France-Presse)—President Nguyen Van Thieu resigned tonight after ten years in office. He appointed Vice President Tran Van Huong to replace him and denounced the United States as "unworthy of trust."

Evening, the Tenth Day

April 22, 1975

THE ROOMS OF IMELDA'S HOTEL on the road between Puerto Princesa and its airport were indeed equipped with refrigerated air-conditioning. Exhaust vents for this frigid air had been installed above the bed and in the bathroom. Unfortunately nothing came out of them. Moon called down to the friendly young man behind the front desk to report this deficiency and received the information that the "machinery was temporarily inoperative" and that "repairs were currently under way." It sounded to Moon as if the young man had either memorized this report or was reading it from a card. Not a good omen.

He forced open his windows and stood beside them, breathing in the hot, humid air.

The last glow was dying from the sky along the western horizon, and the jungle was producing the tropical sounds of twilight. Moon stood listening. He could identify the mating song of frogs, which seemed to be universal. The little chirps would be bats patrolling for mosquitoes, just as they did on summer evenings in Oklahoma and Colorado. But most of the sounds were strange to him: a sequence of whistles (perhaps a lizard of some sort), odd grunting sounds, a sequence of rapid clicks, repeated, and repeated, and repeated. They were sounds that might be from another planet, or a science fiction fantasy, and they gave Moon Mathias a sudden overwhelming sense of being absolutely alone.

He turned away from the window. His suitcase was where he'd tossed it on the bed, waiting for him to finish unpacking. The doorless closet space contained only a cluster of coat hangers waiting to be used. The room, even the door to the bathroom, had been painted a color Moon couldn't identify—what a mortician would think of as flesh tone.

Moon hurried out into the hallway, down the stairs, and into the lobby. Mr. Docoso was sitting there with a middle-aged Japanese couple and a man who looked Arabic. They were watching something on the television set in the corner. The set produced the sound of laughter. Mr. Docoso motioned Moon to join him on the lobby sofa.

"I'm going out for a walk," Moon said. "I have to get some exercise."

He took it slowly in this darkness at first, going carefully down the front steps and across the gravel pathway to the parking spaces. But there was still a faint glow of twilight. A first-quarter moon hung halfway up the eastern sky, and Moon's eyes adjusted quickly. By the time he'd reached the road leading toward town he was walking his standard U.S. Army pace.

The road surface seemed to be a mixture of clay and

gravel, packed hard and pocked with deep potholes. The roadside ditches produced frog sounds that his passage affected—loud ahead of him, silent beside him, and rising again to full cry behind him. This phenomenon reminded Moon that he was an intruder in this world of South Asian frogs and South Asian cultures. It reminded him of what he had come here to do.

A roadside palm had fallen there. Someone had sawed off the part that intruded into the roadway, but the remainder still spanned the ditch. Moon sat on it and reviewed his plans.

They were simple. His letter from the consulate had included a note from Assistant Warden Elogio Osoor. Warden Osoor said visiting hours were from one P.M. until two P.M. in the visiting room in the administration building. Convict Rice would be available for an interview. A guard would be present in the room at all times. No weapons or other contraband should be brought into the prison. This note should be shown to the guards at the perimeter.

Fair enough. He would ask Mr. Rice if he knew what the devil had happened to Ricky's daughter. If he had any idea how to find her. And if Moon was lucky, Rice would say he didn't have the slightest idea and he knew of no one else who had an idea, and that the child was probably safe with her Cambodian grandmother somewhere in Thailand by now, and one of these days, when all this trouble was over and Southeast Asia returned to normal, Victoria Mathias would probably be receiving a letter from the Cambodian granny soliciting money for the child's upbringing.

Whereupon Moon would be free to fly back to Los Angeles, make sure Victoria Mathias was getting proper care, and resume his life as a third-rate managing editor on a third-rate newspaper, sleeping with Miss Southern

Rockies when she decided it was a good idea to have sex and trying to persuade her to marry him.

"Aaah!"

The cry came from the darkness down the road and was accompanied by a clatter and then an exclamation, which, while Moon couldn't understand the language, was clearly an expression of anger and frustration.

He waited. Now the faint sound of footsteps coming toward him. The figure taking shape was tall, slender, female. Carrying a suitcase and a small handbag. Osa van Winjgaarden.

Moon didn't want to startle her. He said, "Good evening, Mrs. van Winjgaarden."

She produced what would have been a startled shriek, had she not instantly suppressed it, and said, "Who?"

"It's just Ricky's brother," Moon said, getting to his feet. "I didn't mean to startle you."

"Oh," she said. "Oh." And put down the bag.

What was she doing out here carrying a suitcase? When they'd left the airport she'd said she was going to check into a hotel in Puerto Princesa. She hadn't said why.

"Have a seat," Moon said. He gestured to the palm trunk. "It's comfortable."

"Thank you," she said. She left the bag on the road and sat. Even in the dim moonlight, he could see she was trembling.

"I'm sorry," he said.

She laughed. "It wasn't your fault I'm so spooky. What could you do? Just sit there and hope I didn't notice you when I walked past? That would have scared me to death."

"Ah, well," Moon said. "Anyway, it's a nice night for a walk."

"If you don't break your ankle. I stepped in a hole back there."

"I heard you," Moon said.

Brief silence. Then she laughed. "I hope you don't understand Dutch. Or the Indonesian Dutch we speak out here. You would have been shocked at my language."

"I translated it to mean something like 'Oh, shoot!' in English."

A chuckle. "That was kind of you," she said. "And close enough, I guess."

Moon had exhausted his small talk. He wanted to ask her what she was doing out here. Walking from her hotel in the town to Imelda's hotel, apparently. Surely not all the way to the airport. But why not take a cab? Was she out of money? If the rates here were as cheap as Manila, it would have been less than half an American dollar. Moon's lack of response didn't seem to bother her. She sat motionless, looking at the night sky.

"You're Dutch, then?"

"Van Winjgaarden," she said. "That's as Dutch as windmills and tulip fields."

"It's your husband's name, though," Moon said. "Your maiden name might be French, or Italian, or Spanish, or just about anything."

Silence. "No. Winjgaarden is my family name. Only the Mrs. isn't really mine. I never married."

"Oh," Moon said.

"In my work I have to travel a lot. All over. In Asia, a woman traveling alone attracts attention—the wrong kind of attention. So I use the Mrs. and I bought myself the wedding ring."

"Does it work?"

"It seems to be effective." And she laughed. "Or maybe I just flatter myself with this. Maybe I just *think* I need the Mrs. and the ring."

Moon thought about that. And about her. Remembering how he had first seen her walking into the hotel restaurant. A handsome woman, really. Graceful. Feminine. The sort of woman one saw in Cadillac commercials, escorted by a man in a tux. Not the sort of woman Moon would even think of approaching. But he knew a lot of men who would.

She glanced at him now, and away. It occurred to Moon that her remark wasn't one to be left hanging. Silence would seem a confirmation.

"No," he said. "I think you need the ring and the Mrs. I'm surprised they keep the wolves at bay."

"Wolves at bay?"

"Wolves," Moon said. "American slang for men who go around trying to connect with unattached women. I'm surprised you don't attract them even with the ring and the title."

"Oh," Mrs. van Winjgaarden said. "Thank you." And in an obvious effort to change the subject, added, "Have you noticed the constellation just above the horizon? The Southern Cross. I don't think you see that in the United States. Aren't you too far north of the equator?"

"We are in Colorado," Moon said. "Can I ask where you are going with your suitcase?"

"To the new hotel. The one in the town was much cheaper, and I thought— Well, when I was here once before, the little hotel in the town wasn't so bad. The ships' officers stayed in it, and I guess the tourists stopped there when there were any, and a few businesspeople who came here. So they made the plumbing work and it was clean. Well, so-so. And the screens kept the mosquitoes out. But that was four years ago, and now the businesspeople come out to this new hotel, and the old one—" She shuddered. "The old one is awful. The smell. The roaches."

"The new one is pretty good," Moon said. It didn't seem the time to mention the lack of refrigerated air.

"And of course I couldn't get a taxi." She laughed. "Puerto Princesa has only four with motors and then some pedicabs. But they all seem to quit at night."

"Noplace much to go," Moon said. "But weren't you nervous? I mean, walking all the way out here in the dark. Alone."

"No," she said. "No tigers out there. But I was thinking of other things and when your voice came out of the dark, calling my name, then I was surprised."

"What did you buy in Puerto Princesa? When you came four years ago?"

"Let me remember," she said. "Yes. I bought ten dozen bamboo blowguns with pigskin quivers, four bamboo darts in each quiver. And one hundred fetish figures, carved out of bamboo, and some little things made out of shark bones, and—" She stopped. "Things like that. Then we sell them to exporters who resell them to importers, and someday they end their travels on the wall of someone's parlor in Tokyo or Bonn or New York."

"Could you buy poison for the darts if you wanted it?"

"I never asked," she said. "But I think they still hunt with blowguns back in the hills, so they'd have to make the poison. It would be trouble for the importers, though."

"Just imagine. You could carry one of those right through the metal detectors at airport security and then hijack the airliner," said Moon, who found he was enjoying this conversation. "I wonder why the terrorists haven't thought of it."

The frogs had become used to them by now and reassured by their silences. Now there was frog song all around them, and from somewhere near, a whistling, and from somewhere far away, the sound of something huffing and grunting.

"We don't have many night sounds in the mountains,"

Moon said. "Just silence in the winter. In the summer, sometimes you hear the coyotes, and that starts the dogs barking."

"You're a long way from home," she said. "Halfway around the world."

Moon thought about that. This was like a totally different planet.

"Did you hear any news today?"

"No," Moon said.

"There was a radio—shortwave I think—playing at the hotel in town. It said ARVN troops had commandeered two evacuation planes at one of the big airports. They threw off the civilians. Running away."

"Um," Moon said.

"They said Vietcong and North Viet troops had captured the provincial capital just north of Saigon. And the airport north of Saigon had been hit by rockets."

Moon could think of nothing to say.

"And they had a report from Bangkok. Refugees from Cambodia were saying that the Khmer Rouge were forcing city people out into the country. That whole towns were being totally emptied and the Khmer Rouge were killing those who looked professional."

"It doesn't sound reasonable," Moon said. "It sounds like propaganda. Don't you think so?"

She sat looking out through the sound of the frogs, across the road, across the rice paddy, into the jungle. The moonlight illuminated her face, but the jungle was dark.

She said, "Are you ever afraid?"

She was looking at him now and Moon studied her expression, not sure exactly what she meant. She was hunched forward, hugging herself.

"I'm afraid sometimes," she added. "When I let myself think of going into Cambodia, I'm terrified."

Moon had parted his lips, beginning the standard reassurance, which was something like, There's nothing to be afraid of. But he bit that off. There was a hell of a lot to be afraid of.

"I don't blame you," he said. "I don't think you should go. Surely your brother will come out."

"No," she said. "He won't. So I am also terrified that I won't be able to get to him there. And then I am terrified that I will be able to get there, and the Khmer Rouge will get me. Afraid of what they would do to me. Afraid that Damon already is dead." She paused. "Just scared. Of everything. Of failing. Of being alone. Of being alive. Of dying. I really doubt if you can understand this business of being afraid."

"I can," Moon said. He saw she was shivering.

"Did you ever wish you could be little again? Just a child with somebody taking care of you?"

"Yes," Moon said.

"Really?"

"Sure," Moon said. "To tell the truth, I'm afraid too. Right now."

"I don't believe that."

"I don't know what I'm getting into. I don't know who I can trust. It's like—" He tried to think of an analogy. "Like walking around with a blindfold on."

She laughed. "You're trying to make me feel better. To make me cheerful. I can't imagine you being afraid. Ricky told me too much about you."

"Ricky didn't know what he was talking about," Moon said.

The faintest hint of a breeze stirred the palm fronds somewhere behind them. Moon smelled dampness, the yeasty smell of decaying vegetation, and the perfume of flowers. The frogs were totally reassured now; their calls rose to full volume.

"I should go and see if they have a room for me," Mrs. van Winjgaarden said. She pushed herself, wearily, up from the palm trunk.

Of course, Moon thought. She would be exhausted. He'd taken a shower, rested awhile, had a drink. She'd spent the time inspecting cockroaches, trying to get a cab, and making the long dark trek through the darkness up the potholed road.

He carried her bag. She explained that the whistling was the mating signal of the male of a species of tree lizard, and the odd high-note low-note call they were hearing now was from the gecko, another climbing lizard, and the huffing came from water buffaloes resting after a day's work in the rice paddies.

"And how about that sweet smell?" Moon asked. "Sort of like vanilla?"

Mrs. van Winjgaarden gave him the name of the vine that produced that aroma. It was a Dutch word. As he repeated it after her, Moon became aware that he no longer felt quite so lonely.

PARIS, April 22 (Agence France-Presse)—The French government today urgently appealed for speedy resumption of negotiations to carry out the 1973 Paris agreement on Vietnam and for an immediate cease-fire.

The Eleventh Day

April 23, 1975

THE SOUND OF RAIN pounding against his window had awakened Moon during the night. But by midmorning it had blown out over the South China Sea. The sky over Palawan Island wasn't the dark deep blue that Moon had learned to expect in the Colorado high country, but it was as blue as it gets in the tropics. And the sun was bright enough to raise Moon's spirits. It also produced a barely visible haze of steam from the potholes, rice paddies, and roadside ditches and sent the humidity up to steambath levels.

"I still don't think they're going to let you in," he told Osa van Winjgaarden, who was jolting along beside him in the back seat of their converted jeep taxi. "Prisons aren't going to let strangers in without any sort of credentials or passes."

"If they don't, then they don't," Osa said. "Then I will

just follow your plan. I'll take the taxi back to the hotel and get out and send it back to pick you up."

The tone was complacent, however. Moon glanced at her. Clearly Osa van Winjgaarden didn't expect she would be taking the taxi back to the hotel.

Neither did the cabdriver, a tiny middle-aged man with a bushy mustache. Moon, who was trying to develop a better eye for things Asiatic, thought he might be part Chinese. Or perhaps, this far south, it was a Malay look. His cab, however, was distinctly Filipino. It was painted with pink, purple, and white stripes, with the name COCK SLAYER superimposed on both sides in a psychedelic yellow. Plastic statues of two fighting cocks facing each other in attack positions were mounted on the hood, a location that forced the cabbie to tilt his head to see past them when he rounded a curve. The cabbie had quickly lost patience with the argument in the back seat over Osa's admissibility to the prison.

"They let her in," he said, waving a hand impatiently. "No question. We all go in. I park at the office in there. I write down the time I wait for you. All right?"

The gate to the Palawan Island Federal Security Unit proved to be a large palm log blocking the narrow road. The log was overlooked by a palm-thatched bamboo hut, which rose on bamboo stilts from the roadside ditch. A neatly printed sign above its door read IWAHIG PRISON AND PENAL FARM. The cab stopped. Two men wearing blue coveralls emerged from the hut. If either of them was armed, Moon saw no evidence of it.

Cabbie and guards exchanged pleasantries and information in a language that wasn't English and didn't sound like the Tagalog Moon had been hearing in Manila. The older of the security men tipped his cap to Osa, gave Moon a curious stare, and held out his hand.

"He wants to see your pass," the cabbie said.

Moon handed him the letter.

The guard examined it, stared at Moon again, returned the letter, and said something to the cabbie. All three laughed, and the older guard, still grinning, waved them through.

"Like I told you," the cabbie said. "No trouble about the lady."

Moon could see no sign that the inside of the Iwahig Prison and Penal Farm differed in any way from the outside. The potholed road still ran between rice paddies; hills rose a mile or two distant on either side of the road. The hills were covered by the deep green of the jungle, and at the margin of the jungle, bamboo shacks were scattered. Just ahead, two men were walking up the road, shovels over their shoulders. They stepped off into the grass, grinning, and made the universal hitchhiker's signal.

"We're inside the prison now?" Moon asked.

"Inside now," the cabbie said. He laughed. "Don't try to get away." He slowed the jeepney to walking speed. The shovel bearers climbed onto the back.

"But who lives in the houses? Out beyond the rice paddies."

"The colonists," the cabbie said, gesturing toward his newly acquired passengers. "These guys." He laughed. "They call 'em colonists. After they've been here awhile, not done anything wrong for a while, they can bring their women in and build a house and get some land to raise their crop."

"Really?" Moon said. He was remembering the cabbie laughing with the guards. Clearly this cabdriver liked his little jokes at the expense of tourists. The hitchhikers were actually prison employees, of course.

"And the prison keeps some buffaloes. So the prisoners can rent them when they need to plow. And then they turn in part of their rice, and the warden sells it and keeps part of the money to pay for the seed and the fertilizer and the rent." The cabbie laughed again and held up his hand—rubbing his fingers together in all of suffering humanity's symbol of extortion. "And a little something for the warden, I think. And a little something to buy Imelda a present too."

"They used a system a lot like that in Java too," Osa said. "When it was Dutch." She turned and said something to one of the hitchhikers. The man grinned a gap-toothed laugh and produced a lengthy answer.

"He said you have to serve a fifth of your sentence before you can bring your wife," Osa explained. "For him that was four years. And now he's growing vegetables."

"Not everybody wants to be a farmer, though," the cabbie said. "Some of them work in the shop. Carve things. Make antique canes, chairs. Nets to fish with. Blowguns. Things to sell in the market."

"What were you telling the guards back there at the gate?" Moon asked.

"I told them the lady was a lawyer the government sent down from Manila to investigate something. I told them you were her bodyguard."

This time Moon laughed. "You'll have trouble getting me to believe that story," he said. "They looked at the letter."

Now Osa chuckled. "I'll bet they don't read," she said. "Is that right?"

"That right," the cabbie said. "I had to tell them what it said. And I don't read either."

The man who came down the steps when the cab stopped at the administration building certainly could read. "I am Lieutenant Elte Creso," he said, and took Moon's letter. He glanced at it. "You are Malcolm Mathias," he said, and looked at Osa. "It says nothing about a woman. Do you have a pass for the woman?"

"This is Mrs. van Winjgaarden," Moon said. "My secretary. In Manila they said the letter would suffice for both of us. They said the authorities here would understand that one would be accompanied by one's secretary."

The lieutenant looked surprised. He considered this, looked at the letter again, sighed, shook his head, and motioned them up the steps.

The building reminded Moon of buildings he had seen in coastal Louisiana. It was a two-story concrete structure, whitewashed but stained by whatever those organisms are that grow on buildings in the tropics. It was raised some five feet off the earth on posts in tropical fashion and surrounded on both levels and all sides by broad verandas. Moon guessed it had been built early in the century, and not as part of a prison. Perhaps it was a hospital once, or a school. It dominated a broad, grassy plaza, the other three sides of which were lined by one-story buildings. They looked like barracks, Moon thought, but probably were quarters for the nonfarming inmates. He paused in the shade of the portal and looked back. Nothing stirred in the noonday heat.

It was very little cooler in the whitewashed room where they sat waiting for George Rice to be delivered to them. High ceiling, high windows, and a brass plaque beside the door declaring that Iwahig Prison was built in 1905 by the United States Philippine Commission. Overhead the blades of an ornate ceiling fan made their leisurely effort to stir the humid air. Even the lieutenant, wearing knee-length shorts and a short-sleeved shirt, was wilted. He was also a bit confused. His stare made his suspicious dislike of Moon apparent. But somehow Mrs. van Winjgaarden had charmed him.

"You know the rules," he said, glowering at Moon and then smiling shyly at Osa. "Visits are limited to twenty minutes for colonists during the first month of their incarceration. Colonist Rice has not been here long enough to qualify for a longer visit. Nothing can be passed to the inmate. Nothing can be received from the inmate. The rules require that a guard will be present at all times."

This recitation completed, the lieutenant gave Moon a final warning stare and backed out, bowed to Osa, and closed the door behind him.

They sat in straight-backed wooden chairs behind a long wooden table. And waited.

"Here we are, then," Osa said. "I think this will be it. I think Mr. Rice will tell us what we have to know. I have prayed for that."

Moon nodded. "Maybe so," he said. And maybe this would be an appropriate time for prayer. He closed his eyes. *Lord,* he thought, *let this Rice guy be the end of it. Let me just go home. Let this man tell us he doesn't know where the kid is, and he doesn't know how to get to this crazy preacher's mission, and he doesn't know a damned thing useful.* He opened his eyes. Closed them again. *And, Lord, let my mother be well again. And let her forgive me if I disappoint her again. Let her know it just wasn't possible. That I really did—*

The door opened and a small man walked through it. George Rice. He wore a loose cotton blouse with broad horizontal stripes in black and white. And under the blouse, loose pants with the same stripes. Exactly like the costumes cartoonists put on convicts, Moon thought. But the man didn't look like a convict even in that uniform. He had bright blue eyes, and a broad grin showed perfect white teeth. He had a well-trimmed white beard and mustache. Moon thought of Santa Claus.

A guard walked in behind him, even smaller. The guard looked about seventeen, and nervous.

"Well, howdy do!" George Rice said, beaming at Osa. "It is so good to see you agin, darlin'. So very, very good."

The guard pointed to the chair on the other side of the table and said, "Sit, please."

Rice sat.

"Mr. Rice," Osa said, "this is Ricky's brother. We hope you can give us some information."

"Moon Mathias," Rice said, extending a hand. "I'll be damned. You finally got here. Ricky thought you were the greatest thing since sliced bread."

The guard stepped forward. "No touch," he said. His expression said he was embarrassed by this rudeness. He looked at Moon, his eyes asking forgiveness.

"I'm glad to meet you," Moon said. "Ricky told me a lot about you too. I guess you were his right-hand man." A small white lie, but harmless as it was, Moon regretted it, just as he regretted the small ones he told Debbie. All Moon remembered hearing about Rice was a couple of anecdotes about his escapades.

"Don't believe all you hear," Rice said, grinning. And then, to Osa, "Darlin', did you come like the prince came to the tower where the princess was"—he searched for the proper word—"was incarcerated against her will? I trust that is your motive."

"It would be nice if we could," Osa said. "But we—"

Rice interrupted her. He turned to the guard. "This is my friend Mr. Preda. Mr. Preda, these are my good old friends, Mrs. van Winjgaarden and Mr. Moon Mathias. Good people. Good friends of President Ferdinand Marcos and Imelda."

"How do you do," Moon said. Osa said something that sounded like it might be in Tagalog, and Mr. Preda smiled shyly and nodded.

"Mr. Preda speaks English," Rice said. "But when it comes to *la lengua* of Shakespeare, to the multiple-syllable latinate vocabulary, then it's a different ball game. You two will understand without any explanation from me the advantage this linguistic situation will have for us." He looked back at Preda, who smiled and nodded.

Rice smiled back.

"I understand," Moon said glumly.

"You don't have to be a Houdini for the first step," Rice said. "I guess you noticed that coming in. A low hurdler could do the palm log. This isn't Sing Sing. That's not the problem. The problem is getting a drawbridge across the moat."

"The Sulu Sea," Moon said. He wasn't happy about the direction this conversation was taking.

"Exactly," Rice said. "Or, in our case, it would be the South China Sea."

"Mr. Rice," Osa said, "to tell the truth, we don't have any way to build bridges over moats. We are trying to find the baby. Eleth's baby. And Ricky's. She was supposed to be brought out to Manila, but she didn't get there. And we want to get my brother out of his mission too. Mr. Brock told us that you might—"

"Little Lila didn't get to Manila?" Rice said, frowning. "Well, now, she should have."

"And I would also like you to tell me some way I can reach my brother."

"Oh," Rice said. He leaned his elbows on the table, hands folded, lip caught between his teeth, thinking. He looked at Moon, blue eyes bright under bushy white eyebrows. And then at Osa. And then down at his hands.

Young Mr. Preda took a small step backward, leaned against the wall, looked out the window, exhaled a great sigh. Moon became conscious of the perspiration running down his cheekbone, down the back of his neck. The smell of mildew reached him, reminding him of something he couldn't quite place.

"Where would she be?" Rice asked himself. He glanced up at Moon. "I take it you're telling me they didn't get her onto the flight to Manila," he said.

"Apparently not," Moon said.

Rice sighed. "The way it was supposed to work, we'd handle it at the Nam end and that lawyer—Castenada, I think his name is, the one that Ricky retained for R. M. Air—was supposed to meet the plane and get the kid sent along to the grandmother in the States." Rice paused, lip between teeth again, remembering.

"I flew her up to Saigon," Rice said. "Lo Tho Dem was there at the airport. He had his wife with him. They took the little girl. Dem said he thought everything was going to be okay but he might need a little more cash"—he glanced up at Moon as he rubbed his fingers together, making sure he understood such things—"because things were getting tense in Saigon already. The rich folks wanting out. People standing in line at the embassy for papers and visas. There was already a big run on the airlines for tickets. But Dem—"

Moon interrupted. "Who is Lo Tho Dem?"

Rice laughed. "I never was quite sure who the hell he was," he said. "Anyway, he was Ricky's man in Saigon. Your brother had a talent for finding useful people. I'm pretty sure Mr. Dem sometimes did a little work for the CIA. That must have been where Ricky got acquainted with him: when Dem was working on one of those little jobs for the Company."

"Oh," Moon said. "And Ricky sometimes did a little work for them too?"

"And that's why Dem figured he could get the paper-work through in a hurry. And get the airline ticket. All that.

From what little I know about it, the Company owed your brother a few favors."

"You think that was the problem?" Moon asked. "Dem couldn't get a visa?"

"Well, now," Rice said, "when you get right down to it I gotta admit the real problem was me being stupid. The problem was, Ricky was dead. To make it worse, the Company knew he was dead. No more favors expected from Ricky Mathias. And the CIA don't have a reputation for paying off favors to people who can't do 'em any more good."

Rice was biting his lip again. He gave Moon an apologetic look and slammed his fist into his palm.

"Son of a bitch! I should have thought of that."

Mr. Preda shifted his weight against the wall, looked at his watch, sighed.

"So how can we find the child now?" Moon asked. "Did you have some sort of backup plan? Would this Dem guy keep her, or what?"

"I don't know," Rice said.

"How can I find Dem, then?"

"He lived in Saigon. Ricky had his address and telephone number in his file."

"At Can Tho?" Moon asked.

"We were pulling out of there," Rice said. "I guess Ricky's files would be downriver at Long Phu." He shook his head. "That is, if they got all the stuff out of Ricky's office moved."

"This Dem had a Saigon telephone," Moon said. "How's chances of calling information, getting it that way?"

"From what I've been hearing in here about the war the past few days, I say about a snowball's chance in hell. You can't get a call through to Saigon without some sort of special pull. And if you got it through, you couldn't get the number. And if you got the number, the system wouldn't be working. Not out to the residences."

"So what do you recommend?" Moon asked.

Rice leaned back in the chair and rubbed his beard, thinking about it.

He will tell me we will have to just forget it. It's absolutely impossible, like finding a needle in a haystack. He will tell Osa there's no way to reach her brother. That the Khmer Rouge have already found him and made a martyr out of him and she should go home and pray for the repose of his soul.

"You have to have a pilot," Rice said. "Ricky wanted you to come out and help run the place. But he said you didn't fly."

"I don't," Moon said. "And while you're thinking, do you have any ideas about an urn Ricky was bringing out of Cambodia for an old Chinese man named Lum Lee?"

"Urn? Oh, yeah. Lee's ancestral bones, wasn't it? I'd forgotten about that job."

"Know where it is?"

"Sure," Rice said. "Or where it was. Ricky had gone up-country to get it. And he called in to say he had it. And then he stopped at the Vinh place and dropped off the kid to visit Eleth's mother there. And there wasn't any sign of an urn in what was left of the helicopter. So I'd say it had to be back in the Vinh village."

"Just a matter of getting there," Moon said.

"Yep," Rice said. "And getting yourself out again. Alive and with all your arms and legs still in place."

Osa had been sitting silently, hands folded in her lap. She leaned forward. "I think we could do it easily enough in a helicopter," she said. "Just as we did last summer when you flew me up there. It took less than an hour."

"I remember, darlin'," he said. "It was a most pleasant

little trip. But that was last summer. Pol Pot's bloody little bastards, with their tripod-mounted antiaircraft machine guns and little handheld missile launchers, had not yet come down from the north."

"Are there any copters left at your hangars? Would any pilots still be there?"

"Copters, I'd say yes. We had eight or nine being fixed when I left, some of them ready to go. And two pilots. That was then. Now I'd say you could subtract two pilots and two copters from that number."

"No pilots?" Osa said.

"Not if they have any sense. And they were sensible fellows. Smart enough to know the Vietcong wouldn't like 'em." He thought about it. "It's Viet Cong territory—the Mekong Delta is. If the ARVN Yellow Tiger Battalion is still there, maybe. But I doubt it. Why stay? They could fly one of those copters away to Bangkok or get it down to Jakarta or Singapore and get a ton of money for it."

"Without any proof of ownership?" Moon asked.

Rice grinned at him. "Mr. Mathias," he said, "we are now in Southeast Asia. I don't think the Republic of Vietnam is going to be around long enough to file suit."

Mr. Preda cleared his throat and pushed away from the wall. "It is about used up, all the time you have. You have to go pretty quick now."

"Back to the subjects of moats and drawbridges," Rice said, voice urgent. "Getting across. What was the blueprint you had in mind?"

"We don't have any," Moon said.

"I do," Rice said. "You good at memorizing?"

Moon nodded.

"Eighty-one. Ninety. Twenty-two. You got it?"

"Eighty-one, ninety, twenty-two," Osa said.

"The man's name is Gregory. He does the same thing a

robin does. Or a crow. Or a seagull. Tell him the aviary for the robin will be at the end of the Puerto Princesa runway." Rice paused. "What day is today?"

"April twenty-third," Moon said, feeling sick as he said it. "But wait a minute now."

"April twenty-fifth, then," Rice said. "In the wee wee hours. The witching hour."

Moon said, "Hold on now. We—"

Mr. Preda said, "Now we go." He put his hand on Rice's shoulder, nodded to Osa. "Have a good day."

Rice, moving toward the door, turned suddenly. "At Imelda's?"

Osa said yes.

Rice said, "Until the wee hours." And to Moon he said, "Across the moat and I can find that little girl for you."

MANILA, April 22 (UPI)—The U.S. Navy has assembled a fleet of five aircraft carriers, eleven destroyers, four amphibious landing craft and other vessels off the coast of South Vietnam for a possible evacuation mission, a well-informed source at the Subic Bay Naval Base said today.

The Thirteenth Day and the Fourteenth Day

April 25–26, 1975

IT DEPENDED on how you looked at it.

You could call it a coup. A stroke of good fortune. Gregory, whoever he might be, would fly in from wherever. They'd get George Rice aboard undetected. Gregory would transport them across the South China Sea to the R. M. Air repair hangars on the Mekong. There Rice would fire up a copter, they'd fly away to the Vinhs' village and pick up Mr. Lee's urn, hop up to the Reverend Damon van Winjgaarden's mission to collect him, and then out of there. Safely. Then Rice, the old Asia hand, would talk to the right people, pull the right strings, find where Lila had been dropped off. They'd make another copter flight, snatch up the kid, and away they'd go.

On the other hand, it could be an unmitigated nightmare, which is the way it seemed to be working out, with Osa and he doing about twenty years, plowing rice paddies, for scheming to break a convict out of a Philippine prison. Having had plenty of time to think about it, Moon sat in the dim moonlight behind Imelda's hotel wondering how he could have been so stupid.

Recognizing the stupidity had been quick enough.

"You know what we've done?" he asked Osa as soon as the log gate had been pulled across the road behind them and they were jolting away from the Palawan prison. "We have conspired to commit a felony."

Osa put a finger to her lips and signified the cabbie with her other hand.

"Okay," Moon said. "So we don't need another witness against us. But you know what I mean?"

"Of course I know," Osa said. "Exactly, I know. But what else could we do?"

Moon had thought of several things they might have done by the time the jeepney dropped them off at the hotel. But instead of doing any of them, he had just sat there like a ninny and let Rice take charge of the conversation.

Now it was almost dawn, a day and half after the conversation, and no sign of George Rice. If Moon had enough optimism left to hope for any luck, he would have been hoping that Rice had fallen fatally down a cliff or become victim to whatever predators Palawan Island's jungles provided. Probably snakes, at least. But Moon's optimism was all used up. Rice would appear, probably at the worst possible time, and they'd have to talk him into going right back to the palm-log gate and turning himself in. And what if he wouldn't?

There was nothing else they could do with him. Except perhaps strangle the bastard and drag his body out into the bushes.

They'd placed the call to Gregory from the telephone in Moon's room, checking first with the desk to be sure making a connection across the Sulu Sea on a Filipino telephone required no special skill. It didn't.

The telephone made the expected ringing sounds, then clicked. A woman's voice said, "What number were you calling?"

Moon told her the number, and waited, trying not to think about how dreadful this was going to be if—

"I'm sorry, sir. That number is no longer in service."

"What?" Moon said. "You mean it's out of order?"

"No, sir. That number has been disconnected."

"Could you try again? Could you check? Maybe he just left the receiver off the—"

"Of course."

Moon waited, listening to the sounds telephones make during this sort of operation, thinking there would be no one named Gregory flying in to make George Rice disappear.

"I'm sorry, sir. That number has been disconnected."

"When?"

"I'm sorry, sir. You will have to check with our business office for that information. Shall I transfer your call?"

"No. Thanks. Just let it go," Moon said. He put down the phone.

"He wasn't there," Osa said.

"The telephone has been disconnected," Moon said. Osa would say maybe he just wasn't in. Osa would say maybe he left the telephone off the hook. Osa would ask—

Osa raised her eyebrows, made a wry face, said, "I don't think Mr. Rice gave us the wrong number. I think Mr.

Gregory moved away." She paused, staring past him, deep in thought. She grimaced. "Now, what to do with Mr. Rice? The prison people, I think they will come looking for him." She paused. "And looking for us."

"How about we kill him and bury him?" Moon said.

"He won't want to go back," she said. "I don't think so. He'll want us to hide him somewhere." She shook her head, gave Moon a wry smile, tapped her purse. "I can't fit him in here."

They sat side by side on Moon's bed. The sound of the lobby television drifted up through the floor. Canned laughter, then drums, then music, then what seemed to be a life insurance commercial.

Osa put her hand on his knee.

"Don't worry, Mr. Mathias. You've had too much to worry about. Your mother. Your poor little niece. And back home there must be the job you had to leave so quickly. Too much to worry about. Don't worry about this."

Surprised, he looked at her. He saw nothing but total sympathy. Her eyes glistened with it. She was ready to cry for him.

Moon wasn't sure what emotion this provoked in him. Whatever it was, it caused him to give a shout of laughter, thrust his arm around her shoulder, and hug her to him. "Mrs. van Winjgaarden," he said. "Osa, you are absolutely something else." He laughed again. "What do you mean, don't worry about this? We're standing here on the edge of the cliff, and it's crumbling under our feet, and Osa van Winjgaarden is advising me not to worry."

"Ooh," Osa said. "Too tight. You hug too strongly."

"We have a magazine in the States," Moon said. He eased his grip. "*Mad* magazine, with this stupid guy grinning on the cover and saying, 'What? Me worry?' It's the American symbol for craziness."

Osa was free now. "Well," she said. "The Italians have a useful phrase. *Che sará sará.* You know it?"

"It's the same in Spanish," he said. "And I guess they're both right."

And so he had picked up the telephone again and repeated the process with the number Rice had given them. The operator was different but the results were the same: disconnected.

"I think you should be calling me Osa," she said. "Mrs. van Winjgaarden is too long. And you never get it quite right."

"And everybody calls me Moon."

Then he called information and got the number of the Pasag Imperial Hotel in Manila.

Mr. Lum Lee was in.

"Ah, Mr. Lee," Moon said. "I think I know now the location of your urn of bones."

He heard the sudden sound of Mr. Lee sucking in his breath.

"We found a man named George Rice. He worked closely with my brother. Rice told us that the day Ricky was killed he called in on his radio and said he had picked up the urn someplace up north in Cambodia. He said he was leaving it off at the home of Eleth Vinh's parents. The name is Vin Ba and it's a tiny little village in Cambodia near the Vietnam border."

"Ah," Lum Lee said. "Mr. Mathias, this is very kind of you. Very generous. It is difficult for a Westerner—for anyone who is not a Buddhist—to understand how important these bones are for our family."

"I've read about it," Moon said. "But I'm afraid this information will be too late. I hear the Khmer Rouge are taking over everything. We may not be able to get there. And it may be gone if we do."

"But this is most generous of you, this kindness to a stranger."

"It is a family responsibility," Moon said. "You contracted with my brother—"

Mr. Lee gave him a moment, decided the sentence wouldn't be finished, said, "But that was an accident," cleared his throat, and went on. "I myself was not able to reach Mr. Rice. I was informed he was in prison. In the south."

"He's in the Federal Correction Unit on Palawan Island," Moon said. "Our embassy arranged for me to talk to him."

"Of course," said Mr. Lee, and Moon heard a wry chuckle. "I think the Taiwan embassy would not know me, and the mainland China embassy would not find favor in the present Philippine foreign office. You are there now? On Palawan?"

"At Puerto Princesa," Moon said. "At the Puerto Princesa Filipina hotel."

"And from there you are going over to Vietnam? Or you come back to Manila?"

"I don't know," Moon said. "I have no plans made. But if I can find the urn I will bring it to you. Where? At your hotel in Manila?"

"Yes," Lee said. "They know me here. And where will you be?"

Probably in prison, but no use getting into all those details. "I'll be here for a day or two." Or however many years it takes to serve out a criminal conspiracy term.

And that had been more or less that. A few more expressions of gratitude on Mr. Lee's part, and disclaimers by Moon.

The next call had been to the cardiac ward in Cedars-Sinai hospital in Los Angeles. He'd asked the nurse who answered how his mother was doing.

"Morick," the nurse said. "Oh, yes. Dr. Serna has been trying to reach you in Manila. Just a moment while I page her."

Moon waited, uneasy. Dr. Serna calling him in Manila couldn't be good. It wasn't.

"Ah, Mr. Mathias," she said. "I haven't been able to reach you. The hotel number you gave us in Manila—"

"Is she worse?"

"We couldn't wait," Dr. Serna said. "We tried an angioplasty. Usually they're effective. This one wasn't. So we—"

"Is she dead?"

"She's alive. Her condition is stabilizing. But we must do bypass surgery right away. How soon can you get to Los Angeles?"

"Ah," Moon said. "I don't know. I'm at Puerto Princesa. Little place way down at the wrong end of the Philippines. I'll have to find a way to get back to Manila and then—"

He stopped, thinking of George Rice in the jungle, of the police surely watching the airport. He'd never get to Manila. And if he did, the police there would grab him the minute he showed his passport.

"Look," he said. "I'll get there as soon as I can. Do the surgery. You have my permission. Do whatever you have to do to save her life."

"We can declare it a medical emergency," Dr. Serna said. "Because it is."

"Can I talk to her?"

"She's sedated."

"Would you tell her for me that I love her. And tell her I'm going to find her granddaughter if I can."

Osa and he had decided that they couldn't risk Rice's simply walking up to the hotel and asking for them. They'd split the night watch into shifts, one prowling the grounds while the other slept, hoping to spot him the moment he arrived. Moon had insisted that Osa take the early watch. Being nervous, he'd shared much of it with her. Now it was almost dawn. He'd memorized the night sky of spring ten degrees north of the equator, identifying the familiar constellations and trying to guess the names of those new to him. He'd sorted out the night sounds, lizards, birds, frogs, mammals. He noticed how the mating symphonies and the hunting calls fell almost silent when the moon went down and rose again just before the eastern horizon lightened. But he neither saw nor heard any trace of escaped convict George Rice. Not on the potholed road. Not on the fringes of jungle beyond the hotel grounds. Not anywhere.

Above and behind him a sudden flash of light: the window of Osa's room. A few moments later, it went off. Bathroom call, he thought. He needed one himself and strolled across the grass to a nearby bush. It was flowering, surrounding him with blossoms the size of baseballs, the aroma overpowering the thousand smells of the night.

When he emerged from the bush, Osa was sitting on the ledge under the hotel wall, looking toward the jungle.

She'll say, Have you seen him? Or she'll say, I couldn't sleep.

She patted the ledge beside her, inviting him to sit, and said, "What are we going to do?"

Moon sat, thought about how to answer.

She rephrased the question. "What are you going to do?"

"If Rice doesn't show up?"

"Yes. Or if he does get here. Either way."

"I don't know," Moon said. "I know I have to figure out some way to get to L.A. But it looks impossible. How about you?"

"I'll keep trying," she said. "I don't know exactly how

to do it, but there must be a way." She touched his arm. "Anyway, there's nothing you could do there but pace the floor and wait. You said you had found a good doctor and a good hospital. All you can do is wait."

Moon found himself thinking that he'd liked *What are* we *going to do?* better than *What are* you *going to do?* But he thought of no way to express that thought. So he said, "If Rice is coming, it should be about now. When it's just light enough so he can see what he's getting into. See if we're out here waiting for him."

"He'd come out of the jungle, you think? Not down the road?"

"I would," Moon said. "I'd be scared to death. But I'd be more scared of getting caught than of getting snake-bit."

"I don't think so," Osa said.

"Don't think what? That I'm not scared of snakes?"

"Not scared of anything," she said. "Anyway, not scared to death. Ricky told us you didn't seem ever to be very frightened."

"Well, now you know better," Moon said.

"Know better? That means like I know more strongly?"

"No. It means you know you were wrong about me. I'm easy to scare. I'm scared about the trouble I got us into here. I'm scared about going to Cambodia."

She sighed. "As you said to me last night, I don't blame you. I'm scared too."

"But you would go?"

The pause was so long Moon thought she would ignore the question. But she said. "Yes. Sure. So would you."

Moon didn't answer. She was probably right, and that made his stomach feel uncomfortable.

"Why would I?"

"Because it's the way you are. You think of your mother, sick back there in that hospital. You want to bring a granddaughter for her to see. You think of that little girl. Your brother's daughter. In Asia people are very proud. They don't like those of other races. The Khmers don't like the Laotians, and the Laotians don't like the Thais, and the Vietnamese don't like the Montagnards, and nobody likes the people who are mixed."

Moon couldn't think of an answer. He said, "People are people."

In the dimness he could see her shaking her head. "They had it in the papers about how badly the Vietnamese treated the children left behind by your army. Half white or half black. Half Vietnamese."

He had read it. In fact, he had written a headline on an AP story reporting that. He couldn't forget it. That was part of his problem.

"Things get exaggerated," Moon said. "I'm in the news business. I know."

She was silent, staring into the jungle. It was light enough now to make out the shape of trees, shades of color. Somewhere in the night a water buffalo bellowed.

"I was a child in Java when they tried to overthrow the Sukarno government," she said. "There was supposed to be an assassination first and then a coup. The Communists were working with the dissidents, and so was part of the army, but something went wrong."

"Were you in danger?" he asked, wondering why she had shifted to another subject. But she hadn't.

"There was probably a betrayal," she said. "Usually there is a betrayal. And there was much fighting, and the Suharto people won and then told the people in Malaysia that the Chinese Communists were behind it all, and then the killing of the Chinese began. People in Asia always find a reason to kill the Chinese. The Chinese work hard and save their money and start their little shops and loan people money, so other people envy them. They blame them for things."

"Like the Europeans do with the Jews," Moon said.

"I think so. Yes. And all through Asia the overseas Chinese have networks. Extended family tongs. Sometimes criminal organizations. I remember as a child I used to collect tong signals. They're supposed to be secret but people get careless. I'd pick them up."

"Like what?" Moon asked.

"Like this," Osa said. She cupped one hand, touched fourth finger to thumb on the other. "Or this," and she turned both hands down with the thumbs swallowed in the fists. "Here in the Philippines they say President Marcos is part Chinese and his tong and the Chinese mafia helped get him elected."

Moon had no comment on this. He'd always assumed Douglas MacArthur had picked him.

"Our house was on a slope above the river. I remember seeing the bodies floating down," Osa said. She shifted on the shelf, hugged herself. "All sizes of bodies."

"I remember reading about it," Moon said. "Weren't several hundred thousand people killed?"

"I think all the Chinese," she said. "In our town the Chinese shops were all empty afterward, and the places where the Chinese lived were all burned down. And you never saw any Chinese anymore anywhere in Java or Sumatra."

"You don't have to remind me," Moon said. "I just hope the little girl, my niece, looks exactly like her mother."

"Maybe she will," Osa said. "Do you have a picture?"

"Yes. But I can't tell much from that."

From somewhere far behind them a rooster crowed, touching off a response from other roosters, arousing a dog and another dog and another.

"Tell me about your mother," Osa said. "And about Ricky. And what happened to your father. Everything."

"You first," Moon said.

She'd been born at Serang, not far from Jakarta. Her father worked for Royal Dutch Petroleum and was killed when the Japanese captured Java in 1942, before she was born. After the war, her mother married van Winjgaarden, who owned a warehouse at Jakarta and operated an export-import business. They had moved there, and she went to private school. Her mother spoke English and her foster father spoke German. The housekeeper who took care of her spoke Chinese, and the people around her spoke Malay and Chinese and a local dialect, and she fell in love with languages but wasn't very good at anything else. But that talent had been very useful. When she finished school, she had gone to work for her foster father, scouting the craft markets for handicrafts to export.

"My foster father always seemed like a real father to me. And he loved me like I was his own child," Osa said. "But he seemed to love dangerous things more than people. Always on flights in little planes in bad weather. Always on little boats when the typhoon was coming. Always in places where there was killing going on over politics. And one time—it was the first time I came here to buy things—he said he was going over to Borneo to buy some jade and teak things. And I said, Don't go. The rebels were fighting the government and it was dangerous. But he hugged me and said good-bye."

Silence. End of the story? Moon guessed the end.

"He didn't come back?"

"Never," Osa said. "Neither he nor the pilot."

"He was Damon's father?"

"Yes. And Damon is just like him. I thought Damon would come home then and keep the company going. But he wanted to be a saint. So our mother had to be the boss. I kept being the buyer."

And that was how she had met Ricky: buying in Laos and Cambodia and needing a way to get in and out.

"Your brother, he was a nice man. He wanted you to come and help him. I wondered why you didn't."

Moon let that hang.

"Now it's your turn. Tell me something about Mr. Mathias."

So he told her something. He planned to tell her just a little. Perhaps it was the darkness, as in Father Julian's confessional, or the sympathy he'd felt from her. Whatever it was, he told her a lot. And then he felt intensely embarrassed.

"They put you out of the army? Just because of an accident?"

"I was drunk," Moon said. "I was using an army vehicle without authorization. Rules were violated."

"But still—"

"I don't want to talk about it anymore. If you keep asking, I'll ask you why you never got married. And personal things like that."

"Do you think Mr. Rice is coming?" Osa said.

"I doubt it," Moon said.

And Mr. Rice didn't. But Mr. Lee did.

WASHINGTON, April 22 (CNS)—A Pentagon official just back from Vietnam says he believes the worst threat to Americans remaining in Vietnam may be deserting ARVN combat troops who feel they have been betrayed.

"They're likely to go berserk in their bitterness and attack anyone they feel responsible for their defeat," the general said.

Still the Fourteenth Day

April 26, 1975

MR. LEE ARRIVED AT THE HOTEL in the same taxi that had brought Moon and Osa in from the airport. Osa, standing at the window of Moon's room, saw him climbing out of it.

"Is your Mr. Lum Lee a very small man?" she asked Moon. "And old? And does he wear an old white straw hat?"

"That sounds like Mr. Lee," Moon said. "But what would he be doing here?"

"Well, at least it's not the police coming after us. Not yet, anyway."

"They're probably right behind him," Moon said, too drowsy to care much, thinking that in jail he could at least get some sleep. He had waited, too nervous even for dozing, for his two A.M. telephoning time. He'd learned that Dr. Serna was in surgery and had left a message that she would call him as soon as she had "anything definite to report." Then he had failed to reach Debbie, who was either out somewhere or simply wasn't answering the phone. Finally, he'd called the *Press-Register* to learn how things were going there.

They were not going well.

"Chaos," Hubble said. "Rooney jumped off the wagon. I think he started nipping day before yesterday. I got on him about it. Told him to go home. Then yesterday he didn't show up. And this afternoon he walks in looking like hell warmed over and smelling like the drunk tank and runs right into old Jerry."

Moon had started to say "Oh, shit," but swallowed it because Osa was standing by his window. She'd been there most of the day, waiting and watching. Osa was absolutely certain that the people who ran the prison would have connected the absence of George Rice to their visit with George Rice. But there was nothing they could do but wait. They had to be here when Rice came because, somehow, they had to persuade him to turn himself in.

Moon bit back the expletive and said, "Jerry fired him?"

And Hubble said, "He sure as hell did. He told him to clean out his desk and get his check from Edith."

"Silly bastard," Moon said. "You were already short-handed."

"To say the least," Hubble said. "I've been coming in right after breakfast. Working about a twenty-eight-hour day."

"Well, hang in there," Moon said. "I'll get back as soon as I can."

"You still in Manila? What's the holdup? Before I forget it, the old man wants to talk to you. He's been bitching about you being gone so long."

"Why didn't he call me?" And then he remembered why. "Oh. I guess I didn't give anybody my new number."

Hubble laughed. "That ain't the reason. Overseas calls are expensive. He wants to do it on your nickel."

So Moon sat, holding the telephone to his ear, waiting for the publisher's secretary to get Shakeshaft on the phone and watching Osa standing by the window. A slender woman, graceful. Not Debbie's lush shape but lithe. Classy.

"Mathias!" Shakeshaft shouted into his ear. "How long is this goddam spring vacation of yours going to last?"

"I can't tell yet," Moon said. "I may know by tomorrow."

"I'm having a little trouble understanding all this," Shakeshaft said. "Are you still out there in Manila? And your momma's sick in Los Angeles? That's what I get from Hubble, anyway. You want to tell me what the hell you're doing in Manila while you're on my payroll? You find us some readers out there?"

"Well," Moon said, "it's some important family business. My mother was going to handle it. She got sick, so I had to go do it for her."

"And you don't know how long it's going to take you, this family business?"

"Not yet, I don't. " Moon said. "I think maybe I'll know by tomorrow."

"Well, I got family business too. Which is getting this goddam paper out. And if you remember, we've got the vacation edition coming up. Got enough ads sold already for four special sections and nobody here to write the copy for it. And that Rooney you hired. That wino son of a bitch. Did Hubble tell you about what happened?"

"He said you fired him," Moon said. "Maybe you should have waited."

Shakeshaft did not appreciate the implied criticism. "Maybe you shouldn't have hired him," he said. "I tell you what I'm going to do. I'm going to hold your job open for you. Another day. Twenty-four more hours. You call me tomorrow and tell me you got your tickets and you're on your way back."

"If I can," Moon said. "I'm sorry I had to leave the paper in such a—"

"I don't want to hear any of that 'If I can' shit," Shakeshaft said. "If you can't, I'll get out the application file tomorrow morning and start interviewing people for your replacement."

"I'll—" Moon began, but Shakeshaft had hung up.

Moon put the telephone down and rubbed his ear. Osa was looking at him.

"Everything is good?"

"Everything is about normal," Moon said.

The telephone rang. It was Lum Lee. Mr. Lee hurried through the polite preliminaries. Mr. Lee hoped to confer with Mr. Mathias. Would that be convenient?

"Come on up," Moon said. But he hoped Lee wouldn't hurry. He wanted to think about being fired. If that was what was going to happen, and it sounded like it would, what would he do?

The payment had been due on his truck April fifteenth. He'd missed that already. Then there was the house payment. He had—let's see—about eleven hundred in the bank. Enough to cover those. And Rooney owed him about four hundred dollars, which he'd probably never see. He owed maybe a hundred and fifty on the credit card, depending on how heavily Debbie had used it when he loaned it to her. He had about forty-five bucks of his own money left in his billfold, and his mother's stack of big bills which he hadn't touched so far. But then he must be a couple of thousand into his mother's credit card by now: the expensive Hotel Maynila and the plane ticket to Palawan and the money he'd spent buying himself some clothes. That had to be paid back.

But maybe he'd learn today that Rice hadn't escaped and there was no practical way to find the child and recover her. There would be nothing to do but call Shakeshaft and tell him he was on his way home. He yearned for that to happen. He did yearn for it, didn't he?

He looked at Osa, holding back the dusty curtain, watching for Rice or for the police. He'd miss her.

Mr. Lee's tap on the door was so polite that Moon barely heard it. He gave Moon his frail hand to shake, but in the dark eyes of Osa van Winjgaarden Mr. Lee somehow recognized a fellow Asian. To her he bowed over hands prayerfully pressed together. She returned the gesture exactly.

But otherwise today Mr. Lee made unusually short work of the polite formalities. He sat on the edge of the chair Moon had offered him and got right to the point.

"At the airport there were police," he said, his eyes on Moon's face. "It was said an inmate had left the penal institution without permission. It was said the one who escaped was an American."

"Probably George Rice," Moon said.

"Yes," Lum Lee said. "And why do you say that? Could it be only because you understand there are very few Americans in the prison here?" Mr. Lee's expression suggested he doubted that.

"He told us he planned to get out."

"Ah," Lee said, nodding. "I am told that getting out is easy. Getting off the island is very hard. Did he suggest you help him accomplish that?"

"I think he expected a friend to fly in and pick him up."

"A friend?"

"Just a guess," Moon said, thinking, How much should I tell this little man? Have I already dug us deeper into trouble?

"Ah, yes," Lee said. "A guess. And since the police are still at the airport, and the police are still around the port at Puerto Princesa, I would guess that the friend has not yet come."

"That sounds logical," Moon said, wondering how Mr. Lee knew about the police at the port. Hadn't he come here directly from the airport?

Mr. Lee, deep in thought, extracted his cigar case, opened it, extracted a slim black cigar, and suddenly became aware of his rudeness. He gave Moon an apologetic look.

"If Osa doesn't mind," Moon said, "go ahead and smoke."

"Please do," Osa said.

"A bad habit," Mr. Lee said, lighting it. "But it sometimes seems to help one think. And now one needs to think."

"Trouble is, I can't think of anything helpful," Moon said.

"It all seems strange," Mr. Lee said. "Perhaps the friend of Mr. Rice betrayed him. Or perhaps Mr. Rice did not find a way to notify this friend of his need. Or of his schedule."

"Perhaps," Moon said. "Or—"

He paused, looked at Osa. Osa shrugged. What the hell, Moon thought. "Or perhaps the friend's telephone in Manila had been disconnected. Perhaps there was no way the friend could be contacted."

Mr. Lee exhaled cigar smoke, careful to aim it away from them.

"Yes," he said. "Either way, the problem is the same for Mr. Rice." He looked at Moon, expression quizzical. "And for others."

He considered this, eyes down, hands folded across his waist.

"I would believe Mr. Rice to be a most shrewd man," Mr. Lee continued. "Reckless at times, but most intelligent." He nodded, agreeing with his conclusion. "Yes. He would never think he could simply walk up to the airport buildings in his prison uniform and wait for this friend to arrive. He would need to be certain that the friend was coming, and to know precisely when this friend would arrive. And precisely on what part of the runway he was landing his airplane. I believe that Mr. Rice would wish to conceal himself in the jungle until he saw this aircraft land. Then he would hurry out from the trees and get aboard before being detected."

"Exactly," Moon said.

"So he was coming here? To learn from you what arrangements had been made by his pilot friend?"

Moon nodded. "He was supposed to come last night. But he didn't make it."

"So now the police search for him." Mr. Lee reached for the telephone. Withdrew his hand with an apologetic look at Moon. "May I?—"

Moon gestured his permission.

"It will be necessary to speak in Chinese," Mr. Lee said. "I am afraid neither of you speak that language." He hesitated a moment, looking at Moon and then at Osa for confirmation. "I will apologize that such impoliteness is necessary, but my friend here at Puerto Princesa does not speak English."

It was a long conversation, involving at various times at least three people on the other end of the telephone.

Moon sat on the edge of the bed, looking away, watching Osa van Winjgaarden, who stood motionless at the window. He tried to read significance into the tone of Mr. Lee's voice and learned only that Mr. Lee seemed to be in charge. The tone suggested that Mr. Lee was not asking favors. Only once did he raise his voice in anything that might have been irritation. Once he paused and asked Moon if he remembered the name of the prison official who had been in charge of him. Moon didn't, but Osa provided the name of the lieutenant and Lum Lee repeated it into the telephone.

Osa had looked away from the window then and watched Lee. Her face registered puzzlement, then surprise, then intense interest. It occurred to Moon that Osa as a child had had a Chinese nanny. She would understood Chinese, or at least a little of it.

She looked at him and then moved her hands down where they would not be visible to Mr. Lee and made with her fingers the tong signals she had shown.

Mr. Lee hung up.

"Thank you very much," he said. "Now I think we should go into Puerto Princesa and make some arrangements."

"I'll have to wait for Rice," Moon said. "We can't—"

"We go now," Lum Lee said. "The police are coming."

"For us?" Moon said. Not that he hadn't been expecting it.

"Yes," Mr. Lee said. "I think they would have been here

much earlier, but your lieutenant had the day off." He was moving toward the door. "Quickly, now. Quickly."

The anxiety in Mr. Lee's expression spoke as loud as the words. Moon stuffed everything he had into his bag in a matter of seconds. Even so, he found Osa in the hall, bag packed, waiting.

Mr. Lee was walking, rapidly and silently, down the hallway toward them. "A policeman has just come into the lobby," he said. "Is there another stairway down?"

"There's a little porch at the end of the building, and a door opens out onto it," Moon said. "Maybe it's a fire escape."

It was. They scrambled down the ladder.

"Where are we going?" Moon asked.

"Where the police won't find you," Mr. Lee said. "Until we can collect Mr. Rice."

WASHINGTON, April 23 (AP)—A spokesman for President Ford said today that sixty helicopters have been assembled on three aircraft carriers off the coast of Vietnam prepared for speedy evacuation of Americans if it becomes necessary.

Evening, the Fourteenth Day

April 26, 1975

THE PLACE WHERE MR. LEE had arranged to hide them proved to be a ramshackle two-story house on a potholed street of ramshackle two-story houses near the port that gave Puerto Princesa its name. The house was built partly of concrete blocks, partly of planking, and partly of bamboo logs, roofed partly with tile and partly with palm thatching—pretty much in keeping with the low-income urban architecture Moon had been noticing in the Philippines. What was less common, or so Moon presumed, was the section of flooring in the back hall. Mr. Tung, who Moon now presumed was the homeowner as well as their cabdriver, slid away the hallway rug, lifted this section, exposed a steep stairway, and led them down it into a large room with a concrete floor. Three of the walls and about four-fifths of the remaining one were also of concrete.

The remaining fraction of a wall opened into a screen of bamboo poles. Mr. Tung pulled this back and peered out into what look to Moon like a bamboo forest. Mr. Tung nodded and refastened the cord that held the screen closed. He said, "I hope there will be comfort here," bowed deeply over tented hands, and hurried up the stairway, where, Moon presumed, Mr. Lee was awaiting him.

"I think we have been put in cold storage for a while," Moon said, inspecting the furnishings. They included three small beds, two folding cots, a worn plastic sofa, a fairly new overstuffed chair, and a round wooden table with four wooden chairs. Around the three concrete walls pallets were stacked, the sort on which heavy materials are shipped. Behind the pallets up to about three feet above the floor, the walls were discolored with water stains.

Moon sat on the sofa, feeling dizzy from lost sleep. And maybe a little bit feverish and headachy besides. He decided not to think about this. He was caught up in the tides of fate. He would discontinue thinking until he had something positive and productive to think about. Maybe he'd get some sleep. The last two nights there'd been damned little of that.

Osa had untied the cord, pulled back the bamboo an inch or two, and peered out.

"How clever," she said.

Moon yawned. Clever? He'd look later. But it had been clever the way Mr. Lee had gotten them here unseen. Lee had told them to appear at the side entrance of the hotel with whatever they had to take with them. He told them exactly when to be there. And just as they got to the door, the jeepney cab had pulled up with its rain curtains down. They'd slid into the back seat and left. It was the jeepney with the fighting cocks on the hood, but this time the driver was an older fellow wearing a flowered necktie and a seersucker jacket. His hair was short-cropped and gray. Mr. Lee had introduced him as Mr. Tung. Moon guessed he was a Malay, but Tung and Lum Lee were communicating in something that sounded like Chinese.

"Pretty soon we will get to a house where you will stay for a while," Mr. Lee had said without turning. "Mr. Tung will park his cab beside the side porch. He and I will get out and go into the house, and all the luggage will be carried in. But you will stay for some time in the cab."

"Until all the neighbors get their curiosity satisfied and stop looking out their windows," Moon said.

Mr. Lee had laughed. "Most astute," he said. "I think you must live in a small town."

Now Osa was still fiddling with the bamboo screen.

"You should see this," she said. "It works like what we Dutch would call a water gate." She laughed. "I think maybe our good hosts here do some smuggling."

"Great," said Moon, and dozed off.

He awoke sometime later, aware that Osa was rearranging his foot, which seemed to have fallen off the sofa.

"Uncomfortable," he heard her say. "There's the bed right over there. Not three yards away. Men are so stubborn. Why not sleep on the bed?" And then some muttering in Dutch, or German, or Tagalog, and Moon was asleep again.

Someone was shaking him. Moon came out of his sleep slowly this time, partly involved in a dream in which Gene Halsey and he were in a bar involved in some sort of disagreement with a military policeman and partly aware that Lum Lee was pushing on his shoulder.

"What?" Moon said.

"Sorry," Mr. Lee said. "Very sorry. But now we must do some business."

"Business," Moon said. Halsey, bar, and MP were gone now. He swung his legs around, sat up, and rubbed his face, trying to stifle a yawn. Osa was standing there watching him. Beside her two men were standing. One was their host, Mr. Tung, the cab owner. The other was George Rice.

Moon became wide awake. "Well!" he said. "Mr. Rice. Welcome to Puerto Princesa."

"Happy to be here," Rice said, grinning his bright blue-eyed grin. "Comparatively speaking, of course."

Rice was still in the striped prison garb, now wet and smeared with mud. A dark brown bruise began near the center of his forehead and ended in his right eyebrow. Below that, a small bandage had been taped over the cheekbone.

"You all right?" Moon asked.

"Fine," Rice said. "Relatively speaking. Getting to the moat wasn't as easy as it sounded."

"Do you know how to reach your pal Gregory? His telephone—"

Mr. Lee interrupted. "Excuse me, please. We have covered all this. Mr. Gregory is not in the picture. We must agree on another solution."

"I don't know of any," Moon said. "Not a clue."

"Mr. Lee thinks we can sail across," Osa said.

"Sail across? Across the Sulu Sea?"

"The South China Sea," Mr. Lee said,

Moon didn't want to think about that. Across the South China Sea lay Vietnam. And Cambodia. And Pol Pot's terrible teenage warriors beating people to death. He'd think about that later. Not for a minute or two. Now he had a headache and his stomach felt queasy.

"How did you get here?" he asked Rice.

Rice produced a self-deprecatory expression and nodded toward Mr. Tung. "I got a little confused out there. Got turned around. This gentleman had sent out some of his friends looking for me, and they found me."

Mr. Tung was smiling. "He had gotten down almost to the beach. My boys found him and then we sent a boat."

Mr. Lee wanted to stick to the point. "I think it would take perhaps three days. No more than four."

"To where?" Moon asked.

"To the mouth of the Mekong and then up to Ricky's repair hangars."

"Sailing on what?"

"The *Glory of the Sea,*" Mr. Lee said. "A two-master. A schooner."

"A sailboat?" Moon's headache was right there behind his forehead, just over the eyes, pounding away. Surely they didn't intend to try to cross the Pacific Ocean in a sailboat. And this still was the Pacific, wasn't it? No matter what they called it.

"Two masts," Mr. Lee said. "But also diesel power."

"Oh," Moon said.

"Yes," Mr. Tung said. "It is docked here now to get the diesel running better."

"It won't work? It's broken down?"

"Oh, yes. It works," Mr. Tung said. "But not so very good. Not so very fast." He made a slow *putt-putt-putt*ing sound with his lips.

In his drinking days Moon had become an authority on headaches. He was thinking that if he had a double shot of bourbon with two aspirins dissolved in it, his headache would go away. But he would never, ever drink again.

Mr. Lee was staring at him, waiting.

"When will this *Glory of the Sea* have its diesel fixed? Do you know?"

Mr. Lee looked at Mr. Tung. Mr. Tung shrugged. "In Puerto Princesa things sometimes go slowly," he said.

"Once we had a man here who fixed such things very well. But he moved his shop over to Leyte, where there is more business."

Moon looked at Osa. She must have told them he was a mechanic, told them about what he did in the army, about J.D's pickup engine awaiting his return in Durance, Colorado. Cold, clean, safe, restful Durance, Colorado.

"I believe you were a mechanic in your military career," Mr. Lee said. "Somewhat like your brother, but working on the engines of tanks and big vehicles."

Moon nodded. But not really like his brother. Moon was the grease monkey. Ricky was the boss. "But this will be a marine diesel. Probably much bigger. Much different." Which was probably baloney. A diesel was a diesel, much alike and all knuckle-busters to work on.

"Do you think you could make it run well again?" Mr. Lee asked.

"I don't know what's wrong with it."

"Captain Teele will be able to tell you," Mr. Lee said. "He is waiting upstairs."

Upstairs, for the first time in quite a while, Moon found himself the second largest man in the room. Forced to guess, Moon would have named Teele a Samoan pro football lineman. Certainly not the captain of a schooner named *Glory of the Sea*. He was dressed in a well-worn pinstriped business suit that had probably fit him well enough when he'd bought it but now bulged where he had added muscle. His hair was long and streaked with gray, and his dark face was marred by scarring and weathered by too many years of strong sun and salty winds.

He bowed to Osa and smiled. To Moon and George Rice he offered a large square hand and said something in a language that was new to Moon. By the sound of it, the statement seemed to end with a question.

"He wishes you well," Mr. Lee said, "and he asks if you can fix his engine so it will run better."

"Tell him I need to know what is wrong with it," Moon said. And thereby began one of those three-sided translated conversations that left Captain Teele looking doubtful and Moon wondering if Teele had even the vaguest notion of what caused ignition inside a diesel engine.

"Tell him I have to go see it," Moon said.

"Ah," Mr. Lee said. "Then I think you believe you can fix this problem?"

"Who knows?" Moon said. But as a matter of fact, Moon did think he could fix it. From the captain's admittedly hazy descriptions, it had the sound of a fuel-injection problem. In the glossary of things that can go wrong with engines that depend on pressure-induced heat to ignite vapors, those were the problems Moon preferred.

"We will go to the ship then," Mr. Lee said. "But we will wait awhile first. We will give the police time to go to bed."

Osa, Rice, and Moon waited in the room under the floor. Captain Teele and Lum Lee had bowed them out with smiles and good wishes, and they had climbed back down the stairway, with Mr. Tung lighting their way with a carbide lamp. He left it behind for them.

The lamp hissed and buzzed and added its peculiar chemical odor to the various perfumes the room already offered. But it was better than waiting in the dark. Moon resumed his position on the sofa, sighed, and relaxed. Rice was relating his misadventures in the jungle. Osa was listening. They would wake him when they needed him.

"Why not one of the beds?" Osa asked. "You would be more comfortable."

"I really don't know," Moon said. "I know you're right. I think it's because I have the idea that the lady should get the bed and the man should sleep on the sofa. Or because

I'm stubborn. Or maybe I just enjoy having these cramps in my leg muscles." He thought of another theory that had something to do with his headache. But Osa had lost patience with him. She was talking to George Rice.

"Did you see how they keep the water out of this room? When the high tide comes, these boards pull down into these slots and—see how tightly they fit."

Moon didn't hear the rest of it. He was asleep again.

Special to the ***New York Times***

SAIGON, South Vietnam, April 24—Panic is clearly visible in Saigon now as thousands of Vietnamese try desperately to find ways to flee their country.

Few exits are left and most involve knowing Americans. U.S. Air Force C-141 transports took off all day and night from Tan Son Nhut air base with lucky passengers en route to Clark Air Force Base in the Philippines.

The Fifteenth Day

April 27, 1975

IT TOOK MOON A FEW MOMENTS to focus well enough to read the numbers on his watch: 1:07 A.M. When he blinked, it became 1:08.

Mr. Tung was holding back the bamboo screen. In front of it, five squared timbers had been dropped into place across the opening in the wall. The tide must have come in, because Moon could see the prow of a little boat nudged up against the planks.

"Be careful," Mr. Tung said. "I think maybe you will have to get yourself just a little bit wet."

Careful or not, Moon was soaked to about six inches

above the knees. Cool water. It helped jar him awake. Mr. Tung stepped from the topmost timber into the boat, agile as a monkey. Captain Teele, now wearing a grimy Beatles T-shirt and pants that seemed to be made of canvas, sat amidships, holding a long-handled paddle.

Mr. Tung said, "We go now" in English and something in some other language. Teele slid them soundlessly down the bamboo tunnel and out into open water. Moon could see now that Mr. Tung's hideaway was located behind the Puerto Princesa wharves, and once away from it there was less effort to maintain total silence. Teele allowed his sculling oar to splash. Moon scooped up a handful of water and splashed it on his face. He felt lousy. Tension. Change of food and water. Too little sleep. Someday he would lie down on something soft and sleep forever. If anyone came to wake him he would strangle them.

Captain Teele sculled past the barnacle-encrusted pillars supporting the dock, past what seemed to be some sort of naval auxiliary vessel, rusted and in need of paint. A dim light burned on its mast, but there was no sign that anyone aboard was awake. Probably an old U.S. Navy minesweeper, Moon guessed, turned over to the Philippine navy. They passed under the bow of a barge that smelled of turpentine and dead fish. Then the white shape of the *Glory of the Sea* was just ahead.

Moon had always loved cars and airplanes. In the army, he had even come to feel a rapport with tanks. Nothing that floated had ever interested him, though. But now the sleek white shape of the *Glory of the Sea* rose above its reflection in the still water, and Moon saw the beauty of it. Someone had built this thing with pride. He looked at Captain Teele, now steering their little boat carefully to the boarding ladder. The captain was smiling. As well he should be, Moon thought. A captain should love this ship.

At the moment, however, Moon was feeling no such sentiment himself. He was feeling faintly seasick.

Nor, once on board, did the engine inspire any affection. It was an old Euclid, probably salvaged out of a landing craft left on a beach somewhere after World War II. A burly young man, barefoot and wearing only walking shorts, was standing beside it watching Moon approach, his face full of doubt. His hair hung in a long black braid. A design that suggested either a dragon or a tiger was tattooed on his shoulder, apparently by an amateur.

"Mr. Suhuannaphum," Captain Teele said, "Mr. Moon." Mr. Suhuannaphum bowed over his hands and pointed to the diesel. "Old," he said.

"Do you speak English?"

Mr. Suhuannaphum looked nervously at Captain Teele, seeking guidance. Receiving none, he shrugged, produced a self-deprecatory smile, and said something in a language entirely new to Moon.

"Thai," Captain Teele said, and made a wry face, as if that explained everything.

"Okay," Moon said. "Let's see what we have here."

Moon discovered very quickly that what they had here was very close to the diagnosis he'd made sight unseen. Something was wrong with the fuel-injection system. Apparently Mr. Suhuannaphum had already reached that same conclusion and had done the preliminary dismantling. The injection system was mechanical, a system long since replaced by electronics. Archaic or not, it seemed to work, as Mr. Suhuannaphum demonstrated. At low pressure, diesel oil emerged evenly from each injection jet. Then, with his face registering first surprise and then disapproval, Mr. Suhuannaphum advanced the throttle. He gestured angrily.

Fuel spurted from one jet. The others died away to a trickle. *"Alors,"* Mr. Suhuannaphum said. "Kaput."

"Do it again," Moon said.

Mr. Suhuannaphum stared at him. Moon devised the proper hand signal.

Mr. Suhuannaphum repeated the process. This time he said, "Broke."

Moon thought about it. He removed four screws, lifted a plate, removed the filter from the only jet that operated properly, blew through it, handed it to Mr. Suhuannaphum, and made washing motions. Mr. Suhuannaphum looked surprised, but he washed it.

With that done, Moon reinstalled the filter and replaced the plate. Simple enough, but would it work?

"Start it," Moon said, gesturing to Mr. Suhuannaphum. Mr. Suhuannaphum's expression formed a question.

"Let's see," Moon said, trying to think of a way to explain to this Thai why the old injection systems worked in this perverse way, increasing the pressure when the filter was dirty and thus starving the jets whose filters were clean. He didn't understand it himself.

"Just start it." he said.

It started, but it had started before. The question was whether the tendency to cut out with acceleration had been solved. Now it thumped with slow regularity, like a healthy heartbeat.

Moon had an eye on his watch, giving it a little time to warm. And thinking that if he had fixed it, and he probably had, he had once again cut his own throat. The condemned electrician repairing the electric chair. Moon Mathias, jack-of-all-trades, fixing the engine that would take him into the hands of the Khmer Rouge, who beat people like him to death with sticks.

It was a little after three A.M. and Mr. Suhuannaphum was looking at him anxiously, awaiting instructions.

"Okay," Moon said, "go for it. Give it the gas. V*rooom,*

vrooom, vrooom." He leaned back against the rail, fighting an urgent need to throw up.

The old Euclid diesel went *vroooooom, vroooooom.* Mr. Suhuannaphum eased off the throttle, clapped his hands, and produced a joyful shout. Captain Teele emerged from the darkness, grinning broadly. "Yes!" he said.

"Well, hell," Moon said. "Nothing to stop us now, I guess. Here we go to meet the boogeymen."

And with that, Moon Mathias leaned over the rail and became thoroughly sick.

SAIGON, South Vietnam, April 26 (Havas)—Some of the many signs of panic and desperation in South Vietnam:

Saigon drugstores are sold out of sleeping pills and other medications useful for suicides.

An American economic aid worker is offered $10,000 to marry the pregnant wife of a Vietnamese co-worker so she can qualify for escape.

Deserting ARVN paratroopers seize a transport plane, force the passengers off and fly away.

The Fifteenth Day to, Alas, the Eighteenth Day

April 27–30, 1975

IT WAS EMBARRASSING. He remembered that part of it clearly enough. But much of the rest was either hazy or mixed with the confusing dreams that high fever provokes.

He recalled sitting on the deck after the heaving of his stomach finally wrenched to a stop. He recalled trembling with a chill, and the voice of Mr. Tung saying something in his oddly accented English about this seasickness, this mal de mer as Mr. Tung called it, being unusually premature, and laughing at his joke. And then he remembered the angry voice of Mr. Lee, speaking in a language that might have been Tagalog or Chinese or almost anything but English.

They took him belowdecks then, Captain Teele helping him down a narrow ladder. He'd sprawled on a bunk. And there was Osa van Winjgaarden leaning over him, asking what he thought was the matter, asking about pain, about what might be causing this, and he'd said something like it must have been something he'd eaten, and she had said, "I hope so."

She'd stood over him, he remembered that clearly, frowning at him, holding the back of her hand against his forehead, taking his wrist and checking his pulse, looking worried.

"You are practicing medicine without a license," Moon had said. The fever was back, and Osa's hand felt cold on his skin. "If I have to throw up anymore, I'll call my lawyer and have him file a malpractice—"

But he didn't finish. Didn't feel like trying to be funny. Felt, in fact, like closing his eyes and leaving all this behind. And so he had.

And now it was—what? Three days later? And almost sundown, so that would make it three and a half days.

"Well, it's Wednesday," Osa said. "And we left Puerto Princesa Sunday morning. So, yes. Three days you've been sick."

Moon had just eaten a bowl of soup made of rice and something else—probably some sort of fish. It was very thin and warm and delicious. It sat uneasily in his stomach. But it was going to be all right, he could tell that. In fact, he could use another bowl.

"Good soup," he said. "Excellent soup."

"You should wait a little while," Osa said. "Until we see what happens with your digestion."

He was sitting on a roll of canvas, leaning back on a burlap sack full of something heavy—maybe rice. A bank of dark clouds closed off the horizon to the left, but the sky above was clear and the setting sun felt wonderful. Climbing up the ladder had left Moon feeling weak. But his head no longer ached. His stomach seemed to be dealing handsomely with the soup. No more nausea. A fresh breeze blew across his face and hummed through the rigging above him. The sea was dark blue, and Moon felt absolutely wonderful. I am actually going to find Ricky's kid. I'm actually going to walk into the room and hand this child to Victoria Mathias and say, Well, Mother, here she is. Here's your granddaughter. And then—

He exhaled a huge sigh.

Osa was leaning against the railing, frowning at him. "You're all right?"

"I'm fine," he said. "Hungry. I feel like you should be telling me what I've been missing. First, where are we?"

"Well," Osa said, "we're on the *Glory of the Sea* and we are going to the mouth of the Mekong and I think we get there very soon. Tonight, I think. Captain Teele is just waiting until he believes it is a little safer. Otherwise, I think we have told you everything."

"You did, I guess. But a lot of it—" He tapped his forehead with a finger. "You know. It's all confused. I remember hearing people talking about the Filipino minesweeper. Rice, I think it was, and Mr. Lee. And I seem to remember the minesweeper didn't chase us. And you told me the North Viets were almost at Saigon. Or maybe I dreamed that. And something about an air base being bombed." He shrugged.

"I think I told you the airport had been shelled and no airplanes were landing. And the Vietnamese had put in a new president but the Communists wouldn't negotiate with him."

"I hoped maybe the good guys would have won while I was asleep," Moon said. "Nothing good seems to happen for our side out here while I'm awake."

"I think it's even worse since you got sick. The Communists are winning everywhere."

"Maybe that will solve a problem for us," he said. "I mean, no more war. Peace. Maybe your brother will be safe now."

Osa didn't react to this. She was staring out toward the setting sun.

"Well," he said, "who knows? Why not?"

"Mr. Teele said the Khmer Rouge radio didn't sound very peaceful. He said they announced they had executed eleven government ministers."

"You know how that is," Moon said. "Things like that get exagerated in the excitement. The press hears they've been shot and they're just locked up."

"The Khmer Rouge decapitated them," Osa said. "And the radio was ordering people in the city to turn in all the college professors, lawyers, and doctors. Business people. Everybody like that. And he heard another radio station broadcasting terrible reports. I think it was from a freighter sailing down the Mekong. It said all the people in some of the villages had been killed."

Osa was looking away from him, to where cloud shadows were making their patterns on the sea.

"Awful," she said, and shuddered, and then was silent.

Moon could think of nothing to say.

"Worse even than what I was telling you when you were sick."

"I don't remember much of it," Moon said.

"Don't," she said, and wiped her sleeve across her face. She turned toward him.

"Part of the time you were delirious. Did you know that?" Suddenly she smiled. "Did you know you were calling me Debbie?"

"Oh," Moon said.

"And talking to your mother quite a bit. You must have dreamed you'd done something very bad. You were telling her you were sorry. Several times you said that."

"Well," Moon said, "several times I did things that were bad." Which really wasn't what Osa van Winjgaarden wanted to talk about.

"This Debbie, I think she must be your sweetheart."

"What did I say?" And, as soon as he askd, wished he hadn't. So, apparently, did Osa. She looked slightly abashed.

"Well, personal things sometimes."

Time to change the subject. "I remember hearing you talking to Mr. Lee about getting me off the ship and to a doctor, and Mr. Lee saying there wasn't a doctor, except the prison doctor," Moon said. "And you said prison was better than being buried at sea. And I remember agreeing with you."

"I thought you had dengue fever," Osa said. "That is very bad business. You die from that."

Moon had a sudden surprising thought. "But you would have gone to prison too. Not just me."

Osa shrugged.

"And I think I remember somebody giving me sort of a bath," Moon said. "With a wet towel or something, turning me over. Washing everywhere. Even behind my ears. I think it was you. Or was I dreaming?"

"It was to make you more comfortable," Osa said, still looking out at the darkening sea.

"So I don't guess I have any secrets anymore," Moon said.

"No secrets?"

"I mean, I guess you know I am a little bit too fat around the middle. And have a scar on my hip. So forth."

"Oh, yes. How did you get that terrible scar?"

Moon was silent for a moment. "When I turned over the jeep."

Some slight variation in the wind caused the sail above them to make a flapping sound. Straight ahead, and high, four sea birds were circling. Long pointed wings. Albatross, perhaps, if they flew over the South China Sea. Gooney birds.

"And a man was killed in it," Osa said slowly. "The friend who died in the accident you had. You talked about him when your fever was so high that first day." She looked at him, face sad. "I think he must have been a very good friend. You grieve for him."

"Yes," Moon said. "I do."

Rice appeared at the top of the ladder, looked at them, climbed out, and walked toward the stern, where Captain Teele was doing something at the wheel.

"What did I say to my mother?"

"I didn't listen," Osa said. "Of course not."

"But you heard enough to know I was talking to her. What did I say?"

He decided she wasn't going to answer. Then she said, "I already told you. You said you were sorry."

Rice was walking up.

"You decide you're going to live?"

"With a little bit of luck," Moon said. "And a little more of that soup."

Rice sat on the canvas beside him. "Teele's going to wait until about an hour before dawn. Then he'll haul in the sail and go as close to the mouth as he can get. We'll take the rubber boat and ride on into the new R. M. Air base. Then I'll fire up a copter and we'll get this business over with."

Moon didn't comment. The soup suddenly felt heavy in his stomach.

"If we're lucky, Bob Yager will be there. If he is, we can get maybe four or five of those copters out of there. You know, fly two of them over to Thailand, leave one, fly back in the other, take a couple more. Keep doing it until we got all of 'em out that are ready to go."

It took Moon about a second or two to understand the implications of this. What was a military helicopter worth? The army paid about a million dollars each, he guessed, depending on the model. Used, and a fire sale situation, maybe three or four hundred thousand each. Maybe more. No way to guess.

"Yager," Moon said. "I thought he was on the business end of things."

"He was Ricky's executive officer back when they were both in the service. He'd resigned his commission before Ricky did. Went into some sort of business in Saigon and Phnom Penh, the way I heard it, and then came along right after Ricky started R. M. Air. Chief pilot and deal maker. Last I heard he was in Malaysia, setting up a base down the peninsula for when the South Viets gave up."

"You told us there wouldn't be any pilots left," Moon said. "Remember telling us that?"

Rice's face showed no trace of embarrassment. "Did I say that? I guess I did, didn't I. I was thinking you folks would have just left me there in prison and gone on about your business."

"You're right about that," Moon said.

"It's better this way anyway. First place, Yager will probably be gone by now. So I didn't lie."

Moon shrugged.

"No use leaving those copters for the Commies," Rice said. "I'd rather blow 'em up. And from what the radio is saying, there ain't going to be no Army of the Republic of Vietnam after a few more days. They owe Ricky money now, and they'll be owing a lot more."

"You going to sell them? Is that the plan?"

"We could. But why not expand R. M. Air to Thailand or Malaysia?" Rice asked. "I guess it's your company now. You being Ricky's brother, I guess you inherit it. There's sure as hell plenty of business out here. Hauling things around. And people."

"First we go get Ricky's daughter," Moon said. "And take care of this other business."

"Sure," Rice said. "First things first." He looked thoughtful. "You still have that map?"

"It's with my stuff," Moon said.

Osa brought it, and they spread it on the deck.

"Okay," Rice said. "Here we are." He tapped a fingertip on the blue of the South China Sea a half inch north of the westernmost of the seven mouths of the mighty Mekong. "When it gets a little darker, Captain Teele will pull in close as he can safely get this ship, and we'll run the shore boat up to here." He moved his fingertip to a dot just upstream from the mouth. "Long Phu is the village. Ricky was starting to move things down there the last I saw of things, so it should pretty much all be there by now. The ARVN general Ricky was working with owned a place down there, a dock sticking out into the Mekong with a warehouse. Had living quarters and a bunch of big sheds Ricky had 'em convert into repair hangars."

He grinned at Moon.

"I think the general had been into smuggling. Probably still was. Anyway, when Ricky wanted a safer place for

R. M. Air he worked out a deal with this fella. So we'll pull in there about daylight and see what we find. If R. M. Air is still operating, then no problem. We just take a copter and get our business done. If everybody's gone but some of the birds are left behind, we'll fuel one up and get on with it. Or, if they didn't get the birds moved down there then"—Rice moved his fingertip an inch up the river—"we sail on up the Mekong to the R. M. Air hangars at the airstrip outside Can Tho and take a copter from there."

Rice paused, studying the map. Far out, near the horizon, Moon saw a red light reflecting from a sail. Then two more. Small craft, six or seven miles away, he guessed, and apparently outward bound.

"I'd guess Bob Yager will still be there," he said. "Wherever the copters are. Yager would stick around until the last dog died."

"Yeah," Moon said.

"Sure," Rice said. "Yager will be there. If he's not, we can do it just as well without him."

"You make it sound so easy," Osa said. "Can you find anything in the darkness?"

Rice shrugged. "Sure. Why not?"

Moon was going to say, Because maybe the Vietcong will be shooting at us, but Osa answered the question.

"I remember flying up the river that day you took me to my brother's mission," she said. "It was like flying over green wilderness. Everywhere you looked you could see light reflecting off the water. All tangled up with streams and irrigation canals. Like a maze. I'd think you would get lost. Easy enough, maybe, in a helicopter where you can see the sea behind you and the mountains up ahead. But down on the water in a little boat how could anybody tell? Not in the dark."

"Anybody couldn't," Rice said. "I can. I used to live on that goddam river. Three hitches in the Brown Water Navy. With the Game Warden project."

Rice looked from Osa to Moon and back, waiting for the question.

"Game Warden?" Moon said.

"The navy called the whole operation Market Garden," Rice said. "And the river patrol part down here was Game Warden. The idea being to keep the VC from running their sampans up and down the rivers, hauling troops, ammunition, all that. The navy bought a bunch of little fiberglass boats. Shallow draft, hold four or five crewmen, and do maybe twenty-five knots, and we'd run up and down the rivers and the creeks and canals and raise hell with the VC."

Rice became aware that his pride was showing and stopped. "Shows you how crazy I was," he added.

"When was that?" Moon asked.

"I started with the project in 'sixty-seven. Transferred in. Did two hitches in the little PBRs—anybody but the navy would call 'em River Patrol Boats but the navy made 'em Patrol Boats River. Then I shifted over to the *Floyd County,* one of the LSTs they converted as base ships for the boats. We'd anchor way out in the channel and be mother hen for the PBRs. That's how I got into copters," Rice said. "They fitted the *Floyd* out with a copter deck and we played mama for the Huey gunships."

"How'd you learn to fly?"

"Went along as crew," Rice said. "I was a chief petty officer, a regular navy lifer. You can do pretty much what you want to do after you learn the system. I got friendly with the pilots. Watched how they did it. Took over when the pilot wanted to eat his lunch or take a break. That's how I met your brother."

"He hired you out of the navy?"

"I was quitting anyway," Rice said. "Had in my twenty, and the navy was phasing out to go home. I'd met Ricky when we were transferring our Hueys over to the Vietnam navy and he was doing their maintenance. I told him I didn't want to go back to the States—nothing for me there, and he said stick around, he could use me. Yager was already part of Ricky's team by then, and he sort of gave me the finishing touches." Rice laughed. "Like how to put one down without bouncing it."

Captain Teele was standing by the mast now, studying the sails through binoculars.

"Okay," Moon said. "We get in. We get a copter. Now where do we go to get the child?"

"Here's where we go look," Rice said. He moved his finger westward from Can Tho, across the Cambodian border, into a range of hills the mapmaker had identified as the Elephant Mountains.

"See this little road here along the coast? Little dot there called Kampot. Stream runs through it and dumps into the Gulf of Siam. Well, we fly five miles up the coast beyond that, then turn right and head due north, right up the ridge. Seventeen miles, you come to a series of clearings. Four of 'em. And in the fourth one, a little village. Ten, maybe twelve buildings, cluster of little terraced rice paddies."

Rice looked up at Moon. "You got anything to write with?"

"Afraid not," Moon said. Back in the prison, on the other side of the moat, Rice hadn't been able to remember how to reach this village. He'd said it was something he'd have to sort of find somehow. He'd only remembered the name was Vin Ba and it was near the Vietnam border.

"Here," Osa said, and handed Rice a pen.

Rice made a tiny X on the map. And out in the Gulf wrote *Vin Ba—four clearings in a row.*

Osa was looking over his shoulder. "I think that's not too far from the village where my brother—"

"Right about here," Rice said. "On this next ridge. There's a little village down in the valley—maybe a couple of hundred people with some terraced rice paddies. And up on the ridge in the forest there's a Montagnard settlement where Osa's brother has his little clinic. Osa will remember it." He made a second X, folded the map, and handed it to Moon.

Lum Lee was standing beside Teele now, looking through the binoculars. Without them, Moon could now make out five craft, all small, three with sails.

Rice was looking at Moon, expression curious. "What are you thinking about this business?"

Moon shrugged.

"Scared?"

"Yeah. Matter of fact, I am."

Rice laughed. "But you'll go on in," he said. "Ricky told me about you."

From behind them came the voice of Mr. Lee. "On the radio just a minute ago they were saying that Pol Pot has made a broadcast. They will cleanse Cambodia of oppression and corruption by returning their country to Zero Year. They will go back to the simple, clean ways. No more parasite predators living in the filth of the cities. The cities will be emptied. People will go back to the land."

"My God," Osa said. "What will that mean?"

"Maybe it is political rhetoric," Mr. Lee said. "But we were listening to Radio Jakarta earlier. They said Pol Pot's army was evacuating Phnom Penh. The soldiers were forcing everybody out of their houses and marching them out into the country."

Rice was grinning, the sunset red on his face. "We're just in time," he said. "Everybody is going to be too busy with their own worries to pay attention to us."

"Yes," Mr. Lee said, "maybe so." And he made a sweeping gesture to take the seven little craft now visible in the dying light. "Just in time. In a few hours we are going in. Everybody else is coming out."

RED FORCES WITHIN MILE OF SAIGON
AS TANKS AND ARTILLERY CLOSE IN

—*New York Times,* April 28, 1975

The Nineteenth Day

May 1, 1975

AFTER SUNDOWN the rain had begun. It was warm, soft, and steady, with a mild breeze behind it. But now, maybe an hour before dawn, the clouds broke up again. The full monsoon would be here a little later, Mr. Lee told them. In maybe a week. Then the rain would be steady. But tonight the first third of the moon hung high in the west. There were stars overhead, and just in front of them was the white line of beach and above it the black wall of shoreline vegetation.

Osa was huddled near the stern of what Captain Teele called in his odd mixture of English and Dutch his "shure boot." She was talking to Mr. Lee, who seemed to have perfect sea legs and rarely sat down even when this awkward craft was rolling through the heavy swells out in the blue water. Mr. Suhuannaphum sat beside her—assigned to take the shore boat back to the *Glory of the Sea* but demoted now to the role of passenger. When they neared shore and moved into the brown water flowing out of the Mekong, they entered Rice's territory. Rice had taken over the navigation.

"Here on in we need to keep it quiet," Rice told them. "Normally at night you wouldn't worry much, because the devils come out after dark and these delta farmers like to stay in their hooches with the doors closed. But now things ain't normal."

Things weren't normal, Rice explained, because the Vietnam navy personnel who took over the U.S. Navy patrol boats and their bases were mostly refugees from the north end of the nation.

"They came down here because they hated the Commies, and because they hate the Commies, Saigon figured it could trust them in patrol boats," Rice said. "You know, not to take the boats and go over to the other side. Anyhow, the point is these guys are mostly Christians, or maybe a different kind of Buddhist, whose demons stay home at night. So they patrol just they way we trained 'em to. Sneak along in the dark, listening. Maybe turn off the engine and just float. Hear an infiltrator, turn on the light, and zap 'em. Taking the night away from the Cong, we called it."

"But now," Osa said, "it is so dark I don't know how you can possibly see where you're going."

"You don't exactly see it," Rice said. "Actually, you sort of feel it. Do you notice how choppy it is under the boat now? Just *bump-bump-bump?* No more upsy-downsy rolling from the waves coming in. Here that's being canceled out by the current, the brown water coming out. So when it's dark, you just keep in the middle of the current best you can. And if you think you're lost, you use these night binoculars."

"But so many different mouths to this river," Osa said. "I think they called it 'Nine Dragons.'"

"Two of 'em are silted up and closed. They oughta call

it 'Seven Dragons,' but with the gooks nine is the lucky number."

Moon now could see that the trees lining the shore were some sort of palms. Soon their crowns were outlined against the stars, almost overhead. And then they were past the palm. Inland. The air felt different: hotter, heavy with humidity. Moon was sweating. The soft sound of the current now drowned the murmur of the idling engine.

The sky lightened a little with a false dawn. Moon saw that the forest lining the river was no longer palms. And no longer alive. The jungle was leafless, dead. Barren limbs formed a black tracery against the horizon. He pointed that out to Osa.

"Agent Orange," Osa said. "I think that's what killed everything."

"Only We Can Prevent a Forest," Rice said, spacing the words. "That was the slogan of the C-One-thirty guys who dropped the stuff. They'd zap the jungle so we could see, then we'd come along and zap the Cong."

The smell of the sea was gone now. Moon's nostrils picked up the aroma of flowers, of decayed vegetation, of rancid mud, the perfume of sandalwood and smoke. Sweat ran down from his eyebrows into the corners of his eyes.

Rice throttled down the engine. "Better be quiet now," he said. "This one we're in they call Cu'a Cung Loi, I think it is. Probably means ninth mouth, or something like that. Anyway, it's the mouth furthest from Saigon. Full of Viet-cong before we got 'em—"

Mr. Suhuannaphum was whispering something.

"Something's coming," Osa said in a low, low voice. "Can you hear it?"

Moon heard it. The sound of someone crying. A child's wail. A tinny rattling. Hushed voices. The creak of wood on wood. The steady thumping of a heavy engine.

Rice cut the motor.

It was off somewhere to their right. Coming toward them but farther out in the channel.

"There," Osa whispered, pointing.

A dark shape, looming above the water. And then it came out of the shadows into the moon path: a sampan, Moon guessed. It had a high round bow and a roof from which the light reflected. Probably tin, Moon thought. It moved steadily past them, loaded with whispers, with someone sobbing and someone scolding, the sounds of sorrow and despair. And then they could see only its stern, quickly disappearing again into the shadows of the mangrove trees.

"Well," Rice said, "I wish them luck." He restarted the motor.

"Refugees from that dreadful war," Osa said. "Probably no place to go. They must be frightened."

"Scared to death," Rice said. "Ghosts are out in the dark at night. They call 'em *kwei,* the Hungry Ones. They're the spirits of folks who die without any children to take care of their bones. They get out of the underworld after dark and go around causing bad luck, making people sick."

"And us," Osa said. "I think you should also wish us to be lucky."

"I think we're already being lucky," Moon said.

About dawn they saw a flare arc into the sky, across the river and maybe a mile to the east. Two more flares rose and died away, and then there was the sudden sound of a machine gun. Moon reached out his hand, touched Osa's arm, and she rewarded him with a strained smile. But the gunfire lasted only a few seconds. It aroused frogs and night birds and provoked challenging calls from the same sort of lizards he'd heard on Palawan Island. That, too, quickly died away.

Silence then. Only the purr of the motor, the hiss of the hull sliding through the brown water, the small clatter when Mr. Suhuannaphum shifted his feet. Moon noticed the night was fading fast. He could make out the shape of mangrove trunks, see the pattern of the current on the water surface, discern flotsam moving with the stream. Beside the bank ahead, a man-made shape loomed. It seemed to be a platform raised above the riverbank on stilts with an odd shape built on it.

Rice noticed him staring at it.

"Used to be a house," Rice said. "The VC used it, and we flushed them out and burned it."

The sky was reddening now in the east. A rooster crowed somewhere nearby, exuberant. And awoke another rooster. A dog barked. Something bulky was floating past, a hundred yards out in the current. Cloth. A human body too far out in the river to determine gender. And beyond it something else that looked like a floating bundle. Another body? Too far away to be sure. He glanced at Osa. She was looking inland. So was Rice.

"There's a few rice paddies back there behind the mangroves," Rice said. "Eight or nine hooches, best I remember. The ARVN boys thought they might be Vietcong, but then they thought everybody might be Vietcong. It's the way they stayed alive."

"Do you think the army will still be here?" Osa said. "They must know they've lost the war."

"I don't know," Rice said. "They had this Yellow Tiger Battalion stationed here. Part of an airborne regiment. If they were normal ARVN, I think they'd just shoot some civilians and steal their clothes and pretend to be just plain folks. But these Tigers were tough cookies. Had a colonel named Ngo Diem. Supposed to be mean as a snake." He chuckled. "Even the marines liked 'em, and the marines didn't like nobody."

From far across the river came another sound. It sounded to Moon like a truck engine starting.

"We got to stick close to the bank now," Rice said. "Around that bend behind that bunch of palms there's an old LST anchored. LST," he repeated. "Landing Ship Tank. The *U.S.S. Pott County.* They anchored it out there and used it as a base for our river patrol boats. Then in 'seventy-three they turned it over to the Vietnam navy."

He looked at Moon.

"What do you think? Should we check in with the good gooks, tell 'em what we're doing here?"

"Maybe we should," Moon said, doubtfully. "We're in here illegally, of course. But maybe they'd be too busy this morning to think about that. What do you think?"

"I think first we should sort of take a look and see what we can see," Rice said. "Could be Charley's taken the place over by now."

They took the first look from almost a mile away. Mr. Suhuannaphum extracted a set of very large, very heavy binoculars from somewhere, steadied them against the gunwale of the shore boat, and spent a long time looking. Moon could make out nothing in the dim light except flat dark shapes far out from the distant shore. Mr. Suhuannaphum, however, occasionally muttered under his breath, or sighed, or made disapproving sounds. Finally he handed the binoculars to Rice.

"What did you see?" Moon asked him.

Mr. Suhuannaphum grinned, struggled for words, shrugged, said: "I think bang." He threw up his hands to demonstrate. "Some fire. Nobody home." He shrugged again and added, "Maybe so."

Rice was more expressive but less informative. "Well, shit," he said. He put down the glasses. "Let's get a little closer."

He maneuvered their boat out into the rougher current, angling upstream. Moon picked up the binoculars. First he noticed the smoke. Not much of it, but it rose from the midsection of the *Pott County,* and the *Pott County* seemed to have tilted sharply toward them. He could see the flat deck of a helicopter pad and a half dozen little boats lined against a system of docks tied to the ship. There was no sign of life.

"Sons of bitches," Rice said. "You gotta protect those things from shore attacks. Got to have outposts out there to keep people with rocket launchers from doing that to you."

"Is that what happened?" Moon said. "Hit with a rocket?"

"Probably half a dozen rockets, which set the sucker on fire, so the PBR crews got in their boats and headed for safety."

Moon said, "But they're still there."

"Four or five," Rice said. "Usually there'd be about thirty tied up at the docks. Probably they had a bunch of people killed in the attack. I guess they took as many as they needed." He sighed. "Well, hell," he said. "Let's get a little safer," and he turned their boat back toward the shore.

It was almost full light now, the eastern horizon bright. Upstream, Moon saw a little boat sailing along the far bank, tall mast in front, short one behind. Behind it, farther out in the current, two other boats moved downriver. Rice accelerated the engine to full speed.

"Well, here we are," he said, and pointed to the left bank ahead. A large concrete building stood there, tile-roofed and raised on the stilts that the rise and fall of the Mekong made necessary. A wharf extended from the building into the river, and behind the building stood a row of bamboo structures roofed with tin and surrounded by a high fence surmounted with barbed wire.

"If our luck holds like it's been, Yager will be waiting here," Rice said. "And he'll have a bird all fueled up, and we'll get going on this before the sun gets hot."

Their luck didn't hold. Yager wasn't there. Neither was anyone else. No one came out of the building to greet them as they docked. Rice looped the anchor rope of the shore boat over a piling. Old Mr. Lee hopped onto the planking, helped Osa out, and offered Moon a hand. Rice tossed their gear ashore. Mr. Suhuannaphum reversed the outboard engine and began backing the shore boat away.

"I'll go see if anybody's home," Rice said, and trotted down the dock and into the warehouse.

Mr. Suhuannaphum was also in a hurry. He held up his left hand with his thumb folded in and three fingers extended and shouted something that sounded like "Tree dee."

"Right," Mr. Lee shouted back and held up three fingers too.

"What's that about?" Moon asked.

"That's the promise Captain Teele made," Mr. Lee said. "He will keep *Glory of the Sea* out in international waters for three days. And then he will come back to the mouth of the Mekong to look for us."

"If something goes wrong," Moon said.

Mr. Lee nodded. "Just in case the wind and water have not been right for us."

And then the motor on Mr. Suhuannaphum's shore boat was going *vrooom*. Racing down the river, back toward the clean, clear blue water of the South China Sea. Toward the *Glory of the Sea*. Toward safety.

Special to the *New York Times*

BANGKOK, Thailand, April 28—In an implicit warning to both North Vietnam and international relief organizations, the new government of Cambodia served notice that no "foreign intervention" would be allowed in the country.

The warning was broadcast over Phnom Penh radio and came as refugees flooding into Thailand reported mass executions by Khmer Rouge troops of those accused of being "exploiters of the people."

Morning, the Nineteenth Day

May 1, 1975

WITH THE MORNING LIGHT UPON IT, the Mekong was busy despite the rain. Little boats were everywhere, being sailed, rowed, poled, pushed along with outboard motors. Moon sat on a bundle of something wrapped in burlap, hungrily eating a sticky mixture of rice and pork with his fingers and thinking about the bodies he'd seen floating past in this morning's darkness.

"It's no use trying to be neat," Osa said. "Eating with your fingers neatly, it is simply not possible."

Osa was sitting on the next bale, eating exactly the same rice mixture neatly.

The rain pattered steadily on the tin roof above them, dripped from the warehouse eaves, splashed in the puddles formed on the dock. Moon heard a thumping sound, far away but too regular to be thunder. He recognized the sound of artillery fire, or perhaps heavy mortars. According to Moon's map, the only major town upstream was Can Tho, where Highway One bridged this arm of the Mekong. Perhaps they were fighting for that. Anyway, it must be a lot quieter here than around Saigon. The radio Rice had turned up loud in the hangar was full of bad news. The Tan Son Nhut air base had been bombed. That was next door to the capital, and apparently the planes that bombed it were U.S.-built fighter bombers—either turncoat pilots of the Vietnam Air Force or planes captured on the ground up north when Phan Thiet and its air base were taken. It didn't seem to matter much. One radio report said ARVN marines had seized a C-130 trying to take off from Nha Trang with a load of refugees, forced the civilians out, and flown away. Big Minh, the new president since yesterday, was on the air. The reporter on Rice's wavelength said he appealed to all citizens to be courageous, not to run away, not to abandon the tombs of their ancestors.

Everything was coming apart. Moon didn't want to think about it.

What time would it be in Los Angeles? Evening. If she was lucky, if Dr. Serna had made no mistakes, his mother would be recovering now. Her heart pumping blood through unclogged bypasses, her surgical incisions healing. She might be out of the intensive care unit, in a regular room, reading the *L.A. Times* about disaster in Southeast Asia, watching television news, perhaps thinking of how alone she was, wondering what had happened to her unreliable elder son. Had Dr. Serna given her his promise? And what would she think of it?

Or the other possibility. Messages awaiting him at the hotel in Puerto Princesa and the embassy in Manila regretting to inform him that Victoria Mathias Morick had not survived the operation. That would release her, at last, from her burdens.

"You look sad," Osa said. "I think you are remembering something unhappy."

"Oh, no," Moon said. "Just thinking."

"Of your mother," Osa said. "I remember today is the day you said they would have her in the surgery. She is all alone. Of course you worry about her."

"There's nothing I could do if I were there."

"You would hold her hand," Osa said.

"I should finish here and go back and help Rice," Moon said. Actually there wasn't much he could do right now to help. Rice was stripping the heavy stuff out of the copter he had chosen for their rescue project. There had seemed to be plenty to choose from in the R. M. Air repair hangar, ranging from a little Cayuse too small for their purpose to a huge banana-shaped Vertol Chinook with its twin rotors, which was obviously too large. In between were four Hueys, familiar to Moon from his days with the Armored, an ugly Cobra in camouflage paint, and a Bell Kiowa. All stood on wheeled dollies. Some were obviously in the throes of repair, with panels removed and parts missing. The Kiowa seemed ready to go, but Rice had picked one of the Hueys. It had apparently been left behind by the U.S. Navy, and its original Marine Corps markings showed through the Vietnamese paint job.

"I remember this one," Rice had said. "The radar's off waiting for parts to come down from Saigon, but we won't need radar, and these navy models were modified to increase the range."

Moon had said he hadn't thought they would need the range either. Weren't they just hopping over the border thirty minutes into Cambodia?

"You hear that artillery upriver a while ago?" Rice had asked. "We may not be able to get back here to refuel." What then? Moon had said. And Rice had shrugged and said the best bet would probably be to try for Thailand. So now Rice was removing the machine gun mounts and, as he put it, "everything else that us peace-loving neutrals don't need to get us the hell out of here." The less weight, the more miles, Rice had said.

Now Moon was aware that Osa had been staring at him. "Or maybe you were thinking of your sweetheart," she said. "You must be missing her."

"No," Moon said. He chuckled and shook his head, thinking how Osa, who often was so uncannily right about what was on his mind, could be so wrong on this one. He tried to imagine how he'd deal with Debbie in this damp, odorous warehouse. Or how Debbie would deal with him. And with Rice, and Mr. Lee and the others.

"Not missing her?" Osa was looking surprised. He guessed she hadn't expected his amusement.

"It's not the kind of relationship you'd normally expect. I own a house. The bank and I own it. I rent out two of the rooms: one to a man who works with me at the newspaper and one to Debbie. Well—" He couldn't think how to finish this explanation. How much had he said when he had that fever?

"Just sex then?" Osa said, looking very wise. "I don't think so. When you were so sick you talked about when you would get married. You talked about love."

Moon found himself embarrassed. "Did I?"

Osa too. Her face was flushed. "I apologize," she said. "I am sorry. This is not my business. Why am I prying into your private life? This is terrible of me. Don't answer any of my questions. I am terribly sorry."

"No, no. It's all right."

Osa wasn't saying anything. Moon suspected she might be crying. Or trying not to cry. Why not? Fatigue. Fear. Dirt. Discomfort. Worry about her brother. Too damn much stress for a woman. Too damn much stress for Moon too. He wasn't going to look at her. What was her last question?

"Sometimes love and marriage don't go together," he said. "Sometimes other things have to be considered. For example, my mother married a man she didn't love. Her second husband."

"Oh," Osa said. She made a sniffing sound. Trying not to cry, Moon thought.

"How about you?" he asked. "You ever think about marrying somebody you didn't love? Or not marrying somebody you did love? Or any combination of the above?"

"Yes," Osa said.

"Which one?"

"I guess it was a combination of the above. I was going to marry him, but he went away."

"What happened to him?"

"I don't know. He didn't come back."

Well, at least she wasn't crying anymore. But Moon didn't know exactly how to stop this.

"Was this recently?"

"I was nineteen," she said. "Going to school in Jakarta. He was a teacher there. He taught French."

Moon digested that. Or thought he had. "I think something like that would happen to Debbie," he said. "She's a very pretty girl. Small and blond. The kind of girl that when she walks into a room all the men look at her. But she doesn't use her head. She picks the wrong kind of man and she's going to get dumped. Have her heart broken."

Osa said, "You are a very funny man," and when he looked at her, surprised, she was laughing at him.

She reached out and squeezed his hand. "Men," she said.

"What do you mean?"

She laughed again. "I mean you don't understand women."

"Like how?"

"That's not what happened to me at all. That's not what's happened with Debbie."

"How the hell do you know?" said Moon. He was not in the mood to be a source of Osa's amusement.

"Of course I don't know," she said. "You see, I am doing it again. I'm sorry. We will not talk about it any longer."

"Well," Moon began, but the noise of an approaching vehicle interrupted him. For a former sergeant in an armored outfit it was a familiar noise. A tracked vehicle, which meant armor. Here that meant trouble.

He stood out of sight at the truck entry door of the warehouse. An armored personnel carrier wearing mottled gray-green camouflage paint splashed with mud had stopped with its nose almost touching the gate in the high wire fence that barred access to the compound. Rice was hurrying out of the hangar toward it. As Moon watched, Lum Lee emerged from the door of the little Quonset hut that housed the R. M. Air offices. Mr. Lee stood just outside, watching.

"What is it?" Osa whispered. She was standing just behind him.

"Technically, it's a Model One-hundred-thirteen armored personnel carrier," Moon said. "Armed with one fifty-caliber machine gun on that little mounting on the roof. The one we drove had two benches, six men on each side with their gear stacked in the middle. Driver jammed in against the engine, peeking out through dirty bulletproof glass and no headroom for anyone to stand up unless the roof hatches were open."

Rice seemed to think it was good news. He unfastened the chain holding the heavy gate. A small man wearing the U.S. Army–model helmet of the Army of the Republic of Vietnam and an officer's uniform climbed out of the roof mounting, hopped off the vehicle, and walked through the gate ahead of it. Rice thrust out his hand.

"Looks all right so far," Moon said.

Then he saw the ARVN officer was holding a pistol. Rice's gesture seemed to have been defensive.

"No," Moon said. "Not so good."

"A pistol," Osa said, voice hushed.

The rear hatch of the armored personnel carrier dropped and a soldier emerged, also in an officer's uniform, carrying an M16 rifle. And then the entourage was moving, with Rice, Lum Lee, and two officers in front, and the APC coming along slowly behind them. The men walked into the hangar. The APC parked, the engine died, and a soldier wearing a fatigue cap and carrying a rifle climbed out. He stretched, scratched his hip, and leaned against the vehicle.

"What should we do?" Osa asked.

"I'd say wait. See what happens."

"But—" She didn't finish the thought.

"These are the good guys," Moon said. "R. M. Air was fixing helicopters for them. Maybe they heard the place had been evacuated so they came by to see what's going on."

"Perhaps so," Osa said. "But he pointed a pistol at Mr. Rice."

"Yeah, I noticed." He and Osa should be looking for a

place to hide. Under the bales stacked against the wall. Or in the bales. "Our best bet is to get our things together and be ready in case we need to be. Sort of clean this place up."

"In case they shoot Mr. Rice and Mr. Lee and come looking to see if there is someone else to shoot?"

"Well, yes," Moon said. He picked up his rice bowl and his map, put them both in his bag, and looked around the floor for any other traces that they'd been there.

"We could hide over there," Osa said, indicating the mountainous stacks of burlap bags.

"You watch," Moon said. "Don't leave any evidence we're here. I'll make us a hiding place."

He moved enough bags to make a narrow crevice against the wall, put his bag in the back of it, and added Osa's baggage to the cache. He was arranging two sacks atop the pile to be pulled down behind them when he heard an engine starting.

Osa was standing just inside the doorway, pointing. Moon saw Mr. Lee, looking very wet, climbing the steps into the warehouse. The dolly holding Rice's favored Huey had been rolled out onto the landing pad. The rotor blades turned slowly. Rice was at the controls beside the officer with the pistol. The engine revved, fell to a purr, revved again. As the copter blades picked up speed, the officer with the rifle climbed in through the side door and motioned for the soldier to join them. He ran from the APC, ducked under the rotors, and pulled himself in.

Mr. Lee stood beside them now, watching the copter rise and make a sharp turn out over the Mekong. Over the noise of its engine came the hard crackling sound of automatic rifle fire.

"I believe the Yellow Tiger Battalion has lost one of its company commanders, the leader of its intelligence platoon, and one of its soldiers," Mr. Lee said.

"And have we lost Rice?" Moon asked. "Or is he going to fly them to safety and then come back for us?"

"I think Mr. Rice will not be back," Mr. Lee said. "And I think we should find a place to hide ourselves."

Through the doorway, Moon saw two men slipping through the gate. They carried automatic rifles and wore the black pajamas and conical hats he'd seen in war movies. Five men followed, heading for the hangar.

"Right over here," Moon said, pointing to the great pile of bales. "And hurry."

HANOI, North Vietnam, April 28—(Agence France-Presse) A spokesman for the foreign office here said today that the proposal of the new president of South Vietnam for a negotiated peace had "come too late" and that the war would be ended by "a military solution."

Noon, the Ninteenth Day

May 1, 1975

MOON SAT ON A SACK of something heavy but soft, with his arms hugged around his knees, wondering if it had been proper to have jammed Osa in the very back of their cubbyhole. He'd done it to improve her safety, but that was accomplished at the price of increasing her discomfort. Putting Mr. Lee in the middle in recognition of his age gave Moon the spot adjoining the sacks that closed the entrance of their cave. There it was more spacious but would be most dangerous if their Vietcong visitors detected them and decided to shoot into the cave—although Moon doubted if AK-47 bullets would penetrate whatever it was (probably rice) that filled the sacks. Would Victoria Mathias have approved of his decisions? A nice ethical question, and better than thinking about a lot of other things. Moon did not want to think about how the hell they were going to get out of this mess.

By twisting his head, Moon could peer through a narrow space between the sacks and observe a little of the outside world. The most interesting thing he could see was the bottom two-thirds of the Vietcong standing beside the pile of bales across the warehouse. This person wore the traditional VC attire—loose black trousers. His were torn at one knee, wet, and muddy. He sat on one of the bales, rested a U.S. Army–issue M16 rifle against it, balanced a small bowl on his left knee, and began eating from it with his fingers. Now Moon could see almost all of this fellow. By leaning far forward and pulling down on the burlap of the bag in front of him, Moon could also see another black-clad leg. The man with the bowl was old and frail with a kindly face and a ragged mustache that he brushed aside to insert a little ball of rice into his mouth. His hair was short, in what Victoria Mathias had called a "bowl haircut" when she administered them to her sons.

What would this old rice farmer do if Moon pushed back the sack, emerged, and introduced himself? Any impulse Moon might have had to find out died. The man turned his face toward the owner of the leg sitting beside him, revealing that most of his right ear was missing. The area was pink and rough, and from it toward the corner of the old man's mouth ran a series of round, puckered scars. Cigarettes held against the skin, Moon thought.

The old man stopped eating and began talking. He evoked a response. A woman's voice responded. The old man produced a clasp knife from his pants, unfolded it, cut a small slit in the sack, and extracted a palmful of brown rice kernels. He showed these to someone, said something, and laughed.

Moon felt a poke in the back: Mr. Lum Lee signaling for attention. Mr. Lee pointed to his own ear to indicate listening. Of course, Moon thought. Mr. Lee was Vietnamese. He'd understand. Moon pressed back against the sacks to allow Lee to squeeze his small, bony frame past him.

The motion produced a fresh flood of perspiration, which dripped from his eyebrows, his nose, and his chin and ran down his back and his chest. His hair was wet with it and had been since long before dawn. When they left the blue water of the sea and entered the brown water of the Mekong they had sailed into a kind of heavy humid heat Moon had never known.

"You must take a lot of water," Mr. Lee had told him as they left *Glory of the Sea*. "You're big. You will sweat. You must drink more water and take salt too." They had loaded four fuel cans of water onto the shore boat, and Moon had been drinking like a camel all day. Still he felt a ferocious thirst.

He glanced at Osa. She sat head down, eyes closed, the face of a person enduring. Even in the dim light filtering in between sacks and the warehouse wall he could see her face was glistening with sweat. He tapped her knee, produced what he hoped was a reassuring grin, and received a faint smile in return.

The sound of a shout reached him, then more shouting, followed by laughter. Something clattered. Then a voice very, very close said something loud. Then came a long discourse in a loud, commanding voice. The sound of an order barked out just above them. Moon held his breath. He gripped Osa's knee. More voices, distant now. Then a dragging, scraping sound. Then silence.

Moon exhaled. Released Osa's knee. Looked at Lum Lee. Mr. Lee signaled silence. They listened. Nothing. Perspiration ran from Moon's eyebrow to the corner of his eye, causing it to sting. A bead of sweat dropped from his nose and was replaced by another. Heat and silence surrounded them.

"They are gone," Mr. Lee said.

Mr. Lee was right. The dragging, scraping sound they'd heard had been produced by the Vietcong closing the sliding warehouse door behind them. Moon slid it open an inch and peered out. The muddy yard was empty of people. The APC stood at the hangar entrance, shiny with rainwater. Also shiny with rainwater was the copter landing pad, reminding Moon that George Rice had flown away with their only hope of getting out of here. He pushed the door open another inch, his fingers touching paper tacked to its outside surface.

He detached it. It was handwritten with a felt-tipped marker pen in a language strange to Moon. He handed it to Lum Lee.

"Ah," Lee said. "This warehouse, the rice it contains, and all its other contents are taken into the custody of the Revolutionary Committee of An Loc. Any trespass or theft will be subject to punishment by the court of the people."

"Right," Moon said. "What were they talking about before they left?"

Lee nodded, opened his mouth to respond, and then sat suddenly on one of the sacks. He was gray with exhaustion. Osa put her hand on his shoulder. "You are not well?" she said.

"Tired," Lee said. "Just tired." He looked up at Moon. "At first the man who had been tortured—the man with the ear sliced off and the burned face—he was telling the woman the mistakes they had made in getting here too late to capture the helicopter. He said the helicopter might be useful to the Yellow Tiger Battalion in holding a bridge somewhere upriver. But he said he thought the puppet soldiers who took it would use it to run away from the fight." He offered Moon a weak smile. "I think he is absolutely correct."

"So do I," Moon said. "Is that why they were laughing?"

"They opened some of the bales," Mr. Lee said. "One of them had opium balls buried in the copra."

Moon exhaled. "Opium," he said.

"In the raw form," Mr. Lee said. "They tap the poppies in Burma. In the mountains. Boil it down into tar and roll it into balls. Then they wrap the balls in cloth and move it down into Cambodia. Then it is either—"

Mr. Lee became aware of Moon's expression. He stood silent a moment, cleared his throat.

"I believe Mr. Rice told us that this warehouse was owned by an ARVN general," Mr. Lee said.

"Yes," Moon said. "That's what Rice told us. What else did you hear?"

"A little bit later several people came in," Mr. Lee continued. "A woman speaking now. She told the old man that they had heard on the Saigon radio that the Americans were evacuating their embassy building in Saigon. They talked about a big mob of city people, the ones who had helped the Americans, fighting each other and trying to get into the embassy grounds and the American marines keeping them away, and helicopters flying in and landing on the roof and flying away with the Americans."

"The fat lady sang," Moon said.

Mr. Lee stared at him.

"It's an American saying," Moon said. "It means something is finished. We say, It ain't over till it's over. Now I guess it's over."

"I see," Mr. Lee said.

"I had been thinking maybe we could find a way to go north. Find a way to slip into Saigon and get to the embassy. So much for that. Not a good idea now."

"It was not a good idea ever," Mr. Lee agreed. "I think what's left of the Army of the Republic of Vietnam will be pulling back to Saigon, and the North Vietnam army and the Vietcong units will be moving there too. Gathering in close now, I think, for the last big battle."

"I think so too," Moon said. "And I don't have any other ideas. Not even bad ones." He used the back of his hand to wipe away the perspiration dripping from his eyebrows. "Did you hear anything else?"

"The man with the scarred face asked someone if he had completed an inventory of what was here, and they talked of how many sacks of rice, and sandalwood, and charcoal, and barrels of gasoline and diesel fuel. And what was in the kitchen and the bathroom. And a pistol found in the office was mentioned, and handed to the old man. Then someone who must have been out at the hangars came in and told the old man that Big Minh, the new puppet president at Saigon, was broadcasting a speech. He was telling the puppet army—"

Mr. Lee paused and gave Moon an apologetic glance.

"The Communists always call ARVN that," he said. "I merely quote. The new president told the army to continue the fighting. To defend Saigon. Not to run away. And then another man came in. I think he had been running. I mean, the way he was breathing." Mr. Lee demonstrated the sound of panting. "This one, he said that the commander wanted them to move up along the river and that the old man was needed at the radio to receive their orders."

"So they left," Moon said.

"Yes," Mr. Lee said. "But they will be back. Or someone else will come."

"Is that something you heard?" Moon asked. "Or is it just a good guess?"

Mr. Lee's face was shiny with perspiration, but Moon

saw no signs of dripping. Maybe it was because he was so thin and frail. Maybe it was because he was used to this sort of heavy wet heat. But how could anyone ever get used to it?

Mr. Lee chuckled. "A guess. In a hungry country one does not walk away from food."

"We don't have much time then?" And, as he said it, thought, Time for what?

Mr. Lee shrugged. "Again, I must guess. What is the movement of their wind and water? What is the movement of our own? How can we know what that holds for them? Or for us? Perhaps the Yellow Tiger Battalion will be fierce and chase their Vietcong brothers into the Mekong. Or perhaps the Vietcong will chase the Tigers all the way into the Gulf of Thailand."

"Do you have any ideas?" Moon asked. Osa was sitting beside Mr. Lee now, looking thoughtful.

Mr. Lee said, "Probably the same ones you have. The alternatives. We could stay here. The Vietcong will come back for the rice, or perhaps the Army of North Vietnam will come to collect the aircraft and the other equipment. Then, perhaps, we will be shot or taken into custody. Or perhaps we will not be shot. If all is well we would be returned to our countries or held for questioning. It is all very problematic. Or we could seek some means to escape to the sea. Or we could seek some way to continue our mission."

"I am remembering what Mr. Rice said about the River Patrol Boats," Osa said. "Some people in that ship must have escaped. Ran away in the boats that were missing. Where would they go? We didn't hear such fast boats when we were coming up the river. Where could they be? We should try to find one of those. We should try to get out the way we came in."

To Moon that seemed awfully close to hopeless. But he could think of nothing better. "What do you think of that?" he asked Lum Lee.

Mr. Lee pulled idly at his gray goatee, considering.

"How do we find the boat?" He made a wry face, shook his head. "However, one with no horse must walk. One with no heliocopter must try to float."

Mr. Lee laughed at his own humor. Osa produced a weak chuckle. Moon didn't even try.

"I will go now and see what I can see," Mr. Lee said. "But first I must find something to make me look more like a Communist. More like a Mekong Delta Communist."

"I think you are too tired for that," Moon said. "Rest awhile. Have some food."

Mr. Lee studied him, tugged at his goatee. "I am remembering what Ricky told me about you," he said. "I think you plan to do this yourself. But you are too big, and too white, too American. You would be caught, and then we all would be caught."

"I know," Moon said. "I thought about that. Let's see if we can find anything useful."

The door at the far end of the warehouse opened into an office: two desks, one small, new, and gray metal, and the other big, old, and oak; a tall old-fashioned five-drawer filing cabinet; a small safe, its door standing open; and a long wooden table with four folding chairs beside it. Moon sat in a swivel chair at the bigger desk, felt the smooth wood under his fingertips. Wood polished by Ricky's hands. In front of him, just over the desk, he could see through the rain-streaked window the open door of the hangar from which George Rice, the Huey copter, and all his hopes had flown away.

Mr. Lee had disappeared through the door behind him into the living quarters, followed by Osa. After a while he would go there himself. He'd see Ricky's nest. See whatever Ricky's friends had left when they collected his things to send back to the States. But not now. It could wait a minute while he would simply think.

Moon heard voices, something clattering. The monsoon wind rattled the window with a fresh barrage of rain. Sweat ran down his back, made his shirt slick against the plastic of the chairback. He wiped his face with his sleeve. Today was what? The end of April. Victoria Mathias would be sleeping in her bed in her hospital room.

Mr. Lee emerged, dressed in loose and slightly dirty cotton trousers and an even looser dark blue smock. He was carrying a conical fiber hat.

"Not perfect, but a lot better," Mr. Lee said. "I go now. Mrs. van Winjgaarden said she will take a shower."

"I think you would fool me," Moon said, "but are you going to fool these local Vietnamese? Are there any Chinese around here, do you think?"

"You forget that I, too, am Vietnamese," Mr. Lee said. "And there are Chinese everywhere in Asia."

"But how the hell—? Just what are you going to do?"

Mr. Lee stopped at the door. "I tell anyone I can find that my son was a cook on the *U.S.S. Pott County.* I came to visit him. I learn the ship has been sunk. Someone told me he got ashore on one of the motorboats."

"Um," Moon said.

"Do you have a better idea?"

"No," Moon said.

"Remember that I am an old man. Remember that the Vietnamese respect their old."

"Like the old man with his ear cut off," Moon said.

Mr. Lee stared at him. "The scar was old. Somebody in your CIA was collecting ears that year, I think." With that, Mr. Lee disappeared through the doorway.

Another gust of wind rattled the window. From the living quarters behind him, Moon heard a shower running. Odd, he thought, how we believe that water through a pipe gets us cleaner than the warm rain. Then a shout. Something between a shout and a scream. Osa's voice.

A half dozen running steps to the door, jerk it open, the bedroom; large, mostly bare, a bed, a chest, a chair. No sign of Osa.

Then, through the doorway into the next room, he could see part of Osa: the back of her head, her right shoulder, the right side of her back, right buttock, right leg, the bare suntanned skin glistening with perspiration. She was standing stock still, facing directly away from him, holding a bundle of clothing against herself, looking down, listening to someone.

Moon pushed past her. A small young man was sitting on the floor in the bathroom closet, matted black hair, the side of his face black with clotted blood, holding a grenade launcher pointed at Osa.

He shifted it to point at Moon.

"Hello," Moon said. Not Vietcong, he thought, or he wouldn't be hiding here. An ARVN deserter. He might understand some English. Would he understand the grenade launcher? If he shot it in here, they were all dead. Moon bent forward, reached his hand back, felt his palm press against Osa's bare stomach, pushed hard, was aware she was falling out through the doorway, heard her body hit the floor.

"You're hurt," he said to the man.

"You are an America," the man said. He said it very slowly, mouthing each word carefully, not sure of his English. He grinned at Moon a pained grin, carefully put the grenade launcher on the closet floor, leaned against the doorjamb, and coughed.

Through his open shirt, Moon saw more dried blood, part of a tattoo, and dark bruises.

"There'll be a first aid kit around here somewhere," Moon said. "What happened to you?"

"Yes," the man said, and something else which Moon didn't understand.

Moon picked up the grenade launcher. The same model, he noticed, that they'd trained with at Fort Riley. He leaned it in the corner of the closet.

"Can you stand?"

The man looked puzzled. "Stand?"

Moon helped him up, helped him into the bedroom, helped him sit on the rumpled bed. Mr. Lee was standing in the bedroom door. Osa reappeared beside him, still barefoot but wearing her khaki pants now and a bra, with her shirt over her shoulders.

"Thank you," she said to Moon, looking slightly embarrassed. "I guess neither of us have any secrets now."

"No," Moon said.

She smiled at him. "But you didn't have to push me so hard." She went into the bathroom, turned off the shower, and came out with a wet towel.

"First we need to clean off the cut places," she said to the man. "Mr. Mathias here will go and find the medical box, and then we will see what we can do for you."

He found four of the kits the U.S. Army issues to its aid men in the kitchen cabinet over the sink. Mr. Lee was standing behind him, looking pleased.

"I think we may have some help now, finding a boat," Mr. Lee said. "Our man is one of the Sealord sailors."

"I thought a soldier," Moon said. "He was carrying a grenade launcher."

"Did you notice the tattoo on his chest?" Mr. Lee asked. "It said SAT CONG. That was the slogan of the river sailors of the Republic's navy from the very first. So I think he's one of the men from the base down the river."

"Sat Cong," Moon said. "Means what?"

"It means Kill Communists," Mr. Lee said. "I think that VC officer with his ear cut off would like to capture this one."

WASHINGTON, April 28 (UPI)—President Ford today ordered the emergency evacuation of all Americans remaining in Vietnam. The plan called for picking them up at assembly points in helicopters and flying them to carriers lying off the coast.

Afternoon, the Nineteenth Day

May 1, 1975

IF OSA VAN WINJGAARDEN'S DIAGNOSIS was correct, Nguyen Nung had suffered two cracked ribs, concussion, multiple wounds caused by some sort of shrapnel on his face, neck, chest, and scalp, plus assorted bruises and abrasions.

By Lum Lee's analysis, based on cross-examining Nguyen Nung before the shot of morphine from a U.S. Army aid kit took effect, these damages had been caused when a Vietcong rocket hit the superstructure of the LST where his PBR was based just as Nung was scrambling up a ladder. He remembered being hit by something and flung from the ladder to the deck. The next thing he remembered was awakening in a PBR somewhere out on the river and being aware that they were being shot at. The last time he revived, he'd found himself on the bottom of the boat, with the legs of a dead man across his own. He had extracted himself to find that the PBR had been run aground on the bank of a very narrow, very shallow creek. He had walked. He had come to the warehouse compound about dawn, found the gate unlocked, and entered. When he heard voices, he'd hidden himself in the closet. Could he find the boat again? Of course. How far was it? Nung was too hazy from the morphine by now to answer that coherently.

Osa picked bits and pieces of debris from various wounds, washed everything with soapy water, applied copious amounts of antiseptic, and swathed his face and neck in U.S. Government Issue bandages. Finally, with Moon holding the groggy Nung erect, Osa wrapped his chest in strips torn from a bedsheet.

"We let him down now," she said, glanced up at Moon, and instantly looked away.

"I shouldn't have screamed like that," she said. "I am embarrassed."

"I would have screamed a lot louder," Moon said. "You open a door and see a guy pointing a grenade launcher at you. I might have fainted."

They lowered Nung gently to the bed and were rewarded with a grimace, followed by a dopey smile. Nung said something that sounded to Moon like "tenk," closed his eyes, and surrendered to the morphine.

Osa, leaning over him, closed a long gash on his cheek with the careful application of an adhesive bandage. She stood straight, stretched her back, shook herself.

"We should leave him to sleep a little," she said. "I will go now and take that shower." She laughed. "This time I look in the closet first."

"Good idea. Nothing to do now but wait until we find out if our friend here can help us."

"That tattoo on his chest," she said. "You saw it?"

"Mr. Lee said it means Kill Communists."

"That's what I thought," Osa said. "Poor man. What does he do now?"

Moon hadn't given that much thought. He watched her close the bathroom door behind her and went back into the office. Through the doorway he saw Mr. Lee prowling the warehouse, checking bales and sacks. He had no desire to talk to Mr. Lee at the moment. What could they say? That they were lucky in connecting with this sailor? Probably it was great good luck. Now there seemed to be some chance, at least. He stood at Ricky's window looking out at the armored personnel carrier parked by the hanger. An M-113, the same model they'd used in training at Fort Riley. The ARVN soldiers had left the hatches open, which meant it would be wet inside. Halsey had done that once, leaving Lieutenant Rasko's bedroll to serve as a blotter, soaking up the rainwater from the metal floor.

Moon smiled, remembering how Halsey had talked his way out of that one. What would Halsey suggest to get out of this situation? He'd say something like "*Que sera sera,* so don't sweat it." As good advice as any. And what would Halsey think of Osa van Winjgaarden? He would have been impressed. She was the kind of woman Halsey always wanted him to chase. He'd point them out across the dance floor when they dressed up and went to the classier places. The tall ones wearing pearls. The ones with the long patrician faces, Bermuda tans, and the high-fashion jackets. The ones who handed the parking lot attendant the keys to the Porsche, who knew exactly how to walk, and hold their heads, and tell the world they owned it. The ones who, when they caught him staring, examined him with cool, disinterested eyes.

"Why not?" Halsey would say. "Maybe they can kill you but they can't eat you." He'd say, "Not my type, Gene." And Halsey, who enjoyed the role of philosopher, would say, "Like hell they're not. Unlike myself, a pragmatist happy with the attainable, you are a victim of divine discontent. You yearn for the perfect. But you ain't got no guts."

But in fact, they really weren't his type. He knew it and they knew it. He learned it when he was younger. The hard way. He had been calmly and efficiently rejected. The duck rebuffed by the swan. He'd learned fairly fast, because Moon Mathias was unusually sensitive to the pain of humiliation.

But the water was still dripping into the M-113 armored personnel carrier, getting things wetter and wetter. Moon slid open the warehouse door. Seeing nothing dangerous on the muddy road beyond the fence, he walked out into the rain to check it out.

The rubber cushion on the driver's seat beside the engine was soaking wet, but by then so was Moon. He sat on it and looked around. Basically it was identical to the ones they had driven at Fort Riley. The ARVN outfit had installed racks for GI gas cans, welded a mount beside the second hatch for an M60 machine gun, and covered the floor with bags. Moon widened a tear in one of them and checked. Sand. Something to stop the shrapnel if the treads triggered a mine. He switched on the ignition. The fuel indicator showed two-thirds. He shifted into low gear, drove the APC into the hangar, tugged the big door closed behind it, and went to work. He'd refuel it, get it ready to go. It was good to feel competent again.

Nguyen Nung became more or less awake about four P.M., about thirty minutes after the rain slackened into a drizzle and gradually faded away. When Moon came in from the hangar, the clouds were breaking, there were signs of watery sunlight here and there, and Nung was sitting stiffly in Ricky's office being cross-examined by Mr. Lee.

"He says the boat is about an hour's walk down the river," Mr. Lee said. "It was run up a creek and into heavy brush in a growth of mangroves. He estimates it's about two or three hundred yards down the creek from this road we're on."

"What happened to the crew?" Moon asked.

Mr. Lee spoke to Nguyen. Nguyen shrugged, then produced a lengthy response.

"He doesn't know," Mr. Lee said. "But they came ashore in his boat, the boat he was a gunner on. He knew them. The boat commander was from Hanoi. Two of the other crewmen were also anti-Communist refugees from the north, another was from Hue, and another from near Da Nang. He guesses they would know the war is over and try to go home. The dead man was a local man. Nguyen's family had a rice paddy in the delta. His father had been one of the headmen in the village just downstream before the Vietcong killed him and the family. And then one morning the United States napalmed the village, and the people who survived moved away."

"What we need to know is whether the crew will come back for the boat. It doesn't sound likely, unless they need it to get across the river."

Lum Lee nodded. "We need to know that. And we need to know if the boat is in condition to take us out to the mouth of the Mekong. Mr. Nung remembers there was water in the bottom. They are made of fiberglass and it was hit by bullets."

"Probably could be patched up," Moon said.

"We also need to understand how to survive three days until it is time to go out and meet the *Glory of the Sea*."

"That's the problem," Moon said. "We're living on borrowed time staying here."

"I think of Mr. Nung's village," Mr. Lee said. "He said he and some friends raised chickens there. Not all the buildings were burned."

Since he had watched George Rice fly away, Moon had been kidding himself about their prospects, avoiding despair by not thinking about it. Now he felt a sudden rush of hope.

"Let's go find out," he said. "Can Mr. Nung travel?"

"Sure," Nguyen Nung said, grinning a goofy morphine withdrawal grin. "'Way we go."

Special to the ***New York Times***

SAIGON, South Vietnam, April 28—More than 150 Communist rockets slammed into Tan Son Nhut air base in Saigon today, destroying a C-130 transport plane, killing at least two U.S. Marines and forcing suspension of evacuation flights.

Evening, the Nineteenth Day

May 1, 1975

IT HAD SOUNDED SIMPLE ENOUGH. "If it's pulled up on the south side of the creek, which is where what's-his-name said they left it, then we can't possibly miss it," Moon declared.

But they did miss it. The boat had been run partly up the muddy bank in a snarled tangle of dead mangroves and palms. The trees had been killed many years past by Agent Orange. The fertilizer used to make the defoliant, diluted by monsoon rains and river flooding, had soaked into the soggy earth and fed a fierce undergrowth of deformed and distorted rain-forest brush. Moon and Lum Lee had skirted this almost impenetrable maze and found nothing downstream in the area Nguyen Nung had described. Rechecking on the way back, Moon had waded hip-deep along the stream bank. He had spotted the stern of the craft just about three seconds before he spotted a leech feeding on his flank.

The leech was less of a shock than the boat. Mr. Lee disposed of the insect by heating it with a match, causing it to withdraw from Moon's flesh. The boat contained the corpse of one of Nguyen's former companions. Worse, it was also half full of dirty water. Worse yet, the water seemed to have entered through a multitude of bullet holes.

"Well, shit," Moon said. "So much for that."

As he said it, the sound of explosions reached him. Artillery, or perhaps rockets, or perhaps tank fire. But from where? At the creek bank, engulfed in vegetation, the noise of the explosions seemed to be coming from all around them. But it was probably another attack in the battle upriver at Can Tho. Wherever it was, it reminded Moon that when one needs a boat as badly as he needed a boat, a leaky one is better than none. The APC could get him into Cambodia, providing he had a huge amount of good luck. But even though the army called it amphibious and it could splash its way across a canal or a rice paddy, it was going to take something that really floated to get this bunch back out into the South China Sea. And he wanted it ready to go now, before he left, just in case the huge amount of good luck he needed didn't happen.

He checked. Five of the bullets had punched through the fiberglass hull well above what normally would have been the water line. Three were lower, where they really mattered. Except for one, the holes were neat, round, and about a quarter of an inch in diameter—probably made by a light machine gun or an AK-47 rifle. The exception seemed to be an exit hole, made by a bullet that had struck something hard and deflected through the bottom, leaving a tear longer than Moon's hand.

Lum Lee stood looking at the holes. He was wet despite his conical hat. His shoulders slumped. He looked gaunt, exhausted, and discouraged.

"Well," Moon said, "let's see what else we can see. And what we can do about this."

Almost immediately he saw that being shot at was nothing new for this particular PBR. In the tradition of river boatmen, a set of large staring eyes had been painted on the bow of the craft to scare away demons. The paint partly obscured round fiberglass patches used to cover a cluster of three earlier bullet holes. Moon pointed them out to Mr. Lee.

Mr. Lee merely raised his eyebrows.

"If the navy is like the army, it put stuff in this boat to fix its problems," Moon said. It had. In a compartment beside the engine they found a flare gun, pliers, two hammers, assorted other tools, wires, bolts, a box full of first aid kits with the morphine missing, and a plastic box marked REPAIR KIT, HULL.

The body of the VNN sailor was small, light, and already stiff with rigor mortis. Moon moved it from the boat and laid it out of sight among the mangrove roots. He jammed cloth from the dead man's shirt into the subsurface holes, bailed out the boat, and shifted enough of its heavier contents so that he could tilt the damaged section out of the water. Then he went to work with the epoxy glue and fiberglass patching.

The sun was just setting below the breaking clouds when Moon and Mr. Lee reached the place they'd left the APC, parked out of sight in a bamboo thicket well off the road.

"You found it?" Osa said. She was standing in the hatch, slender, dark hair pulled back into some sort of bun, looking neat and tidy as if protected from the terrible humidity by some sort of invisible screen with which nature guards its few classy women from the troubles that beset usual folks.

"We did," Moon said, climbing into the driver's seat. "Now let's see if Nguyen Nung can show us how to find his picnicking place."

It was no more than two or three miles away, but getting there involved turning the APC off the relatively compact surface of the road, down into the roadside ditch, and then across a series of soggy rice paddies. The U.S. Army specifications for the APC declared it to be amphibious. If Moon remembered what he'd read about it in the maintenance manual, this particular model had been designed specifically with Vietnamese marsh country and the canals of lowland Europe in mind. Therefore it should float a bit better than the one his battalion used in training. But Moon had never quite brought himself to believe it. It was just too much heavy metal, too many tons. Not that they had any choice. If it sank, it sank.

The APC tilted down the slope, skidding and slipping, nosed into the ditch with a great splash of mud and dirty water, and then rose majestically up the other bank and into the paddy. Its treads made a slithering sound in the mud, but it moved steadily, slowed when Moon eased off on the gas, sped when he asked it to, turned with remarkably little sliding. A damn good piece of equipment, Moon thought, even if the army did design it.

Nguyen Nung was standing on the gunner's pedestal behind the driver's seat, his head out the hatch where the .50-caliber machine gun was mounted. He shouted something Moon couldn't understand, laughed, and started singing. To Moon, that seemed a good omen. But maybe it was a Vietnamese dirge.

Nung's father, fortunately, had built his house near the canal that fed the rice paddies here and away from the little village beside the creek. The village had been incinerated, perhaps by a napalm strike, perhaps by VC or ARVN forces who suspected it of harboring supporters of the other side. The elder Mr. Nung had surrounded his house with an earthen dike, and it sat behind this wall amid a cluster of outbuildings like a low-rent castle of bamboo and palm logs in an ocean of mud. Nung untied the gate, an affair of wired-together bamboo poles. He waved them in and closed it behind them. They were greeted by a clamor of excited ducks and chickens penned in a shed behind the house, and by a trio of tethered pigs. Osa and Mr. Lee climbed out of the APC. Moon stood in the driver's hatch, sweating profusely under the slanting, watery sun, and assessed the situation. It was better than he'd expected.

The dike must have been built to hold back the Mekong at its full end-of-monsoon flood, with a stack of sandbags ready to replace the gate when the water rose. Moon could barely see over the wall, and it would make the APC invisible from the road. The roof of the house had been partly burned away. If a napalm bomber had done it he must have arrived on a wet day. Moon guessed the napalm tank had landed short, detonating in the paddy with only the last of it slashing over the dike to hit the roof. A section of palm fronds and their supports had burned out, but the fire hadn't been hot enough to do more than scorch the bamboo walls. The floor—raised on the inevitable stilts—still looked solid.

Moon found himself feeling optimistic again. Osa, Lum Lee, and Nung could stay here until he got back. Or, if he didn't get back, until time to meet the "shure boot" from the

Glory of the Sea. With perfect luck no one would notice them in the bloody confusion of the war's finale. With fair luck anyone who found them would be friendly. Even with bad luck—being found by desperate ARVN deserters or vengeful Vietcong—their prospects were at least as good as his.

Osa was waving to him from the floor. "One room is dry," she said. "And most of another one."

Time to get moving. Moon picked up his Langenscheidt map of Southeast Asia and climbed down into the mud.

Osa was standing in the partly dry room with Nung beside her, grinning and pointing at a charcoal burner and an assortment of cooking gear on the floor around it. The female instinct to make a home, Moon thought. Universal, even in someone who would look—even in a soggy, crumpled shirt—equally at home on Fifth Avenue. But there was no time for that now.

He unfolded the map Rice had marked, spread it on the floor, and squatted beside it.

"Here's the plan," Moon said.

It was a simple plan. Moon would take the APC northwest into Cambodia and collect Osa's brother, his niece, and Mr. Lum Lee's ancestral bones. That done, he would return to this house. Meanwhile, Osa, Lum Lee, and Nguyen Nung would wait here, keeping out of sight. Upon his return, when the third day was up, they would take Nung's boat and sail away to the mouth of the Mekong and their rendezvous with the shore boat from the *Glory of the Sea.*

"Okay?" Moon asked. "Does everybody agree?"

"No," Osa said. "It's crazy. It's insane."

Lum Lee looked thoughtful. Nguyen Nung looked curious, waiting for a translation.

"Why insane?" Moon asked. "If you lie low here, there's a good chance nobody will find you. At least nobody hostile. And if I'm not back by—"

"No," Osa said. "You stay here. We should all go together."

She looked frightened, Moon thought. He hadn't really seen that before. Plenty of chances to be frightened, but she hadn't let it show.

"You'll be all right," he said. "I'll go take care of things. Find your brother. I'll make him come back even if—"

"He's already dead."

That stopped Moon, the illogic of it.

"Yesterday you were sure he'd still be alive. Even this morning. Did you hear something on the radio?"

Moon looked from Osa to Lum Lee. He thought he saw amusement in Mr. Lee's expression, but that must be wrong.

"We heard that Pol Pot has concentrated his forces at Phnom Penh," Lee said. "We picked up a broadcast that sounded official from Kampong Cham. The man was ordering all the people of that city to gather out on the highway for something. I think it was some work project, but the signal faded in and out."

"And from Thailand," Osa said, "they were broadcasting interviews with refugees who'd gotten across the border. They said—" She shuddered. "It was terrible, what they were saying the Khmer Rouge was doing to people. It was even worse than what I remember from Indonesia when they were killing the Chinese."

"But that's not the point," Moon said. "How about your brother? Was there anything to tell you he's not still alive?"

"How could he be? He's exactly the sort of people they were beating to death."

"But if Pol Pot pulled everybody north to clean out

Phnom Penh, then down here in the south end of the country they wouldn't have had time—"

"No, no," Osa said. "He is already dead."

Intuition, Moon thought. That and too much fatigue. Too much stress. No wonder she has given up. It would be much harder on her, not having any control over things. It was more than anyone should have to bear.

"Possibly you're right," he said. "But if I can find him, I'll bring him out."

Osa said something fiercely emphatic that Moon didn't understand, probably in Dutch and, judging from her expression, probably an expletive. But before she looked away, he thought she was crying.

"What?" Moon said.

"I said, Why are men so damned stubborn? So unreasonable. Like donkeys. So stupid."

"Well," Moon said, a little irked by this, "if you will just remember when you met me in Manila, you will remember my purpose in coming here was to get Ricky's daughter and bring her home. There's nothing unreasonable about that."

"But it's not possible now. Mr. Rice flew away in the helicopter. Before that it was possible. Now it's only being stubborn. You just go in and get killed. How does that help anybody?"

"Nguyen can run the boat. Nguyen and Mr. Lee. You don't need me."

Silence. Moon had been looking at Lum Lee when he made that statement. He looked back at Osa. Her face was no longer pale. It was flushed.

"I can run that damned boat myself," she said. "I was just trying to save your stupid life."

"Oh," Moon said.

"Go ahead, then," Osa said. "Go up there among Pol

Pot's savages and let them beat you to death with their bamboo poles."

"Look," Moon said.

"My stubborn brother has to die so he can be a martyr. Why do *you* want to die?"

"I just—" Moon began, but Osa had stalked out into the courtyard.

Leaving behind a strained silence.

Nguyen Nung was smiling foolishly past his bandages, looking abashed, waiting to learn if he needed a translation of all that.

Mr. Lee had his eyes on Moon Mathias, looking thoughtful.

"Well, hell," Moon said, finally. "What brought all that on?"

Mr. Lee looked down at the map, concealing most of a smile.

"Fatigue," Moon said. "Nervous tension. Women. Stress." He glanced at Nung, seeking confirmation. Nung looked puzzled. Mr. Lee was still studying the map and still seemed to be amused. Something was going on here that Moon didn't understand.

"I, too, find a flaw in your plan," Mr. Lee said.

"What?" Moon wasn't in the mood for any more of this.

"I must go with you," Lum Lee said.

"Why? You describe the urn for me. It has to be fairly large to hold a man's bones. I find it and I bring it back. If it turns out you've had to leave to meet *Glory of the Sea,* then I drop the urn off for you at that hotel in Manila. Or you give me another address."

Lee looked at him.

"You can trust me," Moon said.

"Of course I can," Mr. Lee said. "But I confront a task that only one who understands *feng shui* can perform."

"*Feng shui*. So you tell me what to do. Just explain it to me."

Mr. Lee chuckled. "I believe the best explanation was written by a Taoist scholar in the nineteenth century," he said. "It runs to fifty-three volumes."

"Oh," Moon said.

"Very complicated. Perhaps a thousand years before God inspired men in the Middle East with your Western vision of Genesis, he inspired men in India with the word of the relationship between God and humans, how the world works, and how humans must behave to endure and reach a better life. It spread from India to China and through all of Asia. As the centuries passed, more holy inspiration followed. The Lord Buddha taught us and Confucius and others endowed with spiritual wisdom. But behind it all is *feng shui,* our understanding of the cosmic supernatutal."

Mr. Lee got out his cigar case, offered it to Moon, extracted one for himself. He shook his head.

"I must simplify this," he said. "You don't want a doctoral degree lecture."

"Just tell me why I can't do this job for you," Moon agreed.

"In this cosmos we have the visible world of the natural." He pointed to Moon. "You and I, the lizards we hear calling out there, the insects, all we see and hear. And then the world of the supernatural. The spirit world. We die. Our soul crosses the bridge. The link is broken. But it can be restored. We feed the spirit of our ancestors through respect. The spirit has power. *Mana.*"

Mr. Lee paused, thinking. He blew out a great cloud of smoke.

"I will start another way," he said. "We know that all things are decided by fate. Call it luck, good or bad. But we humans have ways to influence luck. We avoid the evil spirits that cause illness. We please those powers that can bring good. The most important of these is the most powerful of our ancestor spirits. Like you Jews and Christians, we know the power of ritual in dealing with the supernatural. We bury them properly. The place is scientifically chosen, the tomb correctly designed, the depth of the grave measured, the skull faced in the proper direction. All this was done when my most revered forebear was buried in our ancestral place. Then the Khmers captured the village. Before the government troops drove them away, they had killed the monks, burned the temple, and destroyed all things religious—including our family tomb. But the bones were recovered. I hired a geomancer to locate the site of a new tomb where the bones will be safe."

"And you hired Ricky to go get them."

"Yes," Mr. Lee said. "And luck intervened. In itself a bad sign."

"This ancestor, was he a great man?"

"He had great *mana,*" Mr. Lee said. "A minister for the great Sun Yat-sen. Great honor. Great power. My family has benefited always with health and luck."

"We need it now," Moon said.

Mr. Lee exhaled more smoke. "I'm afraid it is changing already," he said. "Since his tomb was destroyed, one of my nieces died in an accident. The shop of a grandson in Hong Kong burned. A brother-in-law was arrested by the police in Saigon. These bones must be placed where the *feng shui* is correct. Where the spirit is again comfortable. Where the *mana* works for the family and not against it."

"So you're going," Moon said. "I can't argue."

Lee gestured toward Nguyen Nung, who had been leaning against a wall, listening and looking puzzled.

"I should explain the situation to our friend," Mr. Lee said. "I think he has become part of our partnership. A member of our tour group."

"Apparently," Moon said, and followed Osa out into the growing darkness.

She was standing on the floor of the roofless section, looking through the twilight toward the burned-out village.

He stood behind her, organizing what he wanted to say.

"You haven't changed your mind, have you?" Osa said. "You've come to tell me why you can't go into Cambodia." She paused, drew in a deep breath. "And let them kill you."

"I'd like you to understand," he said. "Remember when we first met in the hotel at Manila? I told you I had come to bring my brother's child back to her grandmother. Nothing has changed that. I still have to get it done."

Osa turned and looked at him for a long, thoughtful moment. "Then I still don't understand you," she said. "I came looking for you because I had heard all about you. From Ricky. When I heard Ricky was dead, I thought you were coming to take over the company. He'd told me he wanted you to come. Had asked you to come."

She shook her head, sorting out the memories.

"Then you told me about the child. But you made it seem that you thought finding her was hopeless. You made me think you just wanted to find Ricky's friends so they would tell you there was no hope and you could go home, having"—she paused again, searching for the best way to say it—"so you could feel you had done your very best."

"I guess that's true enough."

Osa nodded. "You made it seem that way. I didn't want to believe it, though. That wasn't the Moon Mathias that Ricky had described to me. I thought if we could get to Ricky's hangars, you could just get into a helicopter and fly it away and get the child. And my brother."

"Except I couldn't fly."

"But I didn't know that."

Moon laughed. "I think Ricky made people think I could fly without an airplane."

"So I pushed you into this," Osa said. She threw out her hands. "And now here we are, and the helicopter has gone away with our only hope. And now that it really *is* absolutely impossible—like I thought you wanted it to be—now you act like it isn't."

Moon waited, but that seemed to be all she had to say.

"So I just don't understand you. Which Moon are you?"

"I don't know," Moon said. But even as he said it, he knew that whatever the reason, he simply wasn't willing to stop now. It had to be done. No use arguing about it.

"How are you going? In that little tank?"

"I put enough extra gasoline in those GI cans to get me there and back. Or close to it."

She took a deep breath and released it. "You'll just need enough for one way. They'll kill you."

"I don't think so."

"Be reasonable. The Vietcong, maybe not. Maybe they would just lock you up. But the Khmer Rouge? You represent everything they hate."

How could he explain this? It would sound like dialogue out of a bad movie. But it was true, so he said it.

"There's something worse than being killed sometimes. It's living with too much failure. I've got a long list of screwups behind me. Finally you decide you can't stand another one."

She stared at him, waiting for him to explain. He didn't.

She produced a wry smile. "Sometime I think you will tell me what happened to you to make you like this. If you live long enough."

Moon returned the smile, feeling better. "Maybe so. But it's a long story and dull. We don't have time for it now."

"I think we have what's left of three days," she said.

"No," Moon said. "I want to get started tonight. Get out of here in the wee hours of morning. When all the bad guys are getting their sleep."

Osa said nothing to that for a long time. She looked down at her hands, then up at him. She was facing the west, toward where the remnants of broken clouds still reflected a little of the twilight. Beyond her in the clearing skies over the skeletons of the murdered trees along the creek, the moon was rising. Almost full. The moonlight touched her hair and the twilight her face, and Moon realized for the first time just how much he liked to look at this woman. Unless he was very, very lucky, this would be the last time he'd see her.

BANGKOK, Thailand, April 29 (Agence France-Presse)—An estimated 80 South Vietnamese aircraft streamed into U Taphao airport today carrying at least 2,000 refugees fleeing their country. As night fell the landings continued.

A Thai Foreign Ministry spokesman said no permission had been granted for the landings. He said the refugees would be "deported" and that the aircraft—all provided to South Vietnam by the United States—would be "turned over to the new government of South Vietnam."

The Twentieth Day

May 2, 1975

BY THE TIME Moon had lost the big argument, gotten the APC in gear, and rolled it out of the gate of the Nung enclave, he had sorted out what he needed to worry about in chronological order.

Concentrate on the worries. Forget the argument. It had been lost, actually, when Mr. Lee had insisted, adamantly, that he must go along because only he could identify the ancestral bones with any certainty. The territory along the Vietnam-Cambodian border was populated with various Taoist sects. Ancestral shrines were everywhere. With the current Khmer Rouge upheaval and with the destruction of such shrines an important part of Pol Pot's Zero Year program, bone urns might be found anywhere. Enshrining the wrong ones for his own family would cause dangers and misfortunes beyond comprehension.

This ancestral reverence and its importance to family fortunes was beyond Moon's comprehension, but it was clear enough that Lum Lee was going along unless hell froze over or Moon prevented it by force. Which wasn't Moon's style.

How about Nguyen Nung, for whom Moon found himself illogically feeling responsible? After Lee had explained the situation to him, Nguyen knew he absolutely did not want to be left behind. He was certain the Vietcong would come before the time came to meet *Glory of the Sea*. Wherever the Americans went, Nguyen was going.

That left Osa. True, Osa had insisted she could run the river patrol boat out to the South China Sea with no help from anyone. Moon didn't believe it. And now that she wanted to go along, she had decided she would certainly get lost. Which meant there was no way to leave Osa, even if Osa was willing to be left, which she emphatically wasn't.

"I am going with you," Osa had said grimly. "If you won't take me with you, then I go alone. I walk. I came this far to get my brother. I don't stop now." Osa was glaring at him as she finished this statement, a trace of angry tears in her eyes. No use reminding her that just an hour ago she was assuring him that her brother certainly was already dead. No use thinking about it either. Think about the next problem, not the last one.

First came the Vietcong. They would be controlling the territory he had to cross on the first part of this journey. If they spotted a stray APC, what would they think of it? Would they assume it had been abandoned by the Yellow

Tiger Battalion and was now in the friendly custody of some of their own? Possibly. If they didn't and had only small arms, it was no problem. The APC had a top speed of twenty-eight miles per hour and could outrun them. But if the VC had rocket launchers, the game was over. The hardened aluminum of the APC would stop bullets and deflect shrapnel. The bigger stuff would punch right through it.

Moon had attempted to improve their odds by attaching one of Mr. Lee's two Vietcong flags to one of the APC's two radio antennas. Mr. Lee had discovered several of the flags with an assortment of other abandoned souvenirs in the closet of one of the bedrooms. He'd loaded them in, along with conical straw hats and assorted peasant attire, all far too small for Moon himself.

Moon had also gone hunting through the office and Ricky's bedroom. The only useful thing he'd found was a drawer full of maps. Among them were U.S. Army artillery charts of Vietnam's various military districts and just about everywhere else that the military felt might need attention. He extracted ones covering the delta provinces of Vietnam and the south end of Cambodia. Like the APC itself, such maps were familiar territory for ex–Sergeant Moon Mathias. They gave him a feeling of knowing what the hell he was doing. An illusion, he realized, but comforting.

When (and if) they neared Can Tho, worry number two kicked in. It became the Army of the Republic of Vietnam as well as the VC. If the sound of battle, or anything else, suggested that the Yellow Tiger Battalion still held the town or its crucial bridge, then the flag would be tucked away. Moon intended to skirt far east of Can Tho toward the coast of the Gulf of Siam. But if the Tigers were winning, which seemed unlikely, ARVN soldiers might well be patrolling in that direction. On the other hand, if the regiment had been smashed, the territory would be aswarm with ARVN deserters. Would they be dangerous? From the radio reports they'd been picking up from transmitters in Thailand, Laos, and God knew where else, deserters from the collapsing divisions around Saigon had been causing bloody chaos. One report said panicking Vietnamese marines had seized a ship in Saigon's harbor, forced civilian passengers off, and sailed away. Another relayed U.S. Navy reports of commandeered helicopters crashing on the deck of an aircraft carrier. In Saigon and the few other cities still under government control, there was widespread panic, looting, and shooting.

The third and worst worry would come with the Cambodian border: the Khmer Rouge.

Nguyen Nung's foot tapped him on the shoulder.

Moon looked around and up. Nguyen stood on the pedestal seat under the machine gun mount, his upper body out the hatch, visible to Moon only from his bandaged rib cage downward. His right hand came down, giving the old-as-the-Romans combat signal for be quiet and take cover.

Moon cut the engine.

"What?"

Nguyen was leaning down through the hatch, looking frightened and saying something Moon couldn't understand.

"Nguyen says he sees light coming up behind us." Mr. Lee said. "It is moving the same direction we are going. He thinks several vehicles."

Tanks, Moon thought. ARVN Sheridans or NVA Russian models. One would be about as bad as the other.

The driver's compartment of the APC was not designed for either comfort or visibility. Peering through the dirty bulletproof glass of the viewing slots directly in front of his face, he could see a rice paddy lit vaguely by misty moonlight. Through the slot to the left he could see a line of bamboo and brush along a feeder canal. Fifty yards to his right he could see the raised embankment of the road he'd decided to abandon in fear of mines. He saw no lights. But of course they would be blackout lights—small beams aimed down just ahead of the tracks.

Moon pushed himself up out of the driver's seat, tapped Nguyen on the leg, motioned him down, squeezed past the engine compartment, and stepped up on the machine gunner's pedestal.

Out of the smell of diesel oil, burned cordite, and old fish into a faint fresh breeze moving in from the southwest. If Moon's directions were right, it came from the Gulf of Siam. Relatively fresh, but Moon's sensitive nostrils still detected an acrid hint of fungus, the good smell of sandalwood, and a hint of decayed flesh and tropical flowers. From where he stood now, with his body protruding from the APC's steel roof, he could see a light. Two lights. Three. Four. And these weren't blackout lights. They were bright. The headlights of trucks, he guessed. They were moving slowly down the road toward them.

Moon dropped from the pedestal.

"Where are those—"

He didn't finish the question. Mr. Lee was already handing him the case that held the vehicle's night vision binoculars.

A jeep led the procession up the road, followed by three U.S. Army trucks. The jeep was flying a flag from its radio mast. It looked like a Vietcong flag. Moon scanned the landscape ahead, looking for cover and finding it. He dropped down into the driver's seat, restarted the engine, shouted "Hang on!" and raced the APC across the paddy.

The vehicle crashed through the brush into the little canal that fed Mekong water into the field.

Moon shifted into neutral, cut the ignition, climbed up into the machine gunner's hatch, and checked the situation. The APC might be visible from the road now, but only if you knew where to look and what you were looking for. Could he get it out? He had little doubt of that. Army ordnance had produced some notable lemons (the Sheridan tanks in his outfit being an example), but this APC wasn't one of them. He studied the little convoy through the night glasses, close enough now to make out four men in the lead jeep. The jeep was made in America, but the driver and his passengers wore the black peasant's garb of the Vietcong. The trucks following seemed to be loaded with men. Probably a VC unit in captured trucks heading up to join the attack on Can Tho.

Now that the noise of the APC's diesel was gone he could clearly hear the engines. And over that the night sounds. The sky was mostly clear now. The moon was almost overhead, but still a lopsided disk and not the bright white rock that lit the landscape of the Rocky Mountain high country. It would be midmorning in Durance now. But what day was it? He'd lost track of that. Debbie would be at work or, if it was a weekend, off somewhere with J.D. or one of the other men who chased her. How about Shirley's dog? How about J.D.'s engine? How about Rooney being fired? For that matter, how about being fired himself? None of it seemed important. He shifted to another question. What was going on with Osa van Winjgaarden? Her brother dead and let's go home; then her brother alive and requiring her attention.

Moon heard a single distant explosion. It echoed and died away. He heard gecko lizards making their obscene-sounding mating calls, frogs, the song of insects. And then another sort of song. The men on the passing trucks were singing. He bent down into the APC. Lum Lee was standing just below him. Osa and Nguyen Nung sat on a side bench, looking at him.

"You hear that?" Moon asked.

"I think I hear someone singing," Mr. Lee said.

"Four truckloads of Vietcong," Moon said.

"It sounds like one of their songs," Mr. Lee said.

"Like their national anthem?"

Mr. Lee laughed. "I think more like 'Waltzing Matilda.' It has lots of dirty verses. The song is about chasing out the French, and then chasing out the Japanese, and then chasing out the French again, and now—" Mr. Lee, always polite, didn't complete the sentence. Instead he said, "We have been listening to their radio transmissions. I think they have captured Can Tho. They say the Tiger is dead."

That changed Moon's plans a little. He would tag along behind the convoy. No more worry about mines. The VC would know where they'd laid them.

He ran with lights off about half a mile behind the last truck. Nguyen Nung perched in the machine gun hatch as lookout. In the utterly flat terrain the road followed along this arm of the Mekong, there was no problem keeping the lights in sight. A little after midnight Moon noticed another light, a glow on the horizon visible even through his small, smeared viewing window. Can Tho, or some part of it, was burning. The map showed an airport on the north side of town. Probably its fuel dump was ablaze. Probably that was the explosion they'd heard.

He stopped the APC and spread the proper artillery map over the rice sacks on the floor. They studied it. Nguyen proved to understand maps far better than he understood English. He also knew his home landscape. He corrected their present location, moving Moon's marker to a point six kilometers farther west of Can Tho. The narrow road of packed earth that intersected their path just ahead led directly to paved Route 80, which skirted the coast toward the town of Ha Tien right on the Cambodian border. There would be a border crossing checkpoint there. They'd avoid Route 80 by using farm roads through the paddies and dodge the border guards the same way.

"Okay," Moon said. "Let's everybody relieve themselves who needs to. Men to the right, women to the left. And off we go."

Nguyen was grinning. "Hunner klicks. No much time."

The road was drier here. Moon stood with his back against the metal flank of the APC looking through the moonlight at the orange glow of whatever was burning at Can Tho. No explosions now, just the geckos and the frogs and the insects. He was thinking that Nguyen's hundred kilometers was about right. Sixty miles to the border. There the hills began. Another twenty miles, more or less, to Eleth Vinh's village. Another ten or twelve into the higher country to the Reverend van Winjgaarden's mission. The range on the APC he'd worked with at Fort Riley was 120 miles fully loaded, with twelve men, their weapons, spare ammunition, food, water, and gear. This model was the lighter version, made for the swamps. It should do a little better. He'd strapped eight GI cans in the racks the ARVN had added. Forty gallons. Full tank when they left the hangars, but if the gauge was right they'd already burned about 30 percent of that. Enough fuel to get there. There would be some left for getting back. Enough? Probably not.

The glow at Can Tho flared brighter. Perhaps a gasoline tank going up. It died away. Moon thought about what they'd find at the Cambodian border. And across it. Lum Lee said the radio had reported that Pol Pot's new government was announcing it had executed eight members of the old cabinet. A public decapitation. Someone broadcasting from Bangkok had described the Khmer Rouge sending the capital's residents out into the country, setting up labor camps for them, killing the stragglers, killing the Chinese, killing those who were not ethnic Khmers. Killing those who had "the soft hands of the capitalistic exploiters of the people."

Well, maybe they would never reach the border. A dozen things could happen. If nothing bad happened, they should be there about moonset. Then they'd see what they would see.

PHNOM PENH, Cambodia, April 29 (Agence France-Presse)—The Cambodian government today ordered the immediate deportation of more than 600 foreign refugees being sheltered in the French Embassy. The refugees are being trucked to the Thai border.

Before Dawn, the Twentieth Day

May 2, 1975

THERE HAD BEEN a couple of hours of cautious, tense, uneventful driving. Moon sagged in his seat, fighting off the drowsiness of twenty-four hours without sleep, wondering about how his mother's operation had gone, working over the problem of Osa's odd behavior, and considering how to recover his lost job, his mind drifting far from the unreality of the Mekong Delta, far from the tension of running without lights down this rutted dirt road, depending on the moon, with Nguyen Nung perched above him behind the machine gun, giving directions sometimes with a bare foot tapping the proper shoulder, sometimes shouting over the mutter of the diesel.

Moon shook his head violently to drive away sleep

and, glancing back, saw that Osa was still sleeping curled on the bench and Lum Lee was studying the map spread across a rice sack on the floor. Then Nguyen yelled a warning and kicked hard at both of Moon's shoulders.

Moon slammed the APC into neutral, hit the brakes, flicked on the headlights. Two hundred yards down the road, a group of men were pushing an army truck backward across the narrow road. Some wore steel helmets. ARVN soldiers. Probably one of the fragments left from the Yellow Tiger Battalion. Probably the survivors of a platoon fleeing Can Tho. How should he handle this?

Nguyen was shouting something unintelligible.

"He says rocket launcher," Mr. Lee said. Then Moon could see it himself. The man holding it was just behind the truck, wearing a helmet. Kneeling now to aim. Moon cut the lights, slammed the APC in reverse, did the push-pull "bugout" maneuver they'd practiced a hundred times at Fort Riley, felt the machine begin its spin. He heard something like a curse from Nguyen, then the sound of bullets ricocheting from the side armor, then the staccato roar of Nguyen's machine gun.

The APC lurched into the ditch, tilted at an angle of almost forty-five degrees. From behind Moon came the sound of things clanging and crashing as they fell, the slamming, whanging sound of bullets hitting the armor, of sudden bursts from Nguyen's gun, of the left tread spinning in the mud, the groan of twisting metal plates.

Then the deafening blast of an explosion.

Moon's nostrils were filled with the smell of smoke, his ears with Nguyen's scream.

Moon thought, So this is how it ends.

He felt a strange, illogical sense of peace. Behind him Osa was sprawled on the rice sacks. Mr. Lee was invisible. Nguyen's legs were thrashing. Then he realized that the diesel was roaring, both treads were holding again, the APC rolling down them, tilting back to level, moving. Now the *whang* of bullets hitting steel was coming from the closed rear ramp. Whatever had exploded hadn't killed them. Not even Nguyen. The blood trickling down the man's arm and dripping on Moon's back must be from something relatively minor because Nguyen was still at the gun above, firing efficient short fifty bursts.

It had probably been an antipersonnel grenade, designed to kill men but not to penetrate even the thin armor of an APC. They'd decided that after fleeing a mile down the road and turning down an even narrower side road and sitting, with the engine cut, to listen. Moon, who rarely remembered to pray, prayed now not to hear an approaching truck. The truck could easily outrun them on the road. The grenade had merely frightened them and gave Nguyen another shrapnel slash across his shoulder. But if the soldiers had an antitank rocket it would punch right through this thin-skinned little vehicle and turn it into a great blaze of burning diesel fuel.

Which, it occurred to Moon as he sat straining to hear something and hoping not to, was why they were still alive. The truck must be out of fuel. The roadblock was being formed either to snare an operating vehicle or refuel the truck.

Now sounds began to emerge from the eerie silence. No truck, no shots, just the rain-country lizards resuming their lustful shouts, insects taking up their nocturnal songs, and finally the frogs issuing their interrupted mating calls.

Nguyen was sure the blast had been a rocket grenade. He had seen it coming. He had seen them coming before out of the mangrove thickets, out of the half-burned hooches lining the creeks and canals and the Mekong itself. Seen what they would do when they hit the fiberglass hull of a PBR or one of its occupants. That's why he had screamed. But he was embarrassed by that now, because only a little piece of shrapnel had cut his shoulder.

While Osa added to his collection of bandages, Nguyen gave them his analysis of the action, which seemed, despite his wound, to have left him joyful. They had come upon what was left of a Yellow Tiger infantry platoon on the run from their lost war at Can Tho. They were headed for the coast, Nguyen believed, hoping to steal a boat. Their truck had run out of fuel. They had heard the APC coming and were preparing a roadblock to ambush them. Nguyen emphasized that he was navy, not army. A sailor, not a soldier. He had Mr. Lee translate that distinction twice. Even so, he would not have fired upon those cowardly soldiers had they not shot at him first.

They mapped a detour, following the network of little capillary dirt tracks that kept the delta peasants in touch with the villages. It avoided the roadblock, reduced the risk of running into such problems, and added about twenty kilometers to their journey. Moon pushed himself up from the bench, trying to do the math in his head, converting kilometers to miles and dividing the miles per gallon of diesel fuel burned. He felt dizzy. And pessimistic.

"Well," he said, "let's get going."

Osa caught his arm. "My turn," she said. "I've slept. I'm rested. You're exhausted."

"You think you can drive an APC?" Moon's tone implied he didn't.

"Why not? Because I'm a woman?"

"Because you don't know how," Moon said.

"There's the ignition," she said, pointing past him at the switch just left of the driver's seat. "There's the fuel control. The right post controls the right tread, doesn't it? The left post the left tread. And there's the thing to shift the gears."

"I better drive," Moon said.

"Why? You'll go to sleep. We'll run off the road."

"Things might happen," Moon said. To his dismay, he had to stifle a yawn. Being sick on that ship had taken something out of him.

"If something happens you should be up there in the hatch. Nguyen must lie down. He lost blood. I think he is all used up for a while."

"Mr. Lee can be lookout in the hatch," Moon said.

"Mr. Lee lost his glasses."

"Oh," Moon said, lost for words. The other alternative was to have Osa stand in the machine gun hatch. He rejected that. Someone might shoot her.

"You be in the hatch," she said. "Away from the engine fumes. The fresh air would be good for you."

He made sure Osa understood the gearing system, and how to handle the tread control steering if they needed to go into reverse, and how to take directions by a foot tap on a shoulder. Then he climbed onto the pedestal seat, heard the engine start below him, and felt the APC begin to lumber forward.

The moon was lower now but they were driving westward, almost directly toward it, and it made the track they were following a ribbon of light between the dark brush of the ditches alongside. Nguyen had jammed one of the rice sacks between the hatch rim and the machine gun mount, either for padding or protection. Something had torn the sack, allowing rice to dribble out on the APC's steel roof. But it was soft. Moon rested his arms on it and thought.

First he completed the fuel computation, dividing his estimate of round trip miles remaining by the gallons remaining. He came out short of fuel. Nothing to do about that. He thought about Victoria Mathias. If his mother hadn't survived the operation, who would arrange the funeral? If she had, who would be there to take care of her? He should know more about her friends. He should have taken more interest in her life. Too late for that now. And if he didn't make it back, how would she ever know what had happened to him? Would she ever know that he had tried, that he had not simply absconded with her tickets and her eight thousand dollars?

That led him to think about the long odds against getting back to his house in Durance, and about what he'd have to say to get Shakeshaft to rehire him, and about what to do about getting Rooney back on the wagon and reemployed.

He left thinking about Debbie for the last. Nothing had changed in that department. Only that now he knew he didn't really want to marry her. He would, if that was the only way to save her. But now he hoped for some other salvation—just as in Manila he had longed for something to save him from this hopeless duty.

He remembered the subtle way Osa had pushed him to keep him on the hunt for Ricky's friends. Ah, Osa! If only things had somehow been different a long time ago. If only he had been the man Ricky's tall tales made him out to be. And thinking about that, with his nostrils full of the smell of gunny sacking and rice, Malcolm Mathias drifted off into an exhausted sleep—into a dream dark with sorrow and loss.

SAIGON, South Vietnam, April 29 (UPI)—A helicopter shuttle service began evacuating Americans from the roof of the U.S. Embassy today while marine guards kept thousands of desperate Vietnamese from breaking through the gates.

The evacuation began as North Vietnamese tanks and infantry units began fighting their way into the city.

Dawn, the Twentieth Day

May 2, 1975

SOMETHING WAS JERKING at his pants leg. Someone was saying, "Moon, Moon. Wake up. There's a tank!"

Tank! Moon jerked wide awake. It was dawn. Silent. The APC was motionless in the brush at the very edge of a road, the engine not running. He saw no tank.

Nguyen Nung's bandaged head and torso were within touching distance—in the other roof hatch of the APC. Nguyen had the binoculars to his face, aimed down the road and to the left. Moon saw trees, saw that they were among low hills now, out of the delta's flatness. He saw that the road curved away to the left. And then he saw a flutter of motion. A thin black line extended upward, a green pennant flying from it moving in the breeze. And at the base of the line a gray-green shape that could only be the top of a turret.

Osa was tugging at his pants leg again. He looked down.

"Mr. Lee has gone to take a look," she said.

Damn! "Why didn't you wake me? Where are we?"

"At the border. On maybe just inside it. Mr. Lee said he thinks this must be a Cambodian checkpoint."

Moon took another look. Beyond the pennant, the hills rose into the morning mist, green and forested. That would be right, he thought. The map had showed the land rising sharply where Vietnam and its rice delta ended. It showed the Cambodian highlands rising abruptly there, forming a barrier between the Mekong and the Gulf of Siam.

Osa guessed what he was thinking.

"We're right where we are supposed to be," she said. "The map was accurate."

"But there wasn't supposed to be a border control point here," Moon said. "That was supposed to be down on Route Eighty where the traffic is. Down on the coast."

"There's probably one there too," Osa said. "Probably a big one. Here there seems to be just a tank."

"Yeah," Moon said. "Just a tank." He lowered himself stiffly from the machine gunner's pedestal. "I'd better go and help Mr. Lee scout things out."

"Two," said Nguyen Nung from his perch. He held his hand down, two fingers extended.

"Two tanks?"

"Two tanks," Nguyen agreed, sounding pleased by this linguistic advance, if not by the news.

"I wouldn't go," Osa said. She was twisted in the

driver's seat looking back at him. "Mr. Lee is wearing peasant clothing. And he's small. If they see him, he will just look like a local farmer. If they see you—" She left that hanging, unfinished.

"I'll be careful," he said. The rear ramp had been lowered. He ducked and walked out of it. Osa said something loud—probably Dutch, and probably an expletive.

He kept to the roadside brush, angling toward where he'd seen the tank. Ahead of him among the trees, something rustled. Moon crouched behind a growth of young bamboo. It was Mr. Lee. He squatted beside Moon.

"A tank is parked on each side of the road," Mr. Lee said. "And then there is a small bamboo building in the middle of the road." He described it with his hands. "You know. The road goes on each side of it. It is open on the front and both sides. To collect duties, I think."

"Is it empty now?"

"No one is in it unless they are sleeping on the floor. Empty, I think. But there is one other house, made of planks with a palm roof. Is anyone in it? I don't know. One cannot see the inside."

"What kind of tanks?"

"What kind?" The question came as a surprise. Mr. Lee seemed not to have been aware that tanks came in varieties.

"Are they both alike? Do both have round turrets on top?"

"Yes. Just alike."

"Do they have tractor treads, like ours? Or do they roll on big wheels? How big? Try to describe them."

"Treads," Mr. Lee said. He described what sounded to Moon like an M48 tank, mainstay of the U.S. Army and the model it provided its allies. It was what Moon had hoped to hear. If Mr. Lee had described the rounded shape of a Russian-made T54 it would almost certainly have meant the Khmer Rouge were there.

"Did you see any sign of the crew?"

Mr. Lee shook his head. "But maybe they're inside. There was no way to tell that, of course."

"They're not inside," Moon said. "We can bet on that." No sane person would sleep in a tank if there was another place to bed down. Certainly not in this awful climate. "Now we need to find out if anyone is in the house."

Mr. Lee looked at him thoughtfully. "They did not hear our engine when we came up," he said. "I think we could back slowly away. Then turn around. Then we can find another way to cross the border."

"We didn't find another way when we studied the map. No track we could use without going miles back toward the Mekong."

"True," Mr. Lee said. "But that was the map. Just lines on paper. Now we are here. We try, and try again, and try again. And we finally find a way."

"No," Moon said. "We finally run out of diesel fuel."

"Oh," Mr. Lee said. He made a wry face, shrugged. "There is not enough extra oil in those cans you brought along?"

"We have enough to get there. If the roads aren't too steep, I think we'll have a little bit left."

Mr. Lee considered this. He'd pushed the conical hat to the back of his head, and the slanting early morning light emphasized the lines age had left around his eyes. Moon had thought from that first night in Los Angeles that this man's face was unusually expressive. Now it registered something between despair and sorrow as realization sank in and hope drained away. Then he shrugged and managed a small laugh.

"Ah, then," he said. "I think you could carry your

brother's little baby out." He thought again. "And Mrs. van Winjgaarden could lead out her brother—although I really think she no longer has any hope that he's alive. But how can I carry out the *kam taap* that holds my ancestor's bones?" He smiled weakly at Moon. "I think Mr. Nung would be happy to help me, but with those injuries it would not be possible."

"Nguyen couldn't carry much," Moon agreed. "I could help."

"Then we go on?"

"There must be fuel in those tanks," Moon said. "Almost certainly they'll have fuel in them. Why would they park them there empty?"

"Yes," Mr. Lee said. "Of course. Do you know how to get it out?"

Moon laughed. "That's within the range of my talents," he said.

"I would think that when the Cambodian government broadcast the surrender order and Pol Pot took over the government in Phnom Penh, these soldiers just went away," Mr. Lee said.

"Just climbed out and went home," Moon agreed. And hoped fervently that he was right.

It proved to be a good guess. The proud green pennant of the Royal Cambodian Second Division flew from their antennas, but the two M48s had been left to rust.

By sunrise, Moon had drained enough diesel oil from one of them to refill the tank of their M-113 and had them rolling down the track into the Cambodian hills. Within thirty minutes they'd seen the first evidence of Pol Pot's Zero Year campaign. The track had become a narrow dirt road, winding upward into the forest toward, they hoped, Vin Ba. It passed a cluster of a dozen shacks, all apparently deserted. One seemed to have been a store, and on its porch three bodies were hanging by their necks, their hands tied behind them, two men and a woman. One man wore brown trousers, a white shirt, and a vest, the other the saffron robe of a monk. The woman was naked.

A mile beyond that, the track they were following intersected with another. Moon pulled the APC across the roadside ditch and parked it out of sight among the trees. Mr. Lee spread the artillery map on the rice sacks, with the map Rice had marked for them beside it. Their little intersection was on the military chart, but only one track showed on the commercial version. It seemed to be the one they had been following from the checkpoint through the empty village.

Moon was disappointed but not surprised. "I think this other road must be newer. It wasn't there when the commercial map was made."

"So you think we find Vin Ba up the other road?" Mr. Lee said.

"Well," Moon said, "the army screws things up when it can, but this map must have been drawn from aerial photographs. A computer scans them and redraws the photos on paper. The army hadn't even heard of Cambodia until about ten years ago, so the photos have to be fairly new."

"I wish I could say it looks familiar," Osa said. "I must have flown right over this when I went in to see Damon. But, you know, I just remember hills and trees."

"Things look different from the air anyway," Moon said.

"I do remember Ricky pointing down to a little village in a narrow valley and saying that's where his Lila had been born and where her mother lived. Then we flew over terraced fields, and mountain ridges, and we landed at Damon's place."

"This must be Vin Ba then," Mr. Lee said, with his finger on the map. "Very close to here."

It proved to be less than two miles: a long fuel-draining climb uphill, a sudden ridgeline, and then, as the APC tilted downward, they saw cleared fields and terraced paddies. A village was almost directly below them. Moon stopped, got the binoculars from Nguyen, and examined the place.

He saw no sign of life. Three of the houses were roofless, apparently burned out. The Khmer Rouge seemed to have been there. Were they still here? Why would they be?

"Burned," Nguyen said. "Hooches burned." He was standing in the machine gunner's hatch, pointing, looking at Moon. "Too late, you think?"

"Let's go see," Moon said, and squeezed back into the driver's seat.

"'Way we go!" Nguyen said, and Moon heard him slamming a new round into the breach of the .50. The belt rattled as Nguyen adjusted it.

But there was nothing for Nguyen to shoot at. The road dropped off the hill, emerged from the trees, and became an even narrower track following an irrigation canal. Some of the paddies had been newly planted with shoots of rice, but no one was working the fields. The village seemed empty, the only sound the throbbing of the diesel.

Mr. Lee's hand was on his shoulder. "I think they heard our engine far away. It made them afraid the Khmers were returning."

"We'll see," Moon said. Rice had told them that the Vinhs and their neighbors in this village were not ethnic Khmers. It seemed more likely to him that Pol Pot's troops had followed the pattern of atrocities they'd been hearing described on the radio. They'd left no one behind. They would find the bodies of the old and the sick, with the young people swept away to work camps to be taught the Zero Year philosophy.

Moon cut the ignition and climbed up into the hatch, into the sunlight and the silence.

Where now would he look for Ricky's baby?

Nguyen was looking at him, making a wry face and the empty palms-up gesture of failure. Moon nodded. He climbed out of the hatch and dropped to the ground.

From somewhere behind the house just ahead of them came grunting. A pig? Then a rooster crowed. The door of this house Moon faced had been made of bamboo canes wired together hung on leather hinges. It stood open now. Moon looked in at a dirt floor partly covered with a mat, at a cabinet turned on its side with its contents of dishes and pots scattered around it. But the grunting was coming from behind the next house—fifty yards down the community's irrigation ditch.

Two pigs, both lean and mean by American pig standards, were tethered by long leg chains to one of the posts that supported the back porch of the small bamboo-and-thatch hut. The sight of Moon provoked a chorus of frantic grunts and squeals. They had water in a rusty metal trough. They wanted food, expected it, demanded it, competed for it, snapping and pushing.

The pigs suggested that some villager had been there after the Khmer Rouge left. Pol Pot's troops might fail to catch a rooster, but they would hardly have missed two tethered pigs. But swine devoid of their owner could tell him nothing, least of all where to find the swineherd. And these unfed swine might be as abandoned as the empty houses, the trail that had turned itself into a street, the rice paddies, the ditch that irrigated them, the whole little valley and the hills that closed it in. He would find something back at the APC to cut the chains and free them. That should be a job in the range of his competence.

Nguyen the warrior was still standing behind the .50

caliber, conditioned by his dangerous years in the Brown Water Navy to expect ambushes. His expression, as much of it as was visible around the now-grimy bandages, suggested he wouldn't mind a fight. Nguyen had expressed his distaste for Cambodians in general and Khmer Communists in particular when he first understood they were heading for a village across the border. He had provided a half dozen anecdotal examples of Cambodian rudeness, barbarity, dishonesty, laziness, and otherwise slovenly conduct. Mr. Lee, in translating this, added that the feeling was common among Vietnamese, North and South, and was matched by a Cambodian contempt for Vietnamese, and exceeded by the distaste felt by Laotians for Thais, and vice versa.

Nguyen waved and said, "Nobody?"

"Nobody," Moon agreed. "Just two orphaned pigs."

Osa appeared from around the APC, her face and hair wet. Washing in the irrigation ditch, Moon guessed. He'd try it himself. It seemed to be fresh water diverted from the stream they'd crossed on the way in. He would wash, and collect Mr. Lee from wherever he'd wandered, and get to hell out of here. Finish this. Be done with this. End it. Forget it.

Osa was smiling a rueful smile. "Too bad. I guess nobody is left," she said. "I know you had hopes. I did too. It is a terrible disappointment for you."

"Que sera sera," Moon said, thinking of Halsey's standard formula for dealing with hostile fate. Thinking of Sergeant Gene Halsey dead under the jeep. Of course. What would be would be. And for Malcolm Mathias, despite grandiose intentions, this empty village was what would be at the end of the road for him.

Osa was studying him, looking worried. "Maybe—" she began, but could think of no way to finish it.

"Let's find Mr. Lee," Moon said, "and make sure we haven't missed anyone—or anything. And get the hell out of here."

"He said he would be back very quickly," Osa said. "He said he wanted to find his *kam taap*."

They waited. Even Nguyen was quiet, thinking his thoughts.

Finally Osa touched his arm. "When the wars are all over and there is peace again, then you could come and find the little girl."

"Yeah," Moon said, thinking maybe someone could do that. But not Malcolm Mathias.

"I think it would be easier then. There would be refugee agencies to help people find their relatives. It was that way in Java after the war."

"I think I should go and find Mr. Lee. Maybe I could do that."

As Moon said it, he saw Mr. Lee walking down the track toward them. "I find not a thing," Mr. Lee said. "But I think there is a place back there"—and he pointed to field beyond the ditch—"where some people might be buried just a few days ago. And I find where the Khmer Rouge have torn down some tombs and broken the *kam taap* that were left in them." He paused. "But I did not see mine."

"I guess that's our only good news," Moon said.

"Ah, no," Mr. Lee said. "Not so good. It would be better to find it broken than not at all. I could gather up the bones and have another *kam taap* made for them. There are ceremonies that could be done. And then the place would be found for their permanent tomb, where the wind and water are correct." He paused, attempted a smile. "Now they are simply lost. Just as they were when I came to your hotel room in Los Angeles."

His words, and the sorrow in the old man's face,

reminded Moon that delivery of these bones was an unfulfilled Mathias contract and another failure on his list. He tried to think of something reassuring to say, thought of nothing, and the frustration, fatigue, and disappointment turned to anger.

"Why do they do this?" Moon said, gesturing toward the emptied village. "Pol Pot and his army. On the radio they're saying the son of a bitch wants to turn Cambodia back to farming, fishing, the simple life." He gestured at the row of shacks along the ditch. "What's simpler than this?"

Mr. Lee looked away, frowned. "I think it was the religion," he said. "Mr. Rice said he thought the people of Vin Ba followed Lord Buddha very closely. They were very good Taoists. The other villages would know that. If they know that, the Khmer Rouge would soon know it. Or they might see it here in the village. They would hate that. Buddhism is part of the decadence Pol Pot has told them they must wipe away."

Which meant, as it turned out, that Mr. Lee was not going with them. Mr. Lee would stay behind. He must study this village, this valley, as a geomancer would study it, to find a *feng shui,* the place where a devout Taoist would have left his *kam taap* until Mr. Lee came to recover it.

"I will find it," Mr. Lee said. "It will be a place next to the hills. Better, it will be between the protecting spurs of two hills where the energy would flow down to it." These are called the "green dragon" and the "white tiger," Mr. Lee explained, and they kept the wind flow mild. And from this spot between the two, one should be able to see water flowing away. Not toward the place but away from it.

There was a lot more of this explanation, and Moon nodded now and then to indicate he understood. But he didn't want to hear Mr. Lee's pitiful clutching for a last straw of hope. He wanted to get the hell out of there. Back to keeping Shirley's dog, fixing J.D.'s truck, keeping Rooney sober. Back to Durance and the sort of problems someone like Malcolm Mathias could cope with. Back to the sort of women he could understand.

BANGKOK, Thailand, April 28 (UPI)—An embassy spokesman said today that the United States would contest Thai government plans to return aircraft flying Vietnamese refugees here to Vietnam.

He said the aircraft had been provided to the South Vietnamese at a cost of more than $200 million and would fall into the hands of the Communists if returned.

Noon, the Twentieth Day

May 2, 1975

IT LOOKED FAIRLY EASY on the map. Rice had drawn a line in blue ballpoint ink from Vin Ba angling slightly toward the border. He'd made a blue dot and written in *Phum Kampong*. "I remember now that's what Damon called it," Rice had said. "Actually, you should put in one of those little pronunciation hats over the *a*, the way the Cambodians spell Kâmpong."

Back in Puerto Princesa such details hadn't seemed to matter. They still didn't. What mattered now was what Rice had also said. "Over two mountain ridges from Vin Ba and then up the next ridge and Damon's place is right on top." These weren't really mountains—not even close by Moon's Colorado Rockies standards—but they were significant hills. They ran out of road when they left Vin Ba's little valley and the going had been hard even for a tracked vehicle.

But there were footpaths. Moon's technique was to follow the one that went in the right general direction. They'd made a little plateau of stacked rice sacks next to the APC's personnel bench and spread both maps on it. Nguyen manned his .50-caliber lookout post. Osa matched the elevation lines on the artillery chart with the terrain features they were seeing. When things didn't seem to match, they stopped and consulted.

For Osa, this involved bouncing back and forth from sitting beside the rice sacks to standing on the bench with her head stuck out of the second hatch. There she would look for the spur, or the ridge, or the water drainage cut, matching map lines with the real landscape they were passing. For Moon, this involved an opportunity to look away from his viewing slot and study Osa with no risk of being caught at it. Nor was there much risk of running into a tree, since Nguyen was in the hatch above him, kicking him on the proper shoulder if he started letting the APC drift.

So Moon considered Osa's long denim-clad legs, her rear elevation when she turned to look behind them, her ankles above the funny-looking walking shoes she wore, her back, her narrow waist, the way she moved, the way she held herself. Everything about her from the shoulder blades down he memorized. And, of course, made the inevitable comparisons. In a beauty contest, in a Hollywood casting competition, Debbie would be the winner, a ten. Osa was the sort of woman for whom the gurus of fashion in Paris and Milan (and wherever else such things happened) designed clothing. Debbie was the sort for whom clothing manufacturers, faced with human reality, manufactured dresses in the sizes actually purchased in the various middle-class department stores. In other words, in the same places he bought his own stuff.

Bleak thought. But Moon was a realist. Or considered himself one. Had he been the Moon Mathias whom Ricky's exaggerations had created out here, he'd be making his pitch for Osa. Perhaps, if he actually was that super fellow, maybe he'd even be winning her. But the flesh-and-blood Moon was a K mart fellow. He knew it. By now, with Ricky's tales offset by reality, so did Osa van Winjgaarden.

Now they were at the top of the second ridge and Nguyen was tapping a foot against Moon's shoulder, signaling a stop. Time to eat something anyway. Time to take a rest. Moon climbed wearily out to take a look. Based on the Langenscheidt map, there should have been a small village identified as Neap in the valley below them. Moon had presumed this foot trail had led to it. Now he could see no sign of a village below. About two hundred people, Rice had said, and some terraced rice paddies. Instead of the little strip of cultivated fertility one expected, there was some sort of geological deformity where nothing grew. It was a long strip of broken rocks and desolation starting low on the opposite slope and running down the declivity. No place for a village.

True, there'd been no dot labeled Neap on the artillery map. But such maps tend to be more interested in terrain and less in homesites. Moon had expected to find Neap. Had counted on it. It would be proof he hadn't taken a wrong turn. It would have been his final landmark. Beyond it, he would angle the APC to the left up the slope and reach the top. There they would find the village of Phum Kampong waiting, and the Reverend Damon van Winjgaarden—perhaps—alive. Without Neap, Moon was thoroughly lost.

With much pointing Nguyen showed them that the footpath they'd been following faded out on this stonier ground. Which way now? Nguyen had no idea. Then he was pointing eastward and repeating something that sounded like "Mekong."

Indeed it was. The next ridgeline was lower. Over it and through the blue haze beyond was a ribbon of silver. Sunlight was reflecting off the river. Good. At least they were on the proper ridge.

Moon ate a cupful of boiled rice and some of the crackers they'd brought from the R. M. Air base and thought about it. The route they'd planned on the map had taken them away from the Mekong toward the Gulf to cross the border and then circled back in the hills. At least the Mekong was where it should be. At least that had gone right.

But not quite. Moon explained the problem to Osa. Nguyen listened, a mixture of comprehension and bafflement.

"In other words, there should be a little bitty village down there. There isn't and apparently never was. So I must have either gone too far one way or the other. Which means we are looking down into the wrong little valley and now we have some guessing to do."

"Village?" Nguyen asked.

"Yes," Moon said. "I thought there would be a village down there."

"We'll find it," Osa said. "We'll find paths down there, and they'll lead us."

Nguyen was shaking his head in vigorous denial. "No," he said. "No more." He pointed to the irregular line of broken stones. But that turned out to be a reference to the Ho

Chi Minh trail, which snaked through the mountains along the border to feed supplies to the Vietcong in the delta. That finally understood, Nguyen made the sound of an airplane. He created one with two hands and flew it very slowly, very laboriously across his waist. That done, he said, "Very big."

"Ah, yes," Moon said. "The B-Fifty-twos." He turned to Osa, still looking puzzled. "That's why Kissinger started them bombing Cambodia. To cut off supplies to the VC."

Osa was smiling at him. "I think you're finally getting tired," she said. "That's interesting, but how does it help us?"

A good question. Nguyen seemed to understand the thrust of it. He trotted up the rear ramp and emerged with the Langenscheidt map in one hand, the artillery chart in the other. He held the commercial map against the side of the APC, indicated Neap, then created B-52 sounds and walked his fingers across Neap. *"Boom, boom, boom, boom, boom, boom, boom,"* Nguyen said. He held up his hand and flashed his fingers again and again. "I think fifty," he said. He replaced the commercial with the artillery chart, put his finger where Neap should have been, said, "No." He looked at Moon, then at Osa, seeking understanding.

They stood beside the APC looking down at the long strip of ruin below them where two hundred Cambodians had once lived in a village called Neap.

"Why bomb there?" Osa said. "There couldn't be any kind of road down there."

"Dark of night," Moon said. "They would have been flying very high, probably above thirty-five thousand feet. And they'd be coming all the way from Guam. It would be easy to miss by just one ridgeline."

Osa was looking down at where Neap had been, saying nothing.

"Or maybe one of the planes had mechanical trouble. The pilot had to jettison his load."

"One plane? Just one airplane could do all that?"

"I think they carry fifty bombs. Isn't that what Nguyen was trying to tell us? Five hundred pounds of TNT per bomb. Or was it a thousand? Then multiply that by fifty."

Osa was silent again, looking into the valley. "So maybe we're not lost. Maybe the village was down there once."

"Let's say it was," Moon said, thinking they could be on the other ridge in an hour, maybe less. They'd either find Phum Kampong and Reverend Damon or they wouldn't. Either way, they'd be done with this. "Let's get going."

It wasn't necessary. A man emerged from the trees behind the APC and stood watching them, a small thin man, slightly stooped, with gray hair cut short. Then he shouted, "Mrs. van Wing Garden."

Osa remembered him. He was one of her brother's converts from Phum Kampong whom she'd met on her last visit—one of the men Damon had been training to help him spread Christianity in the hills. He squatted beside the APC, small, thin, slightly stooped, his mustache gray, his eating rice with him, very glad to see Osa. In halting English he told them how he had heard their vehicle coming up the mountainside, thought it must be the Khmer Rouge returning, had hidden, had seen Osa standing in the hatch, had recognized her as the sister of Brother Damon, and had hurried along to try to catch them.

"You have come to replace your brother," he said. "We all will thank you for that."

Osa looked down at her feet. "Replace him? Is Damon not with you now?"

"Oh," the man said. "You didn't know about it." He looked at Osa, then at Moon, expression rueful.

"Is he all right?" Moon asked.

"I was not at the village when the Khmer Rouge came. I live here, where I cut my wood and make my charcoal." He motioned toward Vin Ba. "I sell it over in Vin Ba. But not now because nobody is left in Vin Ba. But—"

Moon cut him off. "Where is Damon now? Will we find him at Phum Kampong?"

"They took him away. They took him and some of the Christians, and some of them they killed in the village."

"But they didn't kill Damon? He was still alive?"

"Down there," the man said, pointing into the valley where Neap had once existed. "There we found his body."

SAIGON, South Vietnam, April 30 (UPI)—President Duong Van Minh announced today the unconditional surrender of the Saigon government and its military forces to the Vietcong.

Afternoon, the Twentieth Day

May 2, 1975

RETRACING ONE'S STEPS is easy. Moon simply spun the APC around and headed it down the mountainside following the tracks the treads had made coming up. No problem. He peered downward through the driver's viewing slot: a little pressure on the right steering bar when needed, then a little pressure on the left. Just think about that. No reason to think about strike three and you're out. No niece, no bones, no brother.

Nguyen was perched in the hatch above. Osa slumped on the troopers' bench. When he turned to glance at her, he'd see only the top of her head, looking at the rice sacks. What was she seeing in the burlap? What was she thinking of? He hoped she had been conscious of the probable time of Damon's execution. From what the man had told them, his body had been found and buried about the day they'd slipped out of Puerto Princesa. Even if he had been the super-Moon that Ricky had fantasized, he couldn't have kept that from happening. Or perhaps Osa would be remembering Damon had realized his dream to be a martyr. He hoped that would give her some comfort.

The man had described it as he had heard it from survivors at the village. He told it proudly, with a fair command of English vocabulary but a pronunciation that Moon guessed must be a mixture of Montagnard inflections and Damon's own Dutch-based distortions. The Khmer Rouge had come at dawn, about twenty of them: two young men, a young woman, and the rest just boys. Some barely in their teens, barely big enough to carry their assault rifles. Everyone had been ordered out into the clearing where the villagers prepared their charcoal and joss sticks to be sold.

Then they burned the house that Damon used as his hospital. They untied Damon's arms and the young woman told him to point to the villagers he had made into Christians. But Damon would not tell them.

Here the man had stopped. He had looked at Osa—obviously not wanting someone who had loved Damon to hear this. Go ahead, Osa had said. It was what Damon wanted. And so the man had continued. He said the Khmers would push someone out of the crowd and the question would be repeated, and Damon would say that only the person they were holding there would know whether or not they believed the words of Jesus. Then "they would hurt Brother Damon," the man said, and ask the question again, and hurt him again. Finally one of the women of the village stepped out of the crowd and said she was a Christian. And then others stepped out, men, women, and children. The Khmers bound their arms and tied them all together and ordered the other villagers to kill them with clubs. But nobody would do it, so the woman shot two of those who refused. And one of the Khmer boys shot another one. Then the villagers would beat the Christians a little, but not hard. So another one was shot. Then the woman ordered it stopped. They left the Christians all tied together. The other young men they herded into a group. The woman said these men would be trained to help liberate their homeland from the capitalist oppressors. She hadn't said what would be done with the Christians.

"She didn't tell us, but we found out," the man said. He walked to the edge of the clearing, pointed down into the valley, and said, "We found their bodies down there."

That had ended it. Except the man had embraced Osa, and she had embraced him hard and for quite a while. The man told her something, speaking too low for Moon to overhear even if he had wanted to.

It was a hard climb up the final ridge before Vin Ba's valley. Moon stopped where the trees were thin at the top to let the engine cool and to give everyone what he had been calling a "comfort break." Nguyen stayed inside, fiddling with the radio, telling them something about the U.S. Embassy. About helicopters. "Americans gone home now," he said sadly. "Congs coming in Saigon now." Osa listened a moment, then came down the ramp, wandered into the trees, and sat on a fallen tree trunk. Moon stood beside the APC looking through the binoculars.

From here, too, you could see the Mekong—barely visible through the gap where the valley opened into its narrower Cambodian flood plain. There was just a flash of reflected sunlight through the haze, but it could only be the river. It was a dramatic view and Moon stared at it a long time—though he hated the humid haze and the heat and everything that dirty river represented to him. If he didn't look at it, he would have to look at Osa, sitting on a fallen tree behind the APC. He'd have to try to think of something to say to her. Something sympathetic and consoling but not stupid. Not something that would make her cry. Or maybe that would be better. They said one shouldn't hold grief in.

He turned away from the river and stood beside her, looking down. She looked up, the question in her eyes.

"I'm sorry," Moon said.

She looked down, shook her head. "It's okay."

"Sorry I was too late."

"It has nothing to do with late," she said. "Or early."

What do you say to that? He didn't think of anything.

"I just didn't believe him," she said, looking up at Moon to see if he understood. "My brother, you know. He was always talking big. He was always full of his dreams." She looked down again, studying her hands. "He told me when he went off to the seminary. I thought he was just being silly. Being romantic. We went on a kind of picnic, the day before he caught the plane. I said, 'Damie, you're being silly going off to be a minister. They'll find out about you in a minute and toss you out. You'll be right back here again and all of those girls who've been chasing after you, they'll all be married and gone.' And he said, 'Oh, no. Not Damie. That was the Damie you used to know. Now—'" She stopped, wiped her eyes with the back of her hand. "He'd been reading a biography of Francis of Assisi, I think it was. One of the great medieval saints. He said he was done with chasing after girls. From now on, he would chase after God."

She glanced up at Moon.

"Well," Moon said.

She smiled. "I remember it so well. I punched him on the shoulder. I said, 'Come on, Damie. Snap out of it. You're dreaming.' And he said—all excited—'Yes. Yes. Yes. Yes. I'm dreaming, Osa. I'm going to be one of God's saints. If I am man enough.'"

She looked up at him, waiting.

"Well," Moon said, "he was man enough. And the way I remember what they tried to teach us in our religion class, he made it in as a saint."

"I loved him," Osa said. "He was a crazy little brother, but I loved him."

Just as he had feared, he had started her really crying. He sat on the tree trunk beside her and hugged her against him and let her weep.

On the long roll down the final hillside into Vin Ba, Nguyen Nung's fear of ambush kicked in again. High in the hills he had become relatively relaxed. Osa had stood in the hatch, watching, while Nguyen sat on the bench fiddling with the radio. The news he was hearing seemed overwhelmingly bad—serious enough for Nguyen to tap Moon on the shoulder and try to explain things. First it was more about the Americans being "all gone home." They'd been hearing that the previous evening, that helicopters were flying in and flying out loaded with refugees from the U.S. Embassy. Not much new there. Nguyen's next burst of excitement brought Osa down from the hatch to join him in listening.

"What's happening now?" Moon shouted.

"I guess it's all over," Osa said. "The war. I think Nguyen is saying that North Vietnamese tanks broke into the presidential palace and captured everybody. He thinks the man talking now is the new president, announcing the war is over. They seem to be broadcasting orders to South Vietnamese units, telling them to quit fighting and surrender."

Moon digested that. The Communists had won, then. No more South Vietnam. But from their point of view, maybe the best possible news. He tried to imagine what would be happening. Wild celebrations by the winners.

Confusion. Despair. People fleeing the country. Who would notice an M-113 APC rolling across the delta flying a Vietcong flag? Who would care?

The trail they were following leveled. The trees thinned as they reached the edge of the valley. Moon stopped the APC. Nguyen remained in the hatch above him, methodically studying the houses through the binoculars.

"Ho!" he shouted suddenly. "People!"

Moon reached up for the binoculars, but Nguyen had already handed them to Osa, standing in the other hatch. Moon waited, nervous. What now? What would they do about Mr. Lee?

"I see Mr. Lee," Osa said. "And a woman is with him." She ducked out of the hatch and handed Moon the glasses.

The woman looked to Moon more like a girl. A teenager, perhaps. She sat in the shade of a hut beside one of the houses with Lee sitting across from her. No one else was in sight. A peaceful scene. Moon remembered the pigs. Of course, someone would still be there. The owner of the tethered pigs would have heard their APC approaching this morning. Time enough to hide, but not to hide the pigs.

"Let's go," Moon said. He didn't want to allow hope to revive. It was still impossible. But hope revived without permission.

Through the driver's slit he could see Mr. Lee waiting beside the irrigation ditch, the girl standing at his side. Lee shouted something. Nguyen shouted an answer. They exchanged more shouts. Moon cut the ignition, stretched, forced himself to be patient for a dignified moment. Then he followed Osa and Nguyen out the rear ramp. Mr. Lee was expressing condolences and Osa was accepting them with her usual grace.

"And you," she said. "Did you find your *kam taap*?"

Mr. Lee's tired old face developed a smile of such luminous joy that no other answer was necessary. But he said, "Yes! Yes!" And pressed his hands in front of his chest, and said "Yes!" again. "And even more wonderful," he said, turning toward Moon, "we have good news for Mr. Mathias too. I think we have found the child."

But not quite yet.

The girl with Mr. Lee was Ta Le Vinh, who was twelve and a second cousin of Eleth Vinh. As Mr. Lee described her presence, a villager cleaning the ditch had seen the Khmer Rouge coming and had come running with the warning. A dozen people had headed for the woods without stopping for anything. Others had waited to collect food, or clothing, or valuables. They had been caught and marched away. Five of the villagers who made it to the woods had kept going, intending to cross the mountains and find refuge with relatives until the territory was safe again. Seven stayed behind, including Ta Le, her parents, and Daje Vinh, who was the mother of Eleth Vinh. And with Daje Vinh was Lila Vinh, the baby.

Mr. Lee was explaining this, with Ta Le listening intently. "After you drove away this morning, I went out there." And Mr. Lee indicated a high meadow across the irrigation ditch. "I noticed how the arms of the hill enclosed it, giving it the proper slope. An excellent *feng shui* site. So I walked up there and found several shrines and several *kam taap*. Many of these, too, had been desecrated by the Khmers. They had shot them with their automatic rifles, breaking them to pieces. And one of them was the *kam taap* we have been seeking."

"Wonderful," Osa said. "They hadn't broken it up?"

"Oh, yes," Mr. Lee said, his smile undiminished. "Broken it up. But it doesn't matter. I got a sack and picked everything up and brought it here." He pointed to the house. "Another *kam taap* will be made. It is the bones that are important." He looked at Moon for agreement. "There is where the spirit lives."

"Right," Moon said.

"Even then the good luck was already working. Miss Vinh and her family were watching me. They saw from what I was doing that I was a religious man. One who follows the teachings of the Lord Buddha could not be a Khmer Rouge. So Miss Vinh came out to learn who I was. She went back and told her family. But her parents said they would wait until the brother of Ricky Mathias came back in the vehicle so they could see him for themselves and be sure it was not a trick before they would come out of the woods."

"That was sensible," Moon said.

So Moon, Mr. Lee, and the Miss Vinh who was a second cousin of Eleth Vinh walked up into the meadow. Moon stood there in the hot afternoon sun, feeling foolish, sweat dripping from his nose, his eyebrows, trickling below his shoulder blades, feeling foolish and praying without words. Miss Vinh was pointing at him, shouting something toward the screen of trees. From the trees emerged a man, and just behind him a woman.

The woman carried a baby.

Moon realized he had not been breathing. He whooshed out a huge breath, inhaled another, and looked up at the sky. What is it that Muslims say? It came to him. God is good. God is good.

The adults proved to be the parents of Ta Le Vinh. The required courteous formalities of introduction were handled in an unusual hurry by Mr. Lee. The elder Vinhs were obviously nervous—not happy to be standing here in the open. It was said, they explained, that the Khmer Rouge followed a tactic of raiding a village, leaving just long enough for those who had escaped them to return, and then raiding it again. In another two days, they would return to their homes. Perhaps it would be safe then, and they had no place else to go.

Moon was shown the infant. He looked, hoping to see a family resemblance, perhaps to Victoria Mathias. He saw just another baby. Between one and two, he guessed, but small. Perhaps Ricky's eyes.

The baby examined Moon with the same results, showing no sign she was particularily impressed.

"Ask them if the child's grandmother is here," Moon said to Mr. Lee. "The mother of Eleth Vinh. Is she here?"

Mr. Lee asked a short question. The answer was long and involved pointing. When translated it said that the elder Mrs. Vinh had been one of two refugees shot as they ran into the woods. Mrs. Vinh had been hit twice in the back. She had died last night.

The transaction was completed. Moon was handed the baby, who resisted the transfer by kicking and crying. Mr. Lee was handed a bundle of the supplies that go with babies. The Vinhs were told that the sacks of rice used as mine protection in the APC would be left behind for them. Farewells were said. The Vinhs disappeared into the woods. Moon and Mr. Lee plodded across the meadow, heading for the APC, with Nguyen Nung perched behind its .50, waiting for trouble, with Osa leaning against it, watching them.

Zero for three had turned into two for three.

Now he could go home. If he could get there. But where was the joy he should be feeling?

CAMBODIAN REDS ARE UPROOTING MILLIONS
AS THEY IMPOSE A "PEASANT REVOLUTION"

—*New York Times*, May 9, l975

The Twenty-seventh Day

May 9, 1975

THE DINING ROOM OF THE HOTEL MAYNILA was cool in the way refrigerated air cools places in a humid climate. Despite the clammy dampness, Moon luxuriated in it. The last time he recalled being really cool was the morning he'd sat at this very table waiting for Osa to arrive. That was about three weeks ago. Or a lifetime, depending on how you looked at it. Actually, a lifetime minus a few hours, which was how long it would be before he'd have to say good-bye to her unless he tried to do something about it. And maybe even if he did.

He'd already said his good-byes to Lum Lee. Mr. Lee was staying with what he called a "family connection" elsewhere in Manila. But he'd called from the lobby, and Moon had come down to receive his thanks and hear him declare himself in Moon's perpetual debt. He reported that he'd dealt with the problem of the *Glory of the Sea*. He'd arranged a radio message to Captain Teele to explain what had prevented them from meeting him. Next he'd asked Moon if he'd seen Osa today. Moon said he hadn't.

Mr. Lee had remarked that Osa was "feeling very sad." Moon had said that the death of a brother was a terrible blow. Mr. Lee then said that wasn't exactly what he meant. He said he'd called Osa to bid her farewell and to tell her of the woman who came to Buddha for help because she could not stop grieving the loss of a loved one. Buddha had told the woman to collect five poppy seeds from homes that had never suffered such a loss. And of course she could find no such home, and that was the lesson. But, Mr. Lee had said, she'd told him she wasn't grieving for Damon. Then why did she sound so sad? And she had said, Not only death causes sorrow. Did Moon know what she meant by that?

And Moon had said no, he didn't.

There had been a moment of silence and Mr. Lee had asked if Moon would see Osa today, and he'd said perhaps, but he was extremely busy finishing the paperwork to fly Lila back to the States.

"I, too, have been busy," Mr. Lee had said. "Even though Lord Buddha taught us that we who busy ourselves picking stones from the path cannot see the gold beside us."

Moon had said he guessed that was true.

"And Osa too has been busy. She said she wanted to tell you good-bye but there had been much to do."

And Moon had said, Well, she'd had to call her mother to tell her about Damon.

Instead of commenting on that, Mr. Lee had told him another of his Buddhist parables. A bird with two heads lived in a desert where it often had to go without water. Thus each of the heads became proud of its ability to endure thirst. The rains came. A pool formed below the bird's nesting place, but each of the heads was too proud to take the first drink and so it died of thirst.

"Think of the wisdom in that teaching," Mr. Lee said.

It had been a strange conversation from a strange man. Moon had thought about the teaching. Then he'd picked up the telephone and called Osa at her hotel. She sounded subdued, tired. But she said yes, she could have dinner with him. She wanted to hear how the baby was doing and they should tell each other good-bye. She would meet him at the Maynila.

He sat in the lobby, twenty minutes early, freshly shaven, cleaned and pressed, and with a new Manila haircut that looked an awful lot like the government-issue cuts they'd seen on the crewmen of the aircraft carrier.

The carrier had been quite an experience—a ferryboat for a motley collection of refugees. Its flight deck had resembled a floating flea market when the *U.S.S. Pillsbury* had delivered them, and it had become more and more crowded as other frigates arrived to dump off the desperate people they were fishing from the South China Sea. The crowding became their good fortune. Somebody ordered helicopters to shuttle the surplus over to the Subic Bay Naval Base outside Manila. Their little party had made it onto the second flight.

Osa was walking across the carpet toward him, smiling.

Moon caught his breath. An almost-white skirt, a blouse with just a touch of blue in it here and there, her dark hair soft around her face.

Moon stood. "Wow," he said.

She rewarded that with a wider smile. "Wow to you too. Isn't it good to feel clean again? And have something done with your hair?"

"Or something done *to* it," Moon said, rubbing his hand across what was left of his.

She laughed. "I think you found Nguyen's barber," she said, and sat in the chair across from him.

"Someone told me that time cures bad haircuts. Probably it was Mr. Lee."

"Not tattoos, though," she said. "I worry about that. What will Nguyen do about that awful tattoo when he has to go back to Vietnam?"

"Nguyen will be all right," Moon said. "The navy takes care of its own." Nguyen had been lucky. In fact, they'd all been lucky. Their only really tense moment had come at the Cambodian border checkpoint. The tanks were still there, and now so were the Khmer Rouge. But they had expected no trouble from their rear. He'd kept the APC in normal speed and rolled it right down the trail with Khmer Rouge troopers staring and Nguyen waving happily. He'd held his breath until they were past the tanks. He'd doubted Pol Pot's citizen soldiers would know how to operate them, and he'd drained their fuel tanks onto the ground, but just seeing them there made him nervous.

Needless nerves. By the time the Khmers realized they weren't stopping and the shouting and shooting began, they were out of range of anything that could dent the APC. The rest of it was travel through a public celebration. The only armed men they saw were Vietcong jubilantly returning Nguyen's flag-waving. The only explosions they heard were fireworks.

The PBR had made it down the Mekong, mingling with such a swarm of refugee boats that the country's new rulers had not a hope of stopping the flood even if they'd wanted to. They made it out past the brown water and into the choppy blue of the Gulf of Siam, hoping the *Glory of the Sea* might have arrived a day early. Instead they'd seen the little frigate *Pillsbury,* patrolling the river mouth for lives to save. The red-haired lieutenant peering down into their boat had shouted, "Hey, Gwen. You too damn mean to die?" And Nguyen had shouted something which included "son-a-bitch" and provoked some more yelling and laughter.

The lieutenant's name was Eldon, and Nguyen had been his gunner when Eldon was an ensign running a Swift Boat up the Mekong back in 1969. And before the *Pillsbury* had turned them over to the carrier, Eldon had written a letter on official navy stationery expounding Nguyen's daring deeds and his claims for special treatment as a political refugee. "I doubt if he'll go back," Moon said. "He has no family left."

"But how about a job?" she said. "I taught him some more English on the ship and he learned fast. But still—"

"Don't worry about it," Moon said. "He'll have a job."

He told her about the office Ricky had opened at Caloocan City, and about the potential business. "I talked to Tom Brock this morning. We already have two copters in the hangar there. The general Ricky was dealing with told him to mark them off as unrepairable and keep them instead of paying the repair bills."

Osa had no comment.

"Does that sound sort of dishonest to you?"

"It sounds like Asia. How about you?" Osa said. "Did your embassy get all the paperwork done for Lila?"

"Yeah," Moon said. "Less hassle than I expected."

"Good," Osa said.

"There'll be more of it when I get her back to the States, though. All kinds of forms to fill out. Getting a birth certificate. So forth."

"I can imagine," Osa said. "Where's Lila now?"

"This hotel has a nursery service, complete with nannies," he said. "She's probably being taught how to speak

Tagalog. And how about your documents? You all right?"

"Fine," Osa said.

"You have dual citizenship, don't you? Didn't you tell me you had a Dutch passport as well as the Federation of Malaysia?"

Osa looked surprised. "Yes," she said. "Why are you asking?"

"There are too many important things I don't know," Moon said. "Like whether you enjoy walking."

"I do," Osa said.

"Then I think we should take a walk."

"In the dark?" Osa asked. But she got up.

"The moon will be up," Moon said. "And I will take you on the only walk I know in Manila—down past the yacht basin and along the waterfront. And if we keep walking long enough there's a restaurant I passed called My Father's Mustache. We could have dinner."

The moon was indeed up, but barely and far from full.

"Did you call your mother again? Is she—"

"She was asleep. But the nurse said everything was fine. Her leg is sore where they took the vein for the bypass surgery, but that's usually the worst of it. They said they could discharge her tomorrow, but I asked them to wait until I can be there to take her back to Florida."

"She'll be so happy to see you," Osa said.

"Funny thing," Moon said. "When I told her we'd found Ricky's daughter, I told her I hadn't been calling because we had to go all the way into Cambodia to get the baby. I told her why it took so long. About the trouble we had in the Philippines. And getting to Cambodia. But it was just like she'd taken it for granted. No surprise at all."

"What did she say?"

"She said something like, 'Well, you already told me the baby didn't get to Manila and you thought maybe she'd still be in Vietnam.' So she had known it would take me a little longer." He shrugged, made a wry face. "Can you believe that? 'Take me a little longer!'"

He waited for Osa's surprised response, but Osa was walking along beside him. He glanced at her. She looked amused.

Moon shrugged again. He didn't seem to understand anyone anymore.

"What else did she say?"

"Oh, was I all right? And all about the baby. Is she healthy? Does she look like Ricky? How old is she? What does she weigh? How many words can she say?"

"What did you expect her to say?"

"I don't know," Moon said. "I just thought she'd be—you know, amazed that I actually got the job done."

Osa put her hand on his hand. "Why? Ricky wouldn't have been surprised either. Ricky's friends wouldn't have been surprised. I had just heard about you from other people, but I wasn't surprised. Remember, I came to you with my trouble because I had heard about the kind of man you are."

Moon felt himself flushing. "Oh, sure," he said. "All that brotherly stuff from Ricky."

"You think your brother didn't know you? Your mother certainly knew you."

"She knows me all too well. That's why I thought she'd be amazed."

Osa removed her hand from his hand. "Why do you say that?" she said. "Why do you always have bad things to say about yourself?"

Time to change the subject. "Since we're getting personal," Moon said, "I have a question for you. In fact, two questions."

"Answer mine first. And then I have another one. Does

what you told me at the hotel just now about Caloocan City mean you are going to run the business?"

"I'm going to try," Moon said. "But there's been too much talking about me already. Listen carefully. Question one: Mr. Lee told me that when he called you this morning to say good-bye you seemed very sad. He thought it was because of Damon. And you said it was another loss."

Moon stopped, swallowed. There was no way to say it that wasn't rude, intrusive, presumptuous. Osa was looking at him, attentive, waiting, lips slightly parted, amusement fading into something very serious. Beautiful. Waiting. For what, the Moon of Durance to chicken out or the super-Moon of Ricky's legend to demand a solution to this little oddity?

"I remember," Osa said.

"He asked me if I understood what you meant. I said I didn't." He hesitated again. But to hell with it. Otherwise he was losing her anyway. "But I hoped I did understand. I hoped you meant me."

Osa looked at him, biting her lip. Looked away.

"I have that hope because when we were in the delta you seemed so sure he was dead. You didn't want to go into Cambodia. When I said I had to go anyway, you insisted you'd go along. But when we got there and found he was actually dead, you were genuinely surprised. Shocked."

Moon stopped. Osa walked three steps away from him and stood at the streetside railing staring out into the yacht harbor. The mast lights were making their colored patterns on the water.

"I think all along you really believed Damon was alive. Probably getting him out alive was hopeless, but you still believed you should try."

"Yes," she said. "I did."

"So now I'm going to guess at why you didn't want me

to go into Cambodia to bring him out. And if I guess wrong, you have to tell me I'm wrong. Even though it means I've made myself look like a damned fool."

"You don't have to guess. I'll tell you."

"I guess you didn't want me to get killed. I guess you knew I'd fallen in love with you, and I guess you'd begun caring some about me yourself."

Moon joined her at the railing. He took her hand.

"Anyway, you didn't want me to get killed."

"Oh, Moon," Osa said. Her eyes were wet but she was smiling. "Do you want me to answer the first question?"

"Only if it's the right answer. Only if you feel sad because you think you are losing Moon Mathias. But Mathias is not getting lost. As soon as I get little Lila back in the States and settled in, I'm coming back here. I'll chase you down wherever I can find you and I'll talk you into marrying me. Or try to. So what's the answer to that question?"

"The answer is Moon," she said. And put her cheek against his shoulder, her arms around his waist, and squeezed. "M-O-O-N," she said. "Moon."

He took her in his arms then, engulfed her, surprised at how small she seemed, conscious of the perfume of her hair, of her smooth skin beneath the silk, that when he tilted up her chin she was returning his kiss.

"It shouldn't take me more than eight or ten days," he said. "Where will you be in eight or ten days?"

"You're going to fly back with Lila? You'll try to take care of her on the plane?"

"Why not?" Moon said. "I can change diapers. Feed her. She can say 'Moon' now. I'm learning."

"Not very fast. I watched you on the aircraft carrier. You weren't designed to be a nanny. And that Baby in Space game you play with her is dreadful. You will break her neck. It scares her."

"It just scares people who're watching it. She likes it. Makes her giggle. She knows I won't drop her."

Osa was shaking her head. "And feeding her. Keeping her clean and comfortable. Getting her to sleep."

He hugged her to him. "Can you think of an alternative?"

"Yes," she said.

"So can I," Moon said. "With a Dutch passport you don't need a visa. So I postponed my flight a day and made reservations for Osa van Winjgaarden."

"No Mrs.?"

"No Mrs.," Moon said. "Until we can make it legal."